IN THE STACKS

IN THE STACKS

SHORT STORIES ABOUT
LIBRARIES AND LIBRARIANS

EDITED AND WITH AN INTRODUCTION BY
MICHAEL CART

THE OVERLOOK PRESS
WOODSTOCK & NEW YORK

First published in the United States in 2002 by
The Overlook Press, Peter Mayer Publishers, Inc.
Woodstock & New York

WOODSTOCK:
One Overlook Drive
Woodstock, NY 12498
www.overlookpress.com
[for individual orders, bulk and special sales, contact our Woodstock office]

NEW YORK:
141 Wooster Street
New York, NY 10012

∞ The paper used in this book meets the requirements for paper
permanence as described in the ANSI Z39.48-1992 standard.

Library of Congress Cataloging-in-Publication Data

Cart, Michael.
In the stacks : stories about libraries and librarians / Michael Cart.
p.   cm.
1. Librarians–Fiction. 2. Libraries–Fiction.
3. Short Stories I. Cart, Michael
PN6120.95.L554 I52 2002
808.83'108352092–dc21   2001056043

Book design and type formatting by Bernard Schleifer
Manufactured in the United States of America
FIRST EDITION
1 3 5 7 9 8 6 4 2
ISBN 1-58567-259-9

CONTENTS

INTRODUCTION

I GREW UP IN LOGANSPORT, INDIANA, A SMALL VALLEY TOWN ON THE banks of the Wabash River. Both of my grandfathers worked for the Pennsylvania Railroad, the backbone of the local economy in those long-ago days. A hundred years earlier, however, it was water, not rails, that brought commerce and economic growth to the fledgling community—water in the form of the once famous Wabash and Erie Canal.

By the time I came along all that remained of the old canal were some pilings and abutments, part of an aqueduct that had once borne it across the Eel River just a few blocks from my home.

Like most kids in town I spent a lot of time at, on, and—whenever my foot slipped on a rock—*in* the river. Unlike the others, however, I spent even more time—too much, some people thought—hanging out at a quiet, two story limestone building downtown; the building's entrance faced Broadway, one of the two main streets in our town, and above its door was carved the phrase "Free to All."

It was, of course, the public library.

The public library. When I was twelve, I didn't know what it represented to others—something loftily abstract like the civilizing influence of books, perhaps; or Culture (with a capital "C"), enlightenment, self-education, maybe even the marketplace of free ideas. Who knew? All I knew was that to me the library represented something much more powerfully and emotionally immediate: it represented escape, shelter, sanctuary, the only place where I felt comfortable, where I felt I belonged. It represented home.

And I loved it. With all my heart.

Sadly, though, no matter how much I wanted to, I couldn't actually live there. But when I got my first library card at age seven, I discovered to my delight that I could take at least part of the library home with me, in the form of the books that crowded its shelves and that soon nearly crowded me out of my bedroom.

Like Thomas Jefferson I could not live without books. And the more books I had, the more alive I felt. So is it any wonder that I became a book collector by the time I turned nine or that when I grew up, I became a librarian? Or that my first professional job was as director of my hometown public library, the place that first brought books and me together?

I remained a librarian for twenty-five years, though only six of those years were spent in Logansport. Thomas Wolfe was wrong, I learned: you CAN go home again; you just can't live there very long. And so I moved to California and, in fairly short order, became director of the Beverly Hills Public Library, where I was librarian to the stars.

When I was a kid haunting the stacks of my hometown public library, I never dreamed that I would become a library director or that I would wind up in Beverly Hills. But I did dream of something else, something that became reality a decade ago when I finally gave up the day job to become a writer.

Well, you can take the writer out of the library but you can't take the library out of the writer, I guess, because here I am, editing a collection of short stories about libraries and librarians.

The commonality of subject aside, they're very different, these nineteen stories. For starters, their settings and the nationalities of their authors represent a mini-United Nations of countries—the United States, of course, but also Argentina (Jorge Luis Borges), Canada (Alice Munro), England (M.R. James and Saki), Italy (Italo Calvino), Poland (Maria Dabrowska), and Russia (Isaac Babel).

They are equally diverse in their chronology. The newest story in the book—Lorrie Moore's exquisitely written "Community Life"—is from 1998. The oldest story in the book is Zona Gale's "The Cobweb" which, although it was first published in 1906, is nearly as psychologically acute as Moore's, and wonderfully relevant in its treatment of gender issues and stereotypes. And it reminds us, of course, that until fairly recently librarianship—along with teaching and nursing—was one of the few professions open to women. That the protagonists of eleven of the nineteen stories represented in this collection are women further reflects that reality. Otherwise, though, the characters defy expectations—cheerfully or bravely, blithely or determinedly—surprising the reader and sometimes even surprising themselves, as in the case of Joanne Greenberg's Myra, a southern librarian who discovers the courage to resist racial discrimination and prejudice when they show up at the door of her library. Similarly, in Maria Dabrowska's story a supervising librarian who holds rigid views about responsibility and process is equally surprised by her unexpected feelings of sympathy for a frustratingly inefficient employee.

I had a surprise, too, when I first became a librarian: I was bemused to discover that people who knew me from the library always seemed shocked to encounter me anyplace else. It seemed that I was the only one who knew I had a life larger than the library. Librarians do, of course, and so do the patrons they serve, as the librarian in Francine Prose's story "Rubber Life" discovers the first time she encounters Lewis, the man with whom she is becoming obsessed, "out in the world."

Like "Rubber Life" many of the stories in this collection are works of realism that explore relationships—John Cheever's melancholy "The Trouble of Marcie Flint," Lorrie Moore's haunting "Community Life," Alice Munro's "Hard Luck Stories," and Gina Berriault's "Who Is It Can Tell Me Who I Am," the last two of which also have something astringent and thought-provoking to say about stereotypes.

Two of the stories—Lisa Koger's "The Retirement Party" and Sue Kaufman's "Summer Librarian"—explore the dynamics of daughter-parent relationships in the context of lives that may change or may stay, sadly, inexorably the same.

Not all the stories are works of realism, of course: there is a cleverly plotted mystery from Anthony Boucher, for example, about murder and (shudder) cataloging; there is a story about a dusty ghost in the stacks of a university library from one of the first masters of the form, M.R. James; there is a merrily malevolent story from Saki about a king named Hkrikros and his Royal Librarian; a disquieting, impossible-to-classify story from Ursula K. LeGuin about librarians, duty and responsibility; and a droll, slightly racy comedy from Walter R. Brooks about that famous horse named "Ed" who gets his mind improved while coming to the rescue of the impoverished local library.

And it is the library itself—as book repository and as something more, something metaphorical, perhaps—that distinguishes four of the other stories: Isaac Babel's "The Public Library" reminds us that the institution provides sanctuary for all kinds of people; Italo Calvino's irresistible "A General in the Library" reminds us of the disarming and insidious power of books to humanize; Ray Bradbury's sweetly nostalgic "Exchange" reminds us that in the library, at least, some things never change; and, finally, Jorge Luis Borges' "The Library of Babel" equates the library with the universe—ubiquitous, infinite, everlasting . . .

From his lips to God's ear! Meanwhile, may you enjoy these stories about the many-splendored universe we call "the library" and its multifarious citizens, the librarians.

MICHAEL CART
Chico, California
September, 2001

IN THE STACKS

A GENERAL IN THE LIBRARY

Italo Calvino

ONE DAY, IN THE ILLUSTRIOUS NATION OF PANDURIA, A SUSPICION CREPT into the minds of top officials: that books contained opinions hostile to military prestige. In fact trials and enquiries had revealed that the tendency, now so widespread, of thinking of generals as people actually capable of making mistakes and causing catastrophes, and of wars as things that did not always amount to splendid cavalry charges towards a glorious destiny, was shared by a large number of books, ancient and modern, foreign and Pandurese.

Panduria's General Staff met together to assess the situation. But they didn't know where to begin, because none of them was particularly well-versed in matters bibliographical. A commission of enquiry was set up under General Fedina, a severe and scrupulous official. The commission was to examine all the books in the biggest library in Panduria.

The library was in an old building full of columns and staircases, the walls peeling and even crumbling here and there. Its cold rooms were crammed to bursting with books, and in parts inaccessible, with some corners only mice could explore. Weighed down by huge military expenditures, Panduria's state budget was unable to offer any assistance.

The military took over the library one rainy morning in November. The general climbed off his horse, squat, stiff, his thick neck shaven, his eyebrows frowning over pince-nez; four lanky lieutenants, chins held high and eyelids lowered, got out of a car, each with a briefcase in his hand. Then came a squadron of soldiers who set up camp in the old courtyard, with mules, bales of hay, tents, cooking equipment, camp radio, and signalling flags.

Sentries were placed at the doors, together with a notice forbidding entry, "for the duration of large-scale manoeuvres now under way". This was an expedient which would allow the enquiry to be carried out in great secret. The scholars who used to go to the library every morning wearing heavy coats and scarves and balaclavas so as not to freeze, had to go back home again. Puzzled, they asked each other: "What's this about large-scale manoeuvres in the library? Won't they make a mess of the place? And the cavalry? And are they going to be shooting too?"

Of the library staff, only one little old man, Signor Crispino, was kept so that he could explain to the officers how the books were arranged. He was a shortish fellow, with a bald, eggish pate and eyes like pinheads behind his spectacles.

First and foremost General Fedina was concerned with the logistics of the operation, since his orders were that the commission was not to leave the library before having completed their enquiry; it was a job that required concentration, and they must not allow themselves to be distracted. Thus a supply of provisions was procured, likewise some barrack stoves and a store of firewood together with some collections of old and it was generally thought uninteresting magazines. Never had the library been so warm in the winter season. Pallet beds for the general and his officers were set up in safe areas surrounded by mousetraps.

Then duties were assigned. Each lieutenant was allotted a particular branch of knowledge, a particular century of history. The general was to oversee the sorting of the volumes and the application of an appropriate rubber stamp depending on whether a book had been judged suitable for officers, NCOs, common soldiers, or should be reported to the Military Court.

And the commission began its appointed task. Every evening the camp radio transmitted General Fedina's report to HQ. "So many books examined. So many seized as suspect. So many declared suitable for officers and soldiers." Only rarely were these cold figures accompanied by something out of the ordinary: a request for a pair of glasses to correct short-sightedness for an officer who had broken his, the news that a mule had eaten a rare manuscript edition of Cicero left unattended.

But developments of far greater import were under way, about which the camp radio transmitted no news at all. Rather than thinning out, the forest of books seemed to grow ever more tangled and insidious. The officers would have lost their way had it not been for the help of Signor Crispino. Lieutenant Abrogati, for example, would jump to his feet and throw the book he was reading down on the table: "But this is outrageous! A book about the Punic Wars that speaks well of the Carthaginians and criticizes the Romans! This must be reported at once!" (It should be said here that, rightly or wrongly, the Pandurians considered themselves descendants of the Romans.) Moving silently in soft slippers, the old librarian came up to him. "That's nothing," he would say, "read what it says here, about the Romans again, you can put this in your report too, and this and this," and he presented him with a pile of books. The lieutenant leafed nervously through them, then, getting interested, he began to read, to take notes. And he would scratch his head and mutter: "For heaven's sake! The things you learn! Who would ever have thought!" Signor Crispino went over to Lieutenant Lucchetti who was closing a tome in rage, declaring: "Nice stuff this is! These people have the audacity to entertain doubts as to the purity of the ideals that inspired the Crusades! Yessir, the Crusades!" And Signor Crispino said with a smile: "Oh, but look, if you have to make a report on that subject, may I suggest a few other books that will offer more details," and he pulled down half a shelf-full. Lieutenant Lucchetti leaned forward and got stuck in, and for a week you could hear him flicking through the pages and muttering: "These Crusades though, very nice I must say!"

In the commission's evening report, the number of books examined got bigger and bigger, but they no longer provided figures relative to positive and negative verdicts. General Fedina's rubber stamps lay idle. If, trying to check up on the work of one of the lieutenants, he asked, "But why did you pass this novel? The soldiers come off better than the officers! This author has no respect for hierarchy!", the lieutenant would answer by quoting other authors and getting all muddled up in matters historical, philosophical and economic. This led to open discussions that went on for hours and hours. Moving silently in his slippers, almost invisible in his grey shirt, Signor Crispino would always join in at the right moment, offering some book which he felt contained interesting information on the subject under consideration, and which always had the effect of radically undermining General Fedina's convictions.

Meanwhile the soldiers didn't have much to do and were getting bored. One of them, Barabasso, the best educated, asked the officers for a book to read. At first they wanted to give him one of the few that had already been declared fit for the troops; but remembering the thousands of volumes still to be examined, the general was loath to think of Private Barabasso's reading hours being lost to the cause of duty; and he gave him a book yet to be examined, a novel that looked easy enough, suggested by Signor Crispino. Having read the book, Barabasso was to report to the general. Other soldiers likewise requested and were granted the same duty. Private Tommasone read aloud to a fellow soldier who couldn't read, and the man would give him his opinions. During open discussions, the soldiers began to take part along with the officers.

Not much is known about the progress of the commission's work: what happened in the library through the long winter weeks was not reported. All we know is that General Fedina's radio reports to General Staff headquarters became ever more infrequent, until finally they stopped altogether. The Chief of Staff was alarmed; he transmitted the order to wind up the enquiry as quickly as possible and present a full and detailed report.

In the library, the order found the minds of Fedina and his men prey to conflicting sentiments: on the one hand they were constantly discovering new interests to satisfy and were enjoying their reading and studies more than they would ever have imagined; on the other hand they couldn't wait to be back in the world again, to take up life again, a world and a life that seemed so much more complex now, as though renewed before their very eyes; and on yet another hand, the fact that the day was fast approaching when they would have to leave the library filled them with apprehension, for they would have to give an account of their mission, and with all the ideas that were bubbling up in their heads they had no idea how to get out of what had become a very tight corner indeed.

In the evening they would look out of the windows at the first buds on the branches growing in the sunset, at the lights going on in the town, while one of them read some poetry Out loud. Fedina wasn't with them: he had given the order that he was to be left alone at his desk to draft the final report. But every now and then the bell would ring and the others would hear him calling: "Crispino! Crispino!" He couldn't get anywhere without the help of the old librarian, and they ended up sitting at the same desk writing the report together.

One bright morning the commission finally left the library and went to report to the Chief of Staff; and Fedina illustrated the results of the enquiry before an assembly of the General Staff. His speech was a kind of compendium of human history from its origins down to the present day, a compendium in which all those ideas considered beyond discussion by the right-minded folk of Panduria were attacked, in which the ruling classes were declared responsible for the nation's misfortunes, and the people exalted as the heroic victims of mistaken policies and unnecessary wars. It was a somewhat confused presentation including, as can happen with those who have only recently embraced new ideas, declarations that were often simplistic and contradictory. But as to the overall meaning there could be no doubt. The assembly of generals was stunned, their eyes opened wide, then they found their voices and began to shout. General Fedina was not even allowed to finish. There was talk of a court-martial, of his being reduced to the ranks. Then, afraid there might be a more serious scandal, the general and the four lieutenants were each pensioned off for health reasons, as a result of "a serious nervous breakdown suffered in the course of duty". Dressed in civilian clothes, with heavy coats and thick sweaters so as not to freeze, they were often to be seen going into the old library where Signor Crispino would be waiting for them with his books.

THE PHOENIX

Ursula K. LeGuin

THE RADIO ON THE CHEST OF DRAWERS HISSED AND CRACKLED LIKE burning acid. Through the crackle a voice boasted of victories. "Butchers!" she snarled at the voice. "Butchers, liars, fools!" But there was an expression in the librarian's eyes which brought her rage up short like a dog on a chain, clawing at the air, choked off.

"You can't be a Partisan!"

The librarian said nothing. He might well have said nothing even if he had been able to say anything.

She turned the radio down—you could never turn it off, lest you should miss the last act, the denouement—and came up close to the librarian on the bed. Familiar to her now were the round, sallow face, the dark eyes with bloodshot whites, the dark, wiry hair on his head, and the hair on his forearms and the backs of his hands and fingers, and the hair under his arms and on his chest and groin and legs, and the whole of his stocky, sweaty, suffering body, which she had been trying to look after for thirty hours while the city blew itself apart street by street and nerve by nerve and the radio twitched from lies to static to lies.

"Come on, don't tell me that!" she said to his silence. "You weren't with them. You were against them."

Without a word, with the utmost economy, he evinced a denial.

"But I saw you! I saw exactly what you did. You locked the library. Why do you think I came there looking for you? You don't think I'd have crossed the street to help one of them!" A one-note laugh of scorn, and she awarded the well-delivered line the moment of silence that was its due. The radio hissed thinly, drifting back to static. She sat down on the foot of the bed, directly in the librarian's line of sight, front and center.

"I've known you by sight for I don't know how long—a couple of years, it must be. My other room, there, looks out on the square. Right across to the library. I've seen you opening it up in the morning a hundred times. This time I saw you closing it, at two in the afternoon. Running those wrought-iron gates across the doors in a rush. So what's he up to? Then I heard the cars and those damned motorcycles. I drew the curtain right away. But then. I stood behind the curtain and watched. That was strange, you know? I'd have sworn I'd be hiding under the bed in here as soon as I knew they were that close. But I stood there and watched. It was like watching a play!" she said with the expansiveness of inaccuracy. In fact, peering out between the curtain and the window frame with a running thrill of not disagreeable terror, she had inevitably felt that she was sizing up the house. Was it that revival of emotion that had moved her, so soon afterwards, to act?

"They pulled the flag down first. I suppose even terrorists have to do things in the proper order. Probably in fact no one is more conventional. They have to do everything that's expected of them. . . . Well, I'd seen you go round to that side door, the basement entrance, after you'd locked the gates. I think I'd noticed your coat, without noticing that I noticed, you know, that yellowish-brown color. So, after they'd been all over the front steps, and broken in at the side door—like ants on meat, I kept thinking—and finally all come out again and got onto their damned motorcycles and roared off to go wreck something else, and I was wondering if it was smoke or just dust that was hanging around that side door—then I thought of your coat, because of the color of the smoke, that yellowish brown. I thought, I never saw that coat again. They didn't bring the librarian out with them. Well, so I thought probably they'd shot you, inside there with the books. But I kept thinking how you'd locked the doors and locked the gates and then gone back inside. I didn't know why you'd done that. You could have locked up and left, got away, after all. I kept thinking about that. And there wasn't a soul down in the square. All us rats hiding in our rat-holes. So finally I thought, Well, I can't live with this, and went over to look for you. I walked right across the square. Empty as four A.M. It was peaceful. I wasn't afraid. I was only frightened of finding you dead. A wound, blood. Blood turns me faint, I detest it. So I go in, and my mouth's dry and my ears are singing, and then I see you coming with an armload of books!" She laughed, but this time her voice cracked. She turned left profile to him, glancing at him once sidelong.

"Why did you go back in? And when they were in there, what did you do? You hid, I suppose. And when they left you came out and tried to put out the fire."

He shook his head slightly.

"You did," she said. "You did put it out. There was water on the floor, and a mop bucket."

He did not deny this.

"I shouldn't have thought books would catch fire easily. Or did they pull out some newspapers, or the catalogue, or the overdue file? They certainly got something burning. All that smoke, it was awful. I was choking as soon as I came in. I don't know how you breathed at all up there on the main floor. Anyway, you put out the fire, and you had to get out because of the smoke, or you weren't sure the fire was really out; so you quick picked up some valuable books and headed for the door—"

Again he shook 'his head. Was he smiling?

"You did! You were crawling towards the stairs, crawling on your knees, trying to carry those books, when I came up. I don't know if you would have got out or not, but you were trying to."

He nodded, and tried to whisper something.

"Never mind. Don't talk. Just tell me, no, don't tell me, how you can be a Partisan, after that. After giving your life, all but, for a few books!"

He forced the whisper, like a steel brush on brass, that was all the smoke had left of his voice: "Not valuable," he said.

She had leaned forward to catch his words. She straightened up, smoothed her skirt, and presently spoke with some disdain.

"I don't know that we are really very well qualified to judge whether our life is or is not valuable."

But he shook his head again and whispered, voiceless, meaningless, obstinate. "The books."

"You're saying that the *books* aren't valuable?"

He nodded, his face relaxing, relieved at having explained himself at last, at having got it all straight.

She stared at him, incredulous, angrier than she had been at the radio, and then the anger flipped over like a coin from a thumb, and she laughed. "You're crazy!" she said, putting her hand on his.

His hand was thickset like the rest of him, firm but uncallused, a desk worker's hand. It was hot to her touch.

"You ought to be in hospital," she said with remorse. "I know you shouldn't talk, I can't help talking, but don't answer. I know you should have gone to the hospital. But how could you get there, no taxis, and God knows what the hospitals are like now. Or who they're willing to take. If it ever quiets down and the telephone works again I'll try to call a doctor. If there are any doctors left. If there's anything left when this is over."

It was the silence that made her say that. It was a silent day. On the silent days you almost wanted to hear the motorcycles, the machine guns.

His eyes were closed. Yesterday evening, and from time to time all night, he had had spasms of struggling for breath, like asthma or a heart attack, terrifying. He breathed short and hard even now, but however worn out and uncomfortable, he was resting; he must be better. What could a doctor do for smoke inhalation, anyhow? Probably not much. Doctors were not much good for things like lack of breath, or old age, or civil disorders. The librarian was suffering from what his country was dying of, his sickness was his citizenship of this city. Weeks now, the loudspeakers, the machine guns, the explosions, the helicopters, the fires, the silences; the body politic was incurable, its agony went on and on. You went miles for a cabbage, a kilo of meal. Then next day the sweet shop at the corner was open, children buying orange drink. And the next day it was gone, the corner building blown up, burnt out. The carcase politic. Faces of people like façades of buildings downtown, the great hotels, blank and furtive, all blinds down. And last Saturday night they had thrown a bomb into the Phoenix. Thirty dead, the radio had said, and later sixty dead, but it was not the deaths that outraged her. People took their chances. They had gone to see a play in the middle of a civil war, they had taken their chance and lost. There was both gallantry and justice there. But the old Phoenix, the house itself: the stage where she had played how many pert housemaids, younger sisters, confidantes, dowagers, Olga Prozorova, and for the great three weeks Nora; the red curtain, the red

plush seats, the dirty chandelier and gilt plaster mouldings, all that
fake grandeur, that box of toys, that defenseless and indefensible strut-
ting place for the human soul—to hurt that was contemptible. Better
if they threw their damned bombs into churches. There surely the startled soul would be plucked straight up to downy heaven before it
noticed that its body had been blown to stewmeat. With God on your
side, in God's house, how could anything go wrong? But there was no
protection in some dead playwright and a lot of stagehands and fool
actors. Everything could go wrong, and always did. Lights out, and
screaming and pushing, trampling, an unspeakable sewer stink, and so
much for Moliére, or Pirandello, or whoever they'd been playing
Saturday night at the Phoenix. God had never been on that side. He'd
take the glory, all right, but not the blame. What God was, in fact, was
a doctor, a famous surgeon: don't ask questions, I don't answer them,
pay your fees, I'll save you if I care to but if I don't it's your own fault.

She got up to rearrange the bedside table, reproving herself for
vulgarity of thought. She had to be angry at somebody; there was
nobody there but God and the librarian, and she did not want to be
angry at the librarian. Like the city, he was too sick. And anger would
disturb the purity of her strong erotic attraction to him, which had
been giving her great pleasure. She had not so enjoyed looking at a
man for years; she had thought that joy lost, withered away. Her age
took advantage from his illness. In the normal course of things he
would not have seen her as a woman but as an old woman, and his
blindness would have blinded her, she would not have looked at him.
But, having undressed him and looked after his body, she was spared
hypocrisy, and could admire that stocky and innocent body with the
innocent joy of desire. Of his mind and spirit she knew almost nothing, only that he had courage, which was a good thing. She did not
need to know more. Indeed she did not want to. She was sorry he had
spoken at all, had said those two stupid, boastful words, "Not valuable," whether meaning his own life, or the books he had tried to save
at the risk of his life. In either case what he had meant was that to a
Partisan nothing was valuable but the cause. The existence of a branch
librarian, the existence of a few books—trash. Nothing mattered but
the future.

But if he was a Partisan, why had he tried to save the books?

Would a Loyalist have stayed alone in that terrible brownish-yellow room of smoke trying to put out the fire, to keep the books from burning?

Of course, she answered herself. According to his opinions, his theories, his beliefs, yes, certainly, of course! Books, statues, buildings, lamp posts bearing lighted lamps not strangled corpses, Moliére at eight-thirty, conversation at dinner, schoolgirls in blue with satchels, order, decency, the past that ensures a future, for this the Loyalist stood. Staunchly he stood. But would he also crawl across a floor coughing out his lungs, trying to hang on to a few of the books?—not even valuable books, that's what the librarian had been trying to say, she understood him now, not even valuable ones; there probably were no valuable books in this branch library. Just books, any books, not because he had opinions, not because he had beliefs, there with his life forfeit, but because he was a librarian. A person who looked after books. The one responsible.

"Is that what you meant?" she asked him, softly, because he had fallen asleep. "Is that why I brought you here?"

The radio hissed, but she did not need applause. His sleep was her audience.

GLOSS ON A DECISION OF THE COUNCIL OF NICAEA

Joann Greenberg

THE MAJOR SCHISMS OF THE CHURCH. A LIST OF THE BISHOPS OF SARUM. She knew a great deal about medieval church politics. With luck and God's help, knowledge would save her. Because the jail was so terrifying.

She had seen the demonstrators out there in front of the library, and she had watched them for a few minutes, unemotionally, and then she had gone into her little office and scratched out some words on a piece of cardboard for a sign. Then she had walked out of the library and down the steps to stand with the demonstrators. She had made no conscious decision to do this. Her heart was exploding its blood in rhythmic spasms of panic, but she paid no attention to it; and this frightened Myra, because she had always weighed her choices carefully and measured feeling against propriety.

Now she was standing in a jail cell. V/hat was there to be afraid of? Jails haven't changed much since the Middle Ages; the properties of a jail—the dirt, discomfort, lack of privacy, and ugliness—were the same. Being a student of history, she had pondered many imprisonments. Except for the electric lights, Tugwell's county jail might have been anywhere at any time; and for Myra, who had always respected fighters for a cause, prison had meant Boethius' great hour, Gottschalk, the Albigensian teachers, and John of the Cross. She now understood that the worst, the most horrifying feature of their imprisonment had eluded her; and in her own moment, its sudden presence was almost too much to stand. Captors hate. How could she have missed so plain a fact? Captors hate. When the sheriff had come to "protect" them from the hecklers, she had started forward, trying to get to him. "These Negroes and I are protesting an unjust . . ."

But he had turned, reaching to take her and the girl next to her, and he had looked at them with a look that stopped the words in her mouth. At the jail, as they went past him into the cell, she saw the look again, a loathing, an all-pervading contempt. Before the wave of fear and sickness had passed, the door was closed and he was gone.

There were no statements taken, no charges made. She had wasted the first hours mustering answers from an array of imprisoned giants, the brilliant, searing words of men whose causes, once eclipsed and darkened, were now the commonplace truths of our civilization.

After a while Myra had looked around and counted. There are eight of us. The young men had been taken somewhere else. Eight girls, two beds—an upper and lower bunk—one spigot, two slop buckets, one bare wall, and two square yards of floor to sit on. That was all. The girls had gone to the bunks in an order that seemed natural: two rested or slept on the lower, four sat on the upper bunk, leaving the floor for the remaining two. When anyone had sat or rested enough, she would move and a girl on the floor would take her place.

She had expected choices. There were none, not even a list of rules that they could obey or refuse to obey. It underlined the sheriff's look. One doesn't give choices to an animal; the sheriff, giving such choices, would be recognizing the humanity of his prisoners and their right to make some disposition of their own lives. So, Miss Myra, the careful librarian of Tugwell, who walked in the crosswalks and did not spit where it said *No Spitting*, was forced to put her own boundaries to her day. She decided to spend the mornings mentally recounting history, braiding popes and synods and the heresies they sifted. Perhaps they would shed light on the evolution of secular law, in which she had done a good deal of reading. In the afternoon she would have to find a way to get some exercise, to get a letter out, to wash her clothes. . . . The girls talked a little now and then, the random exchanges of people waiting. Myra sensed that they didn't have her need for formed, measured bits of time, for routines and categories. They seemed to hang free within the terms of imprisonment, simply waiting.

On the evening of the second day Matilda Jane asked her, "Miss Myra, how you come to be with us?"

The others looked over at her, some smiling, no doubt remembering the scene of themselves as they stood and sang in front of the library, hoping they could keep their voices from quavering. They had watched the door, certain of the nose of a gun or the tip of a firehose as it slowly opened. Instead, there had grown only the tiny white edge of Myra's quickly lettered sign, giving them a word at a time: OPEN LIBRARY TO ALL! IGNORANCE IS NOT BLISS. Then, Myra herself had come, slowly, very much alone. It was as if in the expectation of a cannon, they had been shocked by a pop gun. Some of them had even laughed.

"I'd never thought about it, I mean about colored people not using the library, not until Roswell Dillingham came. After that, I had to—well—to protest."

"*Roswell?*" And the other girls sat up, surprised, interested, waiting for something rich. "Heber's little brother?"

"Hey, she mean Sailor."

They laughed.

"What Sailor done now?"

"I didn't know his nickname," Myra said, and Lalie, who was sitting on the bed beside her, guffawed. "Lord, yes! Great big mouth, blowin' an' goin' all the time, two big ears aflappin', ma'am; you be with Sailor, you ain' need no boat!" And they all wanted to know what Sailor had done now. They were all eager to hear Roswell's latest, all except Delphine, who was stretched out on the bed dozing.

"Well," Myra said, "there's not much to tell, really. You see, when Mrs. Endicott left and I took over as county librarian, she simply told me that you—I mean that Negroes—just didn't use the library, but that when a Negro needed to look something up, why he would come to me and I would take the book out myself. I know it will seem odd to you—it does to me now—but before that it had never occurred to me that there were no Negroes coming into the library. Anyway, one day this spring, I was locking up and Roswell came and asked me for a book. I just followed Mrs. Endicott's instructions—I got it for him on my card. In three days he was back. Soon he started asking me to recommend books for him to read. Two or three books every week. I started combing lists for things I thought he would like, and the more he read, the more foolish it seemed not to have him come and browse around and pick out the books for himself. When I told him to come, he looked at me as if I had told him to fly like a bird. Negroes were forbidden to use the library.

"*The library!* That business of my getting the books for him had been designed to make me ask him why he wanted them, and then to decide that he wasn't responsible! I wrote an inquiry to the county commission and never got an answer. I never dreamed of demonstrating. I have to be honest and say that, but *the library*—well—I just couldn't consent to that. So, I suppose it was Roswell who got me to come out."

M.J. looked away and there was silence while everyone groped for a new, less dangerous subject.

Loretta whistled softly and said, "Kin you beat that damn Roswell?"

No getting away now; there it was. "What's the trouble?" Myra asked.

"You in here with us, Miss Myra," M.J. said, "so I'm gonna tell you truly what Roswell been doin'. He been makin' money offa them books."

"I don't see how. They were returned on time and in good shape."

"Ma'am, he bin' liftun' offa them books."

"I'm sorry, M.J., I just don't understand. . ."

"I'm in here in this jail, an' I got to be ashame' for that bigmouth! He takes them books, an' he reads 'em, an' then he take an' make 'em into a play. Then he go an' puts up a sign down to Carters' store an' he an' Fernelle an' one or two of 'em, they acts it out, see. Ten cents a person. He get almost everyone to come an' bring the kids an' make a night out. He ain' stop there. I know there's whole parts of the play that he have just graff right out of the book. I could tell it. Don't shake your head, Lalie, you know good as I do, am' no words like that come out o' Roswell bigmouth! He lays them words down so nice—an' *powerful!* Miss Myra, he been gettin' maybe five, six dollars clear every Saturday, just showin' your books in the meetin' hall of the Hebron Funeral Home!" ·

Echo of Boethius, calling out of a sixth century cell, "Come, Goddess Wisdom, Come, Heart-ravishing Knowledge . . ." Roswell Dillingham, bootlegger of knowledge, echoed that day when knowledge was an absolute and its conquest as sure as the limits of a finite heaven. Myra wished she could tell them about Boethius, broken and condemned, and crying in his agony: "Earth conquered gives the stars!" It would only embarrass them. She said, "Do the people like the plays?"

"Well—yes, they do. See, Roswell's plays—they're about us, about colored people. It's a' interestin' play, an' folks don' have to go all the way in to Winfiel' Station, sit in the balcony. My granmaw say, she gets to see a play she understan', an' they's nobody drinkin', swearin', runnin' aroun' in they underwear. Roswell plays—I mean your plays— they about what happen to our people. Like las' week, he had one call *Oliver Twiss*. Everybody cry in that one. Before that he had one call *Two Cities*."

Myra heard Dickens' story about how Sydney Carton gave himself up to the sheriff, back in the thirties, when the K.K.K. rode patrol out of Tugwell.

"Kite my books, will he . . . I wish I'd known. There's a fine one about a Civil Rights worker who got too rich and comfortable, name of Julius Caesar; one about a girl named Antigone, the freedom play of all time."

There was a snort from the bed. Delphine stretched and then swung her legs over the side and grunted again. "Miss Myra, we don't need white stories made over for black people."

"I wasn't patronizing. The books I gave Roswell were good books. They weren't 'white' stories. They were about people—any people . . ."

"No, *ma'am*, Miss Myra, *ma'am*, not while you got 'em piled up and stored away in the white-only library."

"That's why I was glad about Roswell." Myra looked down at Delphine. The two girls on the floor shifted a little, ready to use their bed places. Delphine got up slowly, and Myra got down, and they stood together in the cell.

From the beginning Delphine was the only one with whom Myra knew she could have no more than an armed truce. Delphine knew it too, probably. They seldom spoke to one another directly; when they had to speak, they used an agonizingly elaborate etiquette, which Myra noted had just gone over into parody. Delphine had a hard, absolute way of speaking that Myra found irritating; but Myra knew that Delphine must find life in the cramped cell more difficult with her there. Delphine was their leader. She had been in protests and sit-ins, and jailed four times. She spoke with hard-won, frightening knowledge.

"Next time, wear pedal-pushers like I got on, plaid or check. They hold up good an' they don't show the dirt."

"When they're going to hit you, the muscles by their eyes cinch up. You can always tell. Never take the smack, let the smack take you. Go with it."

If she had been an Albigensian under the Question, Myra knew that Delphine would wake great admiration in her. She was strong and intelligent; she could duck a blow, parry a question, and make her silence ring with accusation. Somehow, the heroine was also an arrogant bitch. Myra wondered if some straying grain of her own prejudice made Delphine's virtues seem so much like faults. As the pressures built up in the shares of water, slop bucket, and stench, Myra could see, from her neatly labeled and scheduled mental busy-work, that Delphine was trying to separate her from the rest of the girls.

They waited for three days. On the morning of the fourth, the sheriff came around with his notebook. As he stopped on the other side of the bars, Myra spoke to him. They had been arrested and jailed without being given their legal rights, she said. Would this be remedied?

The sheriff looked up slowly from his book, feigning a courteous confusion. "Why you're the little lady works over to the library, ain't you?" Then he let his gaze sift slowly over the others in the cell and come back to her, the expression now one of sympathetic reproof (Now, look at what you have caused to happen to you.)

She had a sudden, terrifying vision of him in all his genial Southern courtesy cutting away their justice, their law, their lives.

"Oh, ma'am, it's a shame! The commissioners only decided last week that we got to do Comminists the same as we do niggers. Comminist wants to live with niggers, why we ain' gonna stop 'em. But, ma'am, I seen you over in church on Sunday, an' all the bazaars, an' you was servin' donuts at the Legion parade." He looked at her earnestly. "It must be a mistake. I'm sure you ain' one of them Comminists."

Myra had never thought of herself as being a perceptive person. A narrow and careful life had never made it a necessity. Sensitivity can be a frightening gift. It was better to depend on more tangible things: hard work, reasonableness, and caution. Now, in the quiet, fear-laced minute, she suddenly knew that this contemptuously play-acting man was offering her a way out. She had only to weep and tell him how con-

fused she was, to ask for his protection. (Lonely spinster-woman—
everybody knows how notional they get. A woman, being more took up
with the biological part of things, why, if she don't get to re-lize that
biological part of her nature, it's a scientific fact she'll go to gettin'
frusterated. Women, why they're *cows!*) It was as if she heard his mind
form words. When he did speak, the words were so close that she was
dumfounded.

"I guess you kinda got turned around here, all this niggers rights
business. I guess you just got confused for a bit. I sure hate to see you
in here like this. It sure is a pity." White women are ladies, the code
said. You crush ladies not with violence but with pleasant contempt.

She didn't want to leave the girls in the cell. She looked at the
sheriff, but she did not speak. The "lady" dealt with, he turned his
attention to the others, and his voice hardened and coarsened as the
code demanded when speaking to Them.

"We got a list here. You answer to your name when I call it." Then
he read the names, stopping between each syllable to allow for their
slow black wits to apprehend his meaning. The girls answered in the
way Delphine had taught them: their voices cool and level, their eyes
straight on him. Myra had been in Tugwell for only three years, having
come in answer to a wildly exaggerated ad in the *Library Journal,* and
staying because she had liked the town. She had never had any deal-
ings with Tugwell's Negroes, except for Roswell; but she knew somehow that this was not the usual way for Negroes to react to authority
in Tugwell. She couldn't trace this knowledge—she had never seen it
directly or heard mention of it—it was just there, a certitude that their
look was treason and would damn them. She also knew that from that
judgment anyway, she was exempt. She might face down the sheriff
and be called an old-maid eccentric, but she wouldn't be hurt. Another
line of difference had been drawn, excluding her; and for a long
moment of the sheriff's passing by, she was overwhelmed with a loneliness so keen that she found herself shivering and on the verge of
tears.

She tried to close this separation. To do it, she had to appeal to
Delphine. "Four days!" she said. "There must be a way we can get hold
of a lawyer . . ."

But Delphine stepped back from the line that the sheriff had
helped to set between them. "You aren't Miss Myra here; you aren't

ma'am. Not with us. Not for giving us white-man heroes or white-man lawyers either. *You* get *your* lawyer. Let him get *you* out."

"Look, Delphine, I don't know anything about the struggle between the races. I know about the library and the books that are in the library; and I know that it is wrong for the library to deny its treasures to those who want them. I know about books and reading. That's what I know about, where I am strong and where I will fight."

But Delphine had turned her back and gone toward a space on the bed which Myra realized shouldn't have been there. It was there for Delphine. She was the complete leader now. She would always have a seat on the bed or a space to lie down on the bed when she wanted it. Having measured the sheriff, the others had chosen his adversary—tyrant for tyrant. Delphine went to rest on "her" bunk, to claim her compensation. "Her" places would now be offered to others only at her discretion. It was wrong. Myra saw it denying the very equality for which they were risking so much; because Myra now knew that her cellmates were facing the sons of the men who had broken Gottschalk's bones. If only she could give them some of his or Boethius' passionate and simple poetry to have when the time came. They might be strengthened by the words of great prisoners whose causes had been so much like their own. They would need grandeur. That sheriff was one who, to the end, would follow the Customs of the Country.

Later, she was sitting next to M.J. on the floor and they were talking quietly about wonderful food they had eaten. After Myra had dismembered a large, delicately broiled lobster and dipped the red claw carapace full of its vulnerable meat into a well of butter, M.J. leaned close and whispered, "Hey, Myra—uh—you ain' a Comminist or nothin', are you?"

Myra turned in wonder from the fading lobster. "What? Whatever gave you that idea?" Some words scurried across her mind in a disorderly attempt to escape being thought.

"I didn' mean to hurt your feelin's," M.J. murmured, "but, see, Delphine don' trust you, because if you was another kind of different person—well—it wouldn' be like it was one of the regular whites comin' over to our side; it would be like you was arguin' for your own difference, see?"

"M.J., you tell Delphine that all I want is to have the Tugwell library open to everybody, regardless of race, creed, color, or national origin."

"I don' think Delphine is really agains' you."

"Where does she come from?" Myra asked, and M.J. said quickly, "Oh, she from here . . ." And then she looked down. "It's the schoolin' make her talk so much nicer, that's all. Her folks don't live but a street away from us. Her daddy work on the railroad, though, made steady money."

"It's not the way she talks," Myra said, stumbling over that other barrier between them. How could she have read the sheriff so well that his predicted words followed like footprints, and yet not be able to show herself to this girl who had the face and voice of a friend? "Delphine is different from you other girls, she . . ."

"It's the same with us as with the white," M.J. said, and she fingered her torn sleeve in a little nervous gesture that Myra had seen her begin to use after the sheriff's visit. "Some people, you fit 'em in with the rest; it don't bother 'em none. Some, they got to be just one an' the mold broke. Delphine, she like that. She always did feel sharp for things that was done wrong to her. I think she felt hurts more, say, than me. It's cause she's smarter; she got more person to hurt. You know, she went up North to the college."

"I didn't know that."

"I can remember her sayin' all the time how learnin' and education was goin' to get her free. Our grade school here in Tugwell, it ain' hardly one-legged to the white school; an' our high school ain' but a butt-patch to the white. Oh, Myra, an' we didn' know it! Delphine come out of Booker T. Washington High all proud an' keen. She made the straight A. Then she went up North to the college. An' all of a sudden, here she was, bein' counted by white folks measure—an' put down, put way low. It shamed her. The white-school diploma she got cost her a extra year just to fill in on what ol' Booker T. High didn' think a Negro had to know."

"But she did succeed . . ."

"That's what I wonder at—why she come back afterward, here to Tugwell, where she ain't no different from any of us that never done what she did. I can't see how anybody that got the college degree would come back here to be put down low again."

"The fight and the fighter have to be close to each other," Myra murmured.

"What?"

Myra felt a gnawing in her mind that was strange to her. She had to wait until it became plain, and then she recognized that it was her mind moving, feeling blindly toward one of its own motives. It came bumping against something, won the shape from the darkness, and with the shape, a meaning. "Not pretty or smart or gifted, but I had one thing that was mine. The pretty and smart ones had the future; the rich ones had the present. I had the past. In a way, in 'having,' I 'owned.' The history and literature were mine to give when I opened that library door every morning. . . . When Roswell told me that Negroes couldn't use the library, I was mad because the town had no right, no right to deny what wasn't theirs to give or withhold. In a way, Delphine and I are alike." Then she said to M.J., "Delphine has a calling; there's no doubt about that."

Why can't I like her? Myra looked at the leader over the soggy bread in her dinner plate. She has everything I've always reverenced. Watching Delphine at the spigot. . . . not running away, standing, as Boethius stood, and Gottschalk and John. The courage is in knowing exactly what will happen, where the wound will gall most cruelly, and still, standing. . . . But the arrogance in Delphine, who was beginning to posture like Savonarola silhouetted by the light of his own fire, made Myra wince. Delphine's arrogance reached into Myra's thoughts and began to move toward all of the heroes Myra had stored there. She began to worry for the giants she venerated, for years of her pity and love. Was courage only the arrogance used to an enemy?

The next morning the sheriff began.

Tactical blunder: He took Delphine first. She came back sick, the brown color of her face grayed. She was bloody and puffy-faced and harder than ever. Now, anyone who followed would have to come to Delphine before and after, and would be judged. When Loretta went in the afternoon and returned still retching, she was greeted by Delphine's wry smile and the slow unfolding of Delphine's bones, one by one, to make a place for her on the bunk throne of honor. The next day Dilsey and Lalie went. They came back trembling and exhausted, embarrassed at where their hurts were, and with a rumor that things were going to be speeded up because the legal machinery was slowly lumbering in to help. In the night, counting the heretics she knew, burned between 890 and 1350 in France, Myra could hear M.J. quietly sobbing with fear.

It had been hardest for M.J., who had seen all the hurts and heard the accumulating voices in their nightmares. Now the untried ones had the floor all the time. Myra crawled over to M.J. and put a hand on her thin back in a forlorn gesture of comfort. M.J.'s back stopped heaving and the crying stopped or, rather, retreated inward. Myra began to feel that someone was observing her; another silence was there, one that seemed to fill its space instead of being there by default of sound. She turned and saw Delphine looking at them from a seat on the top bunk, her face showing nothing in the dimness. She was awake, all right, watching, listening, as if she were waiting to pounce. It made Myra feel guilty of something. She looked down at M.J., who hadn't moved and was pretending to be asleep, and then she stood up. It was painfully slow; she grunted with the effort and the pain; her legs had been bent against the concrete floor for a long time. When she finally stood, her eyes were at the level of Delphine's kneecaps.

"Help M.J. You know, Delphine, we can't all be as tough as you." She realized immediately that such a plea for M.J. was wrong and stupid.

Crying weakness to Delphine was like asking sympathy from a tornado. Were all heroes so frighteningly impersonal? Damn her! Why couldn't that precious martyrs' firelight extend its warmth and radiance to cover M.J., who had waited all these days while the terror grew?

"Listen, Delphine, I know something about you."

Delphine's impassive face did not move. Damn her, I'll make it move.

"I know, for instance," she continued slowly, whispering a word at a time, "that whatever you took from the sheriff, it didn't hurt as much as theirs did . . ." And she gestured around the cell at the sleepers who were shielding their ugly dreams from the forty-watt light that burned in the corridor outside the cell. "Maybe you didn't feel it at all."

"How come?" Delphine said, fastidiously disinterested.

"You knew it before you went in," Myra went on. "It's a nice secret, too, Delphine, because the welts are real and no one can prove they didn't hurt. Maybe they don't even hurt now."

"No!" Delphine hissed. "Nothing hurts! It's the black skin. Makes you immune. Tougher than the white! Less sensitive!"

"Come off it. It's the anger or the hate that makes you immune.

Your anger and hate are better than morphine for shielding you from pain. You were dressed up to the eyes in hate, and you walked in with it to the sheriff and took your licks and came back bleeding. You didn't even have to lie. Did it make you feel superior to the other girls who had to take it raw, without hate?"

That hit. Myra could see it going in to burn behind Delphine's slowly blinking eyes. She was standing close to Delphine, whispering, but they were both aware that M.J. and maybe others were awake and would hear them if their voices got any louder.

Delphine began to negotiate. "What are you going to do about it?"

"You help M.J. to take what she's going to have to take or I'll tell what I know about you."

Delphine laughed, a silent mouth-laugh, whose mirth died long before it reached her eyes.

"I know they won't believe me," Myra said, "but maybe there'll be a minute of doubt, just enough to force you to come right out and claim that bed space and that first drink in the morning."

Delphine sat there, surprised, and Delphine's surprise was a source of pain to Myra. She had no style and she knew it. Her courage looked silly. Nevertheless, she had gotten to Delphine, and Delphine wasn't used to being gotten to.

"I don't want you here!" she hissed. "I don't want what you have to give us! Get your white face out of this cell and let us, for once, do something all by ourselves!"

"I'm here and my white face is here, and you can either like it or lump it."

Where had the words and the strength come from? She had always been a sheltered person, and three years as Miss Myra, the toy librarian in this toy white town of antimacassars and mint tea hadn't done any more than confirm her opinion. Who had she been a week ago that she could be so far from that self right now? Like a rocket, she thought, that had veered a millionth of a degree from the center of its thrust. She had, on the 14th of April, asked a question of a boy named Roswell Dillingham. It was only the smallest shift, a millionth of a degree, and that smallest change was measuring her path at tangent, thousands of miles into strange darkness, to end lost, perhaps, in uncharted spaces that she could not imagine.

Delphine was muttering curses, and Myra turned back to her

place on the floor and sat down. Delphine didn't want her, and she had said so. Why not? What did Myra, and by extension white people, have that Delphine couldn't accept? If Delphine hadn't been to college up North, it might have been a falsely exalted picture of American history, a Parson Weems history that no Negro in slave-holding country could take seriously. It wasn't that. Delphine had read enough and learned enough to know that white men also searched their souls occasionally. Myra knew that she had to get at it, whatever it was, because she needed everything she could use against Delphine's arrogance. She found herself staring at the slop bucket, riveted on it. Exhausted, she thought.

Hard floors and groping, needs and angers, mine and hers, and barely knowing where to separate mine and hers. Why is *she* in this cell? Then she found herself staring at Lalie's back as if to bore through it, and Lalie shifted and moaned so that Myra pulled her eyes away. I have the past. . . . I have the past and two enemies, who both seem to say "nothing personal." It really isn't, I suppose. They are enemies to my history. What a couple they would make: the sheriff, with his fake past, and Delphine, with her fake . . .

It was there, somewhere near, elusive but near, in Delphine's idea of a future. She became alert, groping to more purpose now. It was in a future of which Delphine dreamed, a world that made "white" history irrelevant and Myra a danger. She looked over the sleeping girls. Delphine had given up too, and was curled in a ball, her arm protectively over her face. The only ones who merely pretended to sleep were the two whose turn it would be to go with the sheriff tomorrow. Myra knew that she would not be beaten, and that the law was slowly lumbering toward her. If only Delphine had let it happen, she might have given them a thousand years of prison humor and two thousand years of resistance to the tyrant, eloquent, proud resistance, face to face, as Delphine would have liked it.

And *I* wanted to be in the history too! she thought. Oh, my God, it was as simple as that! I wanted to be in the history even more than I wanted to fight over Roswell's reading. I wanted to come forward where the fire was, feeling that in the fire, I would not be so alone. . . . The thoughts that she had sent out walking for Delphine's weakness had found hers instead. Does it hurt and sear and shatter, that thought? Is it as hard as the sheriff's blows? No, not so hard as that. She wasn't going to be in the history, even though she was in the fire. In the fire, but no less alone. Delphine had fixed that. A segregated fire. She would have to work at not hating Delphine. This cause was right and the cause should take precedence over its leaders. Heaven knows it was an old argument. It showed up as the Montanist Controversy; and it was put to a rule in 325 A.D.: Decision of the Nicene Council, valid sacraments by a lapsed bishop. Very good. It was a comfort to know that the early Church had ruled on Delphine's case.

M.J. rolled over, but her eyes were closed, and she was still pretending to be asleep. She was a nice girl. If Delphine had allowed it, they could have been, all of them, friends together in this cause. Her mind yearned toward M.J. in the night. There were thousands of men and women before you in that room, a thousand rooms, acts, moments. Don't be afraid. You are neighbored all around by people who have screamed or been silent, wept or been brave—all the nations are represented, all the colors of man. Don't be afraid of pleading, of weeping. You are with some shining names.

At the window there was a little gray light coming. The window was almost hidden by the bunks which had been pushed against its bars, but from where Myra sat on the floor, she could see up into a tiny square of the changing sky. The cell looked even worse in the muddy yellow of the electric bulb.

I suppose I shouldn't stop at the heroes of the Middle Ages. There are more recent slaves and conquerers. Dachau and Belsen— they, too, had men who stood in their moment and said, "I am a person; you must not degrade me." Her eye wandered around the cell and fixed on the slop bucket again, and she tried to ease her aching body on the floor. Dachau and Belsen.

In 1910, technology was going to make everybody free and freedom was going to make everybody good. The new cars had rolled up to the gates of death camps. Dreams of the perfecting of man ended in the gas chambers and behind the cleverly devised electric fences. Didn't everybody dream that dream? Didn't we *all*?

Maybe all but one. Is man imperfect by nature? Maybe only white man? There it was. Delphine was answering to everyone who had ever told her that she and hers were outside the elm-street-and-steeple dream of democracy. If the black heroes weren't in the history

books, then they were also not included in the Albigensian Crusade
and the ride to Belsen. The possibility of perfection—that was being
girded, all right. If Delphine took her blows in hate and in the belief
that *her* people could be perfect, not in some millennium but soon,
and by her own good efforts, what would be, could be given her, what
pain could she endure that wasn't worth it? Not for freedom, not for
friendship, certainly not for the right of ingress to the Tugwell library.
Oh, God, who will help M.J. take her hurting now, when all that M.J.
wants is to include in her God-blesses before bed all the misery-run-
ning, sorrow-spawning world of white and black?

It was morning. M.J. was trembling quietly on the floor. She
looked exhausted and ill, and she hadn't even gone yet. Myra got up,
and the aching numbed to her every bone. She went to where
Delphine was perched, sleeping.

"Delphine?"

"What-do-you-want?" It was the too-clear enunciation of an educated Negro to a white who will call him Rastus if he slurs a letter.

"You've got to do something to help M.J."

"I bet you're happy, white gal. If it wasn't for your people putting
us down, she wouldn't *be* scared now!"

So it was true. The blind would see and the halt would rejoice.
No cowards, no sinners, no wrongs. In the jubilee. In the great jubilee.
"Help her, Delphine. The sheriff is looking for weakness. If he finds it,
he might kill her with his hands or with her own shame. Help her, or
I'm going to start talking about you, Delphine. I'm going to start asking
questions that the others have never asked."

Myra could see the gains and losses ticking off in Delphine's head.
Her eyes were clinical and her expression detatched as an Egyptian
funerary statue. Delphine, at the height of her concentration, was
intensely, breathtakingly beautiful. She stayed in her place for a minute,
two. Then she stretched and the odds and possibilities arranged themselves before her. With elaborate, lithe ease she swung down to the floor,
yawning, and bent to where M.J. lay. They began to whisper. Myra was
glad she couldn't hear them. For a moment her eye strayed to the vacant
place, Delphine's place on the bed. She had a sudden urge to climb up
and take it and make Delphine fight to get it back. The place would be
comfortable for a little nap; she was sore all over from the floor. The
place would be dark against the back wall; she could sleep for a while.

No, Delphine was the leader, the place was her place. Only Delphine, however fanatical and blind, could lead the girls through all the questions, the licks and the lawyers. She found her eyes fixed again. What was so fascinating about that slop bucket! We're both on the floor, she thought.

"I wish to record an opinion," she said to it quietly. "In 325 the Council of Nicaea decided that sacraments at the hands of a lapsed bishop were valid where the intent of the communicant was sincere. The baptisms of these bishops stood. I always wondered about that decision. It smacked too much of ends justifying means. I hereby make my statement to the estimable theologians of the Council of Nicaea: 'Avé, fellas, Salvé, fellas, Congratulations and greetings from the Tugwell jail.'"

MISS VINCENT

Maria Dabrowska

JUST BEFORE LEAVING ON HER VACATION IN MID—APRIL, NATALIE Sztumska decided to inspect the army reading room located in a wing of the old stronghold personally, without relying on her assistants.

This reading room did not fall directly within the sphere of her authority. Natalie worked in the central administration of the Society of Cultural Preservation for the Soldier, while the stronghold was supervised by the local section of the society in that area.

For some time, however, there had been talk that the person to whom that post was entrusted was not equal to the task. But however many times Natalie would consult the local section regarding the matter, she always found everyone busy with arrangements for breakfast, afternoon tea, or a regimental celebration or a field mass on the occasion of dedicating a flag. Whenever she came, a major or a captain would always be standing at the table together with the chairwoman, full of feverish anxiety, and they would realize that something else had been forgotten, something had not been ordered, or someone had not been invited. The excited officer would exclaim, "Perhaps there's still time!" and would grab the telephone while the chairwoman, an attractive, prepossessing woman who had a weak heart, would take advantage of the respite to lean down toward Natalie and quietly, so as not to disturb the shouting directed into the telephone receiver, which seemed to penetrate her like the last rites, would beg for a temporary postponement of the irritating question of the reading room, which was called the fortress.

"Please believe me," she said, "that we're simply snowed under with work here. If right now we also start on the stronghold, we won't be able to manage. Our library overseer couldn't even do anything right now because she, poor thing, is doing the work of three people. But later, immediately after the celebration of the twenty-eighth regiment, we'll put things in order there."

Yet after the celebration there immediately arose the need to arrange another; then three clubs were opened, and after waiting in vain for the proper agents to start in, Natalie one day awoke to the conviction that she must step in herself, bypassing, so to speak, the official route.

Thereafter whenever she found a spare moment she would drop into the fortress club during the hours the reading room was open in order to observe how the work there was going. She noticed a multitude of flaws, and each contact with the librarian left a painful and distasteful and simultaneously rather humorous impression, the essence of which was difficult to define for the time being.

The librarian was called Regina Vincent. She had no professional training, but was, as the saying goes, active in social work, and even "distinguished" in it, so it was believed, accordingly, that she could cope.

After several visits to the stronghold and after receiving from the same Miss Vincent many explanations that aroused only skepticism, Natalie informed her one day that the following day she would come in the morning to take stock of the inventory with her and to revise the control cards and the account books, which gave the figures of reader circulation. She ordered the issuing of books to be suspended for two days.

Next day she got up early and by a quarter after eight had caught a tram so as to arrive at nine, according to the telephone agreement.

There had been a rainstorm during the night, after which it had turned significantly colder. At the crossroads where one had to wait for the tram, a powerful wind pounded and cracked as it rushed out from behind the corners. Here and there in the dark gray sky, crowded with clouds, slightly paler scars and cicatrices shining with feeble brightness were visible. The outlines of houses had a fresh and somewhat raw look. The pavements were still wet.

During the ride Natalie's thoughts continually revolved around

Regina Vincent. She recalled some of her answers, sly due to stupidity, and reflected with alarm that in all likelihood the steps now being taken would result in the removal of the incompetent worker. She did not know whether she could win by force so as to bring that about. She felt comfortable only in the midst of a situation of which she could approve—in each conflict she always tended to acknowledge the antagonist's right.

She awoke from these thoughts when she felt herself being crushed. At the beginning there had been lots of room in the tram; past one of the stations, however, the activity had increased.

With someone's dress and overcoat right in her face, Natalie squeezed up as far as she could against the window and watched as the distorted and broken reflection of the tram pushed through the panes increasingly smaller shops with increasingly loud signboards. Now and then she felt the passengers who were boarding and getting off push against her shoulders, arms, and knees,

After a while the pushing decreased in violence. The tram rolled out of the town limits. Along the sides of the street the lawns and the frail shrubs of the new park looked green, and farther beyond them but just as green appeared the oval forts and sloping hillside of the ancient fortress. Finally the tram halted at the last stop. The driver unscrewed the steering wheel with a crack and left, carrying it with him.

The last passengers jumped down off the steps. Inside the empty vehicle a child—a little girl—pretended she did not want to get out yet. Her mother kept calling to her: "Come on, be good!" but she would turn away contrarily and look through the window, laughing.

To get to the fortress one had to go through a viaduct extending over the railroad tracks. The viaduct was old and the wood on it was already blackened, but the steps of the stairs were covered with new tinplate and a couple of moldy planks had been replaced by new ones.

This sight cheered Natalie up. The last time she had walked through here she had worried that it wouldn't occur to anyone to get this viaduct into more decent shape. Yet when the time came someone thought of it.

"Apparently there's a time for everything. Perhaps it will also come for Miss Vincent, and I want to accelerate it needlessly?" she thought, glancing at the bright leaves under her feet.

A train was slowly rolling down the rails. It had only just moved off. One could hear the loose rattle of wheels and the heavy puffing of the engine. Two peasants jostled passersby as they ran along the hand railing to see the train. To the right of the viaduct a soldier was lying in the wild grass below, propped up on his elbow, reading a newspaper which he had folded over four times. On the other side two tar—stained workers were squeezing through the crevice between the hand railing of the steps and the fence that separated the tracks from the road. This way they wished to bypass the viaduct and go directly across the tracks. The entire railing was shaking from their efforts, but they finally got across.

Natalie entered the avenue of large trees leading to the fortress gate.

The wind was less violent here, and the trees swayed heavily, making a monotonous, gushing sound.

Passes were issued nearby beyond the gate in a small vaulted room. A sergeant whose chest was covered with ribbons sat over an enormous register with columns. He was writing out a pass for an old woman with a checkered kerchief.

"Surname?" he asked.

"And yours?" He turned to Natalie next.

She gave her name and address, then started looking in her handbag for the identification that was customarily required. This time, however, the sergeant didn't demand any identification. He didn't demand anything at all. It was the same with the soldier standing at the entrance to the bridge stretched across the moat. Sometimes he asked for the pass only when one was leaving the fortress; at other times, however, he demanded that one show it upon entering.

At the bottom of the moat, potatoes and vegetables grew abundantly. An enormous elder bush in the corner at the gate reached with its white plates of flowers right up to the handrailing of the bridge.

Passing the second inner gate, Natalie walked along a pavement that was unpleasantly full of holes, in the direction of the temporary location of the club. Her heart was pounding. It became increasingly painful for her to think about the confrontation that awaited her with the librarian.

The entrance to the club consisted of several boards placed at a slant from the sidewalk to the threshold. The boards were rotten and full of holes, and the threshold was already no more than a remnant of scratches and splinters. This deplorable sight aroused something akin to combativeness in Natalie.

The spacious stairway disposed her to be more conciliatory, however. It was washed clean. The large door, painted the color of bull's blood, which led to the interior of the club was open. One could enter the reading room either through the room in which the librarian lived or through the hall with the stage for plays. Natalie chose the latter route, again feeling fit to do battle over the reading room.

The hall was adorned with torn red-and-white paper banderoles and portraits of national dignitaries whose faces had been given gloomy and frightened expressions by local painters. The ceiling of this setting for spiritual entertainment leaked, and a puddle had formed on the floor from the night's storm.

When Natalie mounted the stage along the bench that was propped against it, the hollow floor resounded beneath her feet. The frail walls of the set were painted pink with a fiendish flowered border. A piano stood to one side under the stiff painted draperies. To descend from the stage one had to go down several extremely modest steps to a door behind which the reading room was located in a room offstage.

This spacious room was divided into two sections by a thin partition that didn't reach the ceiling. The opening in the wall that comprised the door was blocked off by a table on which lay the inventory register for the reading room, the bracketed catalogues with the covers turned upward, and flat cardboard boxes containing the control cards—all obviously freshly prepared. Inside, one could see a flat closet made of ash, the archetypical office filing cabinet. The librarian wasn't there.

Natalie approached the table, glanced inside, and looked at the closet standing at right angles to the other one and thereby making that area into a kind of small room, Both closets were open wide; all the books lying on the shelves were at a slant. Natalie got the impression that there were surprisingly few of them. She moved the control cards so as to see how many readers there were, but the last card in the row had the number ten. The readers' cards weren't arranged in order; they were simply thrown into boxes without any order or system.

Natalie passed through between the table and the opening in the wooden wall, and going inside, she took off her coat and hat and hung them on the latch of the raised window, through which one could see the green embankment of the fortress and nearer, the large flowering acacias. The wind was tossing the acacias about, and whenever the branches would bend a little more, the overcast sky was visible through them. For a fraction of a minute Natalie couldn't tear her eyes away from the disturbing little leaves and the bunches of flowers whose light clusters were tossed about violently.

Despite herself she was amazed that there was so much strength and resistance in something so flimsy and fragile.

"Just as with humans." She made the comparison unconsciously, and suddenly lost patience.

"There isn't a living soul here," she thought, discouraged.

She looked around urgently in the direction of the door, behind which at that exact moment someone started to tinkle the piano keys and a voice that struggled to become an alto sang:

If not today, then tomorrow, if not today, then tomorrow
You'll be mine, girl. . . .

Natalie opened the door somewhat violently and inside saw Miss Vincent at the piano. Her dark gray dog, Linda, lay beside her, her elongated nuzzle resting on her paws.

Miss Vincent broke off and ran up in little leaps.

"How can that be!" she cried. "You're here! That's impossible. How can it be? How did you get here? How? Linda and I went out; we were across the way. And we didn't meet you. But it's impossible."

"Yet I did get here, unbelievable though that may seem to you," said Natalie, feeling herself grow pale with irritation at this greeting.

For some time longer Miss Vincent couldn't imagine how it could have happened that they'd missed each other en route.

"That's not important," said Natalie, at the same time resisting the dog, whose unexpected lick she suddenly felt on her face. "Go away," she mumbled feebly, removing the dog's paws from her arms.

"She recognized you! She recognized you," Miss Vincent kept crying. "Linda! Don't dance! Oh, do look—she's dancing for joy!"

In fact the dog, barking rhythmically, was executing something resembling a dance beside her. Then, stopping and pricking up her ears, she seemed to be gauging the impression she'd created.

Natalie wanted to laugh. She turned toward the window so that

Miss Vincent would not interpret her merriment as favorable to her.

"Let's get to work," she said, still turned aside. "Even so we'll not be able to finish today."

"Let's!" cried Miss Vincent readily.

And bustling about, she continued talking:

"I always take Linda with me whenever I get the chance because I'm afraid of her becoming too sluggish. She's in a delicate condition, you know," she added with sly boastfulness.

By now Natalie had gained control over herself, and sat down at the table.

"For God's sake," she said loudly and icily, "Let's leave the dog in peace."

"Heavens!" Miss Vincent was astonished. "You speak to me as though I were a child."

Miss Vincent was an unusually tiny and mobile person similar to a little spider. Her frail, thin legs were not exactly crooked, but they weren't quite straight either, which, added to their thinness, gave the impression that any minute they would bend and break right before your eyes. Her mouth lacked the lower and upper front teeth and her smile revealed pale gums that resembled the pulp of a squashed strawberry. The lusterless head of hair, black as ink, appeared to press down upon this frail being, who was characterized by a kind of premature feverish fading. Her black eyes, like hot drops of sealing wax, had something scalding in them.

Before starting work Miss Vincent ran several times first to her room then into the hall, and the indefatigable dog accompanied her there and back.

Natalie began by checking which books were to be found on the shelves. She would read the number off the inventory list while Miss Vincent, at the closet, would announce whether the book with that number was there and what title it bore. During this procedure Natalie noticed that reading out the titles didn't go smoothly. Miss Vincent stammered over the best-known classical literary names and twisted the titles of masterpieces, acquaintance with which is the property of every civilized man to the same degree as washing and combing one's hair. At the same time she seemed totally oblivious both to her mistakes and to Natalie's embarrassed, startled glances. She kept running briskly from shelf to shelf, leaping onto the stool which substituted for a ladder, and moving the stool from one place to another as she threatened the dog with it.

"Bring the ball," she'd command as she did so, stamping her foot. "Come on, bring it! Oh, you mother-to-be, you!"

The dog would leap up heavily, bark, and then dance again in circles around herself.

"Look! Do look!" The librarian was frantic with joy. "Oh you—you heroine!" she added, glancing significantly in Natalie's direction.

"So," she added, tapping Linda with the book she was holding in her hand, "we got a medal for valor at the marketplace in Katowice, didn't we?"

Natalie already knew of the dog Linda's exploits. During the couple of times she had visited the central office, Miss Vincent had managed to tell several times how the dog had run thirty kilometers in freezing weather so as to let a detachment of Silesian insurgents know that her mistress had been imprisoned by the Germans. How she then had led them to the prison door and how it all ended with both heroines being decorated in the marketplace at Katowice.

Natalie, however, did not consider it possible to run the library with the aid of this heroic myth. She was ashamed and angry with herself for simply not knowing how to neutralize the heroic canine and that past heroism which pressed on everything like a stone.

"I've heard that already," she said drily in response to the allusion to Katowice.

"My God," Miss Vincent said in a sorrowful and offended voice. "I don't understand. . . . You're speaking to me again as though you have no use for me whatever."

In answer Natalie called out the number of a book and after a while said in a fairly calm voice:

"I'm angry because you're reading off the titles as though you're hearing about these books and authors for the first time."

"First time?" Miss Vincent said with surprise, in a tone that one hears from peasant women who place their hands on their hips as they shout during an argument, "My God! For the first time! I can't imagine how you can say that."

And she assumed an expression that said she didn't understand what she was being reproached with, but only sensed vaguely that something negative lay in store for her. There was a careful and sly calculation, almost an animal caution, at the bottom of this expression and in the manner in which she became indignant.

"Is she an imbecile or what?" Natalie wondered.

But Miss Vincent appeared to be beginning to understand what it was all about and she disclosed as much in a way in which she could afford to. She said suddenly in reference to the next book:

"I recently recommended this to Józwik. He's our best reader. He was so appreciative. He said, 'You really know how to give us advice.'"

Natalie passed over her words in silence.

Shortly, when they reached the scientific section, Miss Vincent tried her new method once again. Checking one of the following numbers, she read out, after a moment's reflection: *"Studies of Organic Matter in the Universe*—written by Joseph Zapalski."

"Oh, that's good," she cried, "I was going to put this aside to read myself. I've intended to read it for a long time, since I don't know it."

Natalie gave her a long look.

"Oh, is that what you wanted to put aside for yourself?" she asked, "Wouldn't it be better to start with Mickiewicz?"

Miss Vincent was silent for a moment, her eyes wandering about the room as though she couldn't orient herself with regard to the proportions of the danger threatening her. At last she said in her habitual way:

"Oh, Lord! How can you say that? As though I didn't know Mickiewicz."

"Let's get a move on," urged Natalie. "Let's get to the missing books."

"Now that's really not worth talking about," Miss Vincent brightened up, "We've already done the most important thing, and you can see that everything's in order."

Natalie lit a cigarette, staring attentively at the astonishing librarian.

"Are you pretending?" she asked. "Do you really not know what's the most important thing here?"

"Oh, Holy Jesus—here we go again. . . ." Miss Vincent became worried. "What do you mean—pretend? I've never pretended in my life. I know everything perfectly well," she said a trifle uncertainly.

"And have you really not noticed that only a third of the books are to be found on the shelves?"

"Well, what of it?" she retorted, recovering her self—confidence. "They're lent out."

"Lent out?" Natalie smiled tartly, for she had the worst presentiment about the missing books. "We'll see whether they're lent out. Please take the control cards."

An expression of panic appeared on Miss Vincent's face. It looked as though she wished to gain time and she started trying to persuade Natalie to go and have something to eat. It was already two o'clock, as it turned out.

"I'd order a lunch for you from the club," she said, "but I don't know whether it's any good. But in our regimental teashop there are very good pork dishes. Fresh every day. I, however, could do without eating altogether. Properly speaking, man lives by work."

Natalie maintained an inflexible silence. For the moment she hadn't the least desire to enter into any kind of friendly relations, however passing and incidental, with Miss Vincent. After a moment, however, she changed her mind. Perhaps if she let the woman eat and take a rest from her exchange with her, she'd find out quicker and better what kind of person she was.

So they went.

During the short walk to the teashop attached to one of the regiments located in the fortress, Natalie fell into almost complete silence, while Miss Vincent's garrulity increased significantly.

It soon became apparent that this hour's rest was Miss Vincent's hour of triumph, and she now had the upper hand over Natalie, for she knew the way, she knew what was where, could direct her steps.

"Be careful," she exhorted her, "there's a hole there. Here, we go through here. It's faster this way. You're probably surprised that it's so deserted here? The soldiers are at shooting practice. If one wants to be in charge of a club, one has to know about everything!"

"Ah," she sighed further on. "If only my Linda could have a cold spell like this for her day of trial. German shepherd bitches in general take the heat badly, and especially when they give birth, And she's going to any day, any day now. . . ."

The animal was, in fact, fat and heavy; she'd run past, then when the whim took her, would run around peering into yards and thickets, standing at attention in the middle of the road, running far away and returning to fawn at their feet.

"Yesterday I thought the time had come . . .," Miss Vincent babbled on, "but when I began to count when that husband of hers had visited her, I became convinced that there are two more weeks to go. Oh, look! Look," she started shouting suddenly. "That's Linda's husband!"

And stopping Natalie, she excitedly indicated a beautiful German shepherd with a muzzle, which ran indifferently past his "wife" as he bounded stiffly toward some goal he'd spotted earlier.

"The puppies will be thoroughbreds," Natalie murmured almost against her will.

"Of course. What did you think?"

In the courtyard surrounded by a quadrilateral barrack several soldiers were sitting on a bench in front of the guardhouse, while another stood at some distance and sounded the reveille, turning in a different direction each time. His khaki—colored shirt kept wrinkling in the back under the band into a rather uneven frill.

At the counter in the teashop another soldier just like him stood leaning carelessly against the counter behind which a female shop assistant in a white stained apron was bustling about. Behind the glass of the cases along the sides of the counter one could see cheese, cigarettes, and chocolate. A cat was sleeping on the window sill in the midst of empty bottles, beside a jar of strawberries sprinkled with sugar.

"Here's a better place," said Miss Vincent, and they went through to the other room. It was almost empty here too. A corporal was sitting sideways and alone at one of the small tables. Elbow propped against the edge of the table and the arm of the chair, he was examining his own interlaced fingers. There wasn't a trace of food on his table. After a while the corporal rose, stretched, and walked away. On the way, he stopped at the door for a minute and lit a cigarette.

Natalie ordered some bread and tea. Miss Vincent, on the other hand, brought herself two cakes, two small sausages, and a portion of mustard and four ounces of scraps for Linda.

"What was it I'd started to tell you when we were coming in?" she asked, spreading mustard on the small sausages and chasing them down with a cake. And without recalling what it was, she launched into something else.

"Perhaps you're afraid that this butter isn't fresh," she said sooth-

ingly, "but I would have sensed it from afar. I've become terribly sensitive to bad fat since the time the Germans fed us only margarine. And
black coffee."

Her voice quivered.

"Seventeen days of black coffee. Can you imagine?"

And again she started on a tale about her heroic educational
activity, about the Germans' entry into Katowice, about her imprisonment and so forth. When she reached the place where Linda fetched
the soldiers who disarmed the German rear guard and knocked down
the prison door, Miss Vincent's voice failed and she burst into tears,

"Oh," she said, wiping her tears and rummaging about in her
handbag, "here's a photograph of me right after my release. Look at
how I looked. A shadow, a specter, not a human being. And that's
Linda."

Natalie examined the photograph in silence and Miss Vincent
continued her story.

"I only wish you could see how they loved me in Katowice. They
didn't want to let me go at any price, only I was foolishly obstinate
about coming here. And why I came here I don't know. For I'll really
get it here. I was warned right away that they'll hound me here. And
they will."

"The old women will hound me," she added significantly, growing
increasingly bolder,

And then, wiping the tears from her inflamed eyes, she started
again.

"But I don't let it affect me," she assured Natalie, "I work and I
don't care about anything else. And *I* take pains. Everyone ought to
enter into another's situation and judge only afterward. Look at the
flowers on the window sill, for example. All of that's my work. If it
weren't for my influence, there wouldn't be anything here. I don't
even know why it is that I do wield such an influence. Officially I
have no connection with the teashop, but just ask the shop assistant
and she'll tell you how concerned I am about everything here. Just
now, for example, a new commander arrived and he wanted to remove
the shop assistant. But I didn't let him. 'Colonel,' I said, 'One doesn't
treat people like that, you first must be convinced that you're right.'
For I may be this or that; you don't know me yet, but I cannot endure
injustice. That's why I'm respected everywhere. Only the person who

judges by appearances can think I'm superficial. The new commander was also like that at the beginning, but when he saw what I was like, he said, 'I thought you only liked to amuse yourself, because you're so cheerful, but you've done so much here.' To which I replied: 'Colonel, anyone who's lived through what I have, must approach life seriously!'"

She fell silent and finished her cakes. Linda roamed around the room sniffing, crawled under the tables and traced smells in all the corners. Natalie continued drinking tea and in the other room the shop assistant said to a soldier:

"I love it when they play sad tunes. That's the way I am. I don't like to listen to anything cheerful at all."

Shortly Miss Vincent started to spout her nonsense again:

"I'd like you to come to one of our dances sometime. I arrange such dances that a corporal—he's also one of our readers—said to me: 'You know, Madam Director, since getting to know the club, I don't go to town at all.' And what torture it is to arrange a dance like that. Once they brought to the hall a, well . . . in a word—a slut. But I handled it. I at once went and posted everywhere such notices as 'Rank is not what adorns one!' 'Respect your entertainment!' 'Don't degrade the entrance to the reading room!' And naturally she was told—away with you! They wanted to expel the one who'd brought her here, but I told them—no, gentlemen! She's the guilty one, for a woman ought to be able to respect her own dignity."

Her eyes blazed like burning caramel at these words and a dark flush stayed on her thin face. She swallowed and raved on:

"Oh, you can't imagine how difficult it is to deal with soldiers. And the worst was the orchestra. . . . Everyone in the orchestra was so depraved. . . . Had I not dealt with them I don't know what would have happened. And now? They're the best readers, the most decent boys. . . . And they're always willing to play for me. Whether it's a film or a dance, I don't have to worry about the music. . . ." she boasted, as though wanting to get everything out while they were there.

Natalie rested her head against both her palms and the whole time stared diligently at Miss Vincent.

"How helpless honesty is in the face of such a creature," she thought. "What would it help if I told her what I think of her yarns? What do I think, anyway? I don't know myself."

Miss Vincent, in the meantime, after a lengthy pause leaned across and said in a careful, low voice:

"I'm writing a play. It's about librarians, in order to attract readers. It's completely suitable. It's simplified."

"What can I do," she added with a sigh, "that's the kind of artistic nature I have. But that's not at all surprising. I come from an artistic family. . . ."

When she got to that point, Natalie interrupted:

"Let's go," she said, "it's time to get back to work."

"Let's," the librarian agreed with energy. It was impossible to tell how she explained Natalie's long silence to herself. During the walk back she was as amicably disposed as if a joyful friendly encounter had united her with Natalie.

"Oh," she said, looking at Natalie's black-and-white suit. "How I love it when all the colors are coordinated like that. I'm crazy about that. I must remember to do that myself. I'm so ragged."

Natalie glanced sideways at her and noticed that the expression of guarded caution had vanished completely from Miss Vincent's face. It was serene, as if already settled in new circumstances.

Natalie felt herself growing pale with anger at this sight..

"You should be thinking about the missing books," she said bitterly.

Miss Vincent drew her black brows together.

"O Lord," she moaned in grief, as though in the presence of some great disloyalty. "You're starting again. What missing books?"

The state of affairs that was revealed in the course of their further work proved to be worse than Natalie had feared. A lot of time was spent on simply putting the disorderly control cards in order. When Natalie expressed surprise at their not having been put in order prior to her arrival, Miss Vincent said: "Oh, a few stupid cards that are out of order and you immediately fasten onto that. I'll do it in a jiffy."

But she couldn't. Everything soon got mixed up in her hands. Natalie had to do it herself.

Miss Vincent in the meantime strove to maintain the friendly atmosphere which, as she apparently supposed, she'd earned by her confidences in the teashop.

"What do you do," she asked, "to make your hair lie so smoothly? Oh, if only mine were to stay like that without a permanent. Because I don't have time to go from here to the hairdresser in town and that's why I look like a scarecrow. Although, to tell the truth, I have no pretensions."

Changing her intonation, she chirped to the dog:

"My poor little wife, my poor sweet, my heroine! Bring me the ball, bring it here!"

The dog began to romp about the room and instead of the ball she brought out from a corner an enormous gray stone, which she. lowered noisily to the ground.

When Natalie glanced around at this noise, Miss Vincent laughingly explained:

"She had a ball, but chewed it up. I had to bring her this stone. . . . Do you know that she reacts to numbers? When soldiers get counted she looks and barks each time. Hey! Linda! One! Two! Three! Four! See how she jumps and whines. Don't you think it's true that she's qualified for the first step in the area of human nature because she's made a contribution? . . . Then in Katowice. After all, for a dog to run thirty kilometers in such cold to save a human being . . . and that's my Linda, who's so sensitive to everything. . . ."

Natalie looked at her so coldly and piercingly that Miss Vincent fell silent.

Natalie maybe for the first time in her life experienced something like a desire to bang her fist on the table and to abuse someone. She'd always thought that only fear inspires cruelty in a person. She'd feared spiders and centipedes terribly from childhood. And whenever she glimpsed these creatures near her and couldn't escape, she had to kill them, squeezing her eyes shut, breaking into a sweat of revulsion and terror. Now she perceived that the sight of perverse stupidity likewise instigates one to cruelty.

Bristling from the effort with which she'd controlled herself, she informed Miss Vincent that judging by what their work showed, the books missing from the shelves were all, one after another, either incorrectly recorded on the control cards, or overdue, or had been returned long ago by the readers and were lost without a trace.

"You're quick to assume it's 'without a trace.'" "Miss Vincent, already somewhat surprised, now became indignant.

"Well, if they're crossed out on the reader's card and not borrowed by anyone else–and they're not on the shelves—how can I trace them?"

"O Lord!" The librarian was scandalized. "But I'm telling you: they're out, and you keep asking where, where!"

After a while, having calmed down somewhat and now in an even voice, Natalie strove to explain to Miss Vincent that with her system, or rather with the chaos of her work, this unfortunate soldiers' reading room would soon be ruined. Miss Vincent now began to resist openly and desperately. She insisted that, completely to the contrary, the reading room had made advances, for no one could conceive of what had gone on there before. Given the mass of work, it was possible to make two or three mistakes, surely that was understandable. And even so, almost everything about which Miss Sztumska was angry had probably been done by the previous librarian.

"You're saying that books have been kept long overdue. But what about this book, for example? It's recorded, true, that it was borrowed in January. But is there a year specified in the date? It was probably a year and a half ago. In any case, I can recognize the handwriting perfectly. That's not my handwriting. I write the dashes with a different slant from hers. You can tell that at once."

"And this also isn't your handwriting? And this? And this?" Natalie asked, showing her the figures where someone had written in the current year next to the January date of withdrawal.

Miss Vincent started examining it gravely.

"Certainly, I don't deny that. Although . . . the day seems to be in my handwriting—but the month has that other dash. But I'm not arguing—who's there?" she shouted suddenly, listening intently. "Excuse me, I must go and see."

She and the dog both ran out. They returned shortly.

"It wasn't anyone," Miss Vincent informed her. "Yet I was certain someone was knocking."

In a moment, when Natalie was bent over some notes, Miss Vincent started anew:

"Just a minute. I must check whether our professor hasn't come for the lecture. I let him know that it was canceled, but who knows, perhaps he's come. Everyone likes to come here so much that sometimes nothing is on, but they come and sit anyway."

When Miss Vincent disappeared, Natalie glanced about her, straightened up, sighed, and passed her hand over her face.

The light in the room had changed. It had become warmer, had acquired a brightness. Natalie unconsciously glanced out of the window. It was clearing up outside. Precisely at that moment the acacias were standing bathed in sunlight, looking as though someone had dipped them in golden oil. The wind was stopping and at moments the trees would be immobile. Then it would return, however, and would tug at them and shake them.

Miss Vincent returned with the news that a "Michael" had swept the lecture hall badly.

"Perhaps soldiers know how to do everything," she said with regret, "but none of them can sweep with a wet broom."

Here and there outside the building one could hear a door slam. Shortly someone started to walk through the auditorium. The steps halted for a moment, then resounded on the boards of the stage. One could hear the resonant bang of the piano lid, and directly after that, practice passages from some études resounded.

"Can you hear that?" cried Miss Vincent. "Caesar's come to practise."

"He's a member of the orchestra," she added in a confidential whisper. "He attends the conservatory. Oh, if he could only play something decent for us."

She pushed open the door leading to the stageroom.

"Caesar," she called imperiously, "play us something decent."

Caesar, however, implacably continued playing practice exercises.

Miss Vincent said, inspiration in her voice:

"I attended the conservatory."

"Will you please answer only my questions," Natalie snapped all of a sudden.

"Good Heavens!" Miss Vincent was appalled. "In all my life no one has ever spoken to me like that. You keep treating me as though I'm a snot-nosed kid. I know I don't look it, but I'm close to forty."

"You behave as if you were four."

Miss Vincent suddenly started crying.

"I just don't know. You're simply insulting me."

"You're asking to be insulted," Natalie said, ashamed and at the same time controlling herself with difficulty. "Just one of the errors which are swarming here disqualifies you and yet you, in addition to everything, prevaricate and don't want to admit it."

A flash of hope flickered over Miss Regina Vincent's frightened face:

"Admit it?" she cried with animation. "Now no one can reproach me with that. That I shouldn't be able to recognize my own error? It's only that some people don't wish to get an insight into things. If you wanted to get an insight into the situation, you'd see that yes, there are errors, but again, they're not such. . ."

"And how am I to get this insight?" Natalie had the awkwardness to inquire.

The librarian swiftly shook her head and eagerly hurried to reply:

"I think you started badly. I'd begin by writing out on a separate piece of paper. . . ."

Natalie no longer listened to what Miss Vincent would write out on a separate sheet of paper. In a lightning flash she realized that she'd let loose from its hiding place a terrible, invincible nightmare—or rather, a stupid person who knocked every weapon out of her hand while herself wielding only one, but a disabling one—handfuls of sand thrown in one's eyes. She sensed that if she now gave Miss Vincent the freedom to express herself she'd not be able to settle things with her. She overcome her germinating hesitation, and not believing her own ears, said firmly:

"I'm not asking about that. Please be quiet."

And until 8:00 P.M. the work was carried on in silence, in which only Natalie's short questions and Miss Vincent's answers, reluctant, pretentious, and affable, could be heard.

Natalie didn't work any quicker in this atmosphere of injured silence, but she considered it more appropriate and regretted not having arranged it that way earlier.

"So it turns out," she thought, "that all it needed was a good shouting."

After this shouting, however, there remained an unpleasant after-taste, as though a concealed villain had been unmasked. Natalie now had the feeling that since she could shout like that, everything in her that consisted of goodness and benevolence toward people was a lie. She justified herself to herself by saying that one shouldn't be made of putty where everyone is concerned. Everybody is pleasant to some people. And unpleasant to others. The point is the situation in which one is one or the other.

In spite of this she felt that something continued to bother her; she also couldn't restrain herself from casting furtive glances at Miss Vincent, the point of which she herself didn't understand.

Miss Vincent, in the meantime, having restrained herself from speaking for a long time, addressed her quietly:

"Please excuse me. I wanted to ask something else, or I'll forget. . . . Is it absolutely necessary that I make the notes with a fountain pen, or can it be a ballpoint?"

Natalie looked at her without irritation.

"Just note them down any way," she said as mildly as possible. And suddenly she realized with exasperation that the inner sense of spiritual unease that was oppressing her was the fear of having been more unpleasant to Miss Vincent than necessary.

But she, as though sensing the change in Natalie's temper, raised a finger and said, listening intently:

"Oh, the cocks are crowing. If only the weather were fine. Maybe it will be."

Natalie's voice became stiffer again.

"Four hundred ninety-seven?" she asked, and receiving the answer:

"Reader's card number twenty-three—I've checked that on the card specified, the book under number four ninety-seven was noted down, and then crossed out. The reader returned it and it should be in its place."

It wasn't, of course; Natalie checked the inventory to see what book it was that had got lost that way.

"Eeden, *Little Johnny*," she read.

She remembered reading that book once on a hot day, lying on the grass under a blooming snowball bush. She sensed in herself the aroma, color, and melody of that vacation, long since past.

That copy of *Little Johnny* was also lost.

Tearing herself from these reminiscences with an effort, Natalie mentioned a number. Others followed.

One of the books had been checked out the previous year and hadn't been returned yet. Beside the date of withdrawal in the former librarian's hand was written: "Shot himself."

Natalie checked again to see what book hadn't been returned for such a horrible reason. It was Thomas Mann's *A Man and His Dog*.

With surprise and sadness she thought that more or less at the same time as the unfortunate fellow had checked out the book, she too had borrowed it from one of her acquaintances. She'd read it lying in a hammock in a lovely suburban garden owned by her relatives. Then she lent it "for a day" to some friend of hers and now she suddenly remembered that after that she totally forgot about the book.

The further the checking of the control cards advanced, the more completely Natalie's anger subsided, while the silent librarian, who now seemed even smaller than she had until then, appeared to her as a being deserving the utmost pity.

It didn't cost Natalie anything to explain her sighs and the answers given in a thin, low voice as contrition and an acknowledgement, at long last, of her mistakes,

"And I'm not concerned with anything else," she thought, "only her attitude toward her wrongdoing. The wrongdoing itself isn't important."

And she felt more and more sorry for Miss Vincent.

"What do things—books—really mean," she mused, "in comparison with the lot of poor mankind. And what does she have, this poor Miss Vincent. A dog and the illusion that she's surrounded by men, young men, who need something from her. And if any of them stretches out a hand perhaps not for a book but for her, even if it's this Michael who doesn't know how to sweep or this Caesar who didn't want to play anything decent, then, good God, what's surprising about the fact that that pleasure would have a greater value for her than all the libraries in the whole world? Or if, on the contrary, she, poor thing, is yearning in vain for that thing, without which life isn't life, to happen. . . ."

Oh, Natalie knew well, very well, the value of such pleasures.

She wanted to say something to Miss Vincent that would console her. She almost wanted to apologize for her harshness. She wanted to implore her for a little bit of good will, for a crumb of concentration.

What also mitigated her anger to a great degree was that she now saw concrete work before her, She was distinctly aware of what needed to be improved and changed here, what orders to give. Anger has its place only while one is being critical. As soon as one gets down to work, one feels almost divine powers within oneself, one is not afraid to work with the worst and stupidest people, trusting that one will transform them all into good and intelligent beings.

When she finished the work, Natalie wanted to express this confidence to Miss Vincent. She didn't know, however, how to say this to her.

Tying her kerchief around her neck, she said coldly in an official tone:

"I shall be coming here regularly. When we finish the arrears I'll come out and assign you work for the entire summer. I won't make use of what I've discovered here. But if by autumn everything isn't in order, you won't stay here another day. Until then you'll be dealing only with me. Not with anyone from the administration, but privately with me. With me."

And Natalie suddenly blushed with shame as she heard the pride with which this "with me" resounded.

She wanted to leave, but Regina Vincent blocked her path.

"You won't tell on me?" she asked breathlessly. "Don't ridicule me there. . . . You'll s-see that everything will be fine. I'll do everything. I'll find everything . . . I'll replace them."

She writhed during all this like a fly stuck to flypaper and still buzzing.

Natalie shook her finger admonishingly at her. Miss Vincent seized her threatening hand, then the other, and started kissing both with rapture. She began pressing them to her bosom. She had a bosom as hard and dry as a board, and at the same time uncannily hot. Natalie blushed. "That's enough," she said and shook her finger admonishingly again—but now on the threshold.

Miss Vincent ran after her, together with the dog.

When they were crossing the stage, the soldier who was playing exercises rose and bowed, then sat down again and without stopping playing kept turning around until Natalie, the librarian, and the dog left the auditorium.

At the steps Miss Vincent and the dog turned back home.

Natalie went on alone.

The street was empty, not being much frequented, and weeds grew between the stones of the pavement. Not seeing anyone around, Natalie suddenly started to hum loudly. At the same time she made an indefinite gesture with her hand and even jumped and ran a couple of steps, just as little girls do.

"What am I doing?" she whispered, almost bursting out laughing, and it was only when she reached the bridge of the moat that she restrained somewhat these symptoms of unaccountable joy.

It was then too that she realized why she was so happy. She was happy that Miss Vincent had not got offended, had kissed her hand, had shown repentance and a willingness to improve. And the world surrounding her was also full of joy. The wind had stopped. The sky was clear and uncontaminated, as though never touched by the shroud of clouds. In this tranquillity, the light chill was not annoying. The greenery of the moat and the citadel slopes was already overlaid by shadows. Only the tops of the tallest trees were bathed in the ruddy glow. In the distance could be heard the melodious clamor of the city, which was changing its hues to flesh color, pink, and violet.

Along the edge of the streets, cutting across the view of the city, a purple and fiery tram was gliding along, its windowpanes carrying away the golden glow of the sunset.

"It's the kind of evening that we used to have in childhood," whispered Natalie in delight. And as though endowed anew with the absorbing susceptibility of her childhood, she stood on the bridge so as to cast an insatiable glance at the fresh greenery of the moat. Then unexpectedly the doubts that had vanished returned.

"How could I have let myself be duped like that?" she said almost out loud. "This was a classic display of cunning on the part of petty culprits, of pygmies who stupefy the very air around them. There was even the historical legend that one always has on such occasions.

"No, no," she thought, "my anger was holy, my anger was holy."

She longed to excite and kindle it again. But in spite of this, not holy anger, but a powerful sense of sympathy was growing unbidden in her heart. "Tomorrow," she consoled herself, "such things will probably turn up that I'll get mad again. Then I'll tell her that I wanted to let her remain, but I see it's impossible. And I'll immediately submit to the administration the results of my check and will make a motion that this Miss Vincent be dismissed.

"She pulls the wool over one's eyes—but so what?" the thought flashed beneath these resolutions. "Why, there are animals which, when caught, emit an unpleasant odor. Are they to blame for that? They want to defend themselves and live. And on some level they're right and have the right to exist."

Natalie was frequently oppressed by the thought that evil can't be eradicated anywhere or completely reformed. It's canceled out somehow and balanced by the totality of goodness that is scattered as generously over the world. But this doesn't happen visibly during one person's lifetime, and those who see the sowing and the fruit of evil don't see that distribution of justice.

Yet whether they see it or don't see it, there is no other way for poor mankind other than to sow good or evil. But what is that good and evil supposed to be as far as Miss Vincent is concerned?

"To take her by the horns, to force her to work hard, as is becoming, to somehow tighten down those loose screws. Not to let her breathe. Simply not let her breathe until everything is as clear as glass. Whether that's good or bad—I can't act otherwise," Natalie brooded, her thoughts moving ardently.

And the eagerness to accomplish this seized her for a moment with the rapturous power almost of a lover's inspiration.

Suddenly it occurred to her how this would end, The reading room will go tolerably, Miss Vincent will recover her self-confidence, and only then will get offended on account of today's events. An uproar will be raised in the Society of Cultural Preservation about the fact that Natalie is illegally taking over the fortress reading room completely, neglecting the official route—Miss Vincent will create a new legend for herself.

"Ha, it's difficult," she acknowledged superstitiously. "The sacred law of collectiveness decrees thus, Why, it exists to protect the puny and the weak. And that's certainly the way it should be."

Engrossed in her thoughts, Natalie didn't notice when she passed the gate.

"Your pass!" shouted the soldier after her.

She turned round, and handing the pass to the outstretched brown hand, she said:

"Oh, here you are."

As she emerged from the area of the fortress, she saw her train awaiting departure. She started quickening her steps, then ran.

She fell into the carriage as the train started to move. Jerked by the impetus of the train, she staggered and breathlessly sat down on the first end seat.

Opposite sat a man in a worker's shirt. He was holding a bunch of white stock in his lap. His head was bowed low.

"Where's he taking those flowers?" Natalie was surprised. "How sorry I feel for him. What does the fact that I feel so sorry for everybody mean?"

Through the windowpanes one could see for a moment longer at the bend to town the huge ruddy disk of the sun above a strip of violet mist.

The conductor nudged Natalie's arm.

"Ticket, Miss?"

WHO IS IT CAN TELL ME WHO I AM?

Gina Berriault

ALBERTO PERERA, LIBRARIAN, GRANTED NO CREDIBILITY TO POLICE profiles of dangerous persons. Writers, down through the centuries, had that look of being up to no good and were often mistaken for assassins, smugglers, fugitives from justice—criminals of all sorts. But the young man invading his sanctum, hands hidden in the pockets of his badly soiled green parka, could possibly be another lunatic out to kill another librarian. Up in Sacramento, two librarians were shot dead while on duty and, down in Los Angeles, the main library was sent up in flames by an arsonist. Perera loved life and wished to participate in it further.

"You got a minute?"

"I do not."

"Can I read you something?"

"Please don't." Recalling some emergency advice as to how to dissuade a man from a violent deed—*Engage him in conversation*—he said, "Go ahead," regretting his permission even as he gave it. Was he to hear, as the last words he'd ever hear, a denunciation of all librarians for their heinous liberalism, a damnation for all the lies, the deceptions, the swindles, the sins preserved within the thousands of books they so zealously guarded, even with their lives?

With bafflement in his grainy voice, the fellow read from a scrap of paper.

Greet the sun, spider. Show no rancor.
Give God your thanks, O toad; that you exist.
The crab has such thorns as the rose.
In the mollusc are reminiscences of women.
Know what you are, enigmas in forms.
Leave the responsibility to the norms,
Which they in turn leave to the Almighty's care.
Chirp on, cricket, to the moonlight. Dance on, bear.

The fellow granted his listener a moment to think about what he'd just heard. Then, "What do you make of it?"

"What do I make of it?"

"What I make of it," said the intruder, "is you're supposed to feel great if you're an animal. Like if you're talking about a spider or a toad. Am I supposed to do that?"

"Do what?"

"Like thank God because I'm me?"

"That's for you to decide. Take your time with it." Shuffling papers on his desk. "Take your time but not in here."

Watch your step with anybody playing dumb, Perera cautioned himself. They sneak up on you from behind. This fellow knew just what he was doing, pulling out a poem by Rubén Darío, reading it aloud to a librarian so proud of his Spanish ancestry he kept the name his dear mother had called him, Alberto, and there it was, his foreign name in a narrow frame on his desk for all who passed his open door to see. Maybe this fellow had been stabbed in prison by a Chicano with the name Perera, and now Perera, the librarian, a man of goodwill, a humanitarian, was singled out among his fellow librarians.

"What do you figure this guy's saying? Wake up every day feeling great you're you?"

"If that's what you figure he's saying, that's what he's saying. That's the best you can do with a poem."

Out in fistfuls from his parka pockets, more scraps of paper. So many, some fluttered to the floor. Cigarette packets inside out, gum wrappers, scavenged street papers of many colors that are slipped along underfoot by the winds of traffic, scraps become transcendentally unfamiliar by the use they'd been put to: Lines of poetry in a fixatedly careful, cramped handwriting.

"That spider, you take that spider." Entranced by a spider that only he could see, swinging between himself and Perera. "That spider is in its web where it belongs. Made it himself, swinging away. Sun comes out, strands all shiny, spider feels the warm sun on his back. Okay, glad he's a spider. I can see that. Same with the cricket. Makes chirpity-chirp to the moon. I can accept that. That toad, too. I can see he likes the mud, they're born in mud. It's the bear I can't figure out. Would you know if bears dance in their natural state?"

"Would I know if bears dance?"

"When they're on their own?" A cough, probably incited by some highly pleasurable secret excitement from tormenting a librarian. "What I know about bears," answering himself before his cough was over, is bears do not dance. It is not in their genetic code. I'll tell you when they dance. They dance when they got a rope around their neck. That poet slipped up there. A bear with a rope around his neck, do you see him waking up happy, hallooing the sun? Same thing."

"Same thing as what?"

No answer, only another cough, probably called up to cover his amusement over an obtuse librarian with a silk tie around his stiff neck.

"You know anything about the guy who wrote it? The bear didn't write it, that I know."

"No, the bear did not write it. Darío wrote it. A modernist, brought Spanish poetry into the modern age. Born in Chile. No, Nicaragua. Myself, I like Lorca. Lorca, you know, was assassinated by Franco's Guardia Civil." Why that note? Because, if it happened to him, Alberto Perera, here and now, his death might possess a similar meaning. An enlightened heart snuffed out.

"When he says like, Spider, greet the sun, where do you figure he was lying?" Slyly, the fellow waited.

"Was he lying?" Always the assumption that poets lie. Why else do they deliberately twist things around?

"What I mean is," grudgingly patient, "where was he lying when the sun came up?"

"The spider, you mean?" asked Perera. "Lying in wait?"

"The poet."

"The spider was in its web. I don't know where the poet was.

"I'll tell you. The poet was lying in his own bed."

"That's a thought."

"That's not a thought. That's the truth."

"A poem can come to you wherever you are," Perera explained. "Whatever you're doing. Sleeping, eating, even looking in the fridge, or when you think you're dying. I imagine that in his case he wakes up one morning after a bad night, takes a look at the sun, and accepts who he is. He accepts the enigma of himself."

"Are you?"

"Am I what? An enigma?"

"Are you glad you wake up who you are?"

"I can say yes to that."

"You give thanks to God?"

"More or less."

"Great. I bet you wake up in your own bed. That's what I'm saying. What's-his-name wouldn't've thought up that poem if he woke up where he was lying on the sidewalk."

"Darío," said Perera, "could very well have waked up on a sidewalk. He pursued that sort of life. Opium, absinthe. Quite possibly he was visited by that poem while lying on the sidewalk."

"Then he went back to his own bed and slept it off."

With trembling fingers the fellow gathered up his scraps from the desk. Trembling with what? With timidity, if this was a confrontation with a guardian of the virtues of every book in the place? As he bent to the floor to pick up his scraps, the crown of his head was revealed, the hair sprinkled with a scintilla of the stuff of the streets and the culture. How old was he, this fellow? Not more than thirty, maybe younger. Young, with no staying power.

By the door a coughing spell took hold of him. With his back to Perera he drew out from yet another pocket in the murky interior of the parka one of those large Palestinian scarves that Arafat wore around his head and were to be seen in the windows of used-clothing stores, and brought up into it whatever he had tried to keep down. Voiceless, he left, his bare ankles slapped by the grimy cuffs of his pants.

Perera imagined him shuffling down the hall, then down the wide white marble stairs, the grandiose interior stairs, centerpiece of this eternal granite edifice. As for Darío's admonition to the spider to show no rancor, that fellow's rancor was showing all over him. Yet his voice was scratchily respectful and his fingers trembled. Anybody who inquires so relentlessly into the meaning of a poem, and presses the words of poets into the ephemerae of the streets, would surely return, borne up the marble stairs by all those uplifting thoughts in his pockets.

Alberto Perera, a librarian if for just a few months more, shortly to be retired, went out into the cold and misty evening. A rarity in this time when librarians' ranks were shrinking down as his own head had shrunk while bent for so many years over the invaluable minutiae of his responsibilities, including the selection of belles lettres, of poetry, of literary fiction. The cranium shrinks no matter how much knowledge is crammed inside it. A rarity for another reason—a librarian who did not look like one, who wore a Borsalino fedora, his a classic of thirty years, a Bogart raincoat, English boots John Major would covet, a black silk shirt, a vintage tie.

Never as dashing as he wished to appear, however. Slight, short, and for several years now the bronze-color curls gone gray and the romantically drooping eyelids of his youth now faded flags at half-mast. Dashing, though, in the literary realm, numbering among his pen pals, most dead now: Hemingway, a letter to Perera, the youth, on the Spanish Civil War; Samuel Beckett, on critics mired up to their necks in his plays; Neruda, handwritten lines in green ink of two of his poems. What a prize! Also a note from the lovely British actress Vanessa Redgrave, with whom he'd spent an hour in London when he'd delivered to her an obscure little book of letters by Isadora Duncan, whom she'd portrayed in a film. And more, so much more. Everything kept in a bank vault and to be carried away in their black leather attaché case with double locks when he left this city for warmer climes. It was time to donate it all to an auction of literary memorabilia, on condition that the proceeds be used to establish a fund for down-and-out librarians, himself among them soon enough.

Further, he was a rarity for choosing to reside in what he called the broken heart of the city, or the spleen of it, the Tenderloin, and choosing not to move when the scene worsened. Born into a family of refugees from Franco's Spain, Brooklyn their alien soil, he felt a kinship with the dispossessed everywhere in the world, this kinship deep-

ening with the novels he'd read in his youth. Dostoevski's insulted and
injured, Dickens' downtrodden. Eighteen years ago he'd found a
fourth-floor apartment, the top, in a tentatively respectable building, a
walking distance to the main library in the civic center and to the
affordable restaurants on Geary Street. Soon after he moved in, the
sidewalks and entrances on every block began to fill up with a surge of
outcasts of all kinds. The shaven heads, the never-shaven faces, the
battle-maimed, the dope-possessed, the jobless, the homeless, the
immigrants, and not far from his own corner six-foot-tall transvestite
prostitutes and shorter ones, too, all colors. A wave, gathering momen-
tum, swept around him now as he made his way, mornings and
evenings, to and from the library. There was no city in the world that
was not inundated in its time, or would be in time to come, by refugees
from upheavals of all sorts.

On gray days, as this day was, he was reminded of the poor
lunatics, madmen, nuisances, all who were herded out of the towns and
onto the ships that carried them up and down the rivers of the
Rhineland. An idea! The mayor, having deprived the homeless of their
carts and their tents, would welcome an idea to rid the city of the
homeless themselves. Herd them aboard one of those World War II
battleships, rusting away in drydock or muck, and send them out to sea.
The thousands—whole families, loners, runaway kids, all to be dropped
off in Galveston or New Orleans, under cover of a medieval night.

He ate his supper at Lefty O'Doul's, at a long table in company
of other men his age and a woman who looked even older. Retired
souls, he called them, come in from their residence hotels, their winter smells of naphthalene and menthol hovering over the aroma of his
roast turkey with dressing. One should not be ashamed of eating a substantial meal while the hungry roamed the streets. He told himself this
as he'd told himself so many times before, lifelong. He knew from
saintly experiments of his youth that when he fasted in sympathy, punishing himself for what he thought was plenitude, his conscience
began to starve, unable to survive for very long without a body.

A brandy at the long bar, and the bartender slapping down the
napkin, asking the usual. "When you going to sell me that Borsalino?"
Then, "This man's a librarian," to the bulky young man in a broadly
striped sweater on the stool to the left of Perera. "He's read every book
in the public library. Ever been in there?"

"Never was."

"You can ask him anything," said the bartender, and the man to
Perera's right did. "Do you know right off the number of dead both
sides in the Civil War?"

"Whose civil war?"

Taken for a tricky intellectual, he was left alone.

A theater critic, that's what he wished to be mistaken for, passing
the theaters at the right time as the ticket holders were drifting in and
the lines forming at the box office. Women's skirts and coats swinging
out, swishing against him, and a woman turning to apologize, granting
a close glimpse of her face to this man who appeared deserving of it.
A critic, that's who he was, of the musical up there on the stage and of
the audience so delightedly acceptive of the banal, lustily sung.

Past the lofty Hilton at the Tenderloin's edge, whose ultra-plush
interior he had strolled through a time or two, finding gold beyond an
interior decorator's wildest dreams. Its penthouse window the highest
light in the Tenderloin sky, a shining blind eye. Around a corner of the
hotel, and, lying up against the cyclone fence, the bundled and the
unbundled to whom he gave a wide berth as he would to the dead, in
fear and respect. Over the sidewalks, those slips of refuse paper he'd
always noticed but not so closely as now. Alert to approaching figures,
to whatever plans they had in mind for him, and warily friendly with
the fraternal clusters, exchanging with them joking curses on the
weather, he made his way. Until at last he stood before the mesh gate
to his apartment building. A gate from sidewalk to the entrance's upper
reaches, requiring a swift turn of the key before an assault. The gate,
the lock, the fear—none of which had been there when he moved in.

The only man in the Western world to wear a nightcap, he drew
his on. Cashmere, dove color, knitted twelve years ago by his dear
friend and lover, Barbara, a librarian herself, a beautiful one. Syracuse,
New York. Every year, off they'd go. Archaeological tours, walking
tours. Three winters ago he was at her bedside, close by in her last
hours. She, too, had corresponded with writers. Hers were women—
poets, memoirists—and these letters, too, were in his care. Into his
plaid flannel robe, also a gift from her, the seat and the elbows worn
away. He always read in this robe in his ample chair or at the kitchen
table or in bed. Three books lay on the floor by his bed, among the last
he'd ever consider ordering for any library. One had seduced and

deceived him, the second was unbearably vain, and he was put to sleep by the third, already asleep itself, face down on the carpet.

When he lay down the inevitable happened. At once he wondered where the poetry stalker might be, the librarian stalker with the excitable cough. Could Darío have imagined that his earnest little attempt to accept God's ways would wind up in the parka pocket of a sidewalk sleeper, trying to accept the same a hundred years later?

At his desk he was always attuned to the life of this library, as he'd been to every library where he'd spent his years, even the vaster ones with more locked doors, tonnages of archives. This morning his mind's eye was a benign sensor, following the patrons to their chosen areas. He saw them rising in the slow, creaky elevator, he saw the meandering ones and the fast ones climbing the broad marble stairs, those stairs like a solid promise to the climber of an ennobling of the self on the higher levels. The largest concentration of patrons was in the newspaper and periodical section, always and forever a refuge for men from lonely rooms and also now for those without a room, all observing the proper silence, except the man asleep, head down on the table, his glottal breathing quivering the newspaper before his face. In the past, empty chairs were always available; now every chair was occupied. And where was the young man whose pockets were filled with scraps of poetry? In the poetry section, of course, copying down what the world saw fit to honor with the printed page. *Anything in books represents the godlike and anything in myself represents the vile.* Who said that? A writer, born into grim poverty, whose name he'd recall later. If you felt vile in the midst of all these godlike volumes, what restless rage!

"Am I butting in here?"

Same parka, grimier perhaps. But look! His hair rose higher and had a reddish cast, an almost washed look from the rain. His eyes not clearer, not calmer, and in his arms four books, which he let fall onto the desk.

"This is not a checkout desk," said Perera.

"That I know. Never check out anything. No address. If you try to sneak something out you get the guillotine. You get it in the neck."

To touch or not to touch the books. Since there was no real

reason not to touch, Perera set the four books upright, his hands as
bookends.

"Who've we got here? Ah, Rilke, the *Elegies*. Good choice. And
here we've got Whitman. You know how to pick them. Bishop, she's up
there. And who's this? Pound? Sublime, all of them. But don't let yourself be intimidated. Nothing sacred in this place, just a lot of people
whose thoughts were driving them crazy, euphoria crazy or doom crazy,
and they had to get it out, see what *you* think about what they're thinking. That's all there is to it. Librarians in here are just to give it a sem-
blance of order. I'm not a high priest."

"Never thought you were."

"Ah," said Perera, and the books between his hands resumed
their frayed existence, their common humanity. One, he saw, had a bit
of green mildew at the spine's bottom edge. It must have been left out
in a misty rain or someone had read it while in the tub.

"Can I get you some coffee?" inquired the visitor.

"Strange that you should ask," said Perera. "Got my thermos here.
A thirst for coffee comes over me at this hour." How closely he'd been
watched! And now forced to take the plunge into familiarity, a plunge
he would not have taken without further consideration if this man
were the sole homeless man around. They were empowered by their
numbers.

From the bottom drawer he brought up his thermos and his
porcelain cup. The plastic thermos cup held no pleasure and he never
used it. He'd use it now and not bother to guess why, and bring up also
the paper bag of macaroons.

"Suppose I sit down?"

Perera nodded, and the guest sat down in the only other chair, a
hard chair with an unwelcoming look, a chair used until now only by
Alexa Okula, head librarian, and Amy Peck, chief guard, who often
described for him the assaults she had suffered that day and where in
the library they had occurred.

With both hands around the cup, the guest had no trouble holding it. "This is like dessert," he said. "This is great. Got sugar and cream
in it." He was shy around the macaroons. Crumbs were tripping down
the parka and when they reached the floor he covered them with his
beat-up jogging shoes.

At that moment Perera recalled the very recent tragedy at the

Sacramento library When did the shooting occur? Right after a little party celebrating the library's expanded hours. And what did the assassin do then? Fled to the rooftop, where he was gunned down by the police. It was simple enough to imagine himself dead on the floor, but not so easy to imagine this fellow fleeing anywhere, hampered by the bone-cold ankles, the flappy shoes, the body's tremble at the core.

"You remember that poem?" his guest asked.

"Not verbatim," said Perera. "I did not memorize it."

"You can remember the bear, can't you, and the spider and the toad, anyway? How they're supposed to greet the sun because they are what they are?"

"That I remember," said Perera.

"What I'd like to know is, what am I?"

"You can figure you're a human being," said Perera.

"That's what I thought you'd say. What else you were going to say is, you're a human being by the sweat of your brow. Beavers, that don't take into account beavers. Beavers are dam builders. Then you take those birds who get stuff together to make a nest for the female of their choice. Other birds, too, I've seen them. Can't stop pulling up weeds or whatever stuff is around for a hundred miles, pull this out, pull that out, and off they go and back in a second. Then there's animals who dig a burrow, one hell of a long tunnel in the ground. They can't sweat but they work. It's work, but that don't make them human."

"Work does not get to the essence, I see your point," said Perera. At a moment's notice he could not get to the essence himself and he wished he had not used that word. It could only mean further trouble.

"Okay, take you," said the visitor. "Would you say you were human?"

"I've been led to believe that I am," said Perera.

"What you base that on," said his guest, "is you get to keep guard over this library and you got every book where it's supposed to be and in addition you got it up on a computer, what is its title, what is its number, who wrote it, and maybe you got in your head the reason why the guy wrote it. So in that way you can say you're human and maybe you're glad about it even if you don't look it. Okay, now let's say you're through work for the day and you walk home. Or you go on and have yourself a turkey or whatever they got there, roast beef, chicken and dumplings. Then you go along by that theater, maybe even drop in yourself at fifty bucks a seat in the balcony. After that you go on to your apartment, which is in a bad, I mean *baaad* neighborhood, and you unlock that gate. And then what?"

"I can't imagine."

"You don't have to imagine. You're in your own bed. Got a mattress that's just right for the shape you're in. Maybe you even got an electric blanket. Got pillows with real feathers inside, maybe even that down stuff from the hind end of a couple hundred ducks. Nighty-night."

"So now I'm sure I'm human?"

"So then the sun comes up and what do you say? You say what that spider says. Halloo, old sun up there, had me a good sleep in my own web and now I get to eat some more fat flies. Halloo, says the toad, now I get to spend the day in this hot mud some more. Halloo, says the bear, now I get to dance some more with this rope around my neck. Halloo, says this guy, Alberto Perera, now I get to go to the library again and talk to this guy who can't figure out why he can't halloo the sun with the rest of them."

A flush had spread over the fellow's face, over the pallor and over the pits, over all that was more appallingly obvious today. From his parka he brought out the Arafat headpiece and hid his face in it, coughing up in there something tormentingly intimate.

Alexa Okula, head librarian, passing by and hearing the commotion, paused a moment to look in and Perera held up his hand to calm her fears for his safety. Nothing escaped her, only all the years of her life in the protective custody of tons of books and tons of granite. Soon to be released, just as he was to be, all she'd have was her stringy emeritus professor of a husband and her poodles. Unlike himself, who'd have the world.

The fellow sat staring at the floor, striving to recover from the losing battle with his cough.

"You suppose I could spend the night in here?"

With *unthinkable* on the tip of his tongue, Perera said nothing. Accommodations ought to be available for queries of every sort at any time in your life.

"Looks like it ought to be safer in here."

"Unsafe in here, too," said Perera. "This fortress is in a state of abject deterioration. The last earthquake did some damage, along with

the damage done by the budget cuts, along with the damage by vandals. Time's been creeping around in here, too. The whole place could
collapse on you while you slept."

"I can handle it," said the supplicant. "Nobody's going to throw
lighter fuel on me and set me on fire in here. Nobody's going to knife
me in here, at night anyway. Lost my bedroll. I left my stuff with this
woman who's my friend, she got room in her cart. I had a change of
shirt in there, I had important papers, had a letter from a guy I worked
for up the coast. I was good at hauling in those sea urchins they ship
over to Japan, tons of them. They love those things over there, then
there wasn't anymore. Where the sea urchins were, something else is
taking over, messing up the water. I'm telling you this because I don't
drink, don't do dope, don't smoke, so I sure would not set this place on
fire if I was allowed to sleep in here." He was talking fast, outrunning
his cough. "The cops took her stuff, took my stuff, dumped it all into
the truck. Ordered by the mayor. She lost family pictures, lost the cat
she had tied to the cart that sat on top. She was crying. I was in here
talking to you."

"It must be damn cold in here at night," Perera said.

"Maybe, maybe not, and if it's raining maybe the roof don't leak."

"Dark, I imagine," said Perera. "I've never thought about it. I suspect they used to leave a few lights on but now it's dark. Saves money.
Let's say that once the lights go out you can't see a thing. Your sense of
direction is totally lost, you're blind as a bat, and I'm nowhere around
to guide you to the lavatory and I wouldn't know where it was myself.
You might be pissing, on some of the noblest minds that ever put their
thoughts on paper."

"I wouldn't do that."

"They do get pissed on, one time and another, but not by you or
me. So let's say you're feeling your way around, looking for a comfortable place. Okula has a rug in her office and it's usually warm in there.
She exudes a warmth that might stay the night. But how to get there?"

"I know my way around."

"You do seem to," said Perera.

"What you could do when you take off, like your day is done, see?
You just leave me in here and close the door. I wouldn't care if you
locked it."

"I can lock it," said Perera, "but not with you inside."

"Is there some of that coffee left?"

Perera, pouring, was planning to wash that porcelain cup thoroughly. If it was pneumonia gripping this young man, it would get a more merciless grip on him, twice as old. Or if it was tuberculosis, it would bring on his end with rapacious haste and just as he was about to embark on his most rewarding years.

This time the guest took longer to drink it down, the hot coffee apparently feeling its way past the throat's lacerations.

"Let's say it's like that darkness upon the face of the deep," Perera said. "That same darkness the Creationists are wanting to take us back to. Dark, dark, and you need to find yourself a comfortable place. Now let's say you're at the top of our marble stairs and you don't know it. You take a step and down you go. Come morning, they open up and find you there."

"You think so?"

"You'll be on the front pages in New York, Paris, Tokyo. A homeless man, seeking shelter in San Francisco's main library, fell down in there and died. A library, imagine it, that monument to mankind's exalted IQ. I'll say you dropped by to chat about poetry. I'll say we spent many pleasant hours discussing Darío's *Filosofía.*"

Contempt in the eyes meeting Perera's. "What're you telling me? You're telling me to lie down and die?"

"Not at all. All I'm saying is you cannot spend the night in this library."

Scornfully careful, the fellow placed the porcelain cup on the desk and stood up. "You want me to tell you what that poem is saying? Same thing you're saying. If you can't halloo the sun, if you can't go chirpity-chirp to the moon, what're you doing around here anyway?"

"That is not what it is saying," said Perera.

"To hell with you is what I'm saying."

Gone, leaving his curse behind. A curse so popular, so spread around, it carried little weight.

Closing time, the staff and lingering patrons all forced out through one side entrance and into the early dark, into the rain. Perera hoisted his umbrella, one slightly larger than the ordinary, bought in London the day he met the actress, years ago. It will never turn inside out, the clerk promised, not even in Conrad's typhoon. And it hadn't yet. Lives were being turned inside out, but this snob of an umbrella stayed up there. A stance of superiority, that was his problem. A problem he always knew he had and yet that always took him by surprise. And how did he figure he was so smart, this Alberto Perera? Well, he could engage in the jesting the smart ones enjoy when they're in the presence of those they figure are not so smart. He could engage in that jovial thievery, that light-fingered, light-headed trivializing of another person's tragic truth, a practice he abhorred wherever he came upon it.

Onward through this neon-colored rain, this headlight-glittering rain, every light no match for the dark, only a constant contesting. *There is a certainty in degradation.* You can puzzle over lines all your life and never be satisfied with the meanings you get. Until, slushing onward, you've got at last one meaning for sure, because now its time had come, bringing proof by the thousands wherever they were this night in their concrete burrows and dens. There was no certainty in anything else, no matter what you're storing up, say tons of gold, say ten billion library books, and if you think you can elude that certainty it sneaks up on you, it sneaks up the marble stairs and into your sanctum and you're degraded right along with the rest.

For several days at noontime Perera looked for him in the long line at St. Anthony's, men and women moving slowly in for their free meal. After work he climbed the stairs to Hospitality House and looked around at the men in the collection of discarded chairs, each day different men and each man confounded by being among the unwanted many. Here, too, he knew he would not find him. The fellow was a loner, hiding out, probably afraid his cough was reason to arrest him.

A rolled-up wool blanket, a large thermos filled with hot coffee, a dozen packaged handkerchiefs, a thick turtleneck sweater, a package of athletic socks. Perera carried all this into his office, piecemeal, as the days came and went, and these offerings had the same aspect of futility that he saw in the primitive practice of laying out clothing and nourishment for the departed.

He braved the Albatross used-book store not far from the library, trying not to breathe the invisible dust from the high stacks of disintegrating books, and in the dim poetry section came upon some unexpected finds. Ah, hah! Michaux, *My life, you take off without me,* and Trakl, sad, suicidal soul, *Beneath the stars a man alone,* and Anna Akhmatova, *Before this grief the mountains stoop,* and Ah! Machado, *He was seen walking between rifles.* Comments in the margins, someone's own poem on a title page, bus schedules, indecipherable odds and ends of penciled thoughts intermingling with the printed ones. He wanted to keep these thin volumes for himself and instead he did as planned. He bought a green nylon parka in a discount place on Market Street, slid the books into the deep pockets, and folded the parka on top of the pile.

On the morning of the twelfth day, before the hour when the public was admitted, Perera entered by the side door, bringing a pair of black plastic shoes, oxford style, made in China, recommended for their comfort by a street friend wearing a pair. The door guard silently led him to the foot of the marble stairs, where Okula, cops and paramedics and librarians were gathered around a man lying on the lowest step.

Perera had never fainted and was not going to faint now, even though all the strength of his intelligence was leaving the abode of his head to darkness.

"Mr. Perera," Okula was saying but not to him, "was an acquaintance of this man. Wasn't he?"

Nobody was answering, though Perera gave them time.

"Occasionally," he said, "he stepped into my office. My door is usually open." Sweat was rising from his scalp. "Did he fall?"

"More like he lay down and died." The paramedic's voice was inappropriately young. "T.B. Take a look at that rag."

"You say you knew him?" A cop's voice. "Do you know his name? He's got nothing in his pockets."

"No," said Perera.

"Any idea where he concealed himself in here?"

"Hundreds of places." Okula, responding. "We check carefully. However, anyone wishing to stay in can also check carefully."

"What you might be needing is a couple of dogs. German shepherds are good at it. Dobermans, too. A couple of good dogs could cover this whole place in half an hour."

Kneeling by the body, Perera took a closer look at the face, closer than when they sat in the office, discoursing on the animal kingdom.

The young man was now no one, as he'd feared he already was when alive. The absolute unwanted, that's who the dead become.

"Did this man bother you?"

It would take many months, he knew, before he'd be able to speak without holding back. Humans speaking were unbearable to hear and abominable to see, himself among the rest. Worse, was all that was written down instead, the never-ending outpouring, given print and given covers, given shelves up and down and everywhere in this warehouse of fathomless darkness.

"He did not bother me," he said.

The door to his office was closed but unlocked, just as he'd left it. Scattered over his desk were what appeared to be the contents of his wastebasket. But unfamiliar, not his. So many kinds of paper scraps, they were the bits and pieces his visitor had brought forth from that green parka. Throwaway ads, envelopes, a discount drugstore's paper bag, business cards tossed away. On each, the cramped handwriting. By copying down all these stirringly strange ideas, had the fellow hoped to impress upon himself his likeness to these other humans? A break-in of a different sort. A young man breaking into a home of his own.

Perera sat down at his desk, slipped his glasses on, and spread the scraps out before him as heedfully as his shaking hands allowed.

THE PUBLIC LIBRARY

Isaac Babel

YOU CAN FEEL STRAIGHTAWAY THAT THE BOOK REIGNS SUPREME HERE. All the people who work in the library have entered into communion with The Book, with life at second-hand, and have themselves become, as it were, a mere reflection of the living.

Even the attendants in the cloakroom are hushed and enigmatic, full of inward-looking calm, and their hair is neither dark nor fair, but something in between.

It is quite possible that at home they drink methylated spirits on Saturday nights and systematically beat their wives. But in the library they are as quiet as mice, self-effacing, withdrawn, and somber.

Then there is the cloakroom attendant who draws. His eyes are kind and woebegone. Once every two weeks, helping a fat man in a black jacket to take off his coat, he murmurs that "Nikolai Sergeyevich likes my drawings, and so does Konstantin Vasilyevich. I've only had elementary schooling, and where I go from here I really don't know."

The fat man listens. He is a reporter, a married man, fond of his food and overworked. Once every two weeks he goes to the library to rest—he reads about some trial or other, carefully copies out the plan of the building where the murder took place, is perfectly happy and forgets that he's married and overworked.

He listens to the attendant in anxious bewilderment and wonders how he should deal with someone like this. If he gives him a tip when he leaves, the man might be offended—he's an artist, after all. If he doesn't give him anything, he might still be offended—after all, he's an attendant.

In the reading room there are the more exalted members of the staff: the assistants. Some of them stand out by virtue of a pronounced physical defect—one has his fingers all curled up and another has a head which has dropped over on one side and got stuck there. They are dowdily dressed and extremely thin. They look as though they are possessed of some idea unknown to the world at large.

Gogol would have described them well!

Those assistants who don't "stand out" have gentle balding patches, neat gray suits, a prim look in their eyes, and a painful slowness of movement. They are always chewing something and moving their jaws, although they have nothing in their mouths, and they talk in a practiced whisper, Altogether, they have been debilitated by books, by not being able to have a good yawn every now and then.

Nowadays, during the war, the readers have changed. There are fewer students—scarcely any, indeed. Once in a blue moon you may see one pining away, without undue hardship, in a corner. He will be on a "white ticket," that is, will have a military exemption on grounds of health. He will wear horn-rimmed spectacles or cultivate a slight limp. There are also, however, those on state scholarships and hence temporarily exempted. They have a hangdog look, wear drooping mustaches, appear tired of life and very introspective: they keep reading a little, thinking a little, looking at the pattern of the reading lamp and burying themselves in a book again. They're supposed to graduate and go into the army, but they're in no hurry. Everything in its time.

Here's a former student who has come back in the shape of a wounded officer, with a black sling. His wound is healing. He is young and rosy-cheeked. He has had his dinner and taken a stroll down the Nevsky. The Nevsky is already lit up. The evening edition of the *Stock Exchange News* is already making its triumphal rounds. In Yeliseyev's there are grapes cradled in millet seed. He's early for his evening engagement, so the officer, just for old times' sake, goes to the library. He stretches out his long legs under the table at which he is sitting and reads the *Apollon*. It's a little boring. Opposite sits a girl student. She is studying anatomy and copying a drawing of the stomach into her notebook. She looks as though she's from Kaluga or thereabouts— broad-faced, big-boned, rosy-cheeked, thoroughgoing, and tough. If she has a boyfriend, then that's the best thing for her: she's made for love.

Next to her is a picturesque tableau, an inevitable feature of any public library in the Russian Empire: a sleeping Jew. He is worn out. His hair is a burnished black. His cheeks are sunken. His forehead is bruised and his mouth is half open. He makes wheezing noises. Goodness knows where he comes from, or whether he has a residence permit. He reads every day, and he also sleeps every day. His face is a picture of overwhelming weariness and near-madness. He is a martyr to the book, peculiarly Jewish, an inextinguishable martyr.

Next to the assistants' counter there sits reading a large, broad-chested woman in a gray jumper. She is the sort who talks in the library in unexpectedly loud tones, frankly and ecstatically voicing her astonishment at the printed word and engaging her neighbors in conversation. Her reason for coming here is to find a way of making soap at home. She is about forty-five years old. Is she right in the head, they wonder.

Another regular reader is a lean little colonel in a loose-fitting tunic, wide breeches, and brightly polished boots. He has short legs and his mustaches are the color of cigar ash. He dresses them with brilliantine as a result of which they run to all shades of dark gray. In days of yore he was so dumb he couldn't even make the rank of colonel and hence be retired as a major general. In retirement he has been an infernal nuisance to the gardener, the servants, and his grandson. At the age of seventy-three he took it into his head to write a history of his regiment. He writes surrounded by a mountain of materials. He is liked by the assistants, whom he greets with exquisite courtesy. He no longer gets on his family's nerves. The servant gladly polishes his boots.

There are all kinds of other people in the public library—too many to be described.

It is evening. The reading room is almost dark. The silent figures at the tables are a study in weariness, thirst for knowledge, ambition. . . .

Soft snow weaves its weft behind the large windows. Nearby, on the Nevsky, there is teeming life. Far away, in the Carpathians, blood is flowing. *C'est la vie.*

COMMUNITY LIFE

Lorrie Moore

WHEN OLENA WAS A LITTLE GIRL, SHE HAD CALLED THEM LIE-BERRIES—
a fibbing fruit, a story store—and now she had a job in one. She had
originally wanted to teach English literature, but when she failed to
warm to the graduate study of it, its french-fried theories—a vocabulary of arson!—she'd transferred to library school, where everyone was
taught to take care of books, tenderly, as if they were dishes or dolls.

She had learned to read at an early age. Her parents, newly settled in Vermont from Tirgu Mures in Transylvania, were anxious that
their daughter learn to speak English, to blend in with the community
in a way they felt they probably never would, and so every Saturday
they took her to the children's section of the Rutland library and let her
spend time with the librarian, who chose books for her and sometimes
even read a page or two out loud, though there was a sign that said
PLEASE BE QUIET BOYS AND GIRLS. No comma.

Which made it seem to Olena that only the boys had to be quiet.
She and the librarian could do whatever they wanted.

She had loved the librarian.

And when Olena's Romanian began to recede altogether, and in
its stead bloomed a slow, rich English-speaking voice, not unlike the
librarian's, too womanly for a little girl, the other children on her
street became even more afraid of her. *"Dracula'"* they shouted.
"Transylvaniess!" they shrieked, and ran.

"You'll have a new name now," her father told her the first day of
first grade. He had already changed their last name from Todorescu to

Resnick. His shop was called "Resnick's Furs." "From here on in, you will no longer be Olena. You will have a nice American name: Nell."

"You make to say ze name," her mother said. "When ze teacher tell you *Olena*, you say, '*No, Nell.*' Say *Nell*"

"Nell," said Olena. But when she got to school, the teacher, sensing something dreamy and outcast in her, clasped her hand and exclaimed, "Olena! What a beautiful name!" Olena's heart filled with gratitude and surprise, and she fell in close to the teacher's hip, adoring and mute.

From there on in, only her parents, in their throaty Romanian accents, ever called her Nell, her secret, jaunty American self existing only for them.

"Nell, how are ze ozer children at ze school?"

"Nell, please to tell us what you do."

Years later, when they were killed in a car crash on the Farm to Market Road, and the Nell-that-never-lived died with them, Olena, numbly rearranging the letters of her own name on the envelopes of the sympathy cards she received, discovered what the letters spelled: *Olena; Alone*. It was a body walled in the cellar of her, a whiff and forecast of doom like an early, rotten spring—and she longed for the Nell-that-never-lived's return. She wished to start over again, to be someone living coltishly in the world, not someone hidden away, behind books, with a carefully learned voice and a sad past.

She missed her mother the most.

The library Olena worked in was one of the most prestigious university libraries in the Midwest. It housed a large collection of rare and foreign books, and she had driven across several states to get there, squinting through the splattered tempera of insects on the windshield, watching for the dark tail of a possible tornado, and getting sick, painfully, in Indiana, in the rest rooms of the dead-Hoosier service plazas along I-80. The ladies' rooms there had had electric eyes for the toilets, the sinks, the hand dryers, and she'd set them all off by staggering in and out of the stalls or leaning into the sinks. "You the only one in here?" asked a cleaning woman. "You the only one in here making this racket?" Olena had smiled, a dog's smile; in the yellowish light, everything seemed tragic and ridiculous and unable to stop. The flatness of the terrain gave her vertigo, she decided, that was it. The land was windswept; there were no smells. In Vermont, she had felt cradled by mountains. Now, here, she would have to be brave.

But she had no memory of how to be brave, Here, it seemed, she had no memories at all. Nothing triggered them. And once in a while, when she gave voice to the fleeting edge of one, it seemed like something she was making up.

She first met Nick at the library in May. She was temporarily positioned at the reference desk, hauled out from her ordinary task as supervisor of foreign cataloging, to replace someone who was ill. Nick was researching statistics on municipal campaign spending in the state. "Haven't stepped into a library since I was eighteen," he said. He looked at least forty.

She showed him where he might look. "Try looking here," she said, writing down the names of indexes to state records, but he kept looking at *her*. "Or here."

"I'm managing a county board seat campaign," he said. "The election's not until the fall, but I'm trying to get a jump on things." His hair was a coppery brown, threaded through with silver. There was something animated in his eyes, like pond life. "I just wanted to get some comparison figures. Will you have a cup of coffee with me?"

"I don't think so," she said.

But he came back the next day and asked her again.

The coffee shop near campus was hot and noisy, crowded with students, and Nick loudly ordered espresso for them both. She usually didn't like espresso, its gritty, cigarish taste. But there was in the air that kind of distortion that bent you a little; it caused your usual self to grow slippery, to wander off and shop, to get blurry, bleed, bevel with possibility. She drank the espresso fast, with determination and a sense of adventure. "I guess I'll have a second," she said, and wiped her mouth with a napkin.

"I'll get it," said Nick, and when he came back, he told her some more about the campaign he was running. "It's important to get the endorsements of the neighborhood associations," he said. He ran a bratwurst and frozen yogurt stand called Please Squeeze and Bratwursts. He had gotten to know a lot of people that way. "I feel alive and relevant, living my life like this," he said. "I don't feel like I've sold out."

"Sold out to what?" she asked.

He smiled. "I can tell you're not from around here," he said. He raked his hand through the various metals of his hair. "*Selling out*. Like doing something you really never wanted to do, and getting paid too much for it."

"Oh," she said.

"When I was a kid, my father said to me, 'Sometimes in life, son, you're going to find you have to do things you don't want to do,' and I looked him right in the eye and said, 'No fucking way.'" Olena laughed. "I mean, you probably always wanted to be a librarian, right?"

She looked at all the crooked diagonals of his face and couldn't tell whether he was serious. "Me?" she said. "I first went to graduate school to be an English professor." She sighed, switched elbows, sinking her chin into her other hand. "I did try," she said. "I read Derrida. I read Lacan. I read *Reading Lacan*. I read 'Reading *Reading Lacan*'— and that's when I applied to library school."

"I don't know who Lacan is," he said.

"He's, well—you see? That's why I like libraries: No whos or whys. Just 'where is it?'"

"And *where* are you from?" he asked, his face briefly animated by his own clever change of subject. "Originally." There was, it seemed, a way of spotting those not native to the town. It was a college town, attractive and dull, and it hurried the transients along—the students, gypsies, visiting scholars and comics—with a motion not unlike peristalsis.

"Vermont," she said.

"Vermont!" Nick exclaimed, as if this were exotic, which made her glad she hadn't said something like Transylvania. He leaned toward her, confidentially. "I have to tell you: I own one chair from Ethan Allen Furniture."

"You do?" She smiled. "I won't tell anyone."

"Before that, however, I was in prison, and didn't own a stick."

"Really?" she asked. She sat back. Was he telling the truth? As a girl, she'd been very gullible, but she had always learned more that way.

"I went to school here," he said. "In the sixties. I bombed a ware-house where the military was storing research supplies. I got twelve years." He paused, searching her eyes to see how she was doing with this, how *he* was doing with it. Then he fetched back his gaze, like a piece of jewelry he'd merely wanted to show her, quick. "There wasn't supposed to be anyone there; we'd checked it all our in advance. But this poor asshole named Lawrence Sperry—Larry Sperry! Christ, can you imagine having a name like that?"

"Sure," said Olena.

Nick looked at her suspiciously. "He was in there, working late. He lost a leg and an eye in the explosion. I got the federal pen in Winford. Attempted murder."

The thick coffee coated his lips. He had been looking steadily at her, but now he looked away.

"Would you like a bun?" asked Olena. "I'm going to go get a bun." She stood, but he turned and gazed up at her with such disbelief that she sat back down again, sloppily, sidesaddle. She twisted forward, leaned into the table. "I'm sorry. Is that all true, what you just said? Did that really happen to you?"

"*What?*" His mouth fell open. "You think I'd make that up?"

"It's just that, well, I work around a lot of literature," she said.

"'Literature,'" he repeated.

She touched his hand. She didn't know what else to do. "Can I cook dinner for you some night? Tonight?"

There was a blaze in his eye, a concentrated seeing. He seemed for a moment able to look right into her, know her in a way that was uncluttered by actually knowing her. He seemed to have no informa-tion or misinformation, only a kind of photography, factless but true.

"Yes," he said, "you can."

Which was how he came to spend the evening beneath the cheap stained-glass lamp of her dining room, its barroom red, its Schlitz-Tiffany light, and then to spend the night, and not leave.

Olena had never lived with a man before. "Except my father," she said, and Nick studied her eyes, the streak of blankness in them, when she said it. Though she had dated two different boys in college, they were the kind who liked to leave early, to eat breakfast without her at smoky greasy spoons, to sit at the counter with the large men in the blue windbreakers, read the paper, get their cups refilled.

She had never been with anyone who stayed. Anyone who'd moved in his box of tapes, his Ethan Allen chair.

Anyone who'd had lease problems at his old place.

"I'm trying to bring this thing together," he said, holding her in the middle of the afternoon. "My life, the campaign, my thing with you: I'm trying to get all my birds to land in the same yard." Out the window, there was an afternoon moon, like a golf ball, pocked and stuck. She looked at the calcified egg of it, its coin face, its blue neighborhood of nothing. Then she looked at him. There was the pond life again in his eyes, and in the rest of his face a hesitant, warm stillness.

"Do you like making love to me?" she asked, at night, during a thunderstorm.

"Of course. Why do you ask?"

"Are you satisfied with me?"

He turned toward her, kissed her. "Yes," he said. "I don't need a show."

She was quiet for a long time. "People are giving shows?"

The rain and wind rushed down the gutters, snapped the branches of the weak trees in the side yard.

He had her inexperience and self-esteem in mind. At the movies, at the beginning, he whispered, "Twentieth Century-Fox. Baby, that's you." During a slapstick part, in a library where card catalogs were upended and scattered wildly through the air, she broke into a pale, cold sweat, and he moved toward her, hid her head in his chest, saying, "Don't look, don't look." At the end, they would sit through the long credits—gaffer, best boy, key grip. "That's what *we* need to get," he said. "A grip."

"Yes," she said. "Also a *negative cutter.*"

Other times, he encouraged her to walk around the house naked. "If you got it, do it." He smiled, paused, feigned confusion. "If you do it, have it. If you flaunt it, do it."

"If you have it, got it," she added.

"If you say it, mean it." And he pulled her toward him like a dancing partner with soft shoes and the smiling mouth of love.

But too often she lay awake, wondering. There was something missing. Something wasn't happening to her, or was it to him? All through the summer, the thunderstorms set the sky on fire while she lay there, listening for the train sound of a tornado, which never came—though the lightning ripped open the night and lit the trees like things too suddenly remembered, then left them indecipherable again in the dark.

"You're not feeling anything, are you?" he finally said. "What is wrong?"

"I'm not sure," she said cryptically. "The rainstorms are so loud in this part of the world." The wind from a storm blew through the screens and sometimes caused the door to the bedroom to slam shut. "I don't like a door to slam," she whispered. "It makes me think someone is mad."

At the library, there were Romanian books coming in—Olena was to skim them, read them just enough to proffer a brief description for the catalog listing. It dismayed her that her Romanian was so weak, that it had seemed almost to vanish, a mere handkerchief in a stairwell, and that now, daily, another book arrived to reprimand her.

She missed her mother the most.

On her lunch break, she went to Nick's stand for a frozen yogurt. He looked tired, bedraggled, his hair like sprockets. "You want the Sperry Cherry or the Lemon Bomber?" he asked. These were his joke names, the ones he threatened really to use someday.

"How about apple?" she said.

He cut up an apple and arranged it in a paper dish. He squeezed yogurt from a chrome machine. "There's a fund-raiser tonight for the Teetlebaum campaign."

"Oh," she said. She had been to these fund-raisers before. At first she had liked them, glimpsing corners of the city she would never have seen otherwise, Nick leading her out into them, Nick knowing everyone, so that it seemed her life filled with possibility, with homefulness. But finally, she felt, such events were too full of dreary, glad-handing people speaking incessantly of their camping trips out west. They never really spoke *to* you. They spoke toward you. They spoke at you. They spoke near you, on you. They believed themselves crucial to the welfare of the community. But they seldom went to libraries. They didn't read books. "At least they're *contributers to the community*," said Nick. "At least they're not sucking the blood of it."

"Lapping," she said.

"What?"

"Gnashing and lapping. Not sucking."

He looked at her in a doubtful, worried way. "I looked it up once," she said.

"Whatever." He scowled. "At least they care. At least they're trying to give something back."

"I'd rather live in Russia," she said.

"I'll be back around ten or so," he said.

"You don't want me to come?" Truth was she disliked Ken Teetlebaum. Perhaps Nick had figured this out. Though he had the support of the local leftover Left, there was something fatuous and vain about Ken. He tended to do little isometric leg exercises while you were talking to him. Often he took out a Woolworth photo of himself and showed it to people. "Look at this," he'd say. "This was back when I had long hair, can you believe it?" And people would look and see a handsome teenaged boy who bore only a slight resemblance to the puffy Ken Teetlebaum of today. "Don't I look like Eric Clapton?"

"Eric Clapton would never have sat in a Woolworth photo booth like some high school girl," Olena had said once, in the caustic blurt that sometimes afflicts the shy. Ken had looked at her in a laughing, hurt sort of way, and after that he stopped showing the photo around when she was present.

"You can come, if you want to." Nick reached up, smoothed his hair, and looked handsome again. "Meet me there."

The fund-raiser was in the upstairs room of a local restaurant called Dutch's. She paid ten dollars, went in, and ate a lot of raw cauliflower and hummus before she saw Nick back in a far corner, talking to a woman in jeans and a brown blazer. She was the sort of woman that Nick might twist around to look at in restaurants: fiery auburn hair cut bluntly in a pageboy. She had a pretty face, but the hair was too severe, too separate and tended to. Olena herself had long, disorganized hair, and she wore it pulled back messily in a clip. When she reached up to wave to Nick, and he looked away without acknowledging her, back toward the auburn pageboy, Olena kept her hand up and moved it back, to fuss with the clip. She would never fit in here, she thought.

Not among these jolly, activist-clerk types. She preferred the quiet poet-clerks of the library. They were delicate and territorial, intellectual, and physically unwell. They sat around at work, thinking up Tom Swifties: *I have to go to the hardware store, he said wrenchingly.*

Would you like a soda? he asked spritely.

They spent weekends at the Mayo Clinic. "An amusement park for hypochondriacs," said a cataloger named Sarah. "A cross between Lourdes and *The New Price Is Right,*" said someone else named George. These were the people she liked: the kind you couldn't really live with.

She turned to head toward the ladies' room and bumped into Ken. He gave her a hug hello, and then whispered in her ear, "You live with Nick. Help us think of an issue. I need another issue."

"I'll get you one at the issue store,' she said, and pulled away as someone approached him with a heartily extended hand and a false, booming "Here's the man of the hour." In the bathroom, she stared at her own reflection: in an attempt at extroversion, she had worn a tunic with large slices of watermelon depicted on the front. What had she been thinking of?

She went into the stall and slid the bolt shut. She read the graffiti on the back of the door. *Anita loves David S.* Or: *Christ + Diane W.* It was good to see that even in a town like this, people could love one another.

"Who were you talking to?" she asked him later at home.

"Who? What do you mean?"

"The one with the plasticine hair."

"Oh, Erin? She does look like she does something to her hair. It looks like she hennas it."

"It looks like she tacks it against the wall and stands underneath it."

"She's head of the Bayre Corners Neighborhood Association. Come September, we're really going to need her endorsement."

Olena sighed, looked away.

"It's the democratic process," said Nick.

"I'd rather have a king and queen," she said.

The following Friday, the night of the Fish Fry Fund-raiser at the Labor Temple, was the night Nick slept with Erin of the Bayre Corners

Neighborhood Association. He arrived back home at seven in the morning and confessed to Olena, who, when Nick hadn't come home, had downed half a packet of Dramamine to get to sleep.

"I'm sorry," he said, his head in his hands. "It's a sixties thing."

"A sixties thing?" She was fuzzy, zonked from the Dramamine.

"You get all involved in a political event, and you find yourself sleeping together. She's from that era, too. It's also that, I don't know, she just seems to really care about her community. She's got this reaching, expressive side to her. I got caught up in that." He was sitting down, leaning forward on his knees, talking to his shoes. The electric fan was blowing on him, moving his hair gently, like weeds in water.

"A sixties thing?" Olena repeated. "A sixties thing, what is that—like 'Easy to Be Hard'?" It was the song she remembered best. But now something switched off in her. The bones in her chest hurt. Even the room seemed changed—brighter and awful. Everything had fled, run away to become something else. She started to perspire under her arms and her face grew hot. "You're a murderer," she said. "That's finally what you are. That's finally what you'll always be." She began to weep so loudly that Nick got up, closed the windows. Then he sat down and held her—who else was there to hold her?—and she held him back.

He bought her a large garnet ring, a cough drop set in brass. He did the dishes ten straight days in a row. She had a tendency to go to bed right after supper and sleep, heavily, needing the escape. She had become afraid of going out—restaurants, stores, the tension in her shoulders, the fear gripping her face when she was there, as if people knew she was a foreigner and a fool—and for fifteen additional days he did the cooking and shopping. His car was always parked on the outside of the driveway, and hers was always in first, close, blocked in, as if to indicate who most belonged to the community, to the world, and who most belonged tucked in away from it, in a house. Perhaps in bed. Perhaps asleep.

"You need more life around you," said Nick, cradling her, though she'd gone stiff and still. His face was plaintive and suntanned, the notes and varnish of a violin. "You need a greater sense of life around you." Outside, there was the old rot smell of rain coming.

"How have you managed to get a suntan when there's been so much rain?" she asked.

"It's summer," he said. "I work outside, remember?"

"There are no sleeve marks," she said. "Where are you going?"

She had become afraid of the community. It was her enemy. Other people, other women.

She had, without realizing it at the time, learned to follow Nick's gaze, learned to learn his lust, and when she did go out, to work at least, his desires remained memorized within her. She looked at the attractive women he would look at. She turned to inspect the face of every pageboy haircut she saw from behind and passed in her car. She looked at them furtively or squarely—it didn't matter. She appraised their eyes and mouths and wondered about their bodies. She had become him: she longed for these women. But she was also herself, and so she despised them. She lusted after them, but she also wanted to beat them up.

A rapist.

She had become a rapist, driving to work in a car.

But for a while, it was the only way she could be.

She began to wear his clothes—a shirt, a pair of socks—to keep him next to her, to try to understand why he had done what he'd done: And in this new empathy, in this pants role, like an opera, she thought she understood what it was to make love to a woman, to open the hidden underside of her, like secret food, to thrust yourself up in her, her arch and thrash, like a puppet, to watch her later when she got up and walked around without you, oblivious to the injury you'd surely done her. How could you not love her, gratefully, marveling? She was so mysterious, so recovered, an unshared thought enlivening her eyes; you wanted to follow her forever.

A man in love. That was a man in love. So different from a woman.

A woman cleaned up the kitchen. A woman gave and hid, gave and hid, like someone with a May basket.

She made an appointment with a doctor. Her insurance covered her only if she went to the university hospital, and so she made an appointment there.

"I've made a doctor's appointment," she said to Nick, but he had the water running in the tub and didn't hear her. "To find out if there's anything wrong with me."

When he got out, he approached her, nothing on but a towel, pulled her close to his chest, and lowered her to the floor, right there in the hall by the bathroom door. Something was swooping, back and forth in an arc above her. May Day, May Day. She froze.

"What was that?" She pushed him away.

"What?" He rolled over on his back and looked. Something was flying around in the stairwell—a bird. "A bat," he said.

"Oh my God," cried Olena.

"The heat can bring them out in these old rental houses," he said, stood, rewrapped his towel. "Do you have a tennis racket?"

She showed him where it was. "I've only played tennis once," she said. "Do you want to play tennis sometime?" But he proceeded to stalk the bat in the dark stairwell.

"Now don't get hysterical," he said.

"I'm already hysterical."

"Don't get—There!" he shouted, and she heard the *thwack* of the racket against the wall, and the soft drop of the bat to the landing.

She suddenly felt sick. "Did you have to kill it?" she said.

"What did you want me to do?"

"I don't know. Capture it. Rough it up a little." She felt guilty, as if her own loathing had brought about its death. "What kind of bat is it?" She tiptoed up to look, to try to glimpse its monkey face, its cat teeth, its pterodactyl wings veined like beet leaves. "What kind? Is it a fruit bat?"

"Looks pretty straight to me," said Nick. With his fist, he tapped Olena's arm lightly, teasingly.

"Will you stop?"

"Though it *was* doing this whole astrology thing—I don't know. Maybe it's a zodiac bat."

"Maybe it's a brown bat. It's not a vampire bat, is it?"

"I think you have to go to South America for those," he said. "Take your platform shoes!"

She sank down on the steps, pulled her robe tighter. She felt for the light switch and flicked it on. The bat, she could now see, was small and light-colored, its wings folded in like a packed tent, a mouse with backpacking equipment. It had a sweet face, like a deer, though blood drizzled from its head. It reminded her of a cat she'd seen once as a child, shot with a BB in the eye.

"I can't look anymore," she said, and went back upstairs.

Nick appeared a half hour later, standing in the doorway. She was in bed, a book propped in her lap—a biography of a French feminist, which she was reading for the hairdo information.

"I had lunch with Erin today," he said.

She stared at the page. Snoods. Turbans and snoods. You could go for days in a snood. "Why?"

"A lot of different reasons. For Ken, mostly. She's still head of the neighborhood association, and he needs her endorsement. I just wanted to let you know. Listen, you've gotta cut me some slack."

She grew hot in the face again: "I've cut you some slack," she said. "I've cut you a whole forest of slack. The whole global slack forest has been cut for you." She closed the book. "I don't know why you cavort with these people. They're nothing but a bunch of clerks."

He'd been trying to look pleasant, but now he winced a little. "Oh, I see," he said. "Miss High-Minded. You whose father made his living off furs. Furs!" He took two steps toward her, then turned and paced back again. "I can't believe I'm living with someone who grew up on the proceeds of tortured animals!"

She was quiet. This lunge at moral fastidiousness was something she'd noticed a lot in the people around here. They were not good people. They were not kind. They played around and lied to their spouses. But they recycled their newspapers!

"Don't drag my father into this."

"Look, I've spent years of my life working for peace and free expression. I've been in prison already. I've lived in a cage! I don't need to live in another one."

"You and your free expression! You who can't listen to me for two minutes!"

"Listen to you what?"

"Listen to me when I"—and here she bit her lip a little—"when I tell you that these people you care about, this hateful Erin what's-her-name, they're just small, awful, nothing people."

"So they don't *read enough books*," he said slowly. "Who the fuck cares."

The next day he was off to a meeting with Ken at the Senior Citizens Association. The host from *Jeopardy!* was going to be there, and Ken wanted to shake a few hands, sign up volunteers. The host from *Jeopardy!* was going to give a talk.

"I don't get it," Olena said.

"I know." He sighed, the pond life treading water in his eyes. "But, well—it's the American way." He grabbed up his keys, and the look that quickly passed over his face told her this: she wasn't pretty enough.

"I hate America," she said.

Nonetheless, he called her at the library during a break. She'd been sitting in the back with Sarah, thinking up Tom Swifties, her brain ready to bleed from the ears, when the phone rang. "You should see this," he said. "Some old geezer raises his hand, I call on him, and he stands up, and the first thing he says is, 'I had my hand raised for ten whole minutes and you kept passing over me. I don't like to be passed over. You can't just pass over a guy like me, not at my age.'"

She laughed, as he wanted her to.

This hot dog's awful, she said frankly.

"To appeal to the doctors, Ken's got all these signs up that say 'Teetlebaum for tort reform.'"

"Sounds like a Wallace Stevens poem," she said.

"I don't know what I expected. But the swirl of this whole event has not felt right."

She's a real dog, he said cattily.

She was quiet, deciding to let him do the work of this call.

"Do you realize that Ken's entire softball team just wrote a letter to *The Star,* calling him a loudmouth and a cheat?"

"Well," she said, "what can you expect from a bunch of grown men who pitch underhand?"

There was some silence. "I care about us," he said finally. "I just want you to know that."

"Okay," she said.

"I know I'm just a pain in the ass to you," he said. "But you're an inspiration to me, you are."

I like a good sled dog, she said huskily.

"Thank you for just—for saying that," she said.

"I just sometimes wish you'd get involved in the community, help out with the campaign. Give of yourself. Connect a little with something."

At the hospital, she got up on the table and pulled the paper gown tightly around her, her feet in the stirrups. The doctor took a plastic speculum out of a drawer. "Anything particular seem to be the problem today?" asked the doctor.

"I just want you to look and tell me if there's anything wrong," said Olena.

The doctor studied her carefully. "There's a class of medical students outside. Do you mind if they come in?"

"Excuse me?"

"You know this is a teaching hospital," she said. "We hope that our patients won't mind contributing to the education of our medical students by allowing them in during an examination. It's a way of contributing to the larger medical community, if you will. But it's totally up to you. You can say no."

Olena clutched at her paper gown. *There's never been an accident, she said recklessly.* "How many of them are there?"

The doctor smiled quickly. "Seven," she said. "Like dwarfs."

"They'll come in and do what?"

The doctor was growing impatient and looked at her watch. "They'll participate in the examination. It's a learning visit."

Olena sank back down on the table. She didn't feel that she could offer herself up this way. *You're only average, he said meanly.*

"All right," she said. "Okay."

Take a bow, he said sternly.

The doctor opened up the doorway and called a short way down the corridor. "Class?"

They were young, more than half of them men, and they gathered around the examination table in a horseshoe shape, looking slightly ashamed, sorry for her, no doubt, the way art students sometimes felt sorry for the shivering model they were about to draw. The doctor pulled up a stool between Olena's feet and inserted the plastic speculum, the stiff, widening arms of it uncomfortable, embarrassing. "Today we will be doing a routine pelvic examination," she announced loudly, and then she got up again, went to a drawer, and passed out rubber gloves to everyone.

Olena went a little blind. A white light, starting at the center, spread to the black edges of her sight. One by one, the hands of the students entered her, or pressed on her abdomen, felt hungrily, innocently, for something to learn from her, in her.

She missed her mother the most.

"Next," the doctor was saying. And then again. "All right. Next?"

Olena missed her mother the most.

But it was her father's face that suddenly loomed before her now, his face at night in the doorway of her bedroom, coming to check on her before he went to bed, his bewildered face, horrified to find her lying there beneath the covers, touching herself and gasping, his whispered "Nell? Are you okay?" and then his vanishing, closing the door loudly, to leave her there, finally forever; to die and leave her there feeling only her own sorrow and disgrace, which she would live in like a coat.

There were rubber fingers in her, moving, wriggling around, but not like the others. She sat up abruptly and the young student withdrew his hand, moved away. "He didn't do it right," she said to the doctor. She pointed at the student. "He didn't do it correctly!"

"All right, then," said the doctor, looking at Olena with concern and alarm. "All right. You may all leave," she said to the students.

The doctor herself found nothing. "You are perfectly normal," she said. But she suggested that Olena take vitamin B and listen quietly to music in the evening.

Olena staggered out through the hospital parking lot, not finding her car at first. When she found it, she strapped herself in tightly, as if she were something wild—an animal or a star.

She drove back to the library and sat at her desk. Everyone had gone home already. In the margins of her notepad she wrote, 'Alone as a book, alone as a desk, alone as a library, alone as a pencil, alone as a catalog, alone as a number, alone as a notepad." Then she, too, left, went home, made herself tea. She felt separate from her body, felt herself dragging it up the stairs like a big handbag, its leathery hollowness something you could cut up and give away or stick things in. She lay between the sheets of her bed, sweating, perhaps from the tea. The world felt over to her, used up, off to one side. There were no more names to live by.

One should live closer. She had lost her place, as in a book.

One should live closer to where one's parents were buried.

Waiting for Nick's return, she felt herself grow dizzy, float up toward the ceiling, look down on the handbag. Tomorrow, she would get an organ donor's card, an eye donor's card, as many cards as she could get. She would show them all to Nick. "Nick! Look at my cards!"

And when he didn't come home, she remained awake through the long night, through the muffled thud of a bird hurling itself against the window, through the thunder leaving and approaching like a voice, through the Frankenstein light of the storm. Over her house, in lieu of stars, she felt the bright heads of her mother and father, searching for her, their eyes beaming down from the sky.

Oh, there you are, they said. *Oh, there you are.*

But then they went away again, and she lay waiting, fist in her spine, for the grace and fatigue that would come, surely it must come, of having given so much to the world.

THE COBWEB

Zona Gale

EVENINGS, AT SEVEN O'CLOCK, THE NEW TIMBER LIBRARY OPENED for an hour. Unless there was a band concert, or a moving-picture show, or a night that Timber called "real bad and sloppy out," Emmons's store was, for that hour, the center of village life. A corner of the store was the City Library. There Bethany Emmons kept sacred to books a section of shelves, beyond the canned goods and above the salt-fish barrel. The top shelf, too high to be reached by Lissa Bard, the librarian, held the dried-fruit boxes. The grocery was not large; and by seven o'clock, one winter Saturday night, it was filled with women borrowers.

Lissa Bard had not come in. However, it not infrequently happened that Lissa, by the newness of her duties or by her nature, was late at her post. And of this, and of other things about her, three women, near the threshold of the little dark, coffee-smelling back room of the store, talked enjoyably while they waited.

"It's often that way with sisters, so," Mis' Hibbard observed. (Mis' Hibbard always set the *t* in "often," and the *n* in "column," "because," she defended, "there they are, all ready to say 'em. It ain't like the psalm *p*—that's Bible, an' old-fashioned, an' not a real necessary word anyway. But 'often' an' 'column' you hear every day, an' that's all the more reason to take pains with 'em.")

"Yes, you look at the Clark girls," Mis' Arthur, with her challenging emphasis, agreed; "one is light skin an' no life, an' the other one's black hair, an' goes like the wind. An' the Mosses: one of 'em like real folks, an' the other one just kind o' big, an' in the way. But the two Bards: they 're more differ'nt than it's possible *to* be."

"Lissy always was a real scholar," Mis' Main said, sighing, "an' real intelligent, too. But of them two, poor Kate is the only house-keeper."

Mis' Arthur nodded, tapping an emphasis on the cook-hook she was returning.

"Well," she said, "if you ain't a good housekeeper, with all that means, *what are you?* An' Kate is. The run o' books is all very well, an' nobody likes to see 'em in anybody's parlor more than our family, but there's no contradictin': they ain't to eat nor drink, nor sweep the floor with. Kate Bard keeps house like wax-works if Lissy *has* got the brains."

In the moment of strained silence that fell as the three women became conscious of her presence, Kate Bard, who had entered the store through the little dark back room, stood at their elbows, nodded to them all, and looked elaborately as if she had not heard. But they all knew that she must have heard.

Mis' Arthur, as the culprit, did her part, and laughed out, heartily and guiltily.

"Lawsey, Kate," she said, "you listenin'? Well, nobody born keeps house any neater 'n you do, an' you know it."

Kate Bard, little, flat-waisted, her pointed face held slightly down, her large eyes raised, the gray shawl about her head caught tightly beneath her chin, looked at the three with a faint twist of a smile, and briefly-closed lids.

"Shucks," she said, and passed them.

Seeing her, Bethany Emmons took down the lamp from its bracket above his desk, and set it on the deal table of the City Library.

"Lissa's late gettin' started," Kate explained to every one, throwing off her shawl, with a stiff swing of her head to keep her hair free of it. "She wanted't I should come on ahead, an' say't she'd be right over. She was afraid somebody night get tired waitin' an' try to go off."

She sat at the table awkwardly; the librarianship was new to Lissa, and Kate had not before been asked to take her sister's place. She fell to rearranging the little articles: the petrified potato inkwell, the pretty stone, the smart plush case of the thermometer. The movement displayed on her wrists broad, tortoiseshell bracelets over which fell the loose sleeves of her figured blue dressing-sack.

Mis' Arthur, who had followed her to the table, laid down the cook-book.

"I've got to get back home, an' hunt up the clean clothes," Mis' Arthur said, "so mebbe you could give me some book yourself, Kate. I thought of *The Pathfinder*. I've been readin' that all my life, off an' on. I guess I'll get it out, an' read a couple or two more chapters on it. I can't seem to think of the name of any other book."

Kate rose, and took up the lamp, and held it in both hands while she looked along the lowest shelf, squinting in the light, her lips moving as she read the titles. The lowest shelf held the set of Dickens, bound in four volumes, and that of Scott, in eight, and of Dumas in eight: tall, startled-looking tomes, each appearing to wonder at itself for being so many books in one. Half-way across the row Kate turned, frowning a little.

"Know who wrote it?" she inquired.

"Well-a, wasn't his name Cooper, or like that?" Mis' Arthur hesitated. "I've got that name around in my head, anyhow."

"Is it poetry or readin'?" Kate demanded.

"Oh, readin'," Mis' Arthur said hastily. "Land! It's for myself."

"Anybody got it out?" Kate called in a moment. "Anybody got out a book called *Pathfinder?*" she repeated over-shoulder.

"I've read it." "I've read it twice," several volunteered. And, "I ain't ever read it, but I've heard of it," offered Mis' Hibbard pleasantly. "I donno but what you're lookin' at the wrong writers," she added to Kate. "Mr. Cooper ain't a set. He's just that one."

And now Kate's search was extending laboriously over the titles on the Histories and Lives. And at last it touched at a big, black book without a binding, and she set down the lamp to take the volume from the shelf. But when it was in her hands she did not see the title.

"My soul," she said, "look at the dust."

From the top of the black book she blew a fine, quite visible cloud, in evidence for one full breath; and at one more breath there was a little second cloud. And from the book's edge fine tentacles of cobweb clung and outwavered and caught at Kate's hands, and drew about her wrists like airy manacles. Quite instinctively she turned to the side of the shelves, where a dust-cloth might be native; and, the cloth not being there, she opened the table-drawer and reached capably back among its tumbled papers. Evidently Lissa had no dust-cloth, and Kate glanced perplexedly about. "I never come out without my handkerchief, that I ain't sure to need it for something," she observed, and caught up a corner of her dressing-sack, and dusted the black book. Then she took down another book and another—the Histories and the Lives—and from each she blew fine, condemnatory dust, and each she carefully brushed with the dressing-sack until the blue cloth, like her hands, was cobweb-covered.

She was still at her task when the bell above the store's front door jingled noisily, much as if a gay little wind had prevailed against it. The wind—that one or another—entering with the opening of the door, breathed on a kerosene lamp a-swing from the ceiling, and momentarily it flared up and brightened all the store. Then the door was smartly shut, and Lissa Bard came down the room, a little, tender, blown leaf of a figure, wind still in her soft strayed hair. And brightness in her face. She was very tiny—frail of waist and wrist, evidently unable to undertake tasks of the hand, but armored with the distinction of her bookcraft, and with mere charm so that whatever was her excuse,—and no one quite caught it,—it seemed admirably to answer, and no one seemed really to care that, when the librarian reached the City Library, the clock above the cheese pointed to fifteen past seven.

Kate stood hitching her shawl from side to side, upward from waist to shoulder.

"Have you got Cooper's *Pathfinder* in the library?" she asked, and intent on her shawl, missed the shade of amused surprise in Lissa's look.

"Why yes!" Lissa said. Don't you know—"

"Well, somebody must have it out, Kate went on. "It ain't in the shelves. I've read through 'most every name."

Lissa's eyes danced

"Why, *we've* got it out!" she cried. "I read it out loud to you last night." At that the women about the table laughed, frankly and unrestrainedly. On which Kate Bard colored slowly, her thin cheeks burning in two high, bright spots. Then she made her twisted smile, and closed her eyes momentarily, pinning the shawl tightly about her face.

"I ain't no hand to look at the name of a book I'm interested in," she said. "Every man's name that writes 'em sounds just alike to me, anyhow. Goodnight, all."

But as she crossed the alley from the store to the house where, until Lissa's recent home-coming, she had lived alone. Kate's smile went out. She fumbled in the pump-spout for the key, stepped into the chill cheer of the kitchen, went about the unimportant offices of her return; and in her breast something hurt and seemed heavy, so that she felt a sickness almost physical. But then for days she had not been well,—"sort o' spindlin' an' petered out, an' peaked-feelin'," she had described her state to Lissa,—and now she tried to think that this was the weakness that she felt. She knew better than that, though and when she had turned up the wick, and poked at the fire in the cooking-stove, she sat down before the open oven door, her skirt turned back to dry its hem, and tried to brave the thing that hurt. And what she had to brave were Lissa's eyes, dancing to her own reply, and Lissa's light laughter threading the inadvertent, wounding mockery of the women.

From her school, Lissa had lately come into Kate's orderly life and home, and quite casually had accepted both. Kate's surprise, first amused, then grieved grew to an understanding that her own talent in what she called "flyin' 'round the house" was to Lissa a matter of course—as spring must be a matter of course to a tributary wind. Kate observed that Lissa at her "book-readin'" quickened as she never quickened in the presence of that vague spirit of home to which Kate sacrificed with her exquisite house-wifery. And of all this the older sister had come to think with tender tolerance for the child ill-equipped for home-craft, and promptness, and all exactitudes. Yet this child and the women had laughed at her for not knowing about *Pathfinding*, and nobody had laughed at the dust on the City Library books. And Mis' Arthur had used a kind of defense in "Kate Bard keeps house like wax-works if Lissy has got all the brains."

Her resentment toward Lissa could not all have come in that hour, for now it was big in her heart, a living thing. Lissa had laughed with the rest; and since her return home there must have been other things at which she had laughed, secretly. In spite of Kate's own chieftainship in the home, Lissa must have all this time been making allowance for her,—Lissa, who had always been auxiliary in the household and not a burden-bearer, who was temperamentally alien to responsibility, who was of those who never turn the soil for a garden, but merely drop in the seeds. "She's a poor little stick of a housekeeper and always will be," Kate thought miserably; "everybody in Timber knows that. An' yet they'll bow down to her, knee to dust, because she knows a few funny names," So she thought about it, burning, resolutely overcoming her own tenderness.

After a time, as she tended her skirt's hem in the growing warmth, her look fell on her cooking-stove oven, from which she had drawn thousands of loaves and cakes. Behind the sink looking-glass here was a paper on which she had once tried to compute these loaves and to reckon how many times she had turned the clock-key. And by the wood-box stood the little toy broom which she used for sweeping the top of the long stovepipe, where dust and cobwebs never gathered, and of the cupboard, where no spider ever lived a day. The cupboards locked away the dishes which she knew; oh, as Lissa knew the City Library books, Kate knew those dishes, line and crack and nick: knew what should be piled in what on the ordered shelves; knew every stain and knot-hole of the unpainted floor; and the look of the other rooms, lying beyond in the dark—spotless, dustless, their parts adjusted in all the scrupulous nicety with which men should legislate a nation. It was the work of her hands, And suddenly her heart leaped within her, as a heart leaps when eyes rest upon their kingdom. Her glowing was that of the creator who greets his achievement and his waiting material, and lords it over them, and in them passionately sees, for his spirit, the way out. All this was hers, as peculiarly hers as Lissa's little toy kingdom of funny names. Here she was mistress, here her skill was of sovereign importance, here—she sank in the consciousness as into cherishing arms—Lissa could never enter in.

"An' they ain't a housekeeper in Timber but what knows that!" Kate thought, with her little twisted smile.

When her sister came from the library, Kate still sat by the open oven door. Unaccustomed to fathom mood, to divine the tentacle-like, waving things that web it round, Lissa, bright and uncorrelated, chattered while her wraps came off.

"Oh, so many books went out. I haven't started keeping the cards yet, but I guess Bethany could tell how many. Everybody that took a book bought something: *Kenilworth* and ten cents' worth of crackers; *David Copperfield* and a jug of vinegar; *Vanity Fair* and a pound of prunes. We had to stop the whole circulating department while Bethany climbed the library desk to get those prunes down. O Kate! And little Aggie Ellsworth asked me for Thweet Pickelth, and I reached for the catalogue before I saw the tin pail and sent her across to Bethany!"

Kate did not laugh.

"Been me," she said somberly, "I'd 'a' been huntin' along the shelves for it yet. Without," she added, "Aggie'd 'a' spoke the pickle man's name. Them pickle authors I can seem to keep pretty straight in my head."

Something in her sister's attitude, as obvious as drooping wings, arrested Lissa's look as she came to the stove.

"You cold?" she inquired.

"No," Kate answered listlessly. "I donno. I feel some chilly—on my shoulders. But I guess I just like to be warm."

"You aren't well," Lissa said with decision. "You haven't felt well for days. I'll put a flat-iron on. You sit there and toast your feet and I'll read to you while the iron heats."

Without waiting for assent, Lissa brought *The Pathfinder* from the "other" room and set the table lamp on a wooden-bottomed chair drawn to the hearth. She herself sat on the braided hearth-rug. As she read, Kate looked down at her—a frail little figure whose bent head showed her fair curls at their best. The warm light from the open draft fell on the sweet, small-featured face, no longer in its first youth, but having that perennial youth of a body remote from the activities that age, of a spirit without flight, but perpetually fanning little wings. And as she looked, Kate for the first time became conscious of, say, these little wings. Maybe Lissa's "book-readin'" was a kingdom of more than funny names. Maybe it was as real a comfort to her as "flyin' 'round the house" to Kate herself. Maybe it was a bigger, better place to be, and this the women in the store knew, and that was why they had laughed. The perception came to the older woman in an impression as sharp, and as wordless, as a hurt. And the conviction possessed her the more that her perceptions could not be ordered or explained by her, but merely suffered.

"It's somethin' inside of her that I ain't got an' never did hev," Kate thought. "We're differ'nt, but it ain't the same kind of differ'nt, as her likin' her bread thin an' me likin' mine thick, or her openin' her window nights an' me shuttin' mine most down, or her turnin' the lamp wick down an' me blazin' it 'way up. She's got some woke-up thing in her that bites a-hold o' i-dees the way I spy onto dust an' cobwebs. She's more than differ'nt. She's the otherest a person can be."

And as the understanding grew upon her, Kate turned the more passionately to her own place, as if her little way of skill were a very pleasance where her soul might have its ease, take its way out. Lissa might have some dimly-guessed, bigger, better kingdom; but Kate's kingdom was her own. She was like a word, envious of an idea, glorying in the certainty that the idea could not be spelled without her.

Until Lissa had finished a chapter and had gone away to iron the chill sheets of her sister's bedroom, Kate brooded and burned. Then she rose and took the book from the wing of the stove where Lissa had laid it, and turned to the title-page. So many books! So many different names! But it would not be a disgrace not to remember who had been president of the United States in a certain year, and that was far more important than book names. Yet all those women had laughed at her, and Lissa's eyes had laughed. If only Lissa would laugh at her now for that blunder in the library! "No need o' her keepin' such a nasty, delicate silence," Kate thought.

"The bed's all ready when you are," Lissa called.

Kate closed the book and spoke over shoulder to the open door.

"I ain't anywhere near ready," she said tartly. "Lissa Bard! You've let the books down to the City Library get a perfect sight. They's dust on 'em like feathers, an' cobwebs a regular fringe. An' now you've laid Mr. Cooper's book on the stove-wing out here so's it'll get all splattered with the grease. If I was so crazy about book-readin', I declare if I would'nt do differ'nt."

In Lissa's amazed silence, away there in the bedroom, Kate looked about the kitchen. Then she opened the cupboard door, and, tiptoe, laid the book on the top shelf. There, with the toy broom kept for stovepipe cobwebs, she thrust *The Pathfinder* far back beside the cherry pitter.

II

Her chilliness and weariness had foretold the illness which seized Kate that night, and when the Sunday morning came she was hot with fever and throbbing with pain. Lissa woke, vaguely alarmed not to hear her sister already astir, and for a little lay listening, then went softly to her door.

"I do' want no doctor," Kate observed weakly. "I'd just as lives have a cat open the door an' walk around the bed. You heat me a cup o' hot water."

Lissa, trembling, hurried her dressing, built a fire in the frosty kitchen, waited interminably for the kettle to boil. Kate's silence and her inability to drink even the water terrified the girl as if in the little house some sinister presence had appeared. And when it was church time, and from the kitchen window she saw Mis' Arthur and Mis' Hibbard coming down the street, she threw her apron over her head and, not to pass Kate's window, stumbled through the deep snow on the side of the yard that was pathless.

"Oh," she told them. "I don't know what's the matter with Kate. She's sick and in the bed."

The women, accustomed to treat all crises as their own, followed Lissa to the house, accepting the pathless way as a matter of course, and briskly questioning. Was Kate conscious? When was she taken? There was a lots o' colds everywhere an' it was real pneumonia weather. Had she had her sister's hands and feet in good, hot water? They laid their hymn-books by the unwashed dishes, and stalked through the cold dining-room to Kate's little grave of a chamber.

"Lawsey, Kate Bard, thought *you'd* take down to relieve the monotony, did you?" one of them greeted her.

Kate, opening her eyes, saw them standing in a place without walls and from which she was infinitely remote. She knew them, but instantly she was conscious that they were allied against her, and with them was Lissa. Secure in some friendly and infinitely companionable understanding to which she was alien, they were all laughing at her. And so thought drifted out, without her power to grasp at one association to stay its drifting.

In the weeks that followed, her wandering look often rested unseeingly on one or other of those two faces, or on the face of Mis' Main, who forever crossed the alley from her home to bring a covered bowl of something steaming. Sometimes Kate saw them quite clearly; sometimes the faces blurred and flickered, the better to menace her; always they were quick with an understanding of something which she did not know. But even a greater vexation was the face which hovered constantly above her—that of Lissa. The stricken brain, become a thing of sick impressions which outwavered and clung and fled, lay as if webbed about by its last sane sensation. They were all persistently "against her," they all knew something that she did not know—and with them was Lissa, who could not even take care of her books. Lissa's books were all dust and cobwebs. The dust and cobwebs were what shut away the meaning in the books so that she could not know all about them as Lissa knew. And before she, too, could know, the dust and cobwebs must all be swept away with the toy broom.

Dust and cobwebs—dust and cobwebs. In her fever this became to her a kind of refrain. And it was no great gulf to have bridged from fantasy to faculty when at last one day Kate lay quiet, listening to what the women were saying, and realized that she had been listening for some moments before she was self-conscious.

" . . . *awful.* I donno how it is folks can do as they *do* do. Some seems just bent on gettin' along most any way they can. Shouldn't you think she'd a noticed it by now if she was calculatin' to do any noticin'?"

It was Mis' Hibbard's voice; without lifting her tired lids Kate knew that. Mis' Arthur's emphasis seemed as usual to make a kind of groove for her own reply.

"Well," Mis' Arthur put it, "if ever I see anybody no hand to take notice, it's her. She don't seem to go by no rhyme nor rule. If she was a clock you couldn't tell the time by her no more than you could tell time by a wild duck. She just sort o' goes along, an' goes along—"

Kate's little figure lay tense. They meant her!

" . . . for eight days, hand-runnin'," Mis' Main was saying. "And there it is, full the way it was when I first laid look to it—floatin' away as hard as could float, an' just like it was made for floatin'."

And "It don't seem," Mis' Arthur said, "as if two sisters could be so opposite. Do you s'pse Kate Bard in her well days would ever leave a cobweb swingin' that long?"

At that a pang of fierce delight shot through Kate's whole body. It was not she whom they meant. It was not she!

"The idea," the hushed voices went on, "of takin' no more responsibility. It's plumb over Kate's head when she lays on the back pillow. It might drop on her any minute."

"The only wonder is it ain't fell on her long before now. But it's a good strong cobweb—it's old enough to hev body to it, the dear land knows. *How* long do you s'pose Lissy'll leave it be there?"

"I've set an' watched her when she dusts, an' she goes right past it like it hed been a wreath in the border. I s'pose it's mean, but I declare I've got real interested seein' how long it'll stay there. Why, Kate Bard'd die rather'n hev a cobweb in the family that long."

When the women, still talking, had left the room, Kate lay for a long time without opening her eyes. Like a warm lapping bath it rested her, this indignant praise of her, yes, and this arraignment of Lissa. She lay luxuriously glad, smiling a little, alive and praised. And after a very long time she languidly opened her eyes, and, almost with a sense of gratitude, looked about for the cobweb.

In all Kate's lifetime there had never been, in the bare little room, a cobweb like that. It hung from the corner above the bed, attached just where the eagle on the side-wall border met the stars on the ceiling. To eagle and stars it clung by many a visible filament and, escaping these, it floated, in vagrant currents, its full yard of length. It was, Kate thought dreamily, like an attic cobweb, a cobweb of behind the storeroom blinds in house—cleaning. But a house cobweb, a bedroom cobweb like that—her head drooped sidewise on its pillow and her eyes fell on the little toy broom in a corner—she must have brought the little broom in with her from the kitchen on the night of her illness, and Lissa had left it there. Its uselessness and isolation in the face of so obvious a task moved her to laughter, without her knowing why she laughed. She lay for a little, shaken with silent mirth, until from very weakness she fell asleep.

When she awoke, Lissa sat by the bell with a book. If only Lissa had been sewing, the return to life would have been a simpler matter; but Lissa was reading. For some time she did not lift her eyes from the page, and Kate lay watching her. The girl's face was pleased and quiet, and it shut Kate out.

"What you readin'?" Kate demanded abruptly.

Lissa started, tossed aside the book, hung above her sister with little happy exclamations; but these and the many tender questions Kate passed impatiently.

"What you readin'?" she persisted "*Pathfinder?*"

"No," Lissa said. "Kate. I found *The Pathfinder* away on the top shelf of the cupboard, when I was looking for the potato—masher. How do you suppose it ever got up there?"

To which, with closed eyes and a mere shadow of her twisted smile, Kate responded, "Who ever heard o' keepin' anybody's potato-masher on the *top* shelf? What you readin'?"

In some wonder Lissa named her book, a strange, singing name which told Kate nothing.

"Read some out loud," she commanded; and at Lissa's look, "Go on" she added. "I ain't out o' my head. I feel just like life."

So Lissa read to her at random, wondering very much, secretly simplifying, or making in her voice little shallows of shadow and crests of clearness, more safely to bear meaning. But she knew that she was alone as she read, and that it was Kate who could not come to her. When the reading paused—

"Keep it up," Kate said, "I dunno what it means, but it kind o' rubs around nice on the outside o' my brain."

But Lissa, Kate was brooding, did know what it meant. Lissa knew, not just with her brain, outside or inside, but with the "woke-up thing" in her, the thing that somehow could "bite a-hold o' life." She could not have told why she had wanted Lissa to read, whether in some dim wistfulness to try to share whatever Lissa had, or whether for a kind of dogged strengthening of her own resentment. As she lay with closed eyes, listening, her thought returned and beat upon Lissa, and her own irritation increased and mounted and possessed her. So then she turned passionately to the warm spot in her consciousness, the certainty, unformulated but secure, that for her the way of "bitin' a-hold o' life" lay in manipulating those little energies of home which she called "flyin' round the house."

She moved her head, and lay looking up at where the eagle met the stars, above the back pillow. Oh, it was thick and gray and dusty, that cobweb. And all this time in spite of that mysterious, wise, "woke-up thing" within her, Lissa had missed the cobweb,—as of course Lissa would miss it! A little glow crept and warmed Kate. Poor Lissa, she thought. She said it over and over, luxuriously as, lulled by the singing things freed from the book, she fell asleep.

The four o'clock sun streamed across the blue coverlet, illumining the rose wax blossoms of a begonia on the window-sill, wakening Kate as if spirit had signaled to spirit. In the bedroom it was deliciously quiet. A wood-fire was crackling in the parlor stove. On the table a napkin-covered dish of something delectable awaited her mood. Murmur of voices penetrated the closed kitchen door, both eloquent of the gentleness that tended her. The convalescent's sense of well-being filled Kate, like response.

In a week, she thought, she would be about again—flyin' round the house. How long it had been since she had seen her oven. It would be good to shut the hot door on a batch of bread, a tin of cake, a pan of cookies. She must get at her cupboards, and give them "a good going-over." Lissa never could remember what was to be piled in what. She found herself even wanting to wind the clock,—Lissa had probably let it run down and, when she set it, had guessed at the time. (Poor Lissa! she thought pleasurably.) Yes, the whole house must be gone over thoroughly, must be swept and dusted and rid of its cobwebs— the very first day that she was about again, down should come that cobweb wavering there over head. Then, when Mis' Hibbard and Mis' Arthur and Mis' Main dropped in, she would make excuse to lead them into the bedroom. She would pretend not to see them look up in the cobweb corner, not to see them exchange glances of approval of her and of her housekeeping, that was so much better than Lissa's. Poor Lissa.

On that, as at a motif, Lissa came into the room, in her hand, a blue dust-cloth and a feather-duster. From the kitchen still sounded the voices, and Lissa answered Kate's questioning look.

"I was just coming to wipe up the dust a little, if you were awake," she explained," "when Mis' Hibbard and Mis' Arthur and Mis' Main came in. They'd heard you were conscious. They told me to go right ahead, I'd had to neglect this room so long, an' they'd sit there, and get warm, and come in and see you afterward."

"Oh," said Kate, "*that's* how they done it."

She lay quite still while Lissa dusted. When she was well it had immeasurably irritated Kate to see Lissa dust. To all wide, flat, horizontal surfaces the girl gave the prettiest attention, bending to her task till the curls in her neck were at their best. But all narrow edges, the tops of chairs, of splashers, of pictures, she neglected as if these were in another dimension, and flat vertical surfaces she treated as if they were in no dimension at all. For Lissa, dust that was immaterial was non-existent. For Kate, even if dust were non-existent, dusting was dusting. Yet that day it was with definite enjoyment that Kate lay with half-closed eyes and watched.

A gay little wind would have dusted a room much as did Lissa.

The wind—that one, or another—would have entered and breathed on this and that, touching and lifting, rearranging a disorder rather than ordering. And so Lissa did, omitting needs in all the pretty complaisance with which a housekeeper divines them. Ordinarily Kate would have crashed down on the process with the finality of a drawn blind. Now she lay, benignly indulgent—as Mother Spring at the sweet gaucheries of some little tributary wind.

But there had always been, in Kate's attitude to Lissa, much of this attitude of motherhood. Lissa's little body had constantly demanded the guardianship of which her mind was childishly impatient. And this late resentment of Kate's was wholly toward that mysterious, "woke-up thing," unfostered of her, which made Lissa remote, versed in baffling matters. Yet now, as she worked, these matters were no longer evident. Instead, in her own unwonted leisure and supineness, she was suddenly immeasurably struck with the littleness of her sister, with her physical unfitness for tasks of the hand. Her slenderness of throat, of waist, of wrist, her narrowness of shoulder and thigh,—these smote Kate with a sudden pitying sense of the girl's utter inadequacy for her woman's work. Poor little Lissa—poor little Lissa. That was it: *poor little Lissa!*

Lissa came, in her dusting, to the bed's head, and this, presumably because of Kate's presence, she did not touch at all. Lying so that she could see the cobweb, Kate held her breath as Lissa moved about its corner. Because of her long habit of getting good things for her, almost Kate wished that Lissa would look up to where it hung. There came a little still-born impulse to tell her. But Kate watched her turn away without an upward glance toward eagles and stars, and then, when the impulse to tell her had not yet wholly passed, the girl serenely shook the dust-cloth in the room, in the mere general direction of the paper basket.

"Shall I have Mis' Hibbard and Mis' Arthur and Mis' Main come in a minute?" she asked, while she was guilty of this.

"*Yes!*" Kate burst out. "My land yes. Hev 'em in here! An' you get back to your book."

Lissa looked at her inquiringly.

"I've got the supper to get pretty soon now," she said, quite gently.

As one divining the tentacle-like, waving things that web one round, Kate heard the under-note of weariness in the girl's voice. Her fragility had always. made Kate fear that she might be tired or ill, or even merely cold. The older sister threw out her hand on the coverlet.

"Well, you keep 'em out there a minute or two," she said irresolutely. "I'll pound on the wall with the little broom there—you set it by the bed—in just a minute. Then you can let 'em in."

Left alone, Kate shut her eyes tightly, grotesquely, in her unwonted will to think swiftly, and to a purpose. And in that troubled darkness she visualized the faces of the three women, looking her over sympathetically enough, asking their intimate questions, honestly glad of her recovery, but all the while waiting for chance to peer up in that cobweb corner, and then to look at one another, moving confirmatory eyebrows, or lids, or lips. It all came to Kate as a picture only, but she knew its truth. She knew how they would go away telling scornfully about Lissa Bard's housekeeping, and praising, her—Kate—in the comparison; these very women who had laughed at her, as Lissa had laughed. Oh, but they must not laugh at Lissa too, poor little Lissa!

Kate lifted her head tentatively from the pillow, and then drew herself to sit erect, a scant, gaunt figure in its outing flannel, with a thin, tight little braid of gray hair, reaching hardly half-way to the gown's yoke. Something seemed tipping her poor, dizzy head like a weight when, with infinite difficulty, she groped out for the toy broom. In the faintness that seized her as she pulled herself to her knees on the bed, then unsteadily to her feet, the darkness within her closed lids changed to a glow of red. She saw nothing of what she was doing as she laboriously lifted the little broom up the wall, and swept long, random strokes about the corner, freeing from its hold the flaunting filaments which clung and wavered very near her hair, as if they would have webbed her about. Then she sank, her head jarred to dull aching, throbbing and chill in all her body. So she lay, huddled outside the covers until, hearing some stir in the kitchen, she crept into her place, and the toy broom slipped behind the bed to the floor.

Mis' Hibbard and Mis' Arthur and Mis' Main came tiptoeing through the parlor, and pushed the bedroom door.

"We'll just peek in an' see if she's awake, anyhow," they said to Lissa, who had thought to wait the summons. "You 'wake, Kate?" one put it fairly.

In the whimsical, faint answer there was all the old vitality.

"If you're the nightmare, I ain't," she said, "an' if you're a call, I am. Come along in, why don't you?"

They came to the bedside, their shawls, worn for "runnin' round the neighborhood," slipping loosely down blue calico, flannel dressing-sack, and "mornin' house-work dress."

"Showed the sense to get well, didn't you, Kate?" said one. "Well said. I'm real pleased you've come to."

"May be you think we ain't danced round lively over you while you've been lazin' here in the bed," said another.

"My soul, if you're threatenin' well I donno who's got the biggest chore done, you or us."

"Lawsey, Kate Bard," said the third, "I thought one while't your coffin was cut, but I guess it's green wood yet awhile, an' mebbe growin'."

And, having told her like this of their genuine gladness at her recovery, they all three, with one accord, looked up at the corner of the eagle and the stars. Kate saw them look, and look again, and risk peering this way and that. Mis' Hibbard stepped about the foot of the bed to try a new light, Mis' Arthur came close to Kate's head, as if her assurance was almost reluctant. And then, certainty being fully established, they glanced at one another, and moved surprised, commendatory heads.

Lissa, tying on her big gingham apron, came to the bedroom door.

"Well, sir, Kate," Mis' Hibbard said, "I tell you, Lissy's gettin' to be quite a first-class housekeeper. She'll beat you at it if you don't look out."

In Kate's unimportant reply they could not divine the leaping exultation,—as it were, the very romance of renunciation. Nor did they understand her little twisted smile.

THE RETIREMENT PARTY

Lisa Koger

IT IS TWO O'CLOCK ON A FRIDAY AFTERNOON IN APRIL. THE WILLOWS
along the river north of town are a tender grasshopper green; patches
of henbit and bitter cress sprout like tufts of hair in the winter-weary
yards. In the basement of the library on Main Street, Miss Lucy
McKewn, age thirty-six, assistant librarian, cleans up the last of the
cookie crumbs left by the Story Hour children. She is a local woman,
Farlanburg born, a member of that category often referred to as "attractive enough"—though no one ever says attractive enough for what. She
wears her straight brown hair pulled back from her face by barrettes,
which, at a distance, look like hyphens above her ears. Using the side
of her hand, she rakes cookie scraps into piles, eats the chunks, then
sweeps the rest off the table and into the garbage can.

When she finishes cleaning, she goes upstairs to Microfilm and
debates whether she ought to call Jack at the deli to remind him about
Mrs. Worsham's party, which is scheduled for four o'clock this afternoon. She doesn't look forward to the party, but she'd rather be there
than at home, a three-room apartment above the garage of a Mr. and
Mrs. W. T. Tucker on Stringer Street. Come September, Miss Lucy
will have lived in her garage apartment fourteen years—a fact that
might not depress her if she could forget that she originally told the
Tuckers she'd be staying only two.

The cookie crumbs have roused her hunger. Her stomach roils
and growls. As she rewinds film onto the proper spools, a task the
Historical Society ladies are forever forgetting to do, the machine

creaks and sings to her and seems to say, 'Lemon Cremes or Lorna Doones? Lemon Cremes or Lorna Doones?"

At the front desk, Mrs. Worsham, the librarian, prunes her spider plant and talks to Shirley, who teaches Adult Ed. Shirley skims a newspaper. She has assigned her students a difficult math problem. They sit at a table back in Fiction, rubbing their foreheads and chewing on their pencils. Today, Mrs. Worsham and Shirley are having a discussion about "the good life" and the fact that more people have it in small towns than in large ones. Miss Lucy leans against the microfilm machine and listens. "Your small towns are where you find your happy people," says Mrs. Worsham. "In your small towns, you've got your close families, your safe streets, and your clean air."

Shirley smiles as though she has a secret. She says she wonders. She says she's not so sure. Unlike Mrs. Worsham and Miss Lucy, Shirley hasn't lived her whole life in a small town. The only reason she is in this one is because she met and married Russ Keller, a local boy.

"Well I'm sure," says Mrs. Worsham. She snips and coifs her plant as if it were a difficult head of hair. "I had this nephew who lived in a big town. Detroit. They make cars up there you know, and it's nothing but pollution. Last year, this nephew of mine took sick and died. Want to know how old he was?" She arches her brows and looks over her shoulder as if she thinks a Detroit person might sneak up behind her and mug her for her information. "Guess."

"Sixty," says Shirley.

"I said he was my nephew," says Mrs. Worsham. "How could I have a nephew that old?" She purses her lips and frowns. Her hand floats self-consciously to her neck, which appears to be the gathering place for wrinkles. She is a small woman with a face like a book mite; she is not without opinions. Should the county school board be allowed to close the Rocky Branch grade school where so many have received a fine education? She's against it. Should local law enforcement officials be required to exhibit proof of literacy before they are hired? Depends on who they are. A good reader does not always a good lawman make. Cowardice runs in some families.

Just as she thinks it the duty of a county newspaper to report only county news, she has always considered it the obligation of a librarian to know as much about the history of local families as about best sellers and recent titles. There are many in town who say they'd rather

have fifteen minutes with Mrs. Worsham than a six-week trial owner-
ship of a set of the Britannica.

"He was forty-two," says Mrs. Worsham. "They say that when
they cut him open, his lungs were just like cottage cheese and fell to
pieces in the doctor's hands. Just goes to show you the human body
wasn't made to withstand pollution."

Shirley yawns and pats her mouth. "Did he smoke?"

"Of course he smoked," says Mrs. Worsham, in a tone that
implies all good nephews do. "That's got nothing to do with it. The best
doctors can tell the difference between cancer caused by smoking and
cancer caused by pollution. My nephew was a lawyer, and he had the
best doctors, and they said his was the pollution kind."

Shirley stares at Mrs. Worsham. Mrs. Worsham goes to the water
fountain and fills a plastic cup.

Miss Lucy suddenly remembers she is supposed to stop by the
drug store tomorrow to pick up the new salve Doc Harkins ordered for
the infection in her father's foot. All her life she has been healthy
enough to avoid doctors; now she finds herself surrounded by them.
She shares her apartment with her father, and she is always hauling
him to see them. Her father is in his seventies. For a year after Miss
Lucy's mother died, he stayed by himself out on the farm. He called
her every morning and every night. "I'm not eatin' right," he said. "I
reckon I'm starvin'." When he lost a leg because of diabetes, he sold
his house and phoned Miss Lucy. "Come get me," he said, so she did.
She packed him up and lugged him into town.

He hates town. The water tastes like Clorox, and there are no
groundhogs or squirrels to shoot. Miss Lucy buys frozen dinners for his
lunch; Mexican with enchiladas is his favorite. He is always eating
stuff that messes up his bowels. All winter long, he cracks hickory nuts
and flings shells all over the apartment. He sits by the window and
waits for her to come home.

Miss Lucy hears a flicking sound. She removes a spool of microfilm from the machine, puts another one in and continues to crank.

"Think what your life would have been like if you hadn't married
Russ," Mrs. Worsham says to Shirley. She gives her plant a drink.

Shirley moistens her finger with her tongue and turns a page of
the newspaper. She does not always feel compelled to speak when spoken to. Mrs. Worsham says that's because Shirley was raised in New

Jersey where good manners are a thing of the past. "You can't expect her to change overnight," Mrs. Worsham tells the Historical Society ladies when they complain that Shirley is rude.

Shirley met Russ several years ago while he was in the Army and stationed at Fort Dix. For the first few years of their marriage, they lived in New Jersey, but last year, Russ brought Shirley home to Farlanburg. Since then, he has worked for his father, who owns a rock quarry on the outskirts of town. Russ is an only child, and one day, if he behaves himself, he will own a ton of rock. Several hundred tons, in fact. Rumor has it that Shirley says owning a rock quarry is about as exciting as owning the county dump. Just last week, Mrs. Worsham told Miss Lucy she heard that Shirley is leaving; despite nine years of marriage and two kids, Shirley is calling it quits. "I don't know what's the matter with people these days that they can't just settle down and be happy. I'm happy," said Mrs. Worsham. "Thirty years I've worked at one job. Been married to the same man for thirty-seven." Mrs. Worsham shook her head. "Elba Mounts said she heard Shirley is taking the two little boys and going back to New Jersey as soon as school is out. I can't believe Shirley wouldn't say anything to us. You know anything about it?"

"No," said Miss Lucy, but she was sad to hear it. Shirley has worked at the library less than six months. She has triple-pierced ears, short, dark hair, and she's the only woman Miss Lucy knows who has given herself permission to cuss. She seems much younger than thirty-five. Shirley keeps to herself a lot, so Miss Lucy doesn't really know her. "Surly Shirley," Mrs. Worsham calls her. But her presence in Farlanburg gives Miss Lucy something she cannot explain. Coming to the library each morning and seeing Shirley makes Miss Lucy feel the same way she does when she walks into the grocery store and sees a kiwi fruit or a coconut in June.

Mrs. Worsham takes a bottle of Miracle-Gro from her desk and squeezes two green drops onto the soil around her plant. "Personally, I think there's no place like a small town to raise kids."

Shirley shrugs and says she wouldn't know.

"The good thing about a town this size is that it's safe. You can just turn the little devils loose and let them run."

Shirley says that may be, but her boys prefer organized sports and judo.

"Your boys remind me a lot of my boys when they were little," says Mrs. Worsham. "Just think. If you hadn't married Russ, you wouldn't have them. Close your eyes and try to imagine what your life would be like." Mrs. Worsham looks at Miss Lucy, then closes her eyes and tries to imagine. By the distressed look on her face, she clearly can't.

"Everything works out for the best in the long run," says Mrs. Worsham. "Just ask Miss Lucy. If she'd got it into her head to go chasing off somewhere right after she graduated from Farlanburg State, she'd never have the satisfaction of knowing she stayed and took care of her daddy during his old age. A lot of girls wouldn't do it. So many of our young people leave us for the bright lights these days."

Miss Lucy has finished rewinding and is stuffing microfilm into yellow boxes. She looks at Mrs. Worsham, her face expressionless. From her hand, a strip of microfilm curls and dangles like a tail. She tries to picture herself living in a place with bright lights. The closest she can come is a vision of herself in the parking area of Big Lots at Christmas.

"As for me," says Mrs. Worsham, "if I'd moved to Cincinnati and become a doctor like my high school biology teacher advised instead of taking my degree in library science at Farlanburg State, I wouldn't be standing here today knowing I stayed and made a contribution to my hometown. And I wouldn't have met and married my Edgar. True, I might have met and married some other nice man—"One who would pick up his dirty socks," says Shirley. "And not refuse to change his unders."

Mrs. Worsham's face reddens. Hers is the face of a woman who realizes that at some point in the past, following a trivial argument with her husband, she may have sought revenge with her tongue, talked of intimate things, revealed too much. When the redness disappears, she looks wounded but infinitely wiser. "Like I said," she says, curtly, "another man might have been a little easier to take care of, but he wouldn't have been my Edgar. Not as sweet, not as loyal, not as—"

"Edgar," says Shirley.

"Yes," says Mrs. Worsham. "Not as Edgar. And where would I be now?"

"In Cincinnati picking up after someone named Carl," says Shirley. She laughs.

Mrs. Worsham glances at Miss Lucy, sticks out her chin, then turns her attention to her plant, where there is hope. Sarcasm and cynicism are traits that should not be encouraged, she often says. Sarcasm and cynicism have no more place in a library than foul language, bare feet, or shirtless chests.

By the time Miss Lucy finishes with the microfilm, Mrs. Worsham has gone to work on her fern in the foyer. Shirley has returned to her class. Shirley teaches people who did not get an education when they were supposed to. They've come to the library because they know they've missed out on something and have been told they'll finally have it when they get their GED.

Miss Lucy sits at her desk and listens. She got her education when she was supposed to, but she knows she missed out on something, too. She would trade her high school diploma for a husband; her degree from Farlanburg State for a houseful of kids.

When she was in high school and college and still susceptible to wild flights of fancy provoked by a silver moon, she would loop her arms around an invisible neck at night and slow dance in her room. He was tall, more than six feet, and with her cheek against his chest, she listened for the beating of a heart. Later, in her bed, she dreamed she was the mother of nine children, and in her dreams her children were all under two. When she walked through the house, they jumped on her legs and clung there, thirsty for love, tenacious as fleas. They gnawed on her knuckles, used her fingers as teething rings. "Want cookies!" they screamed at all hours. Willingly, at midnight, she baked.

She went to elementary school with many of Shirley's students. They were wild and rowdy when she knew them; now they are older and tamed. Armed with sharp pencils and middle-aged determination, they are ready to learn history and conjugate verbs. At last, they see the value in knowing who defeated the Spanish Armada. "Fools! Go home to your families!" Miss Lucy would say to them if she were the teacher.

"How has a sweet girl like you managed to stay single?" Mrs. Worsham used to tease. When Miss Lucy turned thirty, the teasing stopped. "Somewhere along the line, something tragic must have happened," Mrs. Worsham assured her. "I'll bet you loved a boy, and he died. You hear about that sort of thing all the time."

Miss Lucy supposes something tragic could have happened; she just can't remember what or when. She had a few dates in high school, but most of the boys she knew didn't have a car or gas money, and she lived so far out of town. Once, during the summer, she went out with a preacher's son who was visiting at a neighbor's house. He took Miss Lucy to Meacham's Restaurant for a hamburger, then led her back to the car with a pleading look on his sunburnt, slightly swollen face. He drove her up and down Main Street, through the car wash, past the pizza shop, around and around the Dairy Dip so many times that Miss Lucy had the feeling he was trying to wind her up for something, and she grew dizzy from the heat and queasy from the hamburger and asked to be taken home.

Then there was her date with Freddy Bashem. He wasn't a town boy, and he didn't play a sport, but Miss Lucy still liked him. She curled her hair for him and put on a little makeup. She borrowed one of her mother's dresses and raised the hem above the knees. Freddy was supposed to pick her up at noon, but he was late by a couple of hours. He took her to the stock sale, bought her a Coke, and waved to her from across the pen while he and his father bought calves.

Looking back on it, Miss Lucy wonders whether she loved him. If she did, she didn't know it at the time. And Freddy Bashem didn't die because there is a picture of him in Miss Lucy's yearbook, taken during graduation. He sold his father's farm and bought a bakery in Clendenin. About six years ago, Miss Lucy was up that way, and she stopped in and bought a donut from him. He looked older and had put on a lot of weight, but he was friendly and took time to show her pictures of his family. There was nothing especially wrong with Freddy Bashem, Miss Lucy tells herself, but she can't help feeling slightly disappointed that he might have been the "something tragic" in her life.

At three o'clock, Mrs. Worsham brings Miss Lucy a card file and requests the circulation stats. "Everything all set for the party?"

"Got it all under control," says Miss Lucy. It's not a surprise party. No party in Farlanburg ever is. Mrs. Worsham has threatened to retire twice before, but this time she says she means it. "You people are just going to have to learn to get along without me," she has been saying since January. Officially, she does not retire until mid-May, but she wanted her party early so she wouldn't be tempted to back out.

Mrs. Worsham frowns. "I hope you didn't go to too much trouble."

Miss Lucy dismisses the notion with a wave of her hand. When Mrs. Worsham wanders over to her own desk, Miss Lucy goes downstairs and phones Jack at the deli to remind him about the dip.

"One crab. One onion. And don't forget the vegetable tray."

"Gotcha," says Jack.

"What about the cake?"

"Cake's fine. Don't worry none about the cake. I ain't seen it, but Dovey says she's got it done. Turns 'em out perfect every time."

"It's no big thing," says Miss Lucy.

"I reckon not," says Jack.

"Just a little get-together. Our way of saying good-bye." Miss Lucy applies a crumpled tissue to her nose, which has a tendency to drip this time of year. "Would it be too much trouble to have all the food over here by a quarter till? The party's at four, but I'd like to make sure we have plenty of time. If that's not too much of a problem."

"No problem," says Jack. "You got'er."

Miss Lucy dabs at her nose once more, then goes back upstairs. She sits at her desk, intending to work on the stats, but she has trouble concentrating. Her desk is remarkably free from clutter. A small, yellow pot filled with dry dirt sits on the left, near the back. Once, it contained a begonia—a gift from Mrs. Worsham, whose own desk resembles an oasis. "Your desk is a clue to your personality," Mrs. Worsham explained when she gave Miss Lucy the plant. "You don't want people to think you have no personality, do you?"

On the opposite side of her desk, for balance, is a photograph in a gold frame—a gift Shirley gave her at the library Christmas party. Miss Lucy picks it up and looks at it. In the photograph, a man, woman, and child are holding hands and running through a field. It could be a wheat field. Miss Lucy cannot tell. She has never been up on her grains. "You're supposed to take that picture out and put your own pictures in," Shirley reminded her when a month had passed and Miss Lucy showed no inclination to remove the models from the frame. "Family pictures, for heaven's sake."

The people in the photograph are beautiful, with honeycolored hair, and long, lovely necks exposed to the sun and wind. Miss Lucy cannot imagine a reason for their running. Perhaps a combine is closing in behind them, threatening to separate flesh from bone. Whatever is after them is coming from behind, though, because the photographer has left a generous amount of space for them to run into, and in doing so, he has given them a future. Lately, Miss Lucy has had a feeling that she, too, is being pursued. But whatever is after her is sneaky and has positioned itself in front of her. It stands, big as a mountain, between her and next week.

"God is testing you," Brother Bennett said when Miss Lucy tried to explain the feeling to him over the phone last Sunday. Brother Bennett is the preacher at Miss Lucy's church. He is a pale, humble-faced man whose quiet sermons are full of talk about shepherds and sheep. He baptized Miss Lucy when she was ten, but other than shaking her hand each week and saying, "May the grace and glory of the Father shine upon you and give you peace," he hasn't had to say much to her since. Still, she thought it might help to talk to him.

She wanted to wait until her father was napping. He lay in his bed in the living room, watching a bass fishing tournament on TV. His foot had snaked its way from under the covers. The ankle was swollen more than usual, the skin, plum-colored and cheesy between the toes.

"Your foot worries me, Daddy."

He reached down and covered it without taking his eyes off the TV. Hidden by blankets, his body seemed flattened, as though he were melting into the bed. When Miss Lucy lifted the covers to check his foot, he kicked feebly at the side of her head. "Stop that!" she said, grabbing his shin. She inspected his foot, then tucked the sheet and covers in at the baseboard. 'First thing tomorrow morning, I'm calling one of those new doctors up at the clinic. Fuss and fume all you want. You keep fooling with Doc Harkins, you're gonna lose another leg."

He looked at her, then rolled onto his side, his foot sticking up like a fin as it traveled the width of the bed. "Go to hell. I ain't going to no clinic," he said. Later, he ordered a cup of warm buttermilk. He drank it, then dropped the cup onto the floor. Miss Lucy sat on the couch and watched him settle into sleep. When his breathing was deep and regular, she picked up the phone from the coffee table and dialed Brother Bennett's number. She pulled the kinks and curls out of the cord, stretched it until it reached into the bathroom, then went in, sat down on the commode, and shut the door.

"I can't stand much more of this," she said. She heard a squeaking sound as Brother Bennett shifted in his chair.

"What you're feeling is perfectly normal for a woman in your situation."

Miss Lucy tore off a piece of toilet paper and blew her nose. "Then I want out of my situation."

"Have faith in Him," said Brother Bennett. "He never gives us more than we can handle."

"How do you know?" said Miss Lucy. "Isn't it possible that God is old and forgetful like Doc Harkins? Maybe He overestimates tolerance levels. Gives big red pills to people who ought to have little blue ones."

"Lucy, Lucy," Brother Bennett said, sadly. She could sense his disapproval moving like a clot through the cables, from pole to pole, its weight sagging the wires.

Miss Lucy picks up her pencil and sighs. She stares at the book cards in front of her and makes a half-hearted attempt to tally. The wall clock emits a grinding sound, and she looks up. Her desk is next to a window. Outside, the world is new and pale: the sky, a soft blue; the leaves, still shy and curled. Sunlight filters through the trees. The rays dapple her wrists and fingers.

With the exception of Shirley's students, there are no patrons in the library. There are seldom patrons in the library, despite the fact that the library does its best to find some. "Read six books a year and win a free trip to Burger King," a sign in the front window promises. That sign is for adults. A poster in the children's section shows a picture of a bearded, anemic-looking man reading by lamplight. At the bottom of the poster are the words: "Abraham Lincoln loved books."

"Abraham Lincoln was kweer," a sly, anonymous Farlanburger has penciled in. The people of Farlanburg do not like books. Or libraries. Libraries remind them of school days and Civil War reports, of a time when they first wanted to be somebody besides themselves and discovered they could not.

When Miss Lucy was in high school, she knew people who wanted to be movie stars, pilots, or mercenaries. She and her small circle of friends did not lean in such directions themselves. The year she graduated, her yearbook entry, like many others, said, "Future: Homemaker." Not an ambitious choice by today's standards, she knows. Not an impossible one, she thought at the time. Life was like a trip to the Piggly Wiggly, she assumed in those days. You went in with a vague idea of what you wanted, followed the arrows up and down the aisles, and emerged, like everyone else, with a full cart.

To date, Farlanburg has produced no movie stars, pilots, or mercenaries. It has turned out some secretaries, teachers, truck drivers, and a couple of librarians. When she was younger, Miss Lucy used to imagine leaving town. She pictured herself out on the bypass, thumb out, truck wind whipping her hair. In her second year of college, she started to work part time at the library. When she graduated, Mrs. Warsham asked if she'd like to stay on, full time. Miss Lucy felt lucky to have an offer. She accepted, boxed up her belongings, and moved into town.

She had a cousin who lived in Knoxville. She didn't know him well, but at reunions he seemed happier than anyone else. Miss Lucy planned to work in Farlanburg a couple of years, save her money, and move to Knoxville. The following spring, her mother died.

"Your Daddy's lucky to have you close by," out-of-state relatives, who came home for the funeral, said. "Will you be moving back out to the farm?"

Miss Lucy stayed in her apartment, a difficult decision, and for the first time in her life, she felt alive and in charge. A year later, her father lost his leg. One evening, after visiting him in the hospital, she read a letter in the county paper. The letter was written by a seventy-six-year-old man, a retired auto worker, a former Farlanburger who had moved to Indiana. His subscription was about to expire, and he wanted to renew it. His note appeared as a letter to the editor. "Dear Sirs," the note began. "Enclosed is twelve dollars to pay for my subscription another year. There is nothing like keeping up with hometown news. Forty-five years I have been here in Indiana, worked all over this great country of ours before that. I am a veteran of the Second World War. It's a funny thing about my hometown. Wherever I've gone, a little place of Farlanburg has gone with me." The letter ended with a poem:

No matter how far I roam,
Farlanburg will be home.
God bless you one and all, dear friends,
And a special hello to my wife's brother, Mr. Harlan Avery.

Miss Lucy clipped the letter from the paper and carried it with her for several days until she understood what it meant. There was a message in it for her, and the message, she finally decided, was that regardless of how far you travel, there are some things that simply cannot be outrun.

So, on afternoons like this one, when she has nothing better to do, she sits at her desk, stares out the window and watches former classmates trudge up and down the streets. Like her, they have grown up and out and older. They are the parents of tiny pink and blue bundles nestled among the celery and Rice Krispies in the grocery carts. They have six-year-olds, who run at full throttle up and down the aisles.

These are the people Miss Lucy has envied. But lately, even that has changed. "Envy is at the heart of most misery," Brother Bennett said in his sermon, Wednesday night. "Make a list of the people you envy most, try to determine what those people have in common, then strive to develop those characteristics in yourself." Miss Lucy made a list. On her list are her mother, her Aunt Opal, and a high school friend named Gloria. The characteristic those people have in common is that they're dead.

At 3:30, Shirley finishes with her students. There is no summary, no wrap-up, no sense that anything is winding down. Shirley simply stops talking and waits. For a moment, her students sit there and blink. When they see that nothing more is coming, they pick up their books and go. They are silent as they leave the library, their faces serious, stunned by how much they know.

"Good-bye. See you on Monday," Mrs. Worsham calls to them. "Those people inspire me," she says when Shirley's last student is gone.

"Strange," says Shirley. "They depress the hell out of me."

Mrs. Worsham gives Shirley a reproachful glance. "They remind

me of just how lucky I am. I look at them and that's how I know I've
been blessed."

Jack calls to say he's on his way with the food. Miss Lucy and
Shirley go downstairs to help him carry it in. The basement is stale,
harsh under fluorescent lights. Zebras, hippopotamuses, and exotic
birds decorate the Story Hour wall. At the other end of the room, balloon clusters hang from the ceilings, and two large pink-and-white floral arrangements sit at each end of a table. Miss Lucy decorated early
that morning. She thought the flowers might droop or the balloons lose
air. They haven't.

Miss Lucy takes pink paper plates, cups, and napkins from the
kitchen cabinets and arranges them in rows on the table while Shirley
pours punch from a plastic container into the library's glass serving
bowl. Jack shows up with the vegetable tray. "H-e-e-e-r-e-'s Jack!" he
says. "Where do you want it?"

Miss Lucy points to the center table. "Would you mind putting it
over there?"

Shirley goes outside to carry in the cake. Jack puts the vegetables
on the table and then stands with his hands hanging awkwardly at his
sides. "Nice," he says, as he surveys the room. He is a stout little man
who looks as if he has eaten as many cakes as he's baked.

Miss Lucy inspects the vegetable tray. "Where's the dip?"

Jack frowns. He bends, puts his hands on his knees, and stares
at the tray as if he expects to discover something hidden under the
radishes. "Damn," he says.

Miss Lucy inhales slowly and releases air through her mouth. "I
guess we'll have to get along without it."

"Where does this go?" says Shirley, who has returned with the cake.

Miss Lucy nods toward the kitchen.

Jack shrugs. "Dip ain't all that good for you anyway."

"That's exactly what they say about retirement!" says Mrs.
Worsham, who descends the stairs followed by several Friends of the
Library. "Jack Pearson? Is that you? I thought I recognized your voice."
Mrs. Worsham smiles and shakes Jack's hand as though she hasn't
seen him in a year. She has applied fresh lipstick, Miss Lucy notices.
Her lips are coral and match the punch. She presses her palms
together and shakes her head as she looks around the basement. "You
girls shouldn't have."

Shirley sticks her head out the kitchen door. "You're right," she says, winking at Miss Lucy. Everyone laughs.

Warren Arganbright from City Council and five members of the Library Board arrive. Warren, a retired Army colonel, much sought-after as a speaker by the civic groups in town, is known for his spit-and-polish appearance and eloquent turns of phrase. This afternoon, he smiles broadly as he embraces Mrs. Worsham. "Never let it be said that I passed up an opportunity to spend an afternoon with lovely ladies," he says. Again, everyone laughs. "What'd he say? What'd he say?" Margaret Jones asks.

Miss Lucy nudges the guests toward the refreshment table. "There's plenty of food and punch," she says. "You all just help yourselves."

Someone taps her on the shoulder. It's Jack. He winks and motions for her to follow him to the kitchen. "I want you to see the cake," he says.

In the kitchen, Shirley leans against the counter, smoking a cigarette. "You're not supposed to do that in here," Jack whispers. He points to a "No Smoking" sign on the wall.

Shirley stares at the sign. "What the hell," she says. "Is this a party or not?"

Jack removes a single candle, which has been taped like a small torpedo to the side of the box. "You're gonna like it," he says. He carefully unfastens more tape and lifts the lid. "Ta da!" He watches Miss Lucy's face.

The cake is white with three layers, decorated with pink icing roses, perfectly sculpted. The inscription, written in green, loops and curls like an elegant vine across the top. "TODAY IS THE FIRST DAY OF THE REST OF YOUR LIFE."

Miss Lucy stares at the cake. "What is this?"

"The cake," says Jack.

Miss Lucy shakes her head. "This is not what I ordered. This is not what I told you to put on there."

"You didn't tell me nothing," says Jack.

Shirley smiles and flicks the ash from her cigarette.

"You said it was a retirement cake. That's all you said. You didn't say nothing about what you wanted on it." Jack's fleshy ears have changed from pink to red. He folds his arms and plants his feet farther apart as though preparing to defend his cake. "Dovey saw this in a book and thought you folks'd like it. She put the same thing on Evert Ramsey's cake last year when he retired, and he didn't complain none." Jack frowns at Miss Lucy. He blinks his little black eyes and looks at Shirley.

Shirley makes a disapproving sound with her tongue. She inhales, opens her mouth, and a smoke ring emerges. It floats upward in front of her face, then dissolves in midair.

"Jesus H. Christ," says Jack. "Try to do something nice for someone, and this is the thanks you get." He pulls the bill from his shirt pocket, lays it on the counter, and leaves.

Shirley stubs her cigarette out in the sink. "No big deal. It's just a corny saying. If you don't mention it, no one'll even notice."

Miss Lucy shakes her head and looks at the cake. "That's not the point," she says, bleakly.

Shirley swipes through a clump of icing stuck to the top of the box, then licks her finger. "Ok. What is the point?"

Miss Lucy stares at the cake, then turns her back to it. "It's a message. Just like that old man's letter."

"What old man?" says Shirley.

"A toast!" someone shouts.

"Come on," says Shirley, but Miss Lucy doesn't move. Shirley takes her arm, and Miss Lucy allows herself to be led toward the party. Someone puts an empty cup in her hand and Miss Lucy, like everyone around her, holds the cup aloft as though she is waiting for something to fall out of the air.

Warren Arganbright's deep voice rises above the chatter. "To Mrs. Worsham," he says, solemnly. "May her retirement be as long and productive as her association with this library, and may she continue in good health and in happiness among her many friends in our little town." Mrs. Worsham's eyes fill as her friends drink to her. Kyle Jamison presses forward and presents her with a dozen red roses, and when Shirley carries out the cake, tears spill down Mrs. Worsham's cheeks and hang from her chin.

Later, when the cake has been cut, the guests served, and the punch stands at low tide, Mrs. Worsham works her way through the crowd to Miss Lucy. "I have a little something for you," she whispers. She pulls a small white envelope from behind her back and presses it into Miss Lucy's hand. "It's nothing much, and it wouldn't mean a thing to anyone except us, but I really want you to have it." Mrs. Worsham dabs at her eyes with a handkerchief and hugs Miss Lucy. "Don't open it until you're alone."

Shirley helps Miss Lucy clean up. They stack tables, fold chairs, take down balloons, and scrape leftovers into the garbage. "See, you got all worked up over the cake for nothing," says Shirley. "I don't think any-one even read it. It could've said, 'Today is the last day of your life,' and these people wouldn't have noticed. To them it all tastes the same."

When they finish, Shirley gets her sweater and purse. "I guess that about takes care of it," she says.

Miss Lucy nods. She picks up a white balloon and stares into it as though it were a crystal ball. "I hear you're leaving us."

Shirley is putting on her sweater. She stops, looks at Miss Lucy a moment, then laughs. "If you want to look at it that way," she says, poking her arm through a sleeve. "I thought I was leaving Russ."

"Same thing."

"Not in my book," says Shirley. She buttons her sweater and digs her car keys from her purse.

Miss Lucy hugs the balloon to her chest. "We'll miss you."

"Come visit," says Shirley. "Better yet, move. We have libraries in New Jersey, you know."

Miss Lucy twists the string on her balloon. "I can't," she says. "My father."

"Sure you can. We have fathers in New Jersey, too."

"You don't understand," says Miss Lucy."

Shirley opens the basement door and winks. "Bull's eye," she says. "You're right."

Miss Lucy locks up. She checks to make sure the basement door is shut, then goes upstairs and turns off all the lights. She pauses in the foyer at the front of the library and removes the envelope from her skirt pocket. Inside are two heavy keys on a gold-colored chain. There is a note. "Dear Lucy, I know you already have a set of keys, but I wanted you to have these. They don't fit the new lock because they were given to me thirty years ago when I first started to work at the library. I hope your new position will bring you as much happiness as it has brought me. With fondest regards, Mrs. Worsham."

Miss Lucy puts the note and keys back in the envelope and drops the envelope into her purse. She pulls the door shut, and as she steps into evening on Main Street, a warm wind lifts and plays with her hair. Hopscotch squares decorate the sidewalks; the smell of freshly cut grass lingers in the air. She shifts her purse from shoulder to shoulder as she heads toward home.

When she turns the corner onto Stringer Street, she spots her landlady digging in the yard. Though Mrs. Tucker is a couple of years older than Miss Lucy's father, she still gardens. She's wearing a sun hat and floral print dress, and with her back to Miss Lucy, she is as bright as any flower.

"It's spring," Miss Lucy calls over the fence, so she won't scare her. Mrs. Tucker is hard of hearing, and at the sound of a voice, she stares at her lilac bush as if she thinks it has spoken. "Oh!" she cries, jumping when Miss Lucy comes through the gate. "Did you say something?"

At the window above the garage, the curtains move slightly, and Miss Lucy sees her father's face behind the glass. "I said, 'It's spring!'" she shouts.

Mrs. Tucker smiles vaguely. "Yes," she says after awhile. She moves closer to Miss Lucy. "I took a bunch of green onions up to your Daddy at noon. He told me his foot's paining him pretty bad. You better get someone to take a look at it."

Miss Lucy nods and shuts her eyes. When she opens them, Mrs. Tucker is staring at the sky. Miss Lucy looks up and sees a jet.

"You ever been on one?" says Mrs. Tucker.

Miss Lucy shakes her head.

"I have. Two years ago. I rode one when I went out to see Teddy and his family in California. You remember my boy Teddy, don't you? I bet you went to school with him."

"Not really," says Miss Lucy. "He was a few years ahead of me."

Mrs. Tucker watches Miss Lucy's lips until they stop moving. She is quiet a moment, her cheeks working in and out. "We was good to him," she says, frowning. "I don't know what we did to make him want to move so far from home." She reaches out and wraps her fingers around Miss Lucy's arm. "Your Daddy's lucky having you right here to take care of him. I guess it's different with girls."

A cool wind sweeps through the yard. The jet cuts across the sky, leaving a silver scar behind it, and Miss Lucy watches, hypnotized by the glint of sun on the wings. For a moment, she is flying, not just a passenger but a pilot, while far below her, a daughter goes inside to fix her father's supper and a landlady leans on her hoe and envies an old man's luck.

SUMMER LIBRARIAN

Sue Kaufman

THE LITTLE LIBRARY WAS SET BACK IN A GROVE OF BEECH AND MAPLE, SO
old, so dense, the tightly meshed leaves gave anyone inside the building the illusion of being in the heart of a forest, rather than just off the
main thoroughfare of a busy village. Made of brown shingle, it possessed all the whimsies of a more romantic period in architecture—
dormers, porticoes, eaves, gables, dovecotes—and the rumor ran that
it had once been the caretaker's cottage on a huge estate. Whatever its
original function, it had been the Community Library for over forty
years, and in that prospering, burgeoning town was one of the sole
remnants of another way of life, now almost extinct.

Cruel Time, Obsolescence, Everything Passes (the Old Order
above all)—of such was Mrs. Foss's obsession, and on the dark humid
July morning she and her daughter Maria drove through the village in
their old gray sedan she held forth, glaring out at chrome-and-glass
storefronts and silvery new parking meters, filling the little car with her
smoldering comments. Maria, a mildly pretty, unobsessed girl of twenty,
who had heard all this too many times, merely nodded as her mother
ranted, and with relief finally pulled the car up to the curb fronting the
Woman's Exchange. ". . . heaven only knows what next!" concluded Mrs.
Foss, getting out and slamming the door for emphasis, but then leaned
down and added through the rolled-down window, "I'll be in front of
Humbert's at five. Unless, of course, you want to join us for lunch."

"Five," said Maria, answering the luncheon invitation with a vague
negative nod, and sat waiting to see if her mother, who was becoming

alarmingly absent-minded, had her keys. With detachment she watched the small wiry woman cross the sidewalk, wryly noting how the pastel golf dress, calcimined gumsoles, and visored piqué cap made her look like a clubwoman off for the greens—precisely the desired effect. When she reached the door Mrs. Foss groped for a moment in a purse shaped like a horse's feedbag, but she finally came up with a bunchy key ring and Maria drove off. She proceeded along the still-deserted street for another block and a half, then turned into what seemed a private driveway, but after a few feet opened onto a vast free parking lot neatly bedded with raked gravel and marked off by spanking whitewashed partitions. Neither the lot nor the supermarket which had generously (shrewdly, claimed Mrs. Foss) built it had been there when Maria had been home from college at Christmastime. Because, unlike her mother, Maria loved progress, particularly when it changed the face of this town she had lived in all her life, she ignored her mother's instructions and left the sedan unlocked—one of those small futile gestures that still symbolize so much.

As she hurried out of the lot through another exit, and started down the long block to the library, massed bluegray clouds, already rumbling and shifting with thunder, were heavily pressing down. It had also rained the day before, and when Maria unlocked the glass-paned door she was almost overpowered by the fusty smell of yesterday's dampness, trapped in old boards, moldings, bindings. She rushed about, banging and tugging at all the warped sashes of the windows in the front room. Aside from the new chintz covering the window-seat cushions, and several additional layers of bright blue enamel encrust-ing the tiny ladder-back chairs, it was a room that had not changed at all since the days Maria had first come there as a child. The four large wicker armchairs and the rack filled with adult magazines were mere tokens, for grownups never lingered here. This front room had always been considered a children's reading room, and each time she came in Maria would look at the two long low tables (pocked and incised by two generations of furiously restless little hands), the bookcases crammed with brilliantly colored picture books and primary readers, and she would shiver, briefly haunted by the vision of herself, raptly curled in one of the window seats, lost, lost in a book.

After hanging her raincoat in a closet-bathroom off the back stacks, she came out to the big desk bearing Miss Leonard's brass nameplate. Though Maria was an old favorite of Miss Leonard's, the librarian had made plain her wish to have this part of herself kept intact while she vacationed. So each day Maria was forced to work on a surface cluttered with a heart-shaped faïence penholder from Quimper (stuck with blue and yellow quills), three china bowls of paper clips in three sizes, two jars of rubber bands in two sizes, a family of Doulton scotties, a Lalique bud-vase, and a fistful of jabbing pencils in a Toby mug. Sighing, Maria took a metal file-box and a pack of postcards, mimeographed "Dear _____, Your book is overdue!" from a drawer. As she began fingering through the cards in the little file-box, she saw that all the titles were those of current best-sellers, the names of the renters ones she had never seen before, and she knew that her mother would have pounced on this, claiming it as a further piece of circumstantial evidence against the newcomers, who (Mrs. Foss stated) were coarse and vulgar and had no taste. But it only made Maria consider the fate of the books during the heat of the last two weeks—she could see them, lying forsaken, left splayed open on a towel under the shade of an umbrella, or dropped onto the baking sands of one of the new beach clubs—and she sighed again, heavily, with pure envy this time, and dipping her pen into red ink, began.

By eleven, though the rain had still not started, only five people had been in and out of the library. One, a pale lumpish fourteen-year-old named Carol Danziger, had remained, settling herself in one of the wicker armchairs to read her newest selection (Elizabeth Goudge's *City of Bells*) with much noisy turning of pages and sucking of jujubes. In the week and a half Maria had taken over the library the girl had been in five times, clearly protecting herself from something at home by maintaining a careful distance from it, solacing herself with books and a new, instantaneous attachment to Maria she seemed to think secret. Though Maria felt sorry for the poor child—she was so overwhelmingly unattractive—she was more irritated than flattered by all her admiration, and today the creak of that indolent body in straw, the asthmatic breathing and wet sucking noises so set her teeth on edge she was about to do something drastic, when leaf-muffled shouts suddenly came from the front lawn, drowning out the exasperating girl. "Okay, Rourke, okay for *you!*" called someone just beyond the rhododendron bushes screening the front windows, and this was immediately followed by a shrill scream of girlish pain or delight—it was hard to tell which.

With a gritty clomp Carol Danziger brought her size seven-and-a-half moccasins to the floor. "Please, Miss Foss. Won't you tell them to go away?"

"Why?" asked Maria, staring with undisguised dislike into the gray eyes swimming behind lenses.

"Because. Because they're not *supposed* to play here. Miss Leonard always makes them go away."

Frowning, but knowing it would be simpler in the long run, Maria rose and went out on the front porch. Four boys in jeans and a ponytailed girl in tight cotton slacks were ranged out under the roof of leaves, the boys throwing an unraveled baseball back and forth in a magnificently casual game of catch, arcing it tauntingly high and slow while the girl scurried and leapt between them, hopelessly trying to intercept. Delight, thought Maria, diagnosing the girl's screams, and reluctantly started across the spongy lawn; one of the boys caught then held the ball, five pairs of eyes watched her approach—a small long-haired girl in a chambray dress trying to look stern and imposing, but only succeeding in looking what she felt: foolish. Someone gave a long low whistle. Her face burning, looking to neither side, Maria picked the tallest boy, the seeming leader, a grinning rawboned redhead, and marched straight up to him. Politely, but firmly, she asked would he and his friends mind playing ball somewhere else, people in the library were trying to read. In the following silence she heard suppressed sniggers, from the corner of an eye she saw the ponytailed girl sidle up to one of the other boys and meaningfully nudge him in the ribs.

"Ur. Well now, Miss . . . ah Miss? Well. We thought it being vacation and like that nobody studied in there." The redhead's yellow eyes shone insolently, taking her in, while from behind her, from the same spot the whistle had come, a boy's voice soft with wonder said: "Hey. Are you the librarian?"

"I am the *summer* librarian," Maria said with deadly calm, ignoring the speaker and continuing to address the redhead in front of her, "and it just happens that there *are* people who read in the summer. We will all be spared a great deal of unpleasantness if you just move, without further comment."

"Well, now, ya don't say. . ." mincingly began the redhead as she turned to leave, but a husky blond boy now in her line of vision, undoubtedly the whistler (and leader, she belatedly realized), quietly

said, "Shove that, Rourke," and the mimicry stopped. In a tense, sim-
mering silence, Maria started back to the porch, rage making her catch
her heels in the rain-softened earth, making her clumsily lurch. Once
back inside she stood watching at the window—after a dawdling conference, they finally followed the whistler's lead, straggling across the
patchy lawn, majestically ignoring the gate and pushing out through
the high privet hedge where they left a wounded gap—and she began
to tremble with a fury the situation hardly warranted, a fury left over
from another time.

"You were just wonderful, Miss Foss," Carol Danziger damply
breathed behind her, "just marvelous. Those disgusting boys. Even the
teachers are afraid of them. Of course," she added swiftly, daintily, "I've
only been *going* to the public school since Miss Maitland's closed last
year, and Mummy and Daddy are sending me away to boarding school
next year. But I still had to be with them all this past winter. And you
know the girls are every bit as disgusting as the boys . . . but then,
you wouldn't know." She blushed heavily. "I mean I happen to know
you went to Miss Maitland's because I saw you in one of the hockey
team pictures hanging in the lunchroom. I remembered because you
were by far the prettiest on the team."

Prettiest, thought Maria as she turned from the window and ironically smiled at the girl: the one slender form among eleven beefy ones,
all lined up against an ivied gymnasium wall, right hands stolidly
clutching hockey sticks, left hands vainly trying to hold down navy
serge pinnies whose flapping pleats revealed lumpy, chilblained knees.
"Thank you," she said dryly, inclining her head, then could not resist:
"Actually I do know about boys and girls like that, and disgusting is an
ugly word."

"But how could you possibly know about them?"

"It's quite simple. I went to the high school for my senior year."

"You did?" Gaggling, the girl jabbed her glasses back on the
bridge of her unfortunate nose. "But wasn't that silly? I mean, leaving
Maitland's in such a *crucial* year. I mean, with Miss Maitland so thick
with all the deans at the good colleges?"

"I'm sure it was silly, but it wasn't a question of choice."

"Oh. Dear. I'm terribly sorry, Miss Foss."

"There's no need to be. I really liked the public school very
much." As the poor girl, in an anguish of thrashing and swallowing,

reached for her book, Maria was filled with remorse—why was she being so cruel?—and in a softer voice said, "I'm going out back for a cigarette, will you rap on the window if anyone comes in?" and hastily went out the back door.

The air was now so thick, so filled with moisture, it was difficult to light a match. Succeeding, she fiercely drew in on her cigarette and with troubled eyes stared out at the library's sad ruin of a backyard: on the left, at the end of an unused driveway, a rotting shingled garage was piled with cartons of moldering junk, its doors coming off the hinges; straight ahead and to the right trees, spaced wider than those out front, had let down enough sunlight to nourish a high wild expanse of grass. Neglect. Decay. Waste. Mostly waste. How vicious and pompous, how ironically like her mother she had just been, and all because the poor girl had unwittingly brought just that back: the waste, the needless waste.

But as overbearing as she had been, she hadn't lied. She *had* liked the public school, the jangle of bells and the shouting and laughter in the halls, the warm density of the overcrowded class-rooms, all of it such a relief after the deathly hush of the frame house, and after years of Maitland's chill, sparsely filled rooms. She had also truly liked her wild and noisy schoolmates and had secretly longed to belong, to be taken in, and would have had there been time. For there she had been, a strikingly undistinguished student, suddenly bereft— of a devoted father, of the necessary funds, of the boost of Miss Maitland's invaluable connections—a student who either won a scholarship to college or did not go at all. Since her father had always stressed the importance of college, particularly the right college (though she now did not understand why), she had managed to go; by discovering a dormant "brilliance" of sorts in History, and by living a merciless, constricted life, she had succeeded in winning scholar-ships for three years at the college her father had most admired. For three winters she had supplemented a meager allowance from her mother by waiting tables, typing manuscripts, doing cataloguing in the library, shortening hems and altering dresses for classmates, and for two summers she had gone off with strange families to be a com-bination Mother's Helper and tutor in History for their petulant chil-dren. She had never complained or considered herself any sort of martyr, but at the same time she never permitted herself to dwell on the dangerous thought: None of this would have been necessary had her mother sold the house.

Maria's father, a Philadelphian, had inherited the pretty white Colonial house from an uncle just shortly after the end of the First World War. After much deliberation, he had accepted a long-standing offer from a New York banking firm, and had come up from Philadelphia with his bride and settled in Marberry Pond Park. Since they already knew many people in the Park, they instantly became a part of its quiet, secluded social life, and lived there happily, and uneventfully, but for the arrival of Maria at a time when they had long reconciled themselves to being childless. Maria's mother passionately loved the Park, her house, her garden, her friends. Maria's father liked the Park well enough, but he was an extremely practical, unsentimental man who, sadly enough, had never prospered, and when the town had begun its sudden violent expansion, he had seen opportunity, and wished to act. He wanted to sell and move to the city nearby: the land had quadrupled its value, he wished to spare himself the exhausting daily commute to the Wall Street banking house where he worked. But his wife was almost hysterical in her opposition. She detested the city. She hated apartment life. Life would be unendurable without her garden, her house, her friends, and the subject of friends brought up the most important thing of all: If they sold they would be the first in the Park to do so, which would amount to a betrayal of the other Park residents, their dear friends, since *he* knew the sort of people ready to jump at the chance to invade their private Park. He did not know, for he was the least snobbish of men, and the fate of "their private Park" did not remotely interest him, but the maintenance of precious peace did. He finally gave it up and soon afterwards succumbed to that strange, terrible exhaustion which it turned out had not been caused by the grinding daily commute at all. He was never told the name of what he had (multiple myeloma), nor did he ever learn that the dread disease which literally ate the marrow out of his poor bones also devoured the hard-won savings of many years. "It would kill him right now if he knew," warned Mrs. Foss. Maria, anguished, deeply loving her father, hardly needed any instructions to be silent. But taking root then, and after her father's death putting out tendrils that were never permitted to break through the surface of her conscious mind, was the ugly suspicion that her mother's real motive for silence had not been compassion, the wish to protect her husband, but fear, the deep well-grounded fear that had the dying man learned the true state of their financial affairs, he would have ordered the house sold from under him. And this spring, when the letter from her mother arrived at college, the suspicion burst out in full bloom at last—proven.

The first sentence in the letter, ending with three exclamation points, stated that the house had been sold. The following staccato sentences explained how it had come about: their house, it seemed, along with four others, had been the last ones left, and the contractor for the middle-income development that was to replace Marberry Pond Park, frantic to get on with things, had in desperation offered unheard-of sums to all of them. Quickly scanning paragraphs documenting betrayal—who had sold out first, who next and next—Maria came to the last and most important page. The house had to be vacated by mid-August, the latest: since there was now not only enough money for Maria to have a "carefree" senior year at college, but also to release her from the hateful summer tutoring, she would expect Maria home. Although, of course, she would need Maria's help in dismantling the house, and moving into the apartment she had leased in one of those new buildings on the station plateau, the rest of Maria's time would be her own—she would have her first real summer of freedom in years. Seeing that she had no choice, she had to go home, and knowing all too well what those hours of "freedom" would be like, Maria quickly made a mental note to write Miss Leonard about working at the library, then sat back to contemplate the enormity of what all this meant. It was not the proof that the house and what it stood for always *had* meant more to her mother than her husband or child, but the dark turn her mother's mind had taken, now that the house was doomed, that chilled Maria through and through. Instead of leaving, clearing out, starting a new life somewhere else, her mother had fanatically encamped on the battlefield, as it were, on the scene of her bitter defeat, and with her few friends rallied round her, clearly intended to make some symbolic sort of Last Stand, pathetic, senseless, yet filled with all the fury of obsessive hate.

Shivering, lighting a fresh cigarette, Maria now heard a ripping swishing sound, and looking to her right she saw a tall blond-haired boy, hands in pockets, striding through the tall tangled grass, making for the porch. The whistler, she remembered, as undaunted by her forbidding glare, he came right up the steps and put out a hand: "Hi. I was just going inside to look for you."

Though she pointedly ignored his extended hand, he was not put off. He let it fall, and continued, smiling: "My name's Harry Strickland and I came back to apologize for Rourke. He's a real wise-guy and doesn't know anything. I mean, you shouldn't mind him."

"I didn't," she said precisely. "And it certainly wasn't necessary to come back and apologize."

This time he reddened and began to blink, and she was instantly sorry, for the handsome face under the inevitable slick haircomb was disarmingly innocent, the blue eyes as clear and candid as a child's. "Well, I didn't really come back for that," he began again, taking courage from the sudden softening he perceived in her face. "The truth is I came back to find out what someone like you's doing here, in a dump like this. This town, I mean."

Because she had to forcibly hold back a smile, she said, almost sternly: "As I told your friend, I'm the summer librarian."

"Well, you talk awful funny. You sure don't come from this town and that's what I mean."

"I've lived here all my life."

"Yeah? Then how come I've never seen you before? In the village or anything. You been away?"

"That's right—at college." She flicked her cigarette down into the spongy black loam, and put her cigarettes into the pocket of her cotton shirt-dress.

"College? Phew!" Pursing his lips, he studied her with wide soft eyes; then bent his long neck and watched one of his sneakered feet kick at the rotting top step as though it belonged to someone else. "That must make you about eighteen."

"Twenty," she said with dry finality, and turned and opened the door in the same instant that Carol Danziger began rapping on the window with her garnet ring.

When the firehouse siren went off at noon, she prodded Carol Danziger from her wicker entrenchment, locked the library, and walked into the village for her lunch. Like thousands of growing small towns all over the country, it had completely changed its face in ten years. As low-priced developments mushroomed on its outskirts, and Garden Apartments (restricted to two stories by zoning laws) sprang up in its heart, the merchants had either rallied to the challenge by bravely remodeling and expanding, or had been vanquished by bolder, more inventive new competitors. Maria's route to the drugstore was a purposefully devious one, which took in an extra block of glittering new storefronts, a detour that skirted the Woman's Exchange where her mother's graying sandy head was always visible in the gloom behind the plate glass.

Her first week at the library, to pacify her mother about having arranged for the job in the first place, she had dutifully gone to the Woman's Exchange for lunch every day. The moment she came in her mother, Mrs. Knowles, and Mrs. Hollis stopped whatever they were doing (nothing), and began bustling about like girls, dragging four Hitchcock chairs with peeling gilt stencils (from Mrs. Peterson's dismantled house, and up for sale) into a small alcove formed by a ceiling-to-floor bookcase in the rear of the shop. There, placing them about a beautiful cherry Lazy Susan table (from Mrs. Knowles's dismantled house, and not up for sale), they took out thermoses filled with hot coffee, wrinkled brown paper bags of homemade sandwiches, and sat down to their lunch. When the last sandwich crust was gone, one of them went out front to the case of "home-baked goods" (Mrs. Luther, the cabinetmaker's wife) and brought back a plateful of something crumbling—*Linzer torte, lebkuchen*—or of strudel so damp or brownies so hard they could no longer be decently offered for sale. Maria did not see what they ever *did* sell, since most of the wares were contributed by themselves or by friends who were hardly likely (or able) to repurchase their own handiwork, and since she had witnessed the reception given to strangers, having helplessly watched the whole thing through spaces in the room-divider bookcase that formed the little alcove. The bell over the door would tinkle, there was an aluminum clatter as the young housewife from one of the developments, wearing slacks or shorts, tried to maneuver the baby-in-stroller through the door; whoever had risen from the cherry table and gone out—her mother or Mrs. Knowles or Mrs. Hollis—would come to a stop in the center of the front room and remain there, arms crossed, watching but not attempting to assist, airily asking "Yes?" when the complicated entrance-operations were completed; there was the inevitable shy

murmur, ending ". . . just like to look around," and whoever had gone
out would say "Ah *yes*" like someone successfully grasping a sentence
in a difficult foreign language, and would remain there, arms still
stolidly crossed, while the stranger explored. The poor self-conscious
young woman would then begin to timidly finger and inspect the tin
trays decorated with *découpages* of flowers and fruit and the waste-
paper baskets glued with hunting scenes and Audubon prints (the
work of old Mrs. Davis), the string gloves, potholders, crochet trivets,
tea cozies, baby bibs embroidered with bumblebees (all from deaf
Mrs. Wade), the little satin pillows filled with sachet, netted bags
holding dried potpourri, pomander balls (Mrs. Hammond's special-
ties)—and finally, since nothing was tagged, would shyly ask some
prices. The outrageous sums were always given with a negligible smile,
a smile which changed as the stammered explanations began ("didn't
dream . . . only a tiny present") into a grimace so chilling, accompanied
by a murmur of ". . . but of *course,* my dear," so patronizing, that Maria,
hidden behind the bookcase, had often trembled with rage. She knew
she could not change the three bitter women, but she also knew she
did not have to sit and passively witness their senseless games of spite.
She managed to stick it out through the first week, but then thought
up the lie which would release her for the rest of the summer: on certain days, she told her mother—and she never knew which days they
might be—she could not close the library promptly at noontime, for
there were people there doing special research with a deadline, or
other people who had phoned and asked to come during the lunch
hour; since she did not want to hold up their lunches at the Exchange,
it was best to count her out from then on; she would grab a sandwich in
the village when she could. Though her mother had violently objected
—did she realize that would mean needlessly spending at least six dollars a week?—Maria had been happily eating her lunches at a big new
air-conditioned drugstore ever since, a wonderful lively place full of
clatter and chatter and jukebox din.

Big drops were staining the pastel slates as she hurried back up the
library walk after her lunch. She had only been safely inside a few minutes when the rain came down at last, and the whole building began
reverberating with cozy pittering sounds. She had finished the "over-

due" postcards and dropped them in a mailbox on her way to lunch, so she now went into the musty back stacks and turned on a dim overhead light, browsing in the narrow book-lined aisles which smelled of leather and binder's glue, until at last she found what seemed a light frivolous novel and carried it back inside. To her relief, the rain kept away all comers, even Carol Danziger, and for two hours she traveled about Mayfair, Paris, Rome, worlds away. The library was singingly quiet, the rain closed in the mind. When it finally stopped at four, it lifted the heavy curtain of silence, of rapt peace; tires began wetly cracking out on the boulevard, a horn blew irritably, someone ran thumpingly up the street frantically calling a dog or cat or child named "Kim." Yawning, stretching, she rose and went to the glass-paned door where she stood staring out with amazement at the violent drenched green of the grass, until the front door rattled open behind her and a now-familiar voice said: "Thought I'd see if you drowned."

Without even turning, she put her hand on the knob of the door in front of her and angrily yanked it open. "You leaving just because I came in?" he asked forlornly, and when he got no answer, relentlessly padded across the room and followed her out the door. On the tiny ledge of back porch two colonial settees faced each other, kept dry by the capacious overhang of the roof. When he came out she was sitting resolutely in the dead-center of one of them, but instead of taking the empty bench, he ignored her forbidding glare and jammed himself into a corner of hers. Fury, exasperation—and despite herself, fear—made her fingers so stiff and clumsy she could not light her cigarette. After quietly watching two of her futile attempts, he leaned forward, calmly striking a match from a book he had held hidden and ready in his hand all the time. When a gust of warm damp wind blew it out, he frowned and quickly struck another, cupping big protective hands about the plumy flame. Defeated, Maria bent to light her cigarette, trying to think of something to say that would be so nasty, so cutting, he would go away and never come back, but as she withdrew, puffing on the cigarette, she accidentally glanced into the eyes above the flame. Her face going hot, she hastily retreated to the far corner of the settee: *Never* had any boy, any man, looked at her with such violent worship, such complete and vulnerable surrender, and the sight of these things in his eyes made her almost sick with shame and fear—fear, not of him, but of something struck deep, deep within herself.

"Just tell me one thing," he said in a perfectly ordinary voice that had nothing to do with his swooning eyes, briskly lighting his own cigarette. "It's what we were discussing before. Why aren't you off somewhere on vacation? Why did you come back here?"

"I came back here to help close up the house."

"The house?" he asked in a tone Maria would have recognized as rapture for just this much confidence, had she not been so muddled and distressed by the strange turn of events. "House where?"

"Marberry Pond Road," she snapped tensely and stood up.

"Oh. Where all those fine old houses are coming down for the lousy little ones?"

"They're nothing but white elephants."

"What?"

"Nothing. *Nothing*," she said, finally coming to her senses and realizing she had talked too much. She took a last deep draw on her cigarette.

"Well, why did you have to come? Couldn't your mother and father manage to close the house themselves?"

"My father's dead."

Blinking, mortified by what Maria had deliberately made him feel was a stupid blunder, he fiercely muttered something that sounded like, "You and your big mouth Strickland," and without another glance at her, stood up and went plunging off the porch. As he disappeared around the driveway corner, Maria wondered for the second time that day what was the matter with her—why did she lash out at everyone, particularly at anyone who admired her?—and bewildered, unhappy, stared through tears at a spaniel snuffling among piles of leaves the rain had brought down.

"I got us some pork chops," said Mrs. Foss, putting the brown paper bag between them on the front seat. Saying nothing, Maria started up the car, wanting to say a great deal about the broiler that would have to be lit on such a hot night, the greasy pan *she* would have to scour, not to mention the more appetizing choices they could be having for the same amount of money—frozen crabmeat, African lobstertails, shrimp or chicken salad neatly put up in plastic containers—if her mother and her friends were not crazily involved in a boycott of the new supermarkets, having sworn eternal fealty to Mr. Humbert and his like.

The sun had come back out at four-thirty, bringing a swarm of life to the village. Now, added to the beetling lines of traffic, were the cars coming from the station where the five-seven had just disgorged a load of commuters. At the first chance, Maria took a turnoff to the right, a maneuver which got them out of the honking jam of cars, but which put them on a longer round-about route to their house. "I hear that's coming down in September," said her mother, at last breaking the silence as they passed an ugly turreted building with boarded-up windows, sitting back on several acres of scorched lawn—the remains of Miss Maitland's Country Day.

"Coming down for what?"

"A Recreation Center. Whatever that means." There was a snort.

Maria sighed heavily, but not, as her mother thought, for the soon-to-be-demolished school. She sighed because for the second time that day she was reminded of the waste, of all the money that had been scraped together just so she could walk that building's drafty corridors, sit cheek-by-jowl in its underheated classrooms with girls like herself, daughters of parents not rich enough to manage a good boarding school, yet too proud to consign them to the public high school, parents who fervently hoped that Miss Maitland's one asset— influential connections—would work the saving charm.

The weed-tangled meadow that had once been a neatly taped-off hockey field fell behind, the car sped along roads where the houses became spaced farther and farther apart. Then finally they were on the dirt beginnings of Marberry Pond Road which wound for three mazy miles along the bay's wooded shore. Once a fence with a locked gate had separated Marberry Pond Park from the rest of the world, a gate to which only residents of the Park had possessed keys. Now pointed fence-slats lay fallen, rotting, while the gate itself had been removed from its hinges and carted off, leaving its two fluted supporting pillars standing sentinel on either side of the road, the head of the one on the right nailed with a gaudy green-and-yellow sign shaped like an arrow: MARBERRY ESTATES—$26,500!!! As the old gray car rolled through this doorless portal, sweet earthy smells blew in through the rolled-down windows, sun glanced off Mrs. Hollis' water-beaded trees and shrubs, filling the windshield with glinty brilliance. Then they passed a muddy gouged-out stretch bristling with the toothpick frames of three new houses, the place where the Dixons' lovely old house had once stood surrounded by stately elms, and Maria steeled herself against some remark or gesture from her mother. But tonight her mother was ominously still. And tonight Maria felt a strange and terrible prickling of the skin, for it occurred to her that each evening, as they rolled through that bare and gaping gateway, it was as though they had just passed from the real world of the living into a twilit one like Limbo, all shades of things long dead.

The sun stayed out from that day on. Lawns turned a bleached yellow, leaves hung flaccid on the high old trees. The village was deserted after ten o'clock every morning and all activity at the library stopped. Even Carol Danziger defected, coming by two days after the rain to select three books and to triumphantly announce that Mummy and Daddy were taking her away for two maybe three weeks in the mountains—good-by, good-by, good-*by!*

There was just one daily visitor to the library.

Bent over a book, Maria would first hear him out beyond the high hedge, loudly declaiming to some real or imaginary friend (his way of heralding his impending arrival), and not long after the screen door would twang open, floorboards would creak under sneakered feet. When she finally looked up from her book, he would be standing there all red in the face, wearing a foolish sheepish grin: "Morning. Thought I'd just browse around." Coughing nervously, he would then abruptly turn his back and the game began: for a while he restlessly prowled about the front room, peering at the covers and tables of contents in any new magazines put out in the reading rack, or pulling down children's readers at random, snorting and chuckling at things he found in them; when he tired of this or sensed that she had come to the end of her patience, he padded back into the stacks, and after a long time would emerge carrying something thick and improbable (once, seeing it was Ruskin, she had almost choked) and settle himself in one of the cushioned window seats; there, with much scholarly wetting of thumb and forefinger, he turned pages at a considered pace, his expression irreproachably preoccupied—a deft imitation of the one she wore when she read.

The first few times he came to the library and all this happened, she barely managed to keep from exploding into the green silence of that leaf-shaded room, to keep from asking what on earth was the matter with him, acting like such an idiotic child—had he nothing better to do with his time? Why wasn't he off with his friends, boys and girls his own age, instead of plaguing her? Why wasn't he outside somewhere on such a beautiful hot day, down at the beach like everyone else? As exasperated as she was, she never did explode and ask any of these things, for she knew all the answers. There was nothing the matter with him because he *was* a child, and to his mind there was nothing better to do than hang around the inspiration of his first really serious crush. As for his going to the beach, she had only to look at those carefully mended, washed-thin suntans to see that his family could hardly afford one of the expensive beach clubs commandeering every foot of a shore that had once been free. And after the initial irritation, she began to relax, began to stop being angry and resentful—he was a funny yet somehow pathetic boy—and she even began to enjoy his visits. Not only was the elaborate pantomime he went through rather amusing, it was also strangely touching and even flattering: he was not like the rest of the boorish teenagers who hung about the village, but was a sweet and gentle and well-mannered boy, quite bright, really very bright, and given the proper advantages could do well for himself, a boy whose simple and direct devotion seemed to refresh and restore her, give her a sorely needed lift of the heart. What harm could there be in that?

Too late she saw the harm, saw how much she had come to depend on his visits, when four days went by and he did not come to the library. Despising herself, she nevertheless spent the fourth day listening for the shouts beyond the hedge, waiting, worrying. Was he sick? Had he suddenly gone away? Had he . . . had he found a replacement for herself, someone his own age, someone sensibly accessible to all that adoration?

On the fifth day, a Wednesday, she went to the drugstore later than she ever had, after shamelessly dawdling at the library, waiting. The noontime rush was long over, the place was almost empty, the whirring whoosh of the air-conditioning was the only sound. Without looking around she made straight for a back booth, gave the waitress her order, then sat pushing her leather cigarette case back and forth over the speckled plastic tabletop with her thumbs, wretchedly wondering what had happened to make her sink so low that she fed on the worship of a schoolboy. Had she lost all sense of proportion? When the waitress set down her hamburger and french fries she gave a guilty start. Troubled, dazed, she looked up and immediately saw him beyond the waitress' starched hips, sitting swung around on a stool at the counter, gravely watching her.

As their eyes met he gave one owlish blink, then swung down long legs and nonchalantly sauntered to the booth. "Hello, Maria," he said, towering over the table, sneakered feet planted imperiously wide apart.

It was the first time he had ever dared use her name. "Hello," she said coldly, pointedly not using his.

"Well, isn't this nice," he said with what she guessed to be carefully rehearsed urbanity, lowering himself into the blue leather seat opposite.

She blinked at the trim collegiate haircut replacing the slick blond water-wave and, despite herself, smiled.

"It's cooler this way," he said quickly, blushing as he saw she had guessed the real motive for the visit to the barber.

"I see." To keep from smiling again, she began to eat her hamburger, but found it difficult to chew and swallow under that fixed, rapt gaze. When he finally realized he was making her uncomfortable, he looked away over the low wall of the booth, and keeping his eyes on a tower of Summer Cologne on sale, a tray of Drastically Reduced bathing caps, he began to talk about the beach club where he had spent the last four days as the guest of some well-to-do classmate named Marvin. Maria barely listened to his descriptions of the cabanas with built-in bars and television sets, of the ladies who wore pearls with their bathing suits, but kept covertly glancing at him, with a strange sinking feeling noting the dazzling color changes the sun had wrought in his skin and hair. She also heard the new note of self-assurance in his voice, and from this and his new manner, she realized that he had come to some sort of decision about her—probably that the library relegated him to an insufferably juvenile position, and that he must try to meet her in other places where they would be on a more equal footing. She knew this guess to be correct when he suddenly broke off, got up and went to put a quarter in one of the little chrome machines sitting at each place along the counter, tune-selectors connected to the huge jukebox on the store's back wall. As all the glassy pyramids of bottles and jars began vibrating with the booming bass of some romantic song, he came and sat down with an air of unmistakable satisfaction: Now—they could almost be out on a date together.

Her course clear, she pushed away the plate of untouched french fries. "Exactly how old are you, Harry?"

"Seventeen." He solemnly stared at her, then picked up a paper napkin and began folding it into an airplane. As the eloquent silence from Maria's side of the booth prolonged itself, he glanced up, then down again, sheepishly smiling. "Okay. Sixteen. But seventeen in December . . . and that's the honest to God truth!" He launched the napkin-plane across the booth. It gently nudged her shoulder then fell into her lap. "Four years' difference. Almost three. That isn't much, Maria. That isn't much at all." He spread begging hands flat on the tabletop, and the cold tips of his fingers grazed hers as they nervously toyed with the sugar bowl.

"That's where you're wrong," she said in a choked voice and, trembling, stood up and threw down money for her lunch. "It's all the difference in the world. All the difference there could ever be. And don't you forget it." Then she fled.

A week went by and he did not come to the library. It was their last week in the house on Marberry Pond Road. Since her mother was at the Exchange and she at the library in the daytime, they spent the nights finishing up. Loading the car with cartons of breakable things her mother would not trust with the movers, they shuttled back and forth between the hushed and fragrant cricket-ticking back roads, and the cement station plateau where lighted evening trains clattered emptily in and out, blowing commuter newspapers and chewing-gum wrappers across platforms still hot from the sun.

One stifling night when even this leisurely carting and dumping seemed impossible, they decided to treat themselves to a few hours of relief in one of the new air-conditioned movie houses, and they set off for the village without phoning to see what was playing. They separated in the lobby as they always did, her mother proceeding down a gently inclined aisle to the unpolluted air of the orchestra, Maria climbing a flight of thickly carpeted steps to the smoky balcony. As she settled herself in an empty row, she shivered at icy blasts of air pouring down from a vent above her, and put on the cardigan she had snatched up as they were leaving the house. Then she lit a cigarette and stared hopefully at the screen where multicolored giants moved suavely, their bodiless voices confusingly booming at her from all directions. For a long time she stared and listened, unable to summon any interest, and finally, bored, began glancing about the balcony. Her restless gaze came to a stop on a row two down from hers, where riotous light splashing off the screen variably made silhouettes or bas-reliefs of four long-necked boys and four girls. In a sudden shift to brighter light the head of the boy on the end of the row flashed goldenly, a head, she instantly noted with a sinking feeling, which was not big-eared like the others, and which held nestled, in the hollow between jawbone and clavicle, the tousled dark head of a girl. Going numb with dread and other emotions she could not bear to acknowledge, Maria watched the gold head bend, ministering to the curly one, until, maneuvering to place a more ambitious kiss, the boy turned his head—and revealed a hook-nosed profile with a receding chin.

Rising, Maria stumbled down the steps to the lobby, where she took a seat on a bench next to the soft-drink machine. She stayed there until crashing chords of music announced the end of the film, and her mother, as always, rushed out first to avoid the crush. As she came up to Maria, rising from the bench, she gave a smug little smile: "I see you couldn't even sit it out. Have you *ever* in your life seen such trash?"

Though the moving men were scheduled to come on Monday, they decided to try and finish up the house on Saturday. Late Friday afternoon as Maria was leaving the library, she hung a little wooden sign on the front door—LIBRARY CLOSED TODAY—and told herself it was perfectly all right, Saturdays were always quiet, and one day would hardly matter. But the next morning when she opened her eyes in her stripped bedroom, she saw that the uncurtained windows looked out on a mistfilled garden like blind white eyes, and as she listened to the drops of water softly plopping off the eaves and branches, she knew at once that it was a perfect "library day," it ought to be open, she ought to be there. Groaning, she shut her eyes, trying to postpone the necessity of making a decision, but as she lay there the busy sounds of cupboard doors slamming and quick footsteps on uncarpeted floors made the decision for her: she had to help her mother. She got up at once, threw on a cotton bathrobe, and, as her first move of the day, took the still-warm sheets and pillow and light blanket off the bed where she had slept, and stacked them in a grocery carton in the hall.

At eleven-thirty she methodically went through all the upstairs rooms to make sure none of the small things had been missed, pausing last in the doorway of her father's old room. Light like dark water poured in through the windows over the uneven pegging of the floorboards, the rolled-up mattress on the springs of the bed. A beautiful walnut four-poster, the bed bore blue tags on two of its posts, for it had been sold to a New York dealer for the true and flawless antique it was. As she looked at the bed, and the similarly tagged maple chest-on-chest, Maria thought of how much this would have pleased him, how in fact the sight of that whole dismantled house would have filled him with joy. "Daddy," she said softly to nothing, no one, and fled down the hall, down the stairs.

She went into the living room, filled with crates of books from the shelves on either side of the fireplace, and where the couches, tables, and armchairs were pushed away from the walls in readiness for the movers and stood huddled in the middle of the room like a herd of mute lost beasts. The house was strangely still, still, there was a peculiar smell of sulfur and slate in the air—the dampness in the fireplace, she decided, looking at the charred bricks in the cleaned-out grate. "Mother?" she called uneasily.

"Cooahhh, coo, coo-o-o," answered a mourning dove from the magnolia by the cellar door.

"Mother?" cried Maria on a rising note of fright. "Where are you? Mother? Are you all right?"

She was not. Maria finally found her in the kitchen, sitting in the middle of the floor next to a deep cardboard carton she had been wadding with paper and packing with cooking utensils. She sat holding a cast-iron skillet and a sheet of newspaper in her meager lap, her thin legs pushed straight out in front of her. Though her face, streaming with tears, was strangely calm, the throat beneath the sharp chin was violently working, either in an effort to hold back sobs or to bring out words, which it apparently could not do. Though she was terrified,

Maria calmly went up to her mother and, acting as though this were a place she often sat, quietly raised her up and supported her to the benched inglenook where they took most of their meals. Passive as a child, her mother let herself be led and fussed over, and when Maria was finally inspired to ask, "Should I call Myra? Would you like to see Myra?" her mother nodded almost simple-mindedly.

Five minutes after Maria phoned, Myra Hollis came clomping in, wearing a hooded plastic raincoat that made her look like a cellophane-wrapped package, brogue tongues flapping over muddy rubbers, plump cheeks scarlet from her agitated walk down the road. "Well now, Liz," she said heartily. "Having a bit of a crying jag, are you? It's high time—I'd been wondering when you would. Goodness knows, it's only natural after—what—forty years? Have you packed your kettle? Good." She proudly patted her huge shabby tapestry purse. "I stuck in some tea bags and a little nip of brandy as I went out the door. Now all we need is some sugar and cups. Ah lovely, Maria, *that's* the good girl. Now we're all set."

They accepted Maria's story without question: Now that it was raining so hard, she had better go and see if any books had been left in the little wooden box on the library porch. And as long as she was in the village, suggested Myra, she might as well pick up some sandwiches for their lunch—since they had defrosted and cleaned out the icebox after breakfast, it was silly to bring in any other kind of food.

"No need to hurry," said Myra Hollis, winking at Maria going out the door, as if to say the longer she gave them the more likely it was she would find everything restored to normal by the time she got back.

Once off the muddy back roads Maria drove wildly, blindly, trembling with the horror she had so bravely suppressed for the last half hour, the rain streaming and muddling over the windshield like the tears she could not seem to shed. Ignoring the peeling sign that prohibited parking in the library's driveway at all times, Maria turned in the car and parked it halfway up. She crossed the patchy wet grass, looked in the book-deposit box which was empty, then let herself in with her key, leaving the LIBRARY CLOSED TODAY sign hanging on the door. Though the front room was dark with storm light, she did not turn on the desk lamp. Sitting down, she put her throbbing head into clammy hands. Rain slipped down through the maple and beech leaves, slapping the windows, hitting the roof like hail, making such a rushing racket she did not hear the tapping on the door. When she finally did, she knew without lifting her face from its shelter of icy hands just who it was, and she did not move. The tapping on the glass panes continued. Realizing that the desk was plainly visible from the door and that it was impossible to pretend she was not there, she at last rose and went to the door, throwing it open with a violence that rattled the panes. "Can't you read? Don't you see that sign?" she cried through the screen door, glaring at him as he stood pale and blinking on the frayed WELCOME mat.

"Sure. But you're here," he said implacably, and opening the screen door marched in past her.

"I'm the librarian."

"I know," he said softly, without any irony, and stopped in the center of the room, crossing his arms.

"Please, Harry," she whispered, feeling the tears rushing up on her at last. "Please," she begged. "Please go home. I have work I must do."

"I won't bother you if I just sit and read."

"But you *will*."

His face broke up into quivering brilliant planes. "Maria. That's the nicest thing you ever said to me."

"You have *got* to leave. D'you understand?"

"Listen Maria—I can't stand it anymore. I have to know. Is there someone you love?"

"Oh God," she said weakly, taking her hand from the door and passing it over her face. "Don't start being awful, Harry. You're not that way. Don't start now. Just go home."

"Tell me if there's someone else," he whispered, tortured, coming slowly back to the door.

Helpless, she watched him slam the door shut with one shove of his broad palm.

"I'll bet there isn't," he said, forcing a smile, coming so close she could feel his warm breath on her face as he took her elbows into his hands. "I'll bet you don't really even know how to kiss. Maria. I'll bet."

"How horrible you are! How disgusting!" she cried, passionately throwing out her hands to push him away, out of the library, out of her life. But the hands stopped, splayed on the chest, feeling the scudding racking beats of the heart under the ridges of rib, until he took them away and squeezed them, powerless, in his own.

Silenced, they stared, wide-eyed, dazed. Drowning, she thought. Drowning, drowned. As the hands released hers and went under her hair, she shut her eyes, and the hands pressed the nape of her neck until her burning face rested against his burning throat. Tears scalded her lowered lids. Shame, fear, desire and shame—each as she had never known. She jerked back her head to finally speak but "Don't . . ." was all she ever said, for he found her mouth, and then there was only glassy green underwater light, the fleet image of a child curled reading on the window seat, and the sound of a squirrel jumping from a tree, running teeteringly, crazily, across the slippery roof above their heads.

QL 696. C9

Anthony Boucher

THE LIBRARIAN'S BODY HAD BEEN REMOVED FROM THE SWIVEL CHAIR, but Detective Lieutenant Donald MacDonald stood beside the desk. This was only his second murder case, and he was not yet hardened enough to use the seat freshly vacated by a corpse. He stood and faced the four individuals, one of whom was a murderer.

"Our routine has been completed," he said, "and I've taken a statement from each of you. But before I hand in my report, I want to go over those statements in the presence of all of you. If anything doesn't jibe, I want you to say so."

The librarian's office of the Serafin Pelayo branch of the Los Angeles Public Library was a small room. The three witnesses and the murderer (but which was which?) sat crowded together. The girl in the gray dress—Stella Swift, junior librarian—shifted restlessly. "It was all so . . . so confusing and so awful," she said.

MacDonald nodded sympathetically. "I know." It was this girl who had found the body. Her eyes were dry now, but her nerves were still tense. "I'm sorry to insist on this, but . . ." His glance surveyed the other three: Mrs. Cora Jarvis, children's librarian, a fluffy kitten; James Stickney, library patron, a youngish man with no tie and wild hair; Norbert Utter, high-school teacher, a lean, almost ascetic-looking man of forty-odd. One of these . . .

"Immediately before the murder," MacDonald began, "the branch librarian Miss Benson was alone in this office typing. Apparently" (he gestured at the sheet of paper in the typewriter) "a draft for a list of needed replacements. This office can be reached only through those stacks, which can in turn be reached only by passing the main desk. Mrs. Jarvis, you were then on duty at that desk, and according to you only these three people were then in the stacks. None of them, separated as they were in the stacks, could see each other or the door of this office." He paused.

The thin teacher spoke up. "But this is ridiculous, officer. Simply because I was browsing in the stacks to find some fresh ideas for outside reading. . ."

The fuzzy-haired Stickney answered him. "The Loot's right. Put our stories together, and it's got to be one of us. Take your medicine, comrade."

"Thank you, Mr. Stickney. That's the sensible attitude. Now Miss Benson was shot, to judge by position and angle, from that doorway. The weapon was dropped on the spot. All four of you claim to have heard that shot from your respective locations and hurried toward it. It was Miss Swift who opened the door and discovered the body. Understandably enough, she fainted. Mrs. Jarvis looked after her while Mr. Stickney had presence of mind enough to phone the police. All of you watched each other, and no one entered this room until our arrival. Is all that correct?"

Little Mrs. Jarvis nodded. "My, Lieutenant, you put it all so neatly! You should have been a cataloguer like Miss Benson."

"A cataloguer? But she was head of the branch, wasn't she?"

"She had the soul of a cataloguer," said Mrs. Jarvis darkly.

"Now this list that she was typing when she was killed." MacDonald took the paper from the typewriter. "I want you each to look at that and tell me if the last item means anything to you."

The end of her list read:

Davies: MISSION TO MOSCOW (2 cop)
Kernan: DEFENSE WILL NOT WIN THE WAR
FIC MacInnes: ABOVE SUSP
QL 696. C9

The paper went from hand to hand. It evoked nothing but frowns and puzzled headshakings.

"All right." MacDonald picked up the telephone pad from the

desk. "Now can any of you tell me why a librarian should have jotted down the phone number of the F.B.I.?"

This question fetched a definite reaction from Stickney, a sort of wry exasperation; but it was Miss Swift who answered, and oddly enough with a laugh. "Dear Miss Benson . . ." she said. "Of course she'd have the F.B.I.'s number. Professional necessity."

"I'm afraid I don't follow that."

"Some librarians have been advancing the theory, you see, that a librarian can best help defense work by watching what people use which books. For instance, if somebody keeps borrowing every work you have on high explosives, you know he's a dangerous saboteur planning to blow up the aqueduct and you turn him over to the G-men."

"Seriously? It sounds like nonsense."

"I don't know, Lieutenant. Aside from card catalogues and bird study, there was one thing Miss Benson loved. And that was America. She didn't think it was nonsense."

"I see . . . And none of you has anything further to add to this story?"

"I," Mr. Utter announced, "have fifty themes to correct this evening and . . ."

Lieutenant MacDonald shrugged. "O.K. Go ahead. All of you. And remember you're apt to be called back for further questioning at any moment."

"And the library?" Miss Jarvis asked. "I suppose I'm ranking senior in charge now and I . . ."

"I spoke to the head of the Branches Department on the phone. She agrees with me that it's best to keep the branch closed until our investigation is over. But I'll ask you and Miss Swift to report as usual tomorrow; the head of Branches will be here then too, and we can confer further on any matters touching the library itself."

"And tomorrow I was supposed to have a story hour. Well at least," the children's librarian sighed, "I shan't have to learn a new story tonight."

Alone, Lieutenant MacDonald turned back to the desk. He set the pad down by the telephone and dialed the number which had caught his attention. It took time to reach the proper authority and establish his credentials, but he finally secured the promise of a full file on all information which Miss Alice Benson had turned over to the F.B.I.

"Do you think that's it?" a voice asked eagerly.

He turned. It was the junior librarian, the girl with the gray dress and the gold-brown hair. "Miss Swift!"

"I hated to sneak in on you, but I want to know. Miss Benson was an old dear and I . . . I found her and . . . Do you think that's it? That she really did find out something for the F.B.I. and because she did . . .?"

"It seems likely," he said slowly, "According to all the evidence, she was on the best of terms with her staff. She had no money to speak of, and she was old for a crime-of-passion set-up. Utter and Stickney apparently knew her only casually as regular patrons of this branch. What have we left for a motive, unless it's this F.B.I. business?"

"We thought it was so funny. We used to rib her about being a G-woman. And now . . . Lieutenant, you've got to find out who killed her." The girl's lips set firmly and her eyes glowed.

MacDonald reached a decision. "Come on."

"Come? Where to?"

"I'm going to drive you home. But first we're going to stop off and see a man, and you're going to help me give him all the facts of this screwball case."

"Who? Your superior?"

MacDonald hesitated. "Yes," he said at last. "My superior."

He explained about Nick Noble as they drove. How Lieutenant Noble, a dozen years ago, had been the smartest problem-cracker in the department. How his captain had got into a sordid scandal and squeezed out, leaving the innocent Noble to take the rap. How his wife had needed a vital operation just then, and hadn't got it. How the widowed and disgraced man had sunk until . . .

"Nobody knows where he lives or what he lives on. All we know is that we can find him at a little joint on North Main, drinking cheap sherry by the water glass. Sherry's all that life has left him—that, and the ability to make the toughest problem come crystal clear. Somewhere in the back of that wino's mind is a precision machine that sorts the screwiest facts into the one inevitable pattern. He's the court of last appeal on a case that's nuts, and

God knows this one is. QL 696. C9 . . . Screwball Division, L.A.P.D., the boys call him."

The girl shuddered a little as they entered the Chula Negra Café. It was not a choice spot for the élite. Not that it was a dive, either. No juke, no B-girls; just a counter and booths for the whole-hearted eating and drinking of the Los Angeles Mexicans.

MacDonald remembered which booth was Nick Noble's sanctum. The little man sat there, staring into a half-empty glass of sherry, as though he hadn't moved since MacDonald last saw him after the case of the stopped timepieces. His skin was dead white and his features sharp and thin. His eyes were of a blue so pale that the irises were almost invisible.

"Hi!" said MacDonald. "Remember me?"

One thin blue-veined hand swatted at the sharp nose. The pale eyes rested on the couple. "MacDonald. . ." Nick Noble smiled faintly. "Glad. Sit down." He glanced at Stella Swift. "Yours?"

MacDonald coughed. "No. Miss Swift, Mr. Noble. Miss Swift and I have a story to tell you."

Nick Noble's eyes gleamed dimly. "Trouble?"

"Trouble. Want to hear it?"

Nick Noble swatted at his nose again. "Fly," he explained to the girl. "Stays there." There was no fly. He drained his glass of sherry. "Give."

MacDonald gave, much of the same précis that he had given to the group in the office. When he had finished, Nick Noble sat silent for so long that Stella Swift looked apprehensively at his glass. Then he stirred slightly, beckoned to a waitress, pointed to his empty glass, and said to the girl, "This woman. Benson. What was she like?"

"She was nice," said Stella. "But of course she *was* a cataloguer."

"Cataloguer?"

"You're not a librarian. You wouldn't understand what that means. But I gather that when people go to library school—I never did, I'm just a junior—most of them suffer through cataloguing, but a few turn out to be born cataloguers. Those are a race apart. They know a little of everything, all the systems of classification, Dewey, Library of Congress, down to the last number, and just how many spaces you indent each item on a typed card, and all about bibliography, and they shudder in their souls if the least little thing is wrong. They have eyes like eagles and memories like elephants."

"With that equipment," said MacDonald, "she might really have spotted something for the F.B.I."

"Might," said Nick Noble. Then to the girl, "Hobbies?"

"Miss Benson's? Before the war she used to be a devoted bird-watcher, and of course being what she was she had a positively Kieranesque knowledge of birds. But lately she's been all wrapped up in trying to spot saboteurs instead."

"I'm pretty convinced," MacDonald contributed, "that that's our angle, screwy as it sounds. The F.B.I. lead may point out our man, and there's still hope from the lab reports on prints and the paraffin test."

"Tests," Nick Noble snorted. "All you do is teach criminals what not to do."

"But if those fail us, we've got a message from Miss Benson herself telling us who killed her. And that's what I want you to figure out." He handed over the paper from the typewriter. "It's pretty clear what happened. She was typing, looked up, and saw her murderer with a gun. If she wrote down his name, he might see it and destroy the paper. So she left this cryptic indication. It can't possibly be part of the list she was typing; Mrs. Jarvis and Miss Swift don't recognize it as library routine. And the word above breaks off in the middle. Those letters and figures are her dying words. Can you read them?"

Nick Noble's pallid lips moved faintly. "Q L six nine six point C nine." He leaned back in the booth and his eyes glazed over. "Names," he said.

"Names?"

"Names of four."

"Oh. Norbert Utter, the teacher; James Stickney, the non-descript; Mrs. Cora Jarvis, the children's librarian; and Miss Stella Swift here."

"So," Nick Noble's eyes came to life again. "Thanks, MacDonald. Nice problem. Give you proof tonight."

Stella Swift gasped. "Does that mean that he . . .?"

MacDonald grinned. "You're grandstanding for the lady, Mr. Noble. You can't mean that you've solved that damned QL business like that?"

"Pencil," Nick Noble said.

Wonderingly, Lieutenant MacDonald handed one over. Nick Noble took a paper napkin, scrawled two words, folded it, and handed it to Stella. "Not now," he warned. "Keep it. Show to him later.

Grandstanding . . .! Need more proof first. Get it soon. Let me know about test. F.B.I."

MacDonald rose frowning. "I'll let you know. But how you can . . ."

"Good-bye, Mr. Noble. It's been so nice meeting you."

But Nick Noble appeared not to hear Stella's farewell. He was staring into his glass and not liking what he saw there.

Lieutenant MacDonald drew up before the girl's rooming house. "I may need a lot of help on the technique of librarianship in this case," he said. "I'll be seeing you soon."

"Thanks for the ride. And for taking me to that strange man. I'll never forget how . . . It seems—I don't know—uncanny, doesn't it?" A little tremor ran through her lithe body.

"You know, you aren't exactly what I'd expect a librarian to be. I've run into the wrong ones. I think of them as something with flat shirtwaists and glasses and a bun. Of course Mrs. Jarvis isn't either, but you . . ."

"I do wear glasses when I work," Stella confessed. "And you aren't exactly what I'd expected a policeman to be, or I shouldn't have kept them off all this time." She touched her free flowing hair and punned, "And you should see me with a bun on."

"That's a date. We'll start with dinner and—"

"Dinner!" she exclaimed. "Napkin!" She rummaged in her handbag. "I won't tell you what he said, that isn't fair, but just to check on—" She unfolded the paper napkin.

She did not say another word, despite all MacDonald's urging. She waved good-bye in pantomime, and her eyes, as she watched him drive off, were wide with awe and terror.

Lieutenant MacDonald glared at the reports on the paraffin tests of his four suspects. All four negative. No sign that any one of them had recently used a firearm. Nick Noble was right; all you do is teach criminals what not to do. They learn about nitrite specks in the skin, so a handkerchief wrapped over the hand . . . The phone rang.

"Lafferty speaking. Los Angeles Field Office, F.B.I. You wanted the dope on this Alice Benson's reports?"

"Please."

"O.K. She did turn over to us a lot of stuff on a man who'd been reading nothing but codes and ciphers and sabotage methods and explosives and God knows what all. Sounded like a correspondence course for the complete Fifth Columnist. We check up on him, and he's a poor devil of a pulp writer. Sure he wanted to know how to be a spy and a saboteur; but just so's he could write about 'em. We gave him a thorough going over, he's in the clear."

"Name?"

"James Stickney."

"I know him," said MacDonald dryly. "And is that all?"

"We'll send you the file, but that's the gist of it. I gather the Benson woman had something else she wasn't ready to spill, but if it's as much help as that was . . . Keep an eye on that library though. There's something going on."

"How so?"

"Three times in the past two months we've trailed suspects into that Serafin Pelayo branch, and not bookworms either. They didn't do anything there or contact anybody, but that's pretty high for coincidence in one small branch. Keep an eye open. And if you hit on anything, maybe we can work together."

"Thanks. I'll let you know." MacDonald hung up. So Stickney had been grilled by the F.B.I. on Miss Benson's information. Revenge for the indignity? Damned petty motive. And still . . . The phone rang again.

"Lieutenant MacDonald? This is Mrs. Jarvis. Remember me?"

"Yes indeed. You've thought of something more about—?"

"I certainly have. I think I've figured out what the QL thing means. At least I think I've figured how we can find out what it means. You see . . ." There was a heavy sound, a single harsh thud. Mrs. Jarvis groaned.

"Mrs. Jarvis! What's the matter? Has anything—"

"Elsie . . ." MacDonald heard her say faintly. Then the line was dead.

"Concussion," the police surgeon said. "She'll live. Not much doubt of that. But she won't talk for several days, and there's no telling how much she'll remember then."

"Elsie," said Lieutenant MacDonald. It sounded like an oath.

"We'll let you know as soon as she can see you. O.K., boys. Get along." Stella Swift trembled as the stretcher bearers moved off. "Poor Cora . . .When her husband comes home from Lockheed and finds . . . I was supposed to have dinner with them tonight and I come here and find you . . ."

Lieutenant MacDonald looked down grimly at the metal statue. "The poor devil's track trophy, and they use it to brain his wife. . . . And what the hell brings you here?" he demanded as the lean figure of Norbert Utter appeared in the doorway.

"I live across the street, Lieutenant," the teacher explained. "When I saw the cars here and the ambulance, why naturally I . . . Don't tell me there's been another . . ."

"Not quite. So you live across the street? Miss Swift, do you mind staying here to break the news to Mr. Jarvis? It'd come easier from you than from me. I want to step over to Mr. Utter's for a word with him."

Utter forced a smile. "Delighted to have you, Lieutenant."

The teacher's single apartment was comfortably undistinguished. His own books, MacDonald noticed, were chosen with unerring taste; the library volumes on a table seemed incongruous.

"Make yourself at home, Lieutenant, as I have no doubt you will. Now what is it you wanted to talk to me about?"

"First might I use your phone?"

"Certainly. I'll get you a drink meanwhile. Brandy?"

MacDonald nodded as he dialed the Chula Negra. Utter left the room. A Mexican voice answered, and MacDonald sent its owner to fetch Nick Noble. As he waited, he idly picked up one of those incongruous library books. He picked it up carelessly and it fell open. A slip of paper, a bookmark perhaps, dropped from the fluttering pages. MacDonald noticed typed letters:

43045q7w7qo0oqd3 . . .

"Noble here."

"Good." His attention snapped away from the paper. "Listen." And he told the results of the tests and the information from the F.B.I. and ended with the attack on Mrs. Jarvis. Utter came to the door once, looked at MacDonald, at the book, and at the paper.

"And so," MacDonald concluded, "we've got a last message again. 'Elsie. . . .'"

"'Elsie . . .'" Nick Noble's voice repeated thoughtfully.

"Any questions?"

"No. Phone me tomorrow morning. Later tonight maybe. Tell you then."

MacDonald hung up frowning. That paper . . . Suddenly he had it. The good old typewriter code, so easy to write and to decipher. For each letter use the key above it. He'd run onto such a cipher in a case recently; he should be able to work it in his head. He visualized a keyboard. The letters and figures shifted into

reportatusualplace . . .

Mr. Utter came back with a tray and two glasses of brandy. His lean face essayed a host's smile. "Refreshments, Lieutenant."

"Thank you."

"And now we can—or should you care for a cheese cracker?"

"Don't bother."

"No bother." He left the room. Lieutenant MacDonald looked at the cipher, then at the glasses. Deftly he switched them. Then he heard the slightest sound outside the door, a sigh of expectation confirmed and faint footsteps moving off. MacDonald smiled and switched the glasses back again.

Mr. Utter returned with a bowl of cheese wafers and the decanter. "To the success of your investigations, Lieutenant." They raised their glasses. Mr. Utter took a cautious sip, then coolly emptied his glass out the window. "You outsmarted me, Lieutenant," he announced. "I had not expected you to be up to the double gambit. I underrated you and apologize." He filled his own glass afresh from the decanter, and they drank. It was good brandy, unusually good for a teacher's salary.

"So we're dropping any pretense?" said MacDonald.

Mr. Utter shrugged. "You saw that paper. I was unpardonably careless. You are armed and I am not. Pretense would be foolish when you can so readily examine the rest of those books."

Lieutenant MacDonald's hand stayed near his shoulder holster. "It was a good enough scheme. Certain prearranged books were your

vehicles. Any accidental patron finding the messages, or even the average librarian, would pay little attention. Anything winds up as a mark-
er in a library book. A few would be lost, but the safety made up for
that. You prepared the messages here at home, returned them in the
books so that you weren't seen inserting them in public . . .

"You reconstruct admirably, Lieutenant."

"And who collected them?"

"Frankly, I do not know. The plan was largely arranged so that no
man could inform on another."

"But Miss Benson discovered it, and Miss Benson had to be
removed."

Mr. Utter shook his head. "I do not expect you to believe me,
Lieutenant. But I have no more knowledge of Miss Benson's death
than you have."

"Come now, Utter. Surely your admitted activities are a catamount to a confession of—"

"Is *catamount* quite the word you want, Lieutenant?"

"I don't know. My tongue's fuzzy. So's my mind. I don't know
what's wrong. . . .

Mr. Utter smiled, slowly and with great pleasure. "Of course,
Lieutenant. Did you really think I had underrated you? Naturally I
drugged both glasses. Then whatever gambit you chose, I had merely
to refill my own."

Lieutenant MacDonald ordered his hand to move toward the
holster. His hand was not interested.

"Is there anything else," Mr. Utter asked gently, "which you
should care to hear—while you can still hear anything?"

The room began a persistent circular joggling.

Nick Noble wiped his pale lips, thrust the flask of sherry back into his
pocket, and walked into the Main library. At the information desk in
the rotunda he handed a slip of paper to the girl in charge. On it was
penciled

QL 696. C9

The girl looked up puzzled. "I'm sorry, but—"

"Elsie," said Nick Noble hesitantly.

The girl's face cleared. "Oh. Of course. Well, you see, in this library we . . ."

The crash of the door helped to clear Lieutenant MacDonald's brain. The shot set up thundering waves that ripped through the drugwebs in his skull. The cold water on his head and later the hot coffee inside finished the job.

At last he lit a cigarette and felt approximately human. The big man with the moon face, he gathered, was Lafferty, F.B.I. The girl, he had known in the first instant, was Stella Swift.

". . . just winged him when he tried to get out of the window," Lafferty was saying. "The doc'll probably want us to lay off the grilling till tomorrow. Then you'll have your murderer, Mac, grilled and on toast."

MacDonald put up a hand to keep the top of his head on. "There's two things puzzle me. A, how you got here?"

Lafferty nodded at the girl.

"I began remembering things," she said, "after you went off with Mr. Utter. Especially I remembered Miss Benson saying just yesterday how she had some more evidence for the F.B.I. and how amazed she was that some people could show such an utter lack of patriotism. Then she laughed and I wondered why and only just now I realized it was because she'd made an accidental pun. There were other things too, and so I—"

"We had a note from Miss Benson today," Lafferty added. "It hadn't reached me yet when I phoned you. It was vaguely promising, no names, but it tied in well enough with what Miss Swift told us to make us check. When we found the door locked and knew you were here."

"Swell. And God knows I'm grateful to you both. But my other puzzle: Just now, when Utter confessed the details of the message scheme thinking I'd never live to tell them, he still denied any knowledge of the murder. I can't help wondering . . ."

When MacDonald got back to his office, he found a memo:

The Public Library says do you want a book from the Main sent out to the Serafin Pelayo branch tomorrow morning? A man named Noble made the request, gave you as authority. Please confirm.

MacDonald's head was dizzier than ever as he confirmed, wondering what the hell he was confirming.

The Serafin Pelayo branch was not open to the public the next morning, but it was well occupied. Outside in the reading room there waited the bandaged Mr. Utter, with Moon Lafferty on guard; the tousle-haired James Stickney, with a sergeant from Homicide; Hank Jarvis, eyes bleared from a sleepless night at his wife's bedside; and Miss Trumpeter, head of the Branches Department, impatiently awaiting the end of this interruption of her well-oiled branch routine.

Here in the office were Lieutenant MacDonald, Stella Swift, and Nick Noble. Today the girl wore a bright red dress, with a zipper which tantalizingly emphasized the fullness of her bosom. Lieutenant MacDonald held the book which had been sent out from the Main. Nick Noble held a flask.

"Easy," he was saying. "Elsie. Not a name. Letters L. C. Miss Swift mentioned systems of classification. Library of Congress."

"Of course," Stella agreed. "We don't use it in the Los Angeles Library; it's too detailed for a public system. But you have to study it in library school; so naturally I didn't know it, being a junior, but Mrs. Jarvis spotted it and Miss Benson, poor dear, must have known it almost by heart."

MacDonald read the lettering on the spine of the book. "U.S. Library of Congress Classification. Q: Science."

Stella Swift sighed. "Thank Heavens. I was afraid it might be English literature."

MacDonald smiled. "I wonder if your parents knew nothing of literary history or a great deal, to name you Stella Swift."

Nick Noble drank and grunted. "Go on."

MacDonald opened the book and thumbed through pages. "QL, Zoölogy. QL 600, Vertebrates. QL 696, Birds, systematic list (subdivisions, A—Z)."

"Birds?" Stella wondered. "It was her hobby of course, but . . ."

MacDonald's eyes went on down the page:

e.g., .A2, Accipitriformes (Eagles, hawks, etc.)
    .A3, Alciformes (Auks, puffins)
        Alectorides, *see* Gruiformes
"Wonderful names," he said. "If only we had a suspect named
Gruiformes . . . Point C seven," he went on, "Coraciiformes, see also
. . . here we are: Point C nine, Cypseli. . . ."

The book slipped from his hands. Stella Swift jerked down her
zipper and produced the tiny pistol which had contributed to the
fullness of her bosom. Nick Noble's fleshless white hand lashed out,
knocking over the flask, and seized her wrist. The pistol stopped
halfway to her mouth, twisted down, and discharged at the floor. The
bullet went through the volume of L. C. classification, just over the
line reading

.C9, Cypseli (Swifts)

A sober and embittered Lieutenant MacDonald unfolded the
paper napkin taken from the prisoner's handbag and read, in sprawling
letters:

STELLA SWIFT

"Her confession's clear enough," he said. "A German mother,
family in the Fatherland, pressure brought to bear.

She was the inventor of this library-message system and running
it unknown even to those using it, like Utter. After her false guess with
Stickney, Miss Benson hit the truth with St . . . the Swift woman. She
had to be disposed of. Then that meant more, attacking Mrs. Jarvis
when she guessed too much, and sacrificing Utter, an insignificant
subordinate, as a scapegoat to account for Miss Benson's further hints
to the F.B.I. But how the hell did you spot it, and right at the beginning of the case?"

"Pattern," said Nick Noble. "Had to fit." His sharp nose twitched,
and he brushed the nonexistent fly off it. "Miss Benson was cataloguer.
QL business had to be book number. Not system used here or recognized at once, but some system. Look at names: Cora Jarvis, James
Stickney, Norbert Utter, Stella Swift. Swift only name could possibly
have classifying number."

"But weren't you taking a terrible risk giving her that napkin? What happened to Mrs. Jarvis?"

Noble shook his head. "She was only one knew you'd consulted me. Attack me, show her hand. Too smart for that. Besides, used to taking risks, when I . . ." He left unfinished the reference to the days when he had been the best damned detective lieutenant in Los Angeles.

"We've caught a murderer," said Lieutenant MacDonald, "and we've broken up a spy ring." He looked at the spot where Stella Swift had been standing when she jerked her zipper. The sun from the window had glinted through her hair. "But I'm damned if I thank you."

"Understand," said Nick Noble flatly. He picked up the spilled flask and silently thanked God that there was one good slug of sherry left.

ED HAS HIS MIND IMPROVED

Walter R. Brooks

I SUPPOSE IT'S KIND OF SILLY OF ME TO KEEP ON TELLING PEOPLE ABOUT Wilbur Pope's talking horse. People are awful skeptical. Prove it they say. Prove it. Well I can't prove it. Neither can Mr. Pope prove it because the darn horse *won't* co-operate. He'll talk all right when he's alone with Mr. Pope, but get him out in company where you want him to show what he can do and he shuts up like a clam. I've told everybody you can talk Ed said Mr. Pope and I do think you might back me up. All our neighbors here around Mt. Kisco are beginning to whisper behind their hands when I come into a room and I've lost two of my best accounts because they say they can't leave their advertising in the hands of a man who chats with animals. I appeal to your better nature Ed he said. But Ed just laughed. Yeah? he said Who told you I had one? So Mr. Pope had to go around and tell everybody that he had just been kidding and that Ed couldn't talk at all. But they still act funny to him in Mt. Kisco.

Well I don't live in Mt. Kisco and I'm not an advertising man and so I don't see why I can't tell the truth about things. And particularly about what happened when Ed learned to read because there's a lesson in it for us.

Well Mr. Pope's house was always overrun on Saturdays and Sundays with a noisy crowd of Mrs. Pope's friends—at least I suppose you'd call then friends for most of them were young men who were trying to persuade Mrs. Pope to run away from Mr. Pope and marry them or something. It really wasn't any fun for Mr. Pope. It wasn't good for him either. He was getting a terrible inferiority complex for all of Mrs. Pope's suitors treated him as if he were a sort of oaf. So he bought this horse Ed and spent most of his week-ends riding.

Ed had things the other way round. To him Mrs. Pope was the oaf and Mr. Pope the jewel and he didn't hesitate to say so. He was pretty outspoken even for a horse. Mr. Pope said Tut tut! And Pshaw! And I can't have you saying things about Carlotta Ed. But he liked it. It built him up. He and Ed ambled over the countryside stopping at wayside taverns for beer and lolling and arguing about life under roadside trees.

Well one day they were sitting around like this and Mr. Pope was reading the Sunday paper and every now and then he would read out an item to Ed and they'd argue about it. But by and by Ed said I wish you'd lay off this political and business stuff. Haven't you got any good murders? Murders don't improve your mind Ed said Mr. Pope reprovingly. Neither do the columnists said Ed. I'd like to pick my own news for a change. Well said Mr. Pope suppose I teach you to read?

So after a while they rode home and Mr. Pope sneaked into the house the back way and got a bottle and an old primer from the attic and took them out to the barn. The first lesson wasn't very successful from a cultural point of view because the primer was one of those that starts with A stands for Aardvark. What the hell is an aardvark? said Ed. Why not teach me words I know? Like A stands for Ale? What's this next letter? Mr. Pope said it was B. That's an easy one said Ed B stands for Beer. And what's this? C said Mr. Pope. C stands for Scotch said Ed. No no Ed said Mr. Pope C stands for—let me see—Cognac.

Well this didn't make sense to Ed and Mr. Pope tried to explain and they got into an argument that lasted until it was so dark that they couldn't see the letters any more. The bottle was empty too.

Ed was persistent and he had Mr. Pope nail the primer up over the manger and in a week he could read The Cat Chases the Rat as well as you or I can. Then Mr. Pope brought out an old school reader and Ed went to work on that. But after he'd got through the third selection he struck. This stuff is too darn noble Wilbur he said. I can get all the edification I need out of your conversation. Bring me something a little low. So Mr. Pope got copies of a few of the more ribald magazines. And as a slight corrective to these he brought out The Three Musketeers.

Ed simply ate them up. In the manger Mr. Pope had rigged up a reading light which was small enough so that Mrs. Pope couldn't see it from the house and the horse read far into the night. He got very clever at turning the pages with his nose and for the first few months he would hardly stop reading long enough to speak to Mr. Pope except to demand more books. But before long he had read all the adventure stories and even some of the more serious novels in the house. Mr. Pope wouldn't get him any more magazines with jokes or risqué stories in them because twice Ed had got to roaring with laughter in the middle of the night and Mrs. Pope had sent Mr. Pope out to the barn to see if it was tramps. So then Mr. Pope got Ed a card at the public library.

So two or three nights a week they would ride over to the library and get a couple of books. Of course Mr. Pope had to go in and pick them out and Ed didn't always like his selections That's all right Ed said Mr. Pope but you can't read detective and adventure stories all the time. Some of your reading ought to be to improve your mind. Listen Wilbur said Ed I'm a horse. What good is an improved mind in a stable? Get me a good Western to read tonight will you?

Well along in the early fall Mr. Pope had to go to Detroit to present a new radio plan to one of his accounts. He got some library books and some detective story magazines for Ed and he hired Joe the handy man to take care of the horse while he was away. And the first thing Joe did was to find Ed's library and tell Mrs. Pope about it. Books in the barn? said Mrs. Pope and she went out to look them over. Good heavens what trash! she said. Throw these magazines out at once Joe. And these books seem to be some Mr. Pope got from the library. You'd better take them back. So Joe took them back.

Well Ed stuck it out without literature two days. On the third evening as soon as it got dark he slipped his halter and by cutting across lots and down back roads reached the library unobserved just before closing time. He peeked in a window. Nobody was there but Miss Sigsbee the librarian. Ed pushed the front door open with his nose and clumped up to the desk. Excuse me ma'am he said have you got anything by Edgar Wallace?

Miss Sigsbee gave a kind of faded squeal and went right over backwards chair and all. Sorry I startled you ma'am said Ed. If you got a slug of whisky handy it would make you feel better. I just wanted a book.

Well Miss Sigsbee was an old fashioned blue ribbon teetotaler and Ed's suggestion brought her round quicker than a drink would have. She was up and back in her chair before you could say John Galsworthy. How dare you! she said How dare you! Leave this library at once. I don't get it ma'am said Ed backing away from her. I just wanted a book. A horse! She said staring at him and she shuddered. Then she stiffened again. Horse or no horse she said you dare to come in here and offer me a drink of liquor! O that! said Ed. I didn't offer you a drink. I don't use the stuff myself. But skip it. Can I get a book out on Wilbur Pope's card?

Mr. Pope! Said Miss Sigsbee. You're Mr. Pope's horse. I remember. There was some gossip about his pretending he had a talking horse. People thought he was joking. But then it wasn't a joke! No ma'am said Ed. Now about that book—

Of course we can let you have a book said Miss Sigsbee. But the books Mr. Pope has been selecting for you—Dear me! You won't mind if I select something suitable for you? Well ma'am said Ed if you got any Edgar Wallace—Let me see said Miss Sigsbee: How old are you? Ed said he was rising nine. Nine said Miss Sigsbee going over to a shelf. Now here is just the thing for you. Exciting and at the same time a high moral tone. Have you read any of the Rollo books? Naw! said Ed disgustedly.

See here young man! said Miss Sigsbee sternly . . . Then she stopped and said Gracious! I can't call you young man can I? What should it be—young colt? But at nine you're hardly a colt are you? No ma'am said Ed firmly I'm a grown horse and I don't want my mind or my morals improved. Now can I have an Edgar Wallace? Why of course said Miss Sigsbee we can't force you to improve yourself. And she got an Edgar Wallace and Ed thanked her and trotted off with it in his mouth.

Well Mr. Pope was in Detroit ten days and Ed went over to the library every night and he and Miss Sigsbee got quite friendly.

The library was badly in need of funds and so far all money-raising schemes had failed. Miss Sigsbee didn't have much sense about

such things but she did know that a horse that could read would
draw a crowd. So she put it up to Ed. Would he give a public reading? Well it was against Ed's principles to do such a thing but he
couldn't help being flattered. Gosh ma'am he said it's nice of you to
ask me. But I really couldn't. Nonsense said Miss Sigsbee of course
you could. The library has done a good deal for you and isn't it rather
selfish of you to refuse to do so small a thing for the library? Well
said Ed slowly now you put it that way I suppose it is. Well he said
I'll do it.

The next day Mr. Pope got home and he was pretty sore when
Ed told him. I suppose you know what it means—thousands of
curiosity seekers tramping over the lawn and eating peanuts and
staring at you and news photographers hiding in the oatbin. Never a
moment to yourself any more. No cross no crown Wilbur said Ed. I
expect it's the penalty of fame. And don't forget there'll be
Hollywood scouts too. I'm not forgetting it said Mr. Pope. But what
good would it be if I signed up a Hollywood contract for you? You
wouldn't go through with it and let me make some money. You'd just
refuse to talk again. Probably I would said Ed. But I don't see why
I can't have a little fun when it comes my way. And anyway he said
I promised Miss Sigsbee.

Mr. Pope was pretty upset. The good times he and Ed had
had together would come to an end once the horse was a celebrity.
And Carlotta would be furious at the notoriety. He walked down
to the library that night to plead with Miss Sigsbee. But it wasn't
any good. Anyway I couldn't stop it now if I wanted to she said.
I've taken the matter up with the trustees. I hadn't anticipated that
they would be so skeptical. Frankly Mr. Pope my position and even
my reputation are at stake. Mrs. Dillway and Dr. Polder are the
only trustees in town. Mrs. Dillway has agreed always to double
any amount we take in through our little entertainments. Of
course as there is usually a deficit—but as I was saying I have
always considered her and Dr. Polder very good friends of mine
but when I told them—Dear me it was a very stormy session. I
insisted however and finally they did agree to give me a chance to
prove my assertion. We have arranged to meet quite informally
tomorrow evening in my garden. Now that you are back Mr. Pope
you will of course come over with Ed. You see my position I am

sure. If he doesn't read for them at this little dress rehearsal—Mr. Pope saw all right.

So the next evening he rode Ed over. Mrs. Dillway was a large imposing presence. She did not believe that horses could talk as was manifest in the indignant heave of her massive bosom as she gazed on Ed. The Rev. Dr. Polder didn't believe it either. You see how people really feel toward a talking horse Ed said Mr. Pope as they paused before crossing the lawn toward the three. And here's another thing he said. When the Hollywood producers begin to bid for you I'm going to sign up with the highest bidder. I'm going to sign a bill of sale. Think that over.

What? said Ed. Hey Wilbur you can't do that. You've made your bed Ed said Mr. Pope Come on. No but have a heart Wilb Ed protested. I'm in a spot. If I let Miss Sigsbee down now she'll lose her job. You should have thought of that before said Mr. Pope pulling him forward. Good evening Miss Sigsbee.

Miss Sigsbee got up and presented Ed and Mr. Pope to the trustees. They bowed coldly to Mr. Pope and Dr. Polder gave Ed a timid nod but Mrs. Dillway flipped open a lorgnette and gave the horse her celebrated basilisk once-over. Ed fidgeted for a second and than he threw up his head. You don't need that thing lady he said I'll tell you what I am. I'm a horse.

Mrs. Dillway gave a strong shudder. Don't be impudent! she said. Then she turned and caught Dr. Polder by the wrist. He had been saying O dear me! O dear me! and wringing his hands. Be quiet Dr. Polder, she said. No! said Dr. Polder trying to jerk away. This is witchcraft—sorcery. I cannot countenance such an exhibition. My bishop—Nonsense! Said Mrs. Dillway. It's merely ventriloquism. We shall expose it.

So after a minute Dr. Polder calmed down though he continued to tremble and Miss Sigsbee took a magazine and had Mrs. Dillway open it at random and then held it up for Ed to read while Mr. Pope sat down next to Mrs. Dillway. Ed glanced at the page and shook his head. No he said I can't do it. Why Ed! said Miss Sigsbee. It's hard on you ma'am said Ed but I got to consider my own future. Come on Wilbur let's got out of here.

Mrs. Dillway's lorgnette came up again and she gave a satisfied smile. You see Doctor? she said. Simply ventriloquism. Naturally if this Mr. Pope can't see the page the horse can't read it.

O is that so! Ed burst out and Miss Sigsbee said but Mrs. Dillway the horse really can read. I've heard him. I am sorry to see you persist in this attempt to hoax us Miss Sigsbee said Mrs. Dillway. The outcome can only be unfortunate for you. As for you Mr. Pope it seems to me that you are carrying a silly joke dangerously far.

Well Ed said Mr. Pope resignedly I take back what I said about selling you. You better do your stuff. We're going to get a lot of unpleasant publicity out of this any way of the goods. Leave it to me boss said Ed under his breath. There won't be any public reading and these goofs won't talk either. Then he said to Miss Sigsbee What you want me to read?

So Miss Sigsbee held the page up and Ed began. *The waters of the lake* he read *had changed from lead to silver and from silver to rose.* Good gracious! said Mrs. Dillway he really is reading! Why this—this—Miss Sigsbee I am afraid we owe you an apology. Go, on—er—Ed.

So Ed went on. *The first flush of surprise reddened the naked limbs of the slender*—Ed! Ed! interrupted Miss Sigsbee blushing. It's *sunrise*—not *surprise* Sorry said Ed. This is kind of fine print for a horse. He winked at Mr. Pope and continued.

Well he read a paragraph or two more and gradually the outraged expression faded from Mrs. Dillway's face Then Ed read *As Gregory stepped out of the canoe the girl ran to him. He seized her and. kicked her passionately on the mouth then drew back and booted her in the eyes.* Kissed Ed said Miss Sigsbee. And looked. O said Ed and continued. *'Darling,' She cried 'if father finds you here—'* *'I have my own ways of knowing about your father,' he said. 'He will not find me here for he has found a better thing elsewhere today.' The words were obscene and as she nestled in his embrace—*

Really Ed! said Mr. Pope and Miss Sigsbee said crossly The word is *obscure*—not *obscene.* I'm sorry said Ed. I guess it's the company. I mean naturally I'm a little nervous Let's see—'*Gregory*' she said '*Now damn you*'—Hey wait a minute said Ed interrupting himself. I guess it's *How can you?*

Mrs. Dillway had got to her feet. Come Dr. Polder. We have had quite enough of this obscene exhibition. Please understand Miss

Sigsbee that from today I withdraw all support from the library. Hey just a minute said Ed. He trotted around in front of the departing pair. There's something you ought to know ma'am he said before you pull anything like that. I'm giving a reading tonight down to the Elks' Hall. It'll be announced that it's for the benefit of the library and of course you'll have to stick to your agreement and match what we take in. You're giving no such disgraceful performance for any library I am connected with said Mrs. Dillway angrily. How you going to stop it? asked Ed and as Mrs. Dillway glared he said Now ma'am I don't want to be mean but we got to raise money. If you want to hand Miss Sigsbee a check for double what me and Wilbur estimate tonight's gate at—well we'll call the reading off.

Well Mrs. Dillway was practically speechless. This—this is extortion she said. Yes ma'am said Ed Shall we say fifteen hundred? No! shouted Mrs. Dillway but Dr. Polder drew her aside and after a few minutes came back to say that she agreed.

O dear said Miss Sigsbee when they had gone it is wonderful about the money of course but I am afraid my position is gone. Pooh! said Ed They won't either of them dare say a word about this. No said Mr. Pope they can hardly go around complaining that they were insulted by a horse. Vulgar but effective—that's Ed. Yeah said Ed and the same thing could be said of Shakespeare Dear me said Miss Sigsbee I never thought of it that way. But it's true. Just the same said Ed that fifteen-hundred smackers will buy a lot of Edgar Wallace. O wait a minute lady he said I know I know. But part of it you're going to get Edgar Wallace with aren't you? If you want to make the world better you got to stop trying to improve people's minds and start improving their dispositions. Speaking of which Wilbur how about a can of beer? O excuse me ma'am for mentioning it. Not at all said Miss Sigsbee archly. After all Shakespeare also drank beer. I wonder. . .

She hesitated and Ed winked slowly at Mr. Pope. After all he said we can't any of us never say anything about this evening in pubic can we? So it might as well be a good one, Wilbur, let's creep over to Horley's and bring back half a case.

THE TRACTATE MIDDOTH

M.R. James

TOWARDS THE END OF AN AUTUMN AFTERNOON AN ELDERLY MAN WITH a thin face and grey Piccadilly weepers pushed open the swing-door leading into the vestibule of a certain famous library, and addressing himself to an attendant, stated that he believed he was entitled to use the library, and inquired if he might take a book out. Yes, if he were on the list of those to whom that privilege was given. He produced his card—Mr. John Eldred—and, the register being consulted, a favorable answer was given. "Now, another point," said he. "It is a long time since I was here, and I do not know my way about your building; besides, it is near closing-time, and it is bad for me to hurry up and down stairs. I have here the title of the book I want: is there anyone at liberty who could go and find it for me?" After a moment's thought the doorkeeper beckoned to a young man who was passing. "Mr. Garrett," he said, "have you a minute to assist this gentleman?" "With pleasure," was Mr. Garrett's answer. The slip with the title was handed to him. "I think I can put my hand on this; it happens to be in the class I inspected last quarter, but I'll just look it up in the catalogue to make sure. I suppose it is that particular edition that you require, sir?" "Yes, if you please; that, and no other," said Mr. Eldred "I am exceedingly obliged to you." "Don't mention it I beg, sir," said Mr. Garrett, and hurried off.

"I thought so," he said to himself, when his finger, travelling down the pages of the catalogue, stopped at a particular entry. "Talmud: Tractate Middoth, with the commentary of Nachmanides, Amsterdam, 1707. 11.3.34. Hebrew class, of course. Not a very difficult job this."

Mr. Eldred, accommodated with a chair in the vestibule, awaited anxiously the return of his messenger—and his disappointment at seeing an empty-handed Mr. Garrett running down the staircase was very evident. "I'm sorry to disappoint you, sir," said the young man, "but the book is out." "Oh dear" said Mr. Eldred, "is that so? You are sure there can be no mistake?" "I don't think there is much chance of it, sir, but it's possible, if you like to wait a minute, that you might meet the very gentleman that's got it. He must be leaving the library soon, and I *think* I saw him take that particular book out of the shelf." "Indeed! You didn't recognize him, I suppose? Would it be one of the professors or one of the students?" "I don't think so: certainly not a professor. I should have known him; but the light isn't very good in that part of the library at this time of day, and I didn't see his face. I should have said he was a shortish old gentleman, perhaps a clergyman, in a cloak. If you could wait, I can easily find out whether he wants the book very particularly."

"No, no," said Mr. Eldred, "I won't—I can't wait now, thank you—no. I must be off. But I'll call again tomorrow if I may, and perhaps you could find out who has it."

"Certainly, sir, and I'll have the book ready for you if we—" But Mr. Eldred was already off, and hurrying more than one would have thought wholesome for him.

Garrett had a few moments to spare; and, thought he, "I'll go back to that case and see if I can find the old man. Most likely he could put off using the book for a few days. I dare say the other one doesn't want to keep it for long." So off with him to the Hebrew class. But when he got there it was unoccupied, and the volume marked 11.3.34 was in its place on the shelf. It was vexatious to Garrett's self-respect to have disappointed an inquirer with so little reason and he would have liked, had it not been against library rules, to take the book down to the vestibule then and there, so that it might be ready for Mr. Eldred when he called. However, next morning he would be on the look out for him, and he begged the doorkeeper to send and let him know when the moment came. As a matter of fact, he was himself in the vestibule when Mr. Eldred arrived, very soon after the library opened, and when hardly anyone besides the staff were in the building.

"I'm very sorry," he said; "it's not often that I make such a stupid mistake, but I did feel sure that the old gentleman I saw took out that very book and kept it in his hand without opening it, just as people do, you know, sir, when they mean to take a book out of the library and not merely refer to it. But, however, I'll run up now at once and get it for you this time."

And here intervened a pause. Mr. Eldred paced the entry, read all the notices, consulted his watch, sat and gazed up the staircase, did all that a very impatient man could, until some twenty minutes had run out. At last he addressed himself to the doorkeeper and inquired if it was a very long way to that part of the library to which Mr. Garrett had gone.

"Well, I was thinking it was funny, sir, he's a quick man as a rule, but to be sure he might have been sent for by the librarian, but even so I think he'd have mentioned to him that you was waiting. I'll just speak him up on the toob and see." And to the tube he addressed himself. As he absorbed the reply to his question his face changed, and he made one or two supplementary inquiries which were shortly answered. Then he came forward to his counter and spoke in a lower tone. "I'm sorry to hear, sir, that something seems to have 'appened a little awkward. Mr. Garrett has been took poorly, it appears, and the librarian sent him 'ome in a cab the other way. Something of an attack, by what I can hear." "What, really? Do you mean that someone has injured him?" "No, sir, not violence 'ere, but, as I should judge, attacted with an attack, what you might term it, of illness. Not a strong constitootion, Mr. Garrett. But as to your book, sir, perhaps you might be able to find it for yourself. It's too bad you should be disappointed this way twice over—" "Er—well, but I'm so sorry that Mr. Garrett should have been taken ill in this way while he was obliging me. I think I must leave the book, and call and inquire after him. You can give me his address, I suppose." That was easily done: Mr. Garrett, it appeared, lodged in rooms not far from the station. "And, one other question. Did you happen to notice if an old gentleman, perhaps a clergyman, in a—yes—in a black cloak, left the library after I did yesterday. I think he may have been a—I think, that is, that he may be staying—or rather that I may have known him."

"Not in a black cloak, sir; no. There were only two gentlemen left later than what you done, sir, both of them youngish men. There was Mr. Carter took out a music-book and one of the prefessors with a couple o' novels. That's the lot, sir; and then I went off to me tea, and glad to get it. Thank you, sir, much obliged."

Mr. Eldred, still a prey to anxiety, betook himself in a cab to Mr. Garrett's address, but the young man was not yet in a condition to receive visitors. He was better, but his landlady considered that he must have had a severe shock. She thought most likely from what the doctor said that he would be able to see Mr. Eldred to-morrow. Mr. Eldred returned to his hotel at dusk and spent, I fear, but a dull evening.

On the next day he was able to see Mr. Garrett. When in health Mr. Garrett was a cheerful and pleasant-looking young man. Now he was a very white and shaky being, propped up in an arm-chair by the fire, and inclined to shiver and keep an eye on the door. If, however, there were visitors whom he was not prepared to welcome, Mr. Eldred was not among them. "It really is I who owe you an apology, and I was despairing of being able to pay it, for I didn't know your address. But I am very glad you have called. I do dislike and regret giving all this trouble, but you know I could nor have foreseen this—this attack which I had."

"Of course not; but now, I am something of a doctor. You'll excuse my asking; you have had, I am sure, good advice. Was it a fall you had?"

"No. I did fall on the floor—but not from any height. It was, really, a shock."

"You mean something startled you. Was it anything you thought you saw?"

"Not much *thinking* in the case, I'm afraid. Yes, it was something I saw. You remember when you called the first time at the library?"

"Yes, of course. Well, now, let me beg you not to try to describe it—it will not be good for you to recall it, I'm sure."

"But indeed it would be a relief to me to tell any-one like yourself: you might be able to explain it away. It was just when I was going into the class where your book is—"

"Indeed, Mr. Garrett, I insist; besides, my watch tells me I have but very little time left in which to get my things together and take the train. No—not another word—it would be more distressing to you than you imagine, perhaps. Now there is just one thing I want to say. I feel that I am really indirectly responsible for this illness of yours, and I think I ought to defray the expense which it has—eh?"

But this offer was quite distinctly declined. Mr. Eldred, not pressing it, left almost at once not, however, before Mr. Garrett had insisted upon his taking a note of the class-mark of the Tractate

Middoth, which, as he said, Mr. Eldred could at leisure get for himself. But Mr. Eldred did not reappear at the library.

William Garrett had another visitor that day in the person of a contemporary and colleague from the library, one George Earle. Earle had
been one of those who found Garrett lying insensible on the floor just
inside the "class" or cubicle (opening upon the central alley of a spacious gallery) in which the Hebrew books were placed, and Earle had
naturally been very anxious about his friend's condition. So as soon as
library hours were over he appeared at the lodgings. "Well," he said
(after other conversation), "I've no notion what it was that put you
wrong, but I've got the idea that there's something wrong in the atmosphere of the library. I know this, that just before we found you I was
coming along the gallery with Davis, and I said to him, 'Did ever you
know such a musty smell anywhere as there is about here? It can't be
wholesome.' Well now, if one goes on living a long time with a smell of
that kind (I tell you it was worse than I ever knew it) it must get into
the system and break out some time, don't you think?"
    Garrett shook his head. "That's all very well about the smell—but
it isn't always there, though I've noticed it the last day or two—a sort
of unnaturally strong smell of dust. But no—that's not what did for me,
It was something I *saw*. And I want to tell you about it. I went into that
Hebrew class to get a book for a man that was inquiring for it down
below. Now that same book I'd made a mistake about the day before.
I'd been for it, for the same man, and made sure that I saw an old parson; in a cloak taking it out. I told my man it was out, off he went, to
call again next day. I went back to see if I could get it out of the parson; no parson there, and the book on the shelf. Well, yesterday, as I
say; I went again. This time, if you please—ten o'clock in the morning,
remember, and as much light as ever you get in those classes, and
there was my parson again, back to me, looking at the books on the
shelf I wanted. His hat was on the table, and he had a bald head. I
waited a second or two looking at him rather particularly, I tell you, he
had a very nasty bald head. It looked to me dry, and it looked dusty, and
the streaks of hair across it were much less like hair than cobwebs.
Well, I made a bit of a noise on purpose, coughed and moved my feet.
He turned round and let me see his face—which I hadn't seen before.

I tell you again, I'm not mistaken. Though, for one reason or another I didn't take in the lower part of his face, I did see the upper part; and it was perfectly dry, and the eyes were very deep-sunk; and over them, from the eyebrows to the cheek-bone, there were *cobwebs—thick*. Now that closed me up, as they say, and I can't tell you anything more."

What explanations were furnished by Earle of this phenomenon it does not very much concern us to inquire; at all events they did not convince Garrett that he had not seen what he had seen.

Before William Garrett returned to work at the library, the librarian insisted upon his taking a week's rest and change of air. Within a few days' time, therefore, he was at the station with his bag, looking for a desirable smoking compartment in which to travel to Burnstow-on-Sea, which he had not previously visited. One compartment and one only seemed to be suitable. But, just as he approached it, he saw, standing in front of the door, a figure so like one bound up with recent unpleasant associations that, with a sickening qualm, and hardly knowing what he did, he tore open the door of the next compartment and pulled himself into it as quickly as if death were at his heels. The train moved off, and he must have turned quite faint, for he was next conscious of a smelling-bottle being put to his nose. His physician was a nice-looking old lady, who, with her daughter, was the only passenger in the carriage.

But for this incident it is not very likely that he would have made any overtures to his fellow-travellers. As it was, thanks and inquiries and general conversation supervened inevitably; and Garrett found himself provided before the journey's end not only with a physician, but with a landlady: for Mrs. Simpson had apartments to let at Burnstow, which seemed in all ways suitable. The place was empty at that season, so that Garrett was thrown a good deal into the society of the mother and daughter. He found them very acceptable company. On the third evening of his stay he was on such terms with them as to be asked to spend the evening in their private sitting-room.

During their talk it transpired that Garrett's work lay in a library. "Ah, libraries are fine places," said Mrs. Simpson, putting down her work with a sigh; "but for all that, books have played me a sad turn, or rather a book has."

"Well, books give me my living, Mrs. Simpson, and I should be sorry to say a word against them. I don't like to hear that they have been bad for you."

"Perhaps Mr. Garrett could help us to solve our puzzle, mother," said Miss Simpson.

"I don't want to set Mr. Garrett off on a hunt that might waste a lifetime, my dear, nor yet to trouble him with our private affairs."

"But if you think it in the least likely that I could be of use, I do beg you to tell me what the puzzle is, Mrs. Simpson. If it is finding out anything about a book, you see, I am in rather a good position to do it."

"Yes, I do see that, but the worst of it is that we don't know the name of the book."

"Nor what it is about?"

"No, nor that either."

"Except that we don't think it's in English, mother—and that is not much of a clue."

"Well, Mr. Garrett," said Mrs. Simpson, who had not yet resumed her work, and was looking at the fire thoughtfully, "I shall tell you the story. You will please keep it to yourself, if you don't mind? Thank you. Now it is just this. I had an old uncle, a Dr. Rant. Perhaps you may have heard of him. Not that he was a distinguished man, but from the odd way he chose to be buried."

"I rather think I have seen the name in some guide-book."

"That would be it," said Miss Simpson. "He left directions—horrid old man!—that he was to be put, sitting at a table in his ordinary clothes, in a brick room that he'd had made underground in a field near his house. Of course the country people say he's been seen .about there in his old black cloak."

"Well, dear, I don't know much about such things," Mrs. Simpson went on, "but anyhow he is dead, these twenty years and more. He was a clergyman, though I'm sure I can't imagine how he got to be one: but he did no duty for the last part of his life, which I think was a good thing; and he lived on his own property: a very nice estate not a great way from here. He had no wife or family only one niece, who was myself, and one nephew, and he had no particular liking for either of us—nor for anyone else, as far as that goes. If anything, he liked my cousin better than he did me—for John was much more like him in his temper, and, I'm afraid I must say, his very mean sharp ways. It might have been different if I had not married; but I did, and that he very much resented. Very well here he was with this estate and a good deal of money, as it turned out, of which he had the absolute disposal, and it was understood that we—my cousin and I—would share it equally at his death. In a certain winter, over twenty years back, as I said, he was taken ill, and I was sent for to nurse him. My husband was alive then, but the old man would not hear of *his* coming. As I drove up to the house I saw my cousin John driving away from it in an open fly and looking, I noticed, in very good spirits. I went up and did what I could for my uncle, but I was very soon sure that this would be his last illness; and he was convinced of it too. During the day before he died he got me to sit by him all the time, and I could see there was something, and probably something unpleasant, that he was saving up to tell me, and putting it off as long as he felt he could afford the strength—I'm afraid purposely in order to keep me on the stretch. But, at last, out it came. 'Mary,' he said—'Mary, I've made my will in John's favor: he has everything, Mary.' Well, of course that came as a bitter shock to me, for we—my husband and I—were not rich people, and if he could have managed to live a little easier than he was obliged to do, I felt it might be the prolonging of his life. But I said little or nothing to my uncle, except that he had a right to do what he pleased partly because I couldn't think of anything to say, and partly because I was sure there was more to come: and so there was. 'But, Mary,' he said, 'I'm not very fond of John, and I've made another will in *your* favor. *You* can have everything. Only you've got to find the will, you see: and I don't mean to tell you where it is.' Then he chuckled to himself, and I waited, for again I was sure he hadn't finished. 'That's a good girl,' he said after a time—' you wait, and I'll tell you as much as I told John. But just let me remind you, you can't go into court with what I'm saying to you, for *you* won't be able to produce any collateral evidence beyond your own word, and John's a man that can do a little hard swearing if necessary. Very well then, that's understood. Now, I had the fancy that I wouldn't write this will quite in the common way, so I wrote it in a book, Mary, a printed book. And there's several thousand books in this house. But there! you needn't trouble yourself with them, for it isn't one of them. It's in safe keeping elsewhere: in a place where John can go and find it any day, if he only knew, and you can't. A good will it is: properly signed and witnessed, but I don't think you'll find the witnesses in a hurry.'

"Still I said nothing: if I had moved at all I must have taken hold of the old wretch and shaken him. He lay there laughing to himself, and at last he said:

"'Well, well, you've taken it very quietly, and as I want to start you both on equal terms, and John has a bit of a purchase in being able to go where the book is, I'll tell you just two other things which I didn't tell him. The will's in English, but you won't know that if ever you see it. That's one thing, and another is that when I'm gone you'll find an envelope in my desk directed to you, and inside it something that would help you to find it, if only you have the wits to use it.'

"In a few hours from that he was gone, and though I made an appeal to John Eldred about it—"

"John Eldred? I beg your pardon, Mrs. Simpson—I think I've seen a Mr. John Eldred. What is he like to look at?"

"It must be ten years since I saw him: he would be a thin elderly man now, and unless he has shaved them *off*, he has that sort of whiskers which people used to call Dundreary or Piccadilly something."

"—weepers. Yes, that *is* the man."

"Where did you come across him, Mr. Garrett?"

"I don't know if I could tell you," said Garrett mendaciously, "in some public place. But you hadn't finished."

"Really I had nothing much to add, only that John Eldred, of course, paid no attention whatever to my letters, and has enjoyed the estate ever since, while my daughter and I have had to take to the lodging-house business here, which I must say has not turned out by any means so unpleasant as I feared it might."

"But about the envelope."

"To be sure. Why, the puzzle turns on that. Give Mr. Garrett the paper out of my desk."

It was a small slip, with nothing whatever on it but five numerals, not divided or punctuated in any way: 11334.

Mr. Garrett pondered, but there was a light in his eye. Suddenly he "made a face," and then asked, "Do you suppose that Mr. Eldred can have any more clue than you have to the title of the book?"

"I have sometimes thought he must," said Mrs. Simpson, "and in this way: that my uncle must have made the will not very long before he died (that, I think, he said himself), and got rid of the book immediately afterwards. But all his books were very carefully catalogued: and John has the catalogue: and John was most particular that no books whatever should be sold out of the house. And I'm told that he is always journeying about to booksellers and libraries; so I fancy that he must have found out just which books are missing from my uncle's library of those which are entered in the catalogue, and must be hunting for them."

"Just so, just so," said Mr. Garrett, and relapsed into thought.

No later than next day he received a letter which, as he told Mrs. Simpson with great regret, made it absolutely necessary for him to cut short his stay at Burnstow.

Sorry as he was to leave them (and they were at least as sorry to part with him), he had begun to feel that a crisis, all-important to Mrs. (and shall we add, Miss?) Simpson, was very possibly supervening.

In the train Garrett was uneasy and excited. He racked his brains to think whether the press mark of the book which Mr. Eldred had been inquiring after was one in any way corresponding to the numbers on Mrs. Simpson's little bit of paper. But he found to his dismay that the shock of the previous week had really so upset him that he could neither remember any vestige of the title or nature of the book, or even of the locality to which he had gone to seek it. And yet all other parts of library topography and work were clear as ever in his mind.

And another thing—he stamped with annoyance as he thought of it—he had at first hesitated, and then had forgotten, to ask Mrs. Simpson for the name of the place where Eldred lived. That, however, he could write about.

At least he had his clue in the figures on the paper. If they referred to a press mark in his library, they were only susceptible of a limited number of interpretations. They might be divided into 1.13.34, 11.33.4, or 11.3.34. He could try all these in the space of a few minutes, and if any one were missing he had every means of tracing it. He got very quickly to work, though a few minutes had to be spent in explaining his early return to his landlady and his colleagues. 1.13.34. was in place and contained no extraneous writing. As he drew near to Class 11 in the same gallery, its association struck him like a chill. But he *must* go on. After a cursory glance at 11.33.4 (which first confronted him, and was a perfectly new book) he ran his eye along the line of quartos which fills 11.3. The gap he feared was there: 34 was out. A moment was spent in making sure that it had not been misplaced, and then he was off to the vestibule.

"Has 11.3.34 gone out? Do you recollect noticing that number?"

"Notice the number? What do you take me for, Mr. Garrett? There, take and look over the tickets for yourself, if you've got a free day before you."

"Well then, has a Mr. Eldred called again?—the old gentleman who came the day I was taken ill. Come! You'd remember him."

"What do you suppose? Of course I recollect of him: no, he haven't been in again, not since you went off for your 'oliday. And yet I seem to—there now. Roberts'll know. Roberts, do you recollect of the name of Heldred?"

"Not arf," said Roberts. "You mean the man that sent a bob over the price for the parcel, and I wish they all did."

"Do you mean to say you've been sending books to Mr. Eldred? Come, do speak up! Have you?"

"Well now, Mr. Garrett, if a gentleman sends the ticket all wrote correct and the secketry says this book may go and the box ready addressed sent with the note, and a sum of money sufficient to deefray the railway charges, what would be *your* action in the matter, Mr. Garrett, if I may take the liberty to ask such a question? Would you or would you not have taken the trouble to oblige, or would you have chucked the 'ole thing under the counter and—"

"You were perfectly right, of course, Hodgson—perfectly right: only, would you kindly oblige me by showing me the ticket Mr. Eldred sent, and letting me know his address?"

"To be sure, Mr. Garrett; so long as I'm not 'ectored about and informed that I don't know my duty, I'm willing to oblige in every way feasible to my power. There is the ticket on the file. J. Eldred, 11.3.34. Title of work: T—a—l—m—well, there, you can make what you like of it—not a novel, I should 'azard the guess. And here is Mr. Heldred's note applying for the book in question, which I see he terms it a track."

"Thanks, thanks: but the address? There's none on the note."

"Ah, indeed; well, now . . . stay now, Mr. Garrett, I 'ave it. Why, that note come inside of the parcel, which was directed very thought-ful to save all trouble, ready to be sent back with the book inside; and if I *have* made any mistake in this 'ole transaction, it lays just in the one point that I neglected to enter the address in my little book here what I keep. Not but what I dare say there was good reasons for me not entering of it: but there, I haven't the time, neither have you, I dare say, to go into 'em just now. And—no, Mr. Garrett, I do *not* carry it in my 'ed, else what would be the use of me keeping this little book here—just a ordinary common notebook, you see, which I make a practice of entering all such names and addresses in it as I see fit to do?"

"Admirable arrangement, to be sure—but—all right, thank you. When did the parcel go off?"

"Half-past ten, this morning."

"Oh, good; and it's just one now."

Garrett went upstairs in deep thought. How was he to get the address? A telegram to Mrs. Simpson: he might miss a train by waiting for the answer. Yes, there was one other way. She had said that Eldred lived on his uncle's estate. If this were so, he might find that place entered in the donation-book. That he could run through quickly, now that he knew the title of the book. The register was soon before him, and, knowing that the old man had died more than twenty years ago, he gave him a good margin, and turned back to 1870. There was but one entry possible. 1875, August 14th. *Talmud: Tractatus Middoth cum comm. R. Nachmanida.* Amstelod. 1707. Given by J. Rant, D.D., of Bretfield Manor."

A gazetteer showed Bretfield to be three miles from a small sta-tion on the main line. Now to ask the doorkeeper whether he recol-lected if the name on the parcel had been anything like Bretfield.

"No, nothing like. It was, now you mention it, Mr. Garrett, either Bredfield or Britfield, but nothing like that other name what you coated."

So far well. Next, a time-table. A train could be got in twenty minutes—taking two hours over the journey. The only chance, but one not to be missed; and the train was taken.

If he had been fidgety on the journey up, he was almost distracted on the journey down. If he found Eldred, what could he say? That it had been discovered that the book was a rarity and must be recalled?

An obvious untruth. Or that it was believed to contain important manuscript notes? Eldred would of course show him the book, from which
the leaf would already have been removed. He might, perhaps, find
traces of the removal—a torn edge of a fly-leaf probably—and who
could disprove, what Eldred was certain to say, that he too had noticed
and regretted the mutilation? Altogether the chase seemed very hopeless. The one chance was this. The book had left the library at 10.30: it
might not have been put into the first possible train, at 11.20. Granted
that, then he might be lucky enough to arrive simultaneously with it
and patch up some story which would induce Eldred to give it up.

It was drawing towards evening when he got out upon the platform of his station, and, like most country stations, this one seemed
unnaturally quiet. He waited about till the one or two passengers who
got out with him had drifted off, and then inquired of the stationmas-
ter whether Mr. Eldred was in the neighbourhood.

"Yes, and pretty near too, I believe. I fancy he means calling here
for a parcel he expects. Called for it once to-day already, didn't he,
Bob?" (to the porter).

"Yes, sir, he did; and appeared to think it was all along of me that
it didn't come by the two o'clock. Anyhow, I've got it for him now," and
the porter flourished a square parcel, which a glance assured Garrett
contained all that was of any importance to him at that particular
moment.

"Bretfield, sir? Yes—three miles just about. Short cut across
these three fields brings it down by half a mile. There: there's Mr.
Eldred's trap."

A dog-cart drove up with two men in it, of whom Garrett, gazing back as he crossed the little station yard, easily recognized one.
The fact that Eldred was driving was slightly in his favor—for most
likely he would nor open the parcel in the presence of his servant.
On the other hand, he would get home quickly, and unless Garrett
were there within a very few minutes of his arrival, all would be over.
He must hurry; and that he did. His short cut took him along one
side of a triangle, while the cart had two sides to traverse; and it was
delayed a little at the station so that Garrett was in the third of the
three fields when he heard the wheels fairly near. He had made the
best progress possible, but the pace at which the cart was coming
made him despair. At this rare it *must* reach home ten minutes before

him, and ten minutes would more than suffice for the fulfilment of Mr. Eldred's project.

It was just at this time that the luck fairly turned. The evening was still, and sounds came clearly. Seldom has any sound given greater relief than that which he now heard: that of the cart pulling up. A few words were exchanged, and it drove on. Garrett, halting in the utmost anxiety, was able to see as it drove past the stile (near which he now stood) that it contained only the servant and not Eldred: further, he made out that Eldred was following on foot. From behind the tall hedge by the stile leading into the road he watched the thin wiry figure pass quickly by with the parcel beneath its arm, and feeling in its pockets. Just as he passed the stile something fell out of a pocket upon the grass, but with so little sound that Eldred was not conscious of it. In a moment more it was safe for Garrett to cross the stile into the road and pick up—a box of matches. Eldred went on, and, as he went, his arms made hasty movements, difficult to interpret in the shadow of the trees that overhung the road. But, as Garrett followed cautiously, he found at various points the key to them—a piece of string, and then the wrapper of the parcel—meant to be thrown *over* the hedge, but sticking in it.

Now Eldred was walking slower, and it could just be made out that he had opened the book and was turning over the leaves. He stopped, evidently troubled by the failing light. Garrett slipped into a gate-opening, but still watched. Eldred, hastily looking around, sat down on a felled tree-trunk by the roadside and held the open book up close to his eyes. Suddenly he laid it, still open, on his knee, and felt in all his pockets: clearly in vain, and clearly to his annoyance. "You would be glad of your matches now," thought Garrett, Then he took hold of a leaf, and was carefully tearing it out, when two things happened. First, something black seemed to drop upon the white leaf and run down it, and then as Eldred started and was turning to look behind him, a little dark form appeared to rise out of the shadow behind the tree-trunk and from it two arms enclosing a mass of blackness came before Eldred's face and covered his head and neck. His legs and arms were wildly flourished, but no sound came. Then, there was no more movement. Eldred was alone. He had fallen back into the grass behind the tree-trunk. The book was cast into the roadway. Garrett, his anger and suspicion gone for the moment at the sight of this horrid struggle, rushed up with loud cries of "Help!" and so too, to his enormous relief, did a labourer who had just emerged from a field opposite. Together they bent over and supported Eldred, but to no purpose. The conclusion that he was dead was inevitable. "Poor gentleman" said Garrett to the labourer, when they had laid him down, "what happened to him, do you think?" "I wasn't two hundred yards away," said the man, "when I see Squire Eldred setting reading in his book, and to my thinking he was took with one of these fits—face seemed to go all over black." "Just so," said Garrett. "You didn't see anyone near him? It couldn't have been an assault?" "Not possible—no one couldn't have got away without you or me seeing them." "So I thought. Well, we must get some help, and the doctor and the policeman; and perhaps I had better give them this book."

It was obviously a case for an inquest, and obvious also that Garrett must stay at Bretfield and give his evidence. The medical inspection showed that, though some black dust was found on the face and in the mouth of the deceased, the cause of death was a shock to a weak heart, and not asphyxiation. The fateful book was produced, a respectable quarto printed wholly in Hebrew, and not of an aspect likely to excite even the most sensitive.

"You say, Mr. Garrett, that the deceased gentleman appeared at the moment before his attack to be tearing a leaf out of this book?"

"Yes; I think one of the fly-leaves."

"There is here a fly-leaf partially torn through. It has Hebrew writing on it. Will you kindly inspect it?"

"There are three names in English, sir, also, and a date. But I am sorry to say I cannot read Hebrew writing."

"Thank you. The names have the appearance of being signatures. They are John Rant, Walter Gibson, and James Frost, and the date is 20 July, 1875. Does anyone here know any of these names?"

The Rector, who was present, volunteered a statement that the uncle of the deceased, from whom he inherited, had been named Rant.

The book being handed to him, he shook a puzzled head. "This is not like any Hebrew I ever learnt."

"You are sure that it is Hebrew?"

"What? Yes—I suppose. . . . No—my dear sir, you are perfectly right—that is, your suggestion is exactly to the point. Of course—it is not Hebrew at all. It is English, and it is a will."

It did nor take many minutes to show that here was indeed a will of Dr. John Rant, bequeathing the whole of the property lately held by John Eldred to Mrs. Mary Simpson. Clearly the discovery of such a document would amply justify Mr. Eldred's agitation. As to the partial tearing of the leaf, the coroner pointed out that no useful purpose could be attained by speculations whose correctness it would never be possible to establish.

The Tractate Middoth was naturally taken in charge by the coroner for further investigation, and Mr. Garrett explained privately to him the history of it, and the position of events so far as he knew or guessed them.

He returned to his work next day, and on his walk to the station passed the scene of Mr. Eldred's catastrophe. He could hardly leave it without another look, though the recollection of what he had seen there made him shiver, even on that bright morning. He walked round, with some misgivings, behind the felled tree. Something dark that still lay there made him start back for a moment: but it hardly stirred. Looking closer, he saw that it was a thick black mass of cobwebs; and, as he stirred it gingerly with his stick, several large spiders ran out of it into the grass.

There is no great difficulty in imagining the steps by which William Garrett, from being an assistant in a great library, attained to his present position of prospective owner of Bretfield Manor, now in the occupation of his mother-in-law, Mrs. Mary Simpson.

THE STORY OF ST. VESPALUUS

Saki

"Tell me a story," said the Baroness, staring out despairingly at the rain; it was that light, apologetic sort of rain that looks as if it was going to leave off every minute and goes on for the greater part of the afternoon.

"What sort of story?" asked Clovis, giving his croquet mallet a valedictory shove into retirement.

"One just true enough to be interesting and not true enough to be tiresome," said the Baroness.

Clovis rearranged several cushions to his personal solace and satisfaction; he knew that the Baroness liked her guests to be comfortable, and he thought it right to respect her wishes in that particular.

"Have I ever told you the story of St. Vespaluus?" he asked.

"You've told me stories about grand-dukes and lion-tamers and financiers' widows and a postmaster in Herzegovina," said the Baroness, "and about an Italian jockey and an amateur governess who went to Warsaw, and several about your mother, but certainly never anything about a saint."

"This story happened a long while ago," he said, "in those uncomfortable piebald times when a third of the people were Pagan, and a third Christian, and the biggest third of all just followed whichever religion the Court happened to profess. There was a certain king called Hkrikros, who had a fearful temper and no immediate successor in his own family; his married sister, however, had provided him with a large stock of nephews from which to select his heir. And the most eligible and royally-approved of all these nephews was the sixteen-year-old Vespaluus. He was the best looking, and the best horseman and javelin-thrower, and had that priceless princely gift of being able to walk past a supplicant with an air of not having seen him, but would certainly have given something if he had. My mother has that gift to a certain extent; she can go smilingly and financially unscathed through a charity bazaar, and meet the organizers next day with a solicitous 'had I but known you were in need of funds' air that is really rather a triumph in audacity. Now Hkrikros was a Pagan of the first water, and kept the worship of the sacred serpents, who lived in a hallowed grove on a hill near the royal palace, up to a high pitch of enthusiasm. The common people were allowed to please themselves, within certain discreet limits, in the matter of private religion, but any official in the service of the Court who went over to the new cult was looked down on, literally as well as metaphorically, the looking down being done from the gallery that ran round the royal bear-pit. Consequently there was considerable scandal and consternation when the youthful Vespaluus appeared one day at a Court function with a rosary tucked into his belt, and announced in reply to angry questionings that he had decided to adopt Christianity, or at any rate to give it a trial. If it had been any of the other nephews the king would possibly have ordered something drastic in the way of scourging and banishment, but in the case of the favored Vespaluus he determined to look on the whole thing much as a modern father might regard the announced intention of his son to adopt the stage as a profession. He sent accordingly for the Royal Librarian. The royal library in those days was not a very extensive affair, and the keeper of the king's books had a great deal of leisure on his hands. Consequently he was in frequent demand for the settlement of other people's affairs when these strayed beyond normal limits and got temporarily unmanageable.

"'You must reason with Prince Vespaluus,' said the king, 'and impress on him the error of his ways. We cannot have the heir to the throne setting such a dangerous example.'

"'But where shall I find the necessary arguments?' asked the Librarian.

"'I give you free leave to pick and choose your arguments in the royal woods and coppices,' said the king; 'if you cannot get together some cutting observations and stinging retorts suitable to the occasion you are a person of very poor resource.'

"So the Librarian went into the woods and gathered a goodly selection of highly argumentative rods and switches, and then proceeded to reason with Vespaluus on the folly and iniquity and above all the unseemliness of his conduct. His reasoning left a deep impression on the young prince, an impression which lasted for many weeks, during which time nothing more was heard about the unfortunate lapse into Christianity. Then a further scandal of the same nature agitated the Court. At a time when he should have been engaged in audibly invoking the gracious protection and patronage of the holy serpents, Vespaluus was heard singing a chant in honour of St. Odilo of Cluny. The king was furious at this new outbreak, and began to take a gloomy view of the situation; Vespaluus was evidently going to show a dangerous obstinacy in persisting in his heresy. And yet there was nothing in his appearance to justify such perverseness; he had not the pale eye of the fanatic or the mystic look of the dreamer. On the contrary, he was quite the best-looking boy at Court; he had an elegant, well-knit figure, a healthy complexion, eyes the color of very ripe mulberries, and dark hair, smooth and very well cared for."

"It sounds like a description of what you imagine yourself to have been like at the age of sixteen," said the Baroness.

"My mother has probably been showing you some of my early photographs," said Clovis. Having turned the sarcasm into a compliment, he resumed his story.

"The king had Vespaluus shut up in a dark tower for three days, with nothing but bread and water to live on, the squealing and fluttering of bats to listen to, and drifting clouds to watch through one little window slit. The anti-Pagan section of the community began to talk portentously of the boy-martyr. The martyrdom was mitigated, as far as the food was concerned, by the carelessness of the tower warden, who once or twice left a portion of his own supper of broiled meat and fruit and wine by mistake in the prince's cell. After the punishment was over, Vespaluus was closely watched for any further symptom of religious perversity, for the king was determined to stand no more opposition on so important a matter, even from a favorite nephew. If there was any more of this nonsense, he said, the succession to the throne would have to be altered.

"For a time all went well; the festival of summer sports was approaching, and the young Vespaluus was too engrossed in wrestling and foot-running and javelin-throwing competitions to bother himself with the strife of conflicting religious systems. Then, however, came the great culminating feature of the summer festival, the ceremonial dance round the grove of the sacred serpents, and Vespaluus, as we should say, 'sat it out.' The affront to the State religion was too public and ostentatious to be overlooked, even if the king had been so minded, and he was not in the least so minded. For a day and a half he sat apart and brooded, and every one thought he was debating within himself the question of the young prince's death or pardon; as a matter of fact he was merely thinking out the manner of the boy's death. As the thing had to be done, and was bound to attract an enormous amount of public attention in any case, it was as well to make it as spectacular and impressive as possible.

"'Apart from his unfortunate taste in religions,' said the king, 'and his obstinacy in adhering to it, he is a sweet and pleasant youth, therefore it is meet and fitting that he should be done to death by the winged envoys of sweetness.'

"'Your Majesty means—?' said the Royal Librarian.

"'I mean,' said the king, 'that he shall be stung to death by bees. By the royal bees, of course.'

"'A most elegant death,' said the Librarian.

"'Elegant and spectacular, and decidedly painful,' said the king; 'it fulfils all the conditions that could be wished for.'

"The king himself thought out all the details of the execution ceremony. Vespaluus was to be stripped of his clothes, his hands were to be bound behind him, and he was then to be slung, in a recumbent position immediately above three of the largest of the royal beehives, so that the least movement of his body, would bring him in jarring contact with them. The rest could be safely left to the bees. The death throes, the king computed, might last anything from fifteen to forty minutes, though there was division of opinion and considerable wagering among the other nephews as to whether death might not be almost instantaneous, or, on the other hand, whether it might not be deferred for a couple of hours. Anyway, they all agreed, it was vastly preferable to being thrown down into an evil smelling bear-pit and being clawed and mauled to death by imperfectly carnivorous animals.

"It so happened, however, that the keeper of the royal hives had leanings towards Christianity himself, and moreover, like most of the

Court officials, he was very much attached to Vespaluus. On the eve of the execution, therefore, he busied himself with removing the stings from all the royal bees; it was a long and delicate operation, but he was an expert bee-master, and by working hard nearly all night he succeeded in disarming all, or almost all, of the hive inmates."

"I didn't know you could take the sting from a live bee," said the Baroness incredulously.

"Every profession has its secrets," replied Clovis "if it hadn't it wouldn't be a profession. Well, the moment for the execution arrived; the king and Court took their places, and accommodation was found for as many of the populace as wished to witness the unusual spectacle. Fortunately the royal bee-yard was of considerable dimensions, and was commanded, moreover, by the terraces that ran round the royal gardens; with a little squeezing and the erection of a few platforms room was found for everybody. Vespaluus was carried into the open space in front of the hives, blushing and slightly embarrassed, but not at all displeased at the attention which was being centered on him."

"He seems to have resembled you in more things than in appearance," said the Baroness

"Don't interrupt at a critical point in the story," said Clovis. "As soon as he had been carefully adjusted in the prescribed position over the hives, and almost before the gaolers had time to retire to a safe distance, Vespaluus gave a lusty and well-aimed kick, which sent all three hives toppling one over another. The next moment he was wrapped from head to foot in bees; each individual insect nursed the dreadful and humiliating knowledge that in this supreme hour of catastrophe it could not sting, but each felt that it ought to pretend to. Vespaluus squealed and wriggled with laughter, for he was being tickled nearly to death, and now and again he gave a furious kick and used a bad word as one of the few bees that had escaped disarmament got its protest home. But the spectators saw with amazement that he showed no signs of approaching death agony, and as the bees dropped wearily away in clusters from his body his flesh was seen to be as white and smooth as before the ordeal, with a shiny glaze from the honey-smear of innumerable bee-feet, and here and there a small red spot where one of the rare stings had left its mark. It was obvious that a miracle had been performed in his favor, and one loud murmur, of astonishment or exultation, rose from the onlooking crowd. The king gave orders for Vespaluus to be taken down to await further orders, and stalked silently back to his midday meal, at which he was careful to eat heartily and drink copiously as though nothing unusual had happened. After dinner he sent for the Royal Librarian.

"'What is the meaning of this fiasco?' he demanded.

"'Your Majesty,' said that official, 'either there is something radically wrong with the bees—'

"'There is nothing wrong with my bees,' said the king haughtily, 'they are the best bees.'

"'Or else,' said the Librarian, 'there is something irremediably right about Prince Vespaluus.'

"'If Vespaluus is right I must be wrong,' said the king.

"The Librarian was silent for a moment. Hasty speech has been the downfall of many; ill-considered silence was the undoing of the luckless Court functionary.

"Forgetting the restraint due to his dignity, and the golden rule which imposes repose of mind and body after a heavy meal, the king rushed upon the keeper of the royal books and hit him repeatedly and promiscuously over the head with an ivory chessboard, a pewter wine-flagon, and a brass candlestick; he knocked him violently and often against an iron torch sconce, and kicked him thrice round the banqueting chamber with rapid, energetic kicks. Finally, he dragged him down a long passage by the hair of his head and flung him out of a window into the courtyard below."

"Was he much hurt?" asked the Baroness.

"More hurt than surprised," said Clovis. "You see, the king was notorious for his violent temper. However, this was the first time he had let himself go so unrestrainedly on the top of a heavy meal. The Librarian lingered for many days—in fact, for all I know, he may have ultimately recovered, but Hkrikros died that same evening. Vespaluus had hardly finished getting the honey stains off his body before a hurried deputation came to put the coronation oil on his head. And what with the publicly-witnessed miracle and the accession of a Christian sovereign, it was not surprising that there was a general scramble of converts to the new religion. A hastily consecrated bishop was overworked with a rush of baptisms in the hastily improvised Cathedral of St. Odilo. And the boy-martyr that might-have-been was transposed in the popular imagination into a royal boy-saint, whose fame attracted throngs of curious and devout sightseers to the capital. Vespaluus who was busily engaged in organizing the games and athletic contests that were to mark the commencement of his reign, had no time to give heed to the religious fervour which was effervescing round his personality; the first indication he had of the existing state of affairs was when the Court Chamberlain (a recent and very ardent addition to the Christian community) brought for his approval the outlines of a projected ceremonial cutting-down of the idolatrous serpent-grove.

"'Your Majesty will be graciously pleased to cut down the first tree with a specially consecrated axe,' said the obsequious official.

"'I'll cut off your head first, with any axe that comes handy,' said Vespaluus indignantly; 'do you suppose that I'm going to begin my reign by mortally affronting the sacred serpents? It would be most unlucky.'

"'But your Majesty's Christian principles?' exclaimed the bewildered Chamberlain.

"'I never had any,' said Vespaluus; 'I used to pretend to be a Christian convert just to annoy Hkrikros. He used to fly into such delicious tempers. And it was rather fun being whipped and scolded and shut up in a tower all for nothing. But as to turning Christian in real earnest, like you people seem to do, I couldn't think of such a thing. And the holy and esteemed serpents have always helped me when I've prayed to them for success in my running and wrestling and hunting, and it was through their distinguished intercession that the bees were not able to hurt me with their stings. It would be black ingratitude to turn against their worship at the very outset of my reign. I hate you for suggesting it.'

"The Chamberlain wrung his hands despairingly.

"'But, your Majesty,' he wailed, 'the people are reverencing you as a saint, and the nobles are being Christianized in batches, and neighboring potentates of that Faith are sending special envoys to welcome you as a brother. There is some talk of making you the patron saint of beehives, and a certain shade of honey-yellow has been christened Vespaluusian gold at the Emperor's Court. You can't surely go back on all this.'

"'I don't mind being reverenced and greeted and honoured,' said Vespaluus; 'I don't even mind being sainted in moderation, as long as I'm not expected to be saintly as well. But I wish you clearly and finally to understand that I will not give up the worship of the august and auspicious serpents."

"There was a world of unspoken bear-pit in the way he uttered those last words, and the mulberry-dark eyes flashed dangerously.

"'A new reign,' said the Chamberlain to himself. 'but the same old temper.'

"Finally, as a State necessity, the matter of the religions was compromised. At stated intervals the king appeared before his subjects in the national cathedral in the character of St. Vespaluus, and the idolatrous grove was gradually pruned and lopped away till nothing remained of it. But the sacred and esteemed serpents were removed to a private shrubbery in the royal gardens, where Vespaluus the Pagan and certain members of his household devoutly and decently worshipped them. That possibly is the reason why the boy-king's success in sports and hunting never deserted him to the end of his days, and that is also the reason why, in spite of the popular veneration for his sanctity, he never received official canonization."

"It has stopped raining," said the Baroness.

THE TROUBLE OF
MARCIE FLINT

John Cheever

"THIS IS BEING WRITTEN ABOARD THE S. S. AUGUSTUS, THREE DAYS AT sea. My suitcase is full of peanut butter, and I am a fugitive from the suburbs of all large cities. What holes! The suburbs, I mean. God preserve me from the camaraderie of commuting trains, and even from the lovely ladies taking in their asters and their roses at dusk lest the frost kill them, and from ladies with their heads whirling with civic zeal. I'm off to Torino, where the girls love peanut butter and the world is a man's castle and . . ." There was absolutely nothing wrong with the suburb (Shady Hill) from which Charles Flint was fleeing, his age is immaterial, and he was no stranger to Torino, having been there for three months recently on business.

"God preserve me," he continued, "from women who dress like *toreros* to go to the supermarket, and from cowhide dispatch cases, and from flannels and gabardines. Preserve me from word games and adulterers, from basset hounds and swimming pools and frozen canapés and Bloody Marys and smugness and syringa bushes and P.T.A. meetings." On and on he wrote, while the *Augustus*, traveling at seventeen knots, took a course due east; they would raise the Azores in a day.

Like all bitter men, Flint knew less than half the story and was more interested in unloading his own peppery feelings than in learning the truth. Marcie, the wife from whom he was fleeing, was a dark-haired, dark-eyed woman—not young by any stretch of the imagination but gifted with great stores of feminine sweetness and gallantry. She had not told her neighbors that Charlie had left her; she had not even called her lawyer; but she had fired the cook, and she now took a south-southwest course between the stove and the sink, cooking the children's supper. It was not in her to review the past, as her husband would, or to inspect the forces that could put an ocean between a couple who had been cheerfully married for fifteen years. There had been, she felt, a slight difference in their points of view during his recent absence on business, for while he always wrote that he missed her, he also wrote that he was dining at the Superga six nights a week and having a wonderful time. He had only planned to be away for six weeks, and when this stretched out to three months, she found that it was something to be borne.

Her neighbors had stood by her handsomely during the first weeks, but she knew, herself, that an odd woman can spoil a dinner party, and as Flint continued to stay away, she found that she had more and more lonely nights to get through. Now, there were two aspects to the night life of Shady Hill; there were the parties, of course, and then there was another side—a regular Santa Claus's workshop of madrigal singers, political discussion groups, recorder groups, dancing schools, confirmation classes, committee meetings, and lectures on literature, philosophy, city planning, and pest control. The bright banner of stars in heaven has probably never before been stretched above such a picture of nocturnal industry. Marcie, having a sweet, clear voice, joined a madrigal group that met on Thursdays and a political workshop that met on Mondays. Once she made herself available, she was sought as a committeewoman, although it was hard to say why; she almost never opened her mouth. She finally accepted a position on the Village Council, in the third month of Charlie's absence, mostly to keep herself occupied.

Virtuousness, reason, civic zeal, and loneliness all contributed to poor Marcie's trouble. Charlie, far away in Torino, could imagine her well enough standing in their lighted doorway on the evening of his return, but could he imagine her groping under the bed for the children's shoes or pouring bacon fat into an old soup can? "Daddy has to stay in Italy in order to make the money to buy the things we need," she told the children. But when Charlie called her from abroad, as he did once a week, he always seemed to have been drinking. Regard this sweet woman, then, singing "Hodie Christus Natus Est," studying Karl Marx, and sitting on a hard chair at meetings of the Village Council.

If there was anything really wrong with Shady Hill, anything that you could put your finger on, it was the fact that the village had no public library—no foxed copies of Pascal, smelling of cabbage; no broken sets of Dostoevski and George Eliot; no Galsworthy, even; no Barrie and no Bennett. This was the chief concern of the Village Council during Marcie's term. The library partisans were mostly newcomers to the village; the opposition whip was Mrs. Selfredge, a member of the Council and a very decorous woman, with blue eyes of astonishing brilliance and inexpressiveness. Mrs. Selfredge often spoke of the chosen quietness of their life. "We never go out," she would say, but in such a way that she seemed to be expressing not some choice but a deep vein of loneliness. She was married to a wealthy man much older than herself, and they had no children; indeed, the most indirect mention of sexual fact brought a deep color to Mrs. Selfredge's face. She took the position that a library belonged in that category of public service that might make Shady Hill attractive to a development. This was not blind prejudice. Carsen Park, the next village, had let a development inside its boundaries, with disastrous results to the people already living there. Their taxes had been doubled, their schools had been ruined. That there was any connection between reading and real estate was disputed by the partisans of the library, until a horrible murder—three murders, in fact—took place in one of the cheesebox houses in the Carsen Park development, and the library project was buried with the victims.

From the terraces of the Superga you can see all of Torino and the snow-covered mountains around, and a man drinking wine there might not think of his wife attending a meeting of the Village Council. This was a board of ten men and two women, headed by the Mayor, who screened the projects that came before them. The Council met in the Civic Center, an old mansion that had been picked up for back taxes. The board room had been the parlor. Easter eggs had been hidden here, children had pinned paper tails on paper donkeys, fires had burned on the hearth, and a Christmas tree had stood in the corner;

but once the house had become the property of the village, a consci-
entious effort seems to have been made to exorcise these gentle
ghosts. Raphael's self-portrait and the pictures of the Broken Bridge at
Avignon and the Avon at Stratford were taken down and the walls were
painted a depressing shade of green. The fireplace remained, but the
flue was sealed up and the bricks were spread with green paint. A track
of fluorescent tubing across the ceiling threw a withering light down
into the faces of the Village Council members and made them all look
haggard and tired. The room made Marcie uncomfortable. In its harsh
light her sweetness was unavailing, and she felt not only bored but
somehow painfully estranged.

On this particular night they discussed water taxes and parking
meters, and then the Mayor brought up the public library for the last
time. "Of course, the issue is closed," he said, "but we've heard everyone all along, on both sides. There's one more man who wants to speak
to us, and I think we ought to hear him. He comes from Maple Dell."
Then he opened the door from the board room into the corridor and
let Noel Mackham in.

Now, the neighborhood of Maple Dell was more like a development than anything else in Shady Hill. It was the kind of place where
the houses stand cheek by jowl, all of them white frame, all of them
built twenty years ago, and parked beside each was a car that seemed
more substantial than the house itself, as if this were a fragment of
some nomadic culture. And it was a kind of spawning ground, a place
for bearing and raising the young and for nothing else—for who would
ever come back to Maple Dell? Who, in the darkest night, would ever
think with longing of the three upstairs bedrooms and the leaky toilet
and the sour-smelling halls? Who would ever come back to the little
living room where you couldn't swing a cat around without knocking
down the colored photograph of Mount Rainier? Who would ever
come back to the chair that bit you in the bum and the obsolete TV
set and the bent ashtray with its pressed-steel statue of a naked
woman doing a scarf dance?

"I understand that the business is closed," Mackham said, "but I
just wanted to go on record as being in favor of a public library. It's
been on my conscience."

He was not much of an advocate for anything. He was tall. His
hair had begun an erratic recession, leaving him with some sparse fluff

to comb over his bald brow. His features were angular; his skin was bad. There were no deep notes to his voice. Its range seemed confined to a delicate hoarseness—a monotonous and laryngitic sound that aroused in Marcie, as if it had been some kind of Hungarian music, feelings of irritable melancholy. "I just wanted to say a few words in favor of a public library," he rasped. "When I was a kid we were poor. There wasn't much good about the way we lived, but there was this Carnegie Library. I started going there when I was about eight. I guess I went there regularly for ten years. I read everything—philosophy, novels, technical books, poetry, ships' logs. I even read a cookbook. For me, this library amounted to the difference between life and death. It meant the difference between success and failure. When I remember the thrill I used to get out of cracking a good book, I just hate to think of bringing my kids up in a place where there isn't any library."

"Well, of course we know what you mean," Mayor Simmons said. "But I don't think that's quite the question. The question is not one of denying books to children. Most of us in Shady Hill have libraries of our own.

Mark Barrett got to his feet. "And I'd like to throw in a word about poor boys and reading, if I might," he said, in a voice so full of color and virility that everyone smiled. "I was a poor boy myself," he said cheerfully, "and I'm not ashamed to say so, and I'd just like to throw in—for what it's worth—that I never put my nose inside a public library, except to get out of the rain, or maybe follow a pretty girl. I just don't want anybody to be left with the impression that a public library is the road to success."

"I didn't say that a public library was the road to—"

"Well, you *implied* it!" Barrett shouted, and he seated himself with a big stir. His chair creaked, and by bulging his muscles a little he made his garters, braces, and shoes all sound.

"I only wanted to say—" Mackham began again.

"You *implied* it!" Barrett shouted.

"Just because *you* can't read," Mackham said, "it doesn't follow—"

"Damn it, man, I didn't say that I couldn't read!" Barrett was on his feet again.

"Please, gentlemen! Please! Please!" Mayor Simmons said. "Let's keep our remarks temperate."

"I'm not going to sit here and have someone who lives in Maple

Dell tell me the reason he's such a hot rock is because he read a lot of books!" Barrett shouted. "Books have their place. I won't deny it. But no book ever helped me to get where I am, and from where I am I can spit on Maple Dell. As for my kids, I want them out in the fresh air playing ball, not reading cookbooks."

"Please, Mark. Please," the Mayor said. And then he turned to Mrs. Selfredge and asked her to move that the meeting be adjourned.

"My day, my hour, my moment of revelation," Charlie wrote, in his sun-deck cabin on the *Augustus*, "came on a Sunday, when I had been home eight days. Oh God, was I happy! I spent most of the day putting up storm windows, and I like working on my house. Things like putting up storm windows. When the work was done, I put the ladder away and grabbed a towel and my swimming trunks and walked over to the Townsends' swimming pool. They were away, but the pool hadn't been drained. I put on my trunks and dove in and I remember seeing—way, way up in the top of one of the pine trees—a brassiere that I guess the Townsend kids had snitched and heaved up there in midsummer, the screams of dismay from their victim having long since been carried away on the west wind. The water was very cold, and blood pressure or some other medical reason may have accounted for the fact that when I got out of the pool and dressed I was nearly busting with happiness. I walked back to the house, and when I stepped inside it was so quiet that I wondered if anything had gone wrong. It was not an ominous silence—it was just that I wondered why the clock should sound so loud. Then I went upstairs and found Marcie asleep in our bedroom. She was covered with a light wrap that had slipped from her shoulders and breasts. Then I heard Henry and Katie's voices, and I went to the back bedroom window. This looked out onto the garden, where a gravel path that needed weeding went up a little hill. Henry and Katie were there. Katie was scratching in the gravel with a stick—some message of love, I guess. Henry had one of those broad-winged planes—talismanic planes, really—made of balsa wood and propelled by a rubber band. He twisted the band by turning the propeller, and I could see his lips moving as he counted. Then, when the rubber was taut, he set his feet apart in the gravel, like a marksman—Katie watched none of this—and sent the plane up. The wings of the plane were pale in the early dark, and then I saw it climb out of the shade up to where the sun washed it with yellow light. With not much more force than a moth, it soared and circled and meandered and came slowly down again into the shade and crashed on the peony hedge. 'I got it up again!' I heard Henry shout. 'I got it up into the light.' Katie went on writing her message in the dirt. And then, like some trick in the movies, I saw myself as my son, standing in a like garden and sending up out of the dark a plane, an arrow, a tennis ball, a stone—anything—while my sister drew hearts in the gravel. The memory of how deep this impulse to reach into the light had been completely charmed me, and I watched the boy send the plane up again and again.

"Then, still feeling very springy and full of fun, I walked back toward the door, stopping to admire the curve of Marcie's breasts and deciding, in a blaze of charity, to let her sleep. I felt so good that I needed a drink—not to pick me up but to dampen my spirits—a libation, anyhow—and I poured some whiskey in a glass. Then I went into the kitchen to get some ice, and I noticed that ants had got in somehow. This was surprising, because we never had much trouble with ants. Spiders, yes. Before the equinoctial hurricanes—even before the barometer had begun to fall—the house seemed to fill up with spiders, as if they sensed the trouble in the air. There would be spiders in the bathtubs and spiders in the living room and spiders in the kitchen, and, walking down the long upstairs hallway before a storm, you could sometimes feel the thread of a web break against your face. But we had had almost no trouble with ants. Now, on this autumn afternoon, thousands of ants broke out of the kitchen woodwork and threw a double line across the drainboard and into the sink, where there seemed to be something they wanted.

"I found some ant poison at the back of the broom-closet shelf, a little jar of brown stuff that I'd bought from Timmons in the village years ago. I put a generous helping of this into a saucer and put it on the drainboard. Then I took my drink and a piece of the Sunday paper out onto the terrace in front of the house. The house faced west, so I had more light than the children, and I felt so happy that even the news in the papers seemed cheerful. No kings had been assassinated in the rainy back streets of Marseille; no storms were brewing in the Balkans; no clerkly Englishman—the admiration of his landlady and his aunts—had dissolved the remains of a young lady in an acid bath;

no jewels, even, had been stolen. And that sometime power of the Sunday paper to evoke an anxious, rain-wet world of fallen crowns and inevitable war seemed gone. Then the sun withdrew from my paper and from the chair where I sat, and I wished I had put on a sweater.

"It was late in the season—the salt of change was in the air—and this tickled me too. Last Sunday, or the Sunday before, the terrace would have been flooded with light. Then I thought about other places where I would like to be—Nantucket, with only a handful of people left and the sailing fleet depleted and the dunes casting, as they never do in the summer, a dark shadow over the bathing beach. And I thought about the Vineyard and the farina-colored bluffs and the purple autumn sea and that stillness in which you might hear, from way out in the Sound, the rasp of a block on a traveler as a sailboat there came about. I tasted my whiskey and gave my paper a shake, but the view of the golden light on the grass and the trees was more compelling than the news, and now mixed up with my memories of the sea islands was the whiteness of Marcie's thighs.

"Then I was seized by some intoxicating pride in the hour, by the joy and the naturalness of my relationship to the scene, and by the ease with which I could put my hands on what I needed. I thought again of Marcie sleeping and that I would have my way there soon—it would be a way of expressing this pride. And then, listening for the voices of my children and not hearing them, I decided to celebrate the hour as it passed. I put the paper down and ran up the stairs. Marcie was still sleeping and I stripped off my clothes and lay down beside her, waking her from what seemed to be a pleasant dream, for she smiled and drew me to her."

To get back to Marcie and her trouble: She put on her coat after the meeting was adjourned and said, "Good night. Good night . . . I'm expecting him home next week." She was not easily upset, but she suddenly felt that she had looked straight at stupidity and unfairness. Going down the stairs behind Mackham, she felt a powerful mixture of pity and sympathy for the stranger and some clear anger toward her old friend Mark Barrett. She wanted to apologize, and she stopped Mackham in the door and said that she had some cheerful memories of her own involving a public library.

As it happened, Mrs. Selfredge and Mayor Simmons were the last to leave the board room. The Mayor waited, with his hand on the light switch, for Mrs. Selfredge, who was putting on her white gloves. "I'm glad the library's over and done with," he said. "I have a few misgivings, but right now I'm against anything public, anything that would make this community attractive to a development." He spoke with feeling, and at the word "development" a ridge covered with identical houses rose in his mind. It seemed wrong to him that the houses he imagined should be identical and that they should be built of green wood and false stone. It seemed wrong to him that young couples should begin their lives in an atmosphere that lacked grace, and it seemed wrong to him that the rows of houses could not, for long, preserve their slender claim on propriety and would presently become unsightly tracts. "Of course, it isn't a question of keeping children from books," he repeated. "We all have libraries of our own. There isn't any problem. I suppose you were brought up in a house with a library?"

"Oh yes, yes," said Mrs. Selfredge. The Mayor had turned off the light, and the darkness covered and softened the lie she had told. Her father had been a Brooklyn patrolman, and there had not been a book in his house. He had been an amiable man—not very sweet-smelling—who talked to all the children on his beat. Slovenly and jolly, he had spent the years of his retirement drinking beer in the kitchen in his underwear, to the deep despair and shame of his only child.

The Mayor said good night to Mrs. Selfredge on the sidewalk, and standing there she overheard Marcie speaking to Mackham. "I'm terribly sorry about Mark, about what he said," Marcie said. "We've all had to put up with him at one time or another. But why don't you come back to my house for a drink? Perhaps we could get the library project moving again."

So it wasn't over and done with, Mrs. Selfredge thought indignantly. They wouldn't rest until Shady Hill was nothing but developments from one end to the other. The colorless, hard-pressed people of the Carsen Park project, with their flocks of children, and their monthly interest payments, and their picture windows, and their view of identical houses and treeless, muddy, unpaved streets seemed to threaten her most cherished concepts—her lawns, her pleasures, her property rights, even her self-esteem.

Mr. Selfredge, an intelligent and elegant old gentleman, was waiting up for his Little Princess and she told him her troubles. Mr. Selfredge had retired from the banking business—mercifully, for whenever he stepped out into the world today he was confronted with the deterioration of those qualities of responsibility and initiative that had made the world of his youth selective, vigorous, and healthy. He knew a great deal about Shady Hill—he even recognized Mackham's name. "The bank holds the mortgage on his house," he said. "I remember when he applied for it. He works for a textbook company in New York that has been accused by at least one Congressional committee of publishing subversive American histories. I wouldn't worry about him, my dear, but if it would put your mind at ease, I could easily write a letter to the paper."

"But the children were not as far away as I thought," Charlie wrote, aboard the *Augustus*. "They were still in the garden. And the significance of that hour for them, I guess, was that it was made for stealing food. I have to make up or imagine what took place with them. They may have been drawn into the house by a hunger as keen as mine. Coming into the hall and listening for sounds, they would hear nothing, and they would open the icebox slowly, so that the sound of the heavy latch wouldn't be heard. The icebox must have been disappointing, because Henry wandered over to the sink and began to eat the sodium arsenate. 'Candy,' he said, and Katie joined him, and they had a fight over the remaining poison. They must have stayed in the kitchen for quite a while, because they were still in the kitchen when Henry began to retch. 'Well, don't get it all *over* everything.' Katie said. 'Come on outside.' She was beginning to feel sick herself, and they went outside and hid under a syringa bush, which is where I found them when I dressed and came down.

"They told me what they had eaten, and I woke Marcie up and then ran downstairs again and called Doc Mullens. 'Jesus Christ!' he said. 'I'll be right over.' He asked me to read the label on the jar, but all it said was sodium arsenate; it didn't say the percentage. And when I told him I had bought it from Timmons, he told me to call and ask Timmons who the manufacturer was. The line was busy, and so, while Marcie was running back and forth between the two sick children, I jumped into the car and drove to the village. There was a lot of light in the sky, I remember, but it was nearly dark in the streets. Timmons' drugstore was the only place that was lighted, and it was the kind of place that seems to subsist on the crumbs from other tradesmen's tables. This late hour when all the other stores were shut was Timmons' finest. The crazy jumble of displays in his window—irons, ashtrays, Venus in a truss, ice bags, and perfumes—was continued into the store itself, which seemed like a pharmaceutical curiosity shop or fun house: a storeroom for cardboard beauties anointing themselves with sun oil; for cardboard mountain ranges in the alpine glow, advertising pine-scented soap; for bookshelves, and bins filled with card-table covers, and plastic water pistols. The drugstore was a little like a house, too, for Mrs. Timmons stood behind the soda fountain, a neat and anxious-looking woman, with photographs of her three sons (one dead) in uniform arranged against the mirror at her back, and when Timmons himself came to the counter, he was chewing on something and wiped the crumbs of a sandwich off his mouth with the back of his hand. I showed him the jar and said, 'The kids ate some of this about an hour ago. I called Doc Mullens, and he told me to come and see you. It doesn't say what the percentage of arsenate is, and he thought if you could remember where you got it, we could telephone the manufacturer and find out.'

"'The children are poisoned?' Timmons asked.

"'Yes!' I said.

"'You didn't buy this merchandise from me,' he said.

"The clumsiness of his lie and the stillness in that crazy store made me feel hopeless. 'I *did* buy it from you, Mr. Timmons,' I said. 'There's no question about that. My children are deathly sick. I want you to tell me where you got the stuff.'

"'You didn't buy this merchandise from me,' he said.

"I looked at Mrs. Timmons, but she was mopping the counter; she was deaf. 'God damn it to hell, Timmons!' I shouted, and I reached over the counter and got him by the shirt. You look up your records! You look up your Goddamned records and tell me where this stuff came from.'

"'We know what it is to lose a son,' Mrs. Timmons said at my back. There was nothing full to her voice; nothing but the monotonous, the gritty, music of grief and need. 'You don't have to tell us anything about that.'

"'You didn't buy this merchandise from me,' Timmons said once more, and I wrenched his shirt until the buttons popped, and then I let him go. Mrs. Timmons went on mopping the counter. Timmons stood with his head so bent in shame that I couldn't see his eyes at all, and I went out of the store.

"When I got back, Doe Mullens was in the upstairs hall, and the worst was over. 'A little more or a little less and you might have lost them,' he said cheerfully. 'But I've used a stomach pump, and I think they'll be all right. Of course, it's a heavy poison, and Marcie will have to keep specimens for a week—it's apt to stay in the kidneys—but I think they'll be all right.' I thanked him and walked out to the car with him, and then I came back to the house and went upstairs to where the children had been put to bed in the same room for company and made some foolish talk with them. Then I heard Marcie weeping in our bedroom, and I went there. 'It's all right, baby,' I said. 'It's all right now. They're all right.' But when I put my arm around her, her wailing and sobbing got louder, and I asked her what she wanted.

"'I want a divorce,' she sobbed.

"'What?'

"'I want a divorce. I can't bear living like this any more. I can't bear it. Every time they have a head cold, every time they're late from school, whenever anything bad happens, I think it's retribution. I can't stand it.'

"'Retribution for what?'

"'While you were away, I made a mess of things.'

"'What do you mean?'

"'With somebody.'

"'Who?'

"'Noel Mackham. You don't know him. He lives in Maple Dell.'

"Then for a long time I didn't say anything—what could I say? And suddenly she turned on me in fury.

"'Oh, I knew you'd be like this, I knew you'd be like this, I knew you'd blame me!' she said. 'But it wasn't my fault, it just wasn't my fault. I knew you'd blame me, I knew you'd blame me, I knew you'd be like this, and I...'

"I didn't hear much else of what she said, because I was packing a suitcase. And then I kissed the kids good-by, caught a train to the city, and boarded the *Augustus* next morning."

What happened to Marcie was this: The evening paper printed Selfredge's letter, the day after the Village Council meeting, and she read it. She called Mackham on the telephone. He said he was going to ask the editor to print an answer he had written, and that he would stop by her house at eight o'clock to show her the carbon copy. She had planned to eat dinner with her children, but just before she sat down, the bell rang, and Mark Barrett dropped in. "Hi, honey," he said. "Make me a drink?" She made him some Martinis, and he took off his hat and topcoat and got down to business. "I understand you had that meatball over here for a drink last night."

"Who told you, Mark? Who in the world told you?"

"Helen Selfredge. It's no secret. She doesn't want the library thing reopened."

"It's like being followed. I hate it."

"Don't let that bother you, sweetie." He held out his glass, and she filled it again. "I'm just here as a neighbor—a friend of Charlie's— and what's the use of having friends and neighbors if they can't give you advice? Mackham is a meatball, and Mackham is a wolf. With Charlie away, I feel kind of like an older brother—I want to keep an eye on you. I want you to promise me that you won't have that meatball in your house again."

"I can't, Mark. He's coming tonight."

"No, he isn't, sweetie. You're going to call him up and tell him not to come."

"He's human, Mark."

"Now, listen to me, sweetie. You listen to me. I'm about to tell you something. Of course he's human, but so is the garbage man and the cleaning woman. I'm about to tell you something very interesting. When I was in school, there was a meatball just like Mackham. Nobody liked him. Nobody spoke to him. Well, I was a high-spirited kid, Marcie, with plenty of friends, and I began to wonder about this meatball. I began to wonder if it wasn't my responsibility to befriend him and make him feel that he was a member of the group. Well, I spoke to him, and I wouldn't be surprised if I was the first person who did. I took a walk with him. I asked him up to my room. I did everything I could to make him feel accepted.

"It was a terrible mistake. First, he began going around the school telling everybody that he and I were going to do this and he and I were going to do that. then he went to the Dean's office and had himself moved into my room without consulting me. Then his mother began to send me these lousy cookies, and his sister—I'd never laid eyes on her—began to write me love letters, and he got to be such a leech that I had to tell him to lay off. I spoke frankly to him; I told him the only reason I'd ever spoken to him was because I pitied him. This didn't make any difference. When you're stuck with a meatball, it doesn't matter what you tell them. He kept hanging around, waiting for me after classes, and after football practice he was always down in the locker room. It go so bad that we had to give me the works. We asked him up to Pete Fenton's room for a cup of cocoa, roughed him up. threw his clothes out the window, painted his rear end with iodine, and stuck his had in a pail of water until he damned near drowned.

Mark lighted a cigarette and finished his drink. "But what I mean to say is that if you get mixed up with a meatball you're bound to regret it. Your feelings may be kindly and generous in the beginning, but you'll do more harm than good before you're through. I want you to call up Mackham and tell him not to come. Tell him you're sick. I don't want him in your house."

"Mackham isn't coming here to visit me, Mark. He's coming here to tell me about the letter he wrote for the paper."

"I'm ordering you to call him up.'"

"I won't, Mark."

"You go to that telephone."

"Please, Mark. Don't shout at me.'"

"You go to that telephone."

"Please get out of my house, Mark."

"You're an intractable, weak-headed, God-damned fool!" he shouted. "That's the trouble with you!" Then he went.

She ate supper alone, and was not finished when Mackham came. It was raining, and he wore a heavy coat and a shabby hat—saved, she guessed, for storms. The hat made him look like an old man. He seemed heavy-spirited and tired, and he unwound a long yellow woolen scarf from around his neck. He had seen the editor. The editor would not print his answer. Marcie asked him if he would like a drink, and when he didn't reply, she asked him a second time. "Oh, no, thank you," he said heavily, and he looked into her eyes with a smile of such engulfing weariness that she thought he must be sick. Then he came up to her as if he were going to touch her, and she went into the

library and sat on the sofa. Halfway across the room he saw that he had
forgotten to take off his rubbers.

"Oh, I'm sorry," he said. "I'm afraid I've tracked mud—"

"It doesn't matter."

"It would matter if this were *my* house."

"It doesn't matter here."

He sat in a chair near the door and began to take off his rubbers,
and it was the rubbers that did it. Watching him cross his knees and
remove the rubber from one foot and then the other so filled Marcie
with pity at this clumsy vision of humanity and its touching high purpose in the face of adversity that he must have seen by her pallor or
her dilated eyes that she was helpless.

The sea and the decks are dark. Charlie can hear the voices from the
bar at the end of the passageway, and he has told his story, but he does
not stop writing. They are coming into warmer water and fog, and the
foghorn begins to blow at intervals of a minute. He checks it against
his watch. And suddenly he wonders what he is doing aboard the
Augustus with a suitcase full of peanut butter. "Ants, poison, peanut
butter, foghorns," he writes, "love, blood pressure, business trips,
inscrutability. I know that I will go back." The foghorn blasts again, and
in the held note he sees a vision of his family running toward him up
some steps—crumbling stone, wild pinks, lizards, and their much-
loved faces. "I will catch a plane in Genoa," he writes. "I will go back.
I will see my children grow and take up their lives, and I will gentle
Marcie—sweet Marcie, dear Marcie, Marcie my love. I will shelter her
with the curve of my body from all the harms of the dark."

RUBBER LIFE

Francine Prose

THAT WINTER I READ A LOT AND WORKED IN THE PUBLIC LIBRARY. A FOG settled in on my heart like the mists that hung in the cranberry bogs and hid the ocean so totally that the sound of the waves could have been one of those records to help insomniacs fall asleep. Always I'd been happy when the summer people left, but that fall I couldn't look up when the geese flew overhead and I avoided the streets on which people were packing their cars. Always I'd felt that the summer people were missing something, missing the best part of something, but now it seemed that I was the one being left as they went off, not to their winter office life, but to a party to which I had not been asked, and I felt like you do when the phone doesn't ring and no mail comes and it's obvious no one wants you. Of course I had reason to feel that way. But oddly, I hadn't noticed. How strange that you can be satisfied with your life till the slamming of some stranger's car trunk suddenly wakes you up.

I was trying to be civilized, cooking fresh produce till the market ran out, although it was only for me. The house I was caretaking had a microwave oven that seemed important to resist. The microwave surprised me. It was a colonial whaler's house, white clapboard with a widow's walk, so perfectly restored and furnished so obsessively with period pieces that all the comforts of modern life were tucked away grudgingly in some hard-to-find wing or upstairs. There was a cherry-wood table on which I read while I ate. I had promised myself: no television till 10:30, when *Love Connection* came on. I loved that show with its rituals of video dating, its singles who rarely loved each other as much as they'd loved each other's images on TV.

The house was supposed to be haunted—but so was every house in our town; a resident ghost could double what you could ask for summer rent. The Carsons, who were returning from Italy in the spring, told me their house had a ghost they'd never seen or heard; they could have been referring to some projected termite problem that never materialized. I didn't listen too hard. I'd heard similar stories in several previous houses, and such was my mood that fall that it depressed me to admit that ghosts were yet another thing that I no longer believed in.

I read through the evenings and weekends. I found out how not to OD. When I got tired there were books I could read for refreshment, fat non-fiction bestsellers detailing how rich people contract-murdered close relatives. I skimmed these books as fast as I could and let their simple sentences wash through my brain like shampoo.

I couldn't read at work, except on quiet mornings. We were surprisingly busy. Our town had a faithful daytime library crowd—young mothers, crazies, artists, retirees, the whole range of the unemployed and unattached. The best part of my job was seeing them come in from the briny winter cold, into the shockingly warm, bright library where the very air seemed golden with the fellowship and grateful presence of other people.

At first I read mostly new books, picked indiscriminately from the cartons that came in. Most of them were boring, but I liked knowing how to live with tennis injuries and diseases I hoped never to live with. I preferred these to books about why women lose men, books that made me so anxious I'd fall asleep reading and wake up long before dawn. It was a winter of lengthy biographies: lives that seemed longer than lives lived in actual time. I read a book about Edith Wharton and Henry James, and then I read Edith Wharton. I felt so close to Lily in *The House of Mirth* that when she took opium and died, an odd electric shiver shot across my scalp. We had six Edith Wharton books. When I finished them, nothing else seemed appealing and for a while I felt lost.

Then I became interested in a man named Lewis and the problem of what to read was solved because now I could read what he read. I put aside the books he returned and later took them home. To start, these were mainly cookbooks with photos in which dusty bits of Mexico or Tuscany peeked disconsolately at you from behind shiny platters of food. The first time I noticed Lewis—one of the summer helpers must have issued his card—he was returning a book he opened to show me a huge plate of black pasta on which some mussels had been fetchingly strewn.

"Isn't it wild?" Lewis said. "Isn't it pornographic?"

"How do they make it black?" I said.

"Squid ink," Lewis said. He looked at me almost challengingly, perhaps because our town was very health-conscious, on strict natural and macrobiotic diets that would probably not include squid ink— though you might ask why not. The previous week, at a potluck Sunday brunch, I got up to help clear the dishes and was scraping grapefruit shells into the compost pail when my hostess said, "Stop!" It wasn't compost, it was the tofu casserole main course. After that, the black pasta looked as magnificent as the walled Tuscan city behind it, and when I said, "Have you ever made this?" there was a catch in my voice, as if we were gazing not at pasta but at a Fra Angelico fresco.

Lewis said, "No, I use the pictures for attitude. Then I make up the recipes myself."

I wondered whom he cooked for, but didn't feel I could ask. It crossed my mind he might be gay—but somehow I thought not. After that, I paid attention: Lewis came in about twice a week, often on Mondays and Thursdays; I always wore jeans and sweaters, but on those days I tried to look nice.

One day a Moroccan cookbook seguéd into a stack of books about Morocco which I checked out for him, longing to say something that wasn't obvious ("Interested in Morocco?") or librarian-like ("Oh, are you planning a trip?"). If he was en route to Marrakech, I didn't want to know. When he returned the Morocco books I guiltily sneaked them home. That night I sat at my table and read what he'd read, turned the pages he'd turned, till a hot desert wind seemed to draft through the house, and I felt safe and dozed off.

He chose topics apparently at random, then read systematically: theater memoirs, histories of the Manhattan Project, Victorian social mores, the Dada avant-garde, Conrad, Apollinaire, Colette, Stephen Jay Gould. I read right behind him, with a sense of deep, almost physical connection, doomed and perverse, perverse because to read the same words he'd read felt like sneaking into his room while he slept, doomed because it was secret. How could I tell him that, with so many books in the library, I, too, just happened to pick up *The Panda's Thumb?*

No matter what else Lewis borrowed, there were always a couple of art books. He renewed a huge book on the Sistine Chapel three times and when I finally got it home I touched the angels' faces and ran one finger down the defeated curve of the prophet's shoulders. He often had paint on his clothes, and when I'd convinced myself that it wasn't too obvious or librarian-like, I asked if he was an artist. He hesitated, then went to the magazine shelf and opened a three-month-old *ArtNews* to a review of his New York show. There was a photo of a room decorated like a shrine with tinfoil and bric-a-brac and portraits of the dead in pillowy plastic frames. He let me hold it a minute, then took it and put it back on the shelf. I was charmed that he'd given me it and then gotten shy; other guys would have gone on to their entire résumés. I wanted to say that I understood now how his work was like his reading, but I was ashamed to have been paying attention to what he read. After he left, I got the *ArtNews* and reread it again and again.

Then two weeks passed and Lewis didn't appear. One afternoon a woman brought back Lewis's books. I noticed the proprietary intimacy with which she handled them; they might have been dishes, or his laundry, unquestionably her domain. She had red hair and a pretty, Irish face, endearingly like mine. She looked around, intimidated. Were it anyone else, I would have asked if she needed help, but I have to confess that I liked it when she left without any books.

The next time Lewis came in, he stood several feet from my desk. "Stand back," he said. "I've still got the flu."

I said, "Look, look at this," babbling mostly to cover the fact that my face had lit up when I saw him. As it happened, we'd just received a new book—a history of the 1918 influenza epidemic. He took it and returned from the shelves with an armload of medical history. In one volume of sepia photos, hollow-eyed Civil War soldiers stared into the camera; for all their bandages and obvious wounds, they perched on the edge of their cots, as if, the instant the shutter snapped, they might jump up and go somewhere else. Lewis said, "I think I'll go home and get over this flu and meditate on a new piece."

Nothing is so seductive as thinking you're someone's muse—
even when you aren't—and in that instant the library became for me a
treasure trove of possibilities for conversation with Lewis. The cello-
phane bookcovers seemed to wink with light, and as I browsed among
them, I felt like a fish in clear silver water, swimming from lure to lure.
Each week I set something aside and rehearsed what I wanted to show
him, but always I was defeated by an adrenaline rush.

One day he was practically out the door when I called him back
and flung open a coffee-table book. I turned to a photo of an altar from
a West African tribe that boasted an elaborate dream culture in which
you constructed little personal shrines with doll figures representing
everyone you had ever slept with in a dream.

Lewis studied it awhile. Then he said, "My gallery isn't big enough."
I laughed but it hurt me a little. I thought, Well, it serves me right.
Honestly, I couldn't believe what I'd picked out to finally show him.

Lewis said, "And who do you dream about?" It was a smarmy,
lounge-lizard kind of question he seemed shocked to hear himself ask.
Then he got embarrassed and I got embarrassed and I said, "Last night
I dreamed I was trapped in Iran with terrorists looking for me and—"

"Oh," said Lewis, semi-glazed over. "The evening-news dream.
Do you get cable? The worst dreams I ever have are from falling asleep
watching C-Span government hearings from D.C."

A week or so later I ran into Lewis on Front Street. I had never
seen him out in the world. It took me a second to recognize him; then
my heart started slamming around. I walked toward him, thinking I
would soon get calm, but when I reached him I was quite breathless
and could barely speak. He walked me to the library. I noticed that we
moved slower and slower, the closer and closer we got; it made me feel
I should be looking around for the woman Lewis lived with. He said
he was driving to Rockport next week and did I want to go? He left me
at the library without coming in, even though it was Thursday, one of
his regular days.

On the way to Rockport, Lewis told me his idea. He was planning
to make a kind of wax-museum diorama, all manner of Civil War
wounded and maimed behind a plexiglass panel that tinted everything
sepia except in large gaps through which you could see the scene in all

its full gory color. When I asked what he needed in Rockport he said, "I don't know. Store mannequins. Ace bandages. Ketchup. Half my art is shopping."

I tried to imagine the piece, but kept being distracted by how many layers of meaning everything seemed to have. For example: the ashtray in his car was full and smelled awful. Normally, I'd have shut it, but he wasn't smoking, so it must be the woman he lived with who smoked, and I feared my shutting the ashtray might be construed and even intended as a movement toward him, against her. I felt she was there with us in the car; in fact, it was her car. I can't remember quite what I said but I know that it wasn't entirely connected to Lewis's saying, "It's Joanne's car. Joanne, the woman I live with."

"How long have you lived together?" I asked; my voice sounded painfully chirpy.

"Forever," said Lewis, staring off into space. "Forever and ever and ever."

By then we were walking through Rockport at our usual hypnotized crawl; really, it was so cold you'd think we might have hurried. Lewis bought a wall clock, the plain black-and-white schoolroom kind. In a dry-goods shop, he asked to see the cheapest white bedsheets they had, and the salesman looked at me strangely. We walked in and out of antique stores; several times Lewis made notes. More often, we just window-shopped. In front of one crowded window, Lewis pointed to a large porcelain doll in a rocking chair. He said, "People always say 'life-like' when they just mean nicely painted. But that one really looks like an actual dead child."

"Or a *live* one," I said, overbrightly. Though the doll was fairly extreme, I probably wouldn't have noticed. Whatever I was drawn to in antique shop windows, it wasn't, hadn't been for years, the Victorian doll in the rocker with, the corkscrew curls and christening dress. But when Lewis said look, I looked.

It would have seemed impolite not to ask him in for a drink when he drove me home, and when it got late and I said, "Won't Joanne be expecting you?" and he said, "She's in Boston," it would have seemed silly not to invite him to dinner. Hadn't my asking after Joanne made my good intentions clear? If you believed *that,* you'd believe that my showing him the African dream-lover altar was meant to convey not the fact that I'd dreamed of sleeping with him (which, actually, I hadn't) or that I wanted to sleep with him, but rather that I would be satisfied if it only happened in dreams.

There was never any telling when he would show up. Sometimes at night he would rap on the window, very *Wuthering Heights,* and my heart would jump. I'd think first of psycho killers and then of the house's ghost; then I'd realize it was Lewis and get scared in a different way. We were very discreet because of Joanne. He clearly felt torn for deceiving her and would never come, or say he would come, unless she was gone or too busy to ever suspect or find out.

In the library we were distant, no different from before. It was remarkably erotic. Once more I brought home the books he returned, read what he had read, though now these were sometimes on woodworking and the chemistry of glue. Strangely, I never mentioned this. I think I was superstitious that his knowing might spoil my pleasure, pleasure I badly needed to fill the time between his visits. I was disturbed that time had become something to fill, and sometimes I couldn't help wondering if I hadn't been happier before.

But of course I never wondered that when Lewis was around. I made him watch *Love Connection* with me, and for the first time my feelings for the video-date couples were unmixed with personal fear. He seemed so happy to see me that I thought, without daring to think it in words, that what he felt was love. But how could I know the truth about this when I never knew him well enough to confess we read the same books? There were some things I knew. He used to bring me presents: sewing baskets, beaded purses, bits of antique fluffery that somehow I knew he'd tried out unsuccessfully in his work. Lewis often talked of his work in the most astonishing ways. Once he told me about making a figure for his new piece, a Confederate dummy. Just as he finished painting the face, he was for an instant positive he'd seen it blink, and he felt that if he sat down beside it on its cot he might stay there and never get up.

One night he gave me a cardboard box long enough for a dozen roses, but wider. In it was the Victorian doll we'd seen in the Rockport window. Though it wasn't something I wanted, I nonetheless burst into tears and, like an idiot, I hugged it. I stood there lamely, cradling the doll, wondering where to put it. I thought of pet-shop goldfish and of how one was cautioned to find them a water temperature just like the one they had left, and I remembered the antique mini-rocking chair in the Carsons' living room, with the tiny woven counterpane tossed artfully across it, always at the ready to keep the colonial baby warm. The doll was larger than it appeared, and it was a bit of a squeeze. For a while we remained looking down at it until it had stopped rocking.

That night when we were in bed we heard footsteps from downstairs. "Did you hear that?" I said, though I could tell Lewis had. It had stopped us cold. Lewis put on his pants and picked up a poker from the fireplace in my bedroom, a hearth I suddenly wondered why I had never used. "Wait here," he said, but I put on my nightgown and followed him.

We skulked through the house, flinging doors open, like in the movies. But there was no one there. The door was locked, the windows shut. Nothing had been disturbed. "Mice," Lewis said.

"Mice in tap shoes," I said.

Then Lewis said, "Look at that." The doll we'd left in the rocker was sitting in one corner of the living room couch. He said, "How did you do *that?*"

"I didn't!" I said shrilly. "I was upstairs with you." I felt too defensive to be frightened or even amazed. Did he think I'd staged this for his benefit? I'd read all those books for his benefit, and I couldn't even admit that. "Well, the house is supposed to be haunted," I said, and then got terribly sad. It struck me that finding yourself in a haunted house with someone should unite you in a kind of fellowship, the camaraderie of the besieged, of spookiness and fear. But I didn't sense any of that. What I did feel was that Lewis had moved several steps away. "Put it back in the rocker," he said.

"I don't think it liked it there," I said.

"Put the doll back in the rocker," he said. I did, and we went upstairs. We got into bed and curled back to back, staring at opposite walls. Finally he said, "I'm sorry. I take these things too seriously. I guess it was being raised Catholic. I can't help thinking it has something to do with Joanne."

I couldn't see what a walking doll could have to do with Joanne. I hadn't known he was Catholic—why had that never come up? I didn't know why this was stranger than thinking a Confederate dummy had blinked at him.

"I'm Catholic, too," I said. "But the ghost is a Protestant ghost."

Just then the footsteps resumed. We rolled over and looked at each other. It was exactly like those awful moments when you wake up in the morning and the pain you've been worried about is still there.

Downstairs, we found the doll on the couch. This time I got frightened. Lewis's face looked totally different than I'd ever seen it.

"You know what, Bridget?" he said to me. "You are one crazy chick."

After that, everything changed and ground to a gradual halt. After that, the doll stayed put and we never discussed that night. To mention it would have risked letting him know how wronged I felt, not just over his coolness, his punishing me for what obviously wasn't my fault, but because he'd left me so alone, alone with my own astonishment. I'd been mystified, too, confused, even a little irritated to find myself so chilled by something I couldn't explain and didn't believe in. I kept thinking that meeting a ghost with someone who actually loved you might actually have been fun. Anyway, what was happening with us seemed beyond discussion. In the library, we acted the same as before, but it was no longer exciting. It left me nervous and sad. I stopped reading the books he brought back. All I had to do was look at them and a heaviness overcame me, that same pressure in the chest that on certain days warns you it's not the right time to start leafing through family albums of the family dead.

I no longer read at all. Without that awareness of what Lewis might choose, I'd lost my whole principle of selection. Out of habit, I browsed the shelves; nothing seemed any less boring than anything else. I gave up *Love Connection,* but often fell asleep watching TV, not for entertainment so much as for steadiness, comfort, and noise. For a while I forgot the doll, then considered throwing it out. I wound up tossing the counterpane over its head and leaving it in its chair; the doll showed no reaction. I remember waves of a tingly frostbite chill, a physical burning that sent me racing to the mirror. Naturally, nothing showed. It should not have been so painful, the whole thing had been so short-lived, not nearly so bad as, say, the breakup of a long marriage, losing someone you've shared years and children with. That pain is about everything: your life, your childhood, death, your past. Mine was purely about the future.

That winter the future took a very long time to come. I felt that time had become an abyss I would never get across. And then at last it was spring. The Carsons returned from Italy. Their eyes kept flickering past me till they'd reassured themselves that the house was in perfect shape. Then they thanked me for forwarding their mail, inquired after my winter, told me that Florence had been marvelous fun, and asked if I'd seen the ghost. No, I said. I hadn't.

"No one has," said Mrs. Carson. "But once you know about it . . . Now that you're leaving, I can tell you. I'm always reluctant to lease this place to couples with small children because the ghost, oh, it's horrible, the ghost is supposed to be that of a child."

For just a moment I got the chills. I refused to let this sink in. I wondered if her reluctance really had to do with the supernatural or with damage control. I said, "Well, if that's the case, I'm leaving the ghost a present." I indicated the doll. They weren't exactly thrilled. The doll, after all, was Victorian, hopelessly out-of-period. They seemed already tired of me and impatient for a reunion with their possessions.

Outside, packed, was the car I had just bought; even its monthly-payment book seemed a sign of faith in the future. I was moving to Boston to enroll in a library science program. I said goodbye to the Carsons and got in my car and drove off. On my way out of town, I drove past the golf course on which, from the corner of my eye, I spotted what looked like a sprinkling of brilliant orange poppies. It took me a while to realize that they were plastic tees.

Moments of recovery are often harder to pinpoint than moments of shock and loss, but I knew then at what precise instant I'd stopped grieving over Lewis. It had been late April, or early May, a few weeks before the Carsons came home. The tulips were in bloom. I'd been at work, shelving books, deep in the stacks. A volume on Coptic religious texts had fallen open to reveal a magazine hidden inside. It was a fetish magazine called *The Best of Rubber Life*. Inside were color photos of mostly plump, mostly female couples. Some of the women wore baby-doll pajamas, others were in rubber suits or in the process of putting them on. Most were in quasi-sexual poses though no one seemed to be touching or making love. Everyone gazed at the camera, full frontal stares in some hard-to-read middle between totally blank and bold.

I wondered whose it was. I considered some (mostly elderly) men who seemed like possible candidates. I thought meanly: maybe it was Lewis's. But I didn't think so. Perhaps I should have been disgusted, it was really extremely sordid, or even frightened of being in the library with whoever had hid it there. In fact, I felt nothing like that, but rather a funny giddiness, an unaccountable lightness of heart. I felt remarkably cheered up. Standing there in the stacks, turning the pages, I realized, as never before, what an isolated moment each photograph represents, one flash of light, one frozen instant stolen from time, after which time resumes. It was what I'd thought when I'd first seen those Civil War pictures but had never known how to tell Lewis. Perhaps I'd been worried that if I told him, the camera would click and he'd move.

I looked at the women in the rubber magazine, and I began to laugh, because all I could think of was how soon the strobes would stop flashing, the cameras would click one last time, how that day's session would end, and they would collect their checks and rise from their rubber sheets and fill the air with hilarious sounds as they stripped off their rubber suits. It was almost as if I could hear it, that joyous sigh and snap—the smacky kiss of flesh against flesh, of flesh, unbound, against air.

HARD-LUCK STORIES

Alice Munro

JULIE IS WEARING A PINK-AND-WHITE-STRIPED SHIRTWAIST DRESS, AND A hat of lacy beige straw, with a pink rose under the brim. I noticed the hat first, when she came striding along the street. For a moment I didn't realize it was Julie. Over the last couple of years I have experienced moments of disbelief when I meet my friends in public. They look older than I think they should. Julie didn't look older, but she did catch my attention in a way she had never done before. It was the hat. I thought there was something gallant and absurd about it, on that tall, tomboyish woman. Then I saw that it was Julie and hurried to greet her, and we got a table under an umbrella at this sidewalk restaurant where we are having lunch.

We have not seen each other for two months, not since the conference in May. I am down in Toronto for the day. Julie lives here.

She soon tells me what is going on. Sitting down, she looks pretty, with the angles of her face softened and shaded by the hat, and her dark eyes shining.

"It makes me think of a story," Julie says. "Isn't it like one of those ironical-twist-at-the-end sort of stories that used to be so popular? I really did think that I was asked along to protect you. No, not exactly protect, that's too vulgar, but I thought you felt something and you were being prudent, and that was why me. Wouldn't it make a good story? Why did those stories go out of style?"

"They got to seem too predictable," I said. "Or people thought, that isn't the way things happen. Or they thought, who cares the way things happen?"

"Not to me! Not to me was anything predictable!" says Julie. One or two people look our way. The tables are too close together here.

She makes a face, and pulls the hat down on both cheeks, scrunching the rose against her temple.

"I must be crowing," she says. "I have a tendency now to get light-headed. It just seems to me so remarkable. Is this hat silly? No, seriously, do you remember when we were driving down and you told about the visit you went on, the visit that man took you on, to see the rich people? The rich woman? The awful one? Do you remember you said then about there being the two kinds of love, and the one kind nobody wants to think they've missed out on? Well, I was thinking then, have I missed out on every kind? I haven't even got to tell the different kinds apart."

I am about to say "Leslie," which is the name of Julie's husband.

"Don't say 'Leslie,'" Julie says. "You know that doesn't count. I can't help it. It doesn't count. So I was thinking, I was ready to make a joke about it but I was thinking, how I'd like to get some crumbs, even!"

"Douglas is better than crumbs," I say.

"Yes he is."

When the conference last May had ended and the buses were standing at the door of the summer hotel, waiting to take people back to Toronto or to the airport, I went into Julie's room and found her doing up her backpack.

"I've got us a ride to Toronto," I said. "If you'd rather that than the bus. Remember the man I introduced you to last night? Douglas Reider?"

"All right," said Julie. "I'm mildly sick of all these people. Do we have to talk?"

"Not much. He will."

I helped her hoist her backpack. She probably doesn't own an overnight case. She was wearing her hiking boots and a denim jacket. She wasn't faking. She could have walked to Toronto. Every summer she and her husband and some of their children walk the Bruce Trail. Other things fit the picture. She makes her own yogurt, and whole-grain bread, and granola. You'd think I would have worried about introducing her to Douglas, who is driven by any display of virtue into the most extraordinary provocations. I've heard him tell people that yogurt causes cancer, and smoking is good for your heart, and whales are an abomination. He does this lightheartedly but with absolute assurance, and adds a shocking, contemptuous embroidery of false statistics and invented detail. The people he takes on are furious or confused or wounded—sometimes all of those things at once. I don't remember thinking about how Julie would have handled him, but I suppose, if I did think about it, I must have decided that she would be all right. Julie isn't simple. She knows her own stratagems, her efforts, her doubts. You couldn't get at her through her causes.

Julie and I have been friends for years. She is a children's librarian, in Toronto. She helped me get the job I have now, or at least, she told me about it. I drive a bookmobile in the Ottawa Valley. I have been divorced for a long time, and so it is natural that Julie should talk to me about a problem she says she cannot discuss with many people. It is a question, more than a problem. The question is: should Julie herself try living alone? She says her husband Leslie is cold-hearted, superficial, stubborn, emotionally stingy, loyal, honest, high-minded, and vulnerable. She says she never really wants him. She says she thinks she might miss him more than she could stand, or perhaps just being alone would be more than she could stand. She says she has no illusions about being able to attract another man. But sometimes she feels her emotions, her life, her something-or-other—all that is being wasted.

I listen, and think this sounds like the complaints many women make, and in fact it sounds a lot like the complaints I used to make, when I was married how much is this meant, how deep does it go? How much is it an exercise that balances the marriage and keeps it afloat? I've asked her, has she ever been in love, in love with somebody else? She says she once thought she was, with a boy she met on the beach, but it was all nonsense, it all evaporated. And once in recent years a man thought he was in love with her, but that was nonsense too, nothing came of it. I tell her that being alone has its grim side, certainly; I tell her to think twice. I think that I am in some ways a braver person than Julie, because I have taken the risk. I have taken more than one risk.

Julie and Douglas Reider and I had lunch at a restaurant in an old white wooden building overlooking a small lake. The lake is one of a chain of lakes, and there was a dock where the lake boats used to come in before the road was built; boats brought the holidayers then, and the supplies. The trees came down to the shore, on both sides of the building. Most of them were birch and poplar. The leaves were not quite out here, even though it was May. You could see all the branches with just an impression of green, as if that was the color of the air. Under the trees there were hundreds of white trilliums. The day was cloudy, though the sun had been trying to break through. The water looked bright and cold.

We sat on old, unmatched, brightly painted kitchen chairs, on a long glassed-in verandah. We were the only people there. It was a bit late for lunch. We ate roast chicken.

"It's Sunday dinner, really," I said. "It's Sunday dinner after church."

"It's a lovely place," said Julie. She asked Douglas how he knew it existed.

Douglas said he got to know where everything was, he spent so much time travelling around the province. He is in charge of collecting, buying up for the Provincial Archives, all sorts of old diaries, letters, records, that would otherwise perish, or be sold to collectors outside the province or the country. He pursues various clues and hunches, and when he finds a treasure it is not always his immediately. He often has to persuade reticent or suspicious or greedy owners, and to outwit private dealers.

"He's a sort of pirate, really," I said to Julie.

He was talking about the private dealers, telling stories about his rivals. Sometimes they would get hold of valuable material, and then impudently try to sell it back to him. Or they would try to sell it out of the country to the highest bidders, a disaster he has sworn to prevent.

Douglas is tall, and most people would think of him as lean, disregarding the little bulge over his belt which can be seen as a recent, unsuitable, perhaps temporary, development. His hair is gray, and cut short, perhaps to reassure elderly and conservative diary-owners. To me he is a boyish-looking man. I don't mean to suggest by that a man who is open-faced and ruddy and shy. I am thinking of the hard youthfulness, the jaunty grim looks you often see in photographs of servicemen in the Second World War. Douglas was one of those, and is preserved, not ripened. Oh, the modesty and satisfaction of those faces, clamped down on their secrets! With such men the descent into love is swift and private and amazing—so is their recovery. I watched him as he told Julie about the people who deal in old books and papers, how they are not fusty and shadowy, as in popular imagination, not mysterious old magpies, but bold rogues with the instincts of gamblers and confidence men. In this, as in any other enterprise where there is the promise of money, intrigues and lies and hoodwinking and bullying abound.

"People have that idea about anything to do with books," Julie said. "They have it about librarians. Think of the times you hear people say that somebody is not a typical librarian. Haven't you wanted to say it about yourself?"

Julie was excited, drinking her wine. I thought it was because she had flourished, at the conference. She has a talent for conferences, and no objection to making herself useful. She can speak up in general meetings without her mouth going dry and her knees shaking. She knows what a point of order is. She says she has to admit to rather liking meetings, and committees, and newsletters. She has worked for the P.T.A. and the N.D.P. and the Unitarian Church, and for Tenants' Associations, and Great Books Clubs; she has given a lot of her life to organizations. Maybe it's an addiction, she says, but she looks around her at meetings and she can't help thinking that meetings are good for people. They make people feel everything isn't such a muddle.

Now, at this conference, Julie said, who, who, were the typical librarians? Where could you find them? Indeed, she said, you might think there had been a too-strenuous effort to knock that image on the head.

"But it isn't a calculated knocking-on-the-head," she said. "It really is one of those refuge-professions." Which didn't mean, she said, that all the people in it were scared and spiritless. Far from it. It was full of genuine oddities and many flamboyant and expansive personalities.

"Old kooks," Douglas said.

"Still, the image prevails somewhere," Julie said. "The Director of the Conference Centre came and talked to the Chairman this morning and asked if she wanted a list of the people who were out of their rooms during the night. Can you imagine them thinking we'd want to know that?"

"Wouldn't we?" I said.

"I mean, officially. How do they get that kind of information on people, anyway?"

"Spies," said Douglas. "A.G.P.M. Amateur Guardians of the Public Morality. I'm a member myself, It's like being a fire warden."

Julie didn't pick this up. Instead she said morosely, "It's the younger ones, I guess."

"Envious of the Sexual Revolution," said Douglas, shaking his head. "Anyway I thought it was all over. Isn't it all over?" he said, looking at me.

"So I understand," I said.

"Well that's not fair," said Julie. "For me it never happened. No, really. I wish I'd been born younger. I mean, later. Why not be honest about it?" Sometimes she set herself up to be preposterously frank. There was something willed and coquettish—childishly coquettish—about this; yet it seemed not playful. It seemed, at the moment, necessary. It made me nervous for her. We were working down into our second bottle of wine and she had drunk more than either Douglas or I had.

"Well all right," she said. "I know it's funny. Twice in my life there have been possibilities and both turned out very funny. I mean very strange. So I think it is not meant. No. Not God's will."

"Oh, Julie," I said.

"You don't know the whole story," she said.

I thought that she really was getting drunk, and I ought to do what I could to keep the tone light, so I said, "Yes, I know. You met a psychology student while you were throwing a cake into the sea."

I was glad that Douglas laughed.

"Really?" he said. "Did you always throw your cakes into the sea? Were they that bad?"

"Very good," said Julie, speaking in an artificial, severely joking style. "Very good and very elaborate. Gateau St. Honoré. A monstrosity. It's got cream and custard and butterscotch. No. The reason I was throwing it into the sea—and I've told you this," she said to me, "was that I had a secret problem at the time. I had a problem about food. I was just newly married and we were living in Vancouver, near Kitsilano Beach. I was one of those people who gorge, then purge. I used to make cream puffs and eat them all one after the other, or make fudge and eat a whole panful, then take mustard and water to vomit or else

massive doses of epsom salts to wash it through. Terrible. The guilt. I
was compelled. It must have had something to do with sex. They say
now it does, don't they?

"Well, I made this horrific cake and I pretended I was making it
for Leslie, but by the time I got it finished I knew I was making it for
myself, I was going to end up eating it all myself, and I went to put it
in the garbage but I knew I might fish it out again. Isn't that disgusting? So I put the whole mess in a brown paper bag and I went down
to the rocky end of the beach and I heaved it into the sea. But—this
boy saw me. He gave me a look, so I knew what he thought. What's
naturally the first thought, when you see a girl throw a brown paper
bag into the sea? I had to tell him it was a cake. I said I'd goofed on
the ingredients and I was ashamed it was such a failure. Then within
fifteen minutes' conversation I was telling him the truth, which I never
dreamed of telling anybody. He told me he was a psychology student
at U. B.C. but he had dropped out because they were all behaviorists
there. I didn't know—I didn't know what a behaviorist *was*.

"So," said Julie, resigned now, and marveling. "So, he became my
boyfriend. For about six weeks. He wanted me to read Jung. He had
very tight curly hair the color of mouse-skin. We'd lie behind the rocks
and neck up a storm. It was February or March, still pretty cold. He
could only meet me one day a week, always the same day. We didn't
progress very far. The upshot was—well, the upshot was, really, that I
discovered he was in a mental hospital. That was his day out. I don't
know if I discovered that first or the scars on his neck. Did I say he
had a beard? Beards were very unusual then. Leslie abhorred them.
He's got one himself now. He'd tried to cut his throat. Not Leslie."

"Oh, Julie," I said, though I had heard this before. Mention of
suicide is like innards pushing through an incision; you have to push
it back and clap some pads on, quickly.

"It wasn't that bad. He was recovering. I'm sure he did recover.
He was just a very intense kid who'd had a crisis. But I was so scared.
I was scared because I felt I wasn't too far from being loony myself.
With the gorging and vomiting and so on. And at the same time he
confessed that he was really only seventeen years old. He'd lied to me
about his age. That really did it. To think I'd been fooling around with
a boy three years younger than I was. That shamed me. I told him a
pack of lies about how I understood and it didn't matter and I'd meet

him next week and I went home and told Leslie I couldn't stand living in a basement apartment any more, we had to move. I cried. I found us a place on the North Shore within a week. I never would go to Kits Beach. When the kids were little and we took them to the beach I would always insist on Spanish Banks or Ambleside. I wonder what became of him.

"Probably he's okay," I said. "He is probably a celebrated Jungian."

"Or a celebrated behaviorist," said Douglas. "Or a sportscaster. You don't look as if you ate too many cream puffs now."

"I got over it. I think when I got pregnant. Life is so weird."

Douglas ceremonially poured out the rest of the wine.

"You said two occasions," he said to Julie. "Are you going to leave us hanging?"

It's all right, I thought, he isn't bored or put off, he likes her. While she talked I had been watching him, wondering. Why is there always this twitchiness, when you introduce a man to a woman friend, about whether the man will be bored or put off?

"The other was weirder," said Julie. "At least I understand it less. I shouldn't bother telling such stupid stuff but now I'm on the brink I suppose I will. Well. This puzzles me. It bewilders me totally. This was in Vancouver too, but years later. I joined what was called an Encounter Group. It was just a sort of group-therapy thing for ordinary functioning miserable mixed-up people. That sort of thing was very in at the time and it was the West Coast. There was a lot of talk about getting rid of masks and feeling close to one another, which it's easy to laugh at but I think it did more good than harm. And it was all sort of new. I must sound as if I'm trying to justify myself. Like saying, I was doing macramé fifteen years ago before it was the fad. When it's probably better never to have done macramé, ever."

Douglas said, "I don't even know what macramé is."

"That's best of all," I said.

"A man from California, named Stanley, was running several of these groups. He wouldn't have said he was running them. He was very low-key. But he got paid. We did pay him. He was a psychologist. He had lovely long curly dark hair and of course he had a beard too, but beards were nothing by then. He sort of barged around in an awkward innocent way. He'd say, 'Well, this is going to sound kind of crazy but I wonder—' He had a technique of making everybody feel they were smarter than he was. He was very sincere. He'd say, 'You—don't—realize—how *lovable* you are.' No. I'm making him sound such a phony. It's got to be more complicated than that. Anyway, before long he wrote me a letter. Stanley did. It was an appreciation of my mental and physical and spiritual qualities and he said he had fallen in love with me.

"I was very mature about it. I wrote back and said he hardly knew me. He wrote oh, yes, he did. He phoned to apologize for being such a nuisance. He said he couldn't help himself. He asked if we could have coffee. No harm. We had coffee various times. I'd be doing the cheery conversation and he'd break in and say I had beautiful eyebrows. He'd say he wondered what my nipples were like. I have very ordinary eyebrows. I stopped having coffee and he took to lurking around my house in his old van. He did. I'd be shopping in the supermarket and there he'd be beside me peering into the dairy goods, with his woebegone expression. I'd get sometimes three letters a day from him, rhapsodies about myself and how much I meant to him and confessions of self-doubt and how he didn't want to turn into a guru and how good I was for him because I was so aloof and wise. What rot. I knew it was all ludicrous but I won't deny I got to depend on it, in a way. I knew the exact time of day the postman came. I decided I wasn't too old to wear my hair long.

"And about half a year after this started, another woman in our group phoned me up one day. She told me all hell had broken loose. Some woman in one of the groups had confessed to her husband she was sleeping with Stanley. The husband got very mad, he wasn't a group person, and the story got out and then another woman, and another and another, revealed the same thing, they confessed they were sleeping with Stanley, and pretty soon there was no blame attached, it was like being a victim of witchcraft. It turned out he'd been quite systematic, he'd picked one from each group, and he already had one in the group I was in so presumably it wasn't to be me. Always a married woman, not a single one who could get bothersome. Nine of them. Really. Nine women."

Douglas said, "Busy."

"All the men took that attitude," Julie said. "They all chortled. Except of course the husbands. There was a big sort of official meeting of group people at one of the women's houses. She had a lovely kitchen with a big chopping block in the middle and I remember thinking, did they do it on that? Everybody was too cool to say they were shocked about adultery or anything like that so we had to say we were mad at Stanley's betrayal of trust. Actually I think some women were mad about being left out. I said that, as a kind of joke. I never told a word about how he'd been acting with me. If there'd been anybody else getting the same treatment I was, she didn't tell either. Some of the chosen women cried. Then they'd comfort each other and compare notes. What a scene, now when I think of it! And I was so bewildered. I couldn't put it together. How can you put it together? I thought of Stanley's wife. She was a nice-looking rather nervous girl with lovely long legs. I used to meet her sometimes and to think: little do you know what your husband's been saying to me. And there were all those other women meeting her and thinking, little do you know, etcetera. Maybe she knew about them all, us all, maybe she was thinking: little do you know how many others there are. Is it possible? I'd said to him once, you know this is really just a farce, and he said, don't say that, don't say that to me! I thought he might cry. So what can you make of it? The energy. I don't mean just the physical part of it. In a way that's the least of it."

"Did the husbands get him?" Douglas said.

"A delegation went to see him. He didn't deny anything. He said he acted in good faith and from good motives and their possessiveness and jealousy was the problem. But he had to leave town, his groups had collapsed, he and his wife and their little kids left town in the van. But he sent back bills. Everybody got their bills. The women he'd been sleeping with got theirs with the rest. I got mine. No more letters, just the bill. I paid. I think most people paid. You had to think of the wife and kids.

"So there you are. I only attract the bizarre. And a good thing, because I'm married all along and virtuous at heart in spite of whatever I may have said. We should have coffee."

We drove on the back roads, in the sandy country, poor country, south of Lake Simcoe. Grass glows on the dunes. We hardly saw another car. We got out the road map to see where we were, and Douglas sidetracked to drive us through a village where he had once almost got his hands on a valuable diary. He showed us the very house. An old woman had burned it, finally—or that was what she told him—because parts of it were scandalous.

"They dread exposure," Douglas said. "Unto the third and fourth generation."

"Not like me," said Julie. "Laying bare my ridiculous almost-affairs. I don't care."

"Back and side lay bare, lay bare," sang Douglas. "Both foot and hand go cold—"

"I can lay bare," I said. "It may not be very entertaining."

"Will we risk it?" Douglas said.

"But it is interesting," I said. "I was thinking back at the restaurant about a visit I went on with a man I was in love with. This was before you came down to Toronto, Julie. We were going to visit some friends of his who had a place up in the hills on the Quebec side of the Ottawa River. I've never seen such a house. It was like a series of glass cubes with ramps and decks joining them together. The friends were Keith and Caroline. They were married, they had children, but the children weren't there. The man I was with wasn't married, he hadn't been married for a long time. I asked him on the way up what Keith and Caroline were like, and he said they were rich. I said that wasn't much of a description. He said it was Caroline's money, her daddy owned a brewery. He told me which one. There was something about the way he said 'her daddy' that made me see the money on her, the way he saw it, like long lashes or a bosom—like a luxuriant physical thing. Inherited money can make a woman seem like a treasure. It's not the same with money she's made herself, that's just brassy and ordinary. But then he said, she's very neurotic, she's really a bitch, and Keith's just a poor honest sod who works for the government. He's an A.D.M., he said. I didn't know what that was."

"Assistant Deputy Minister," Julie said.

"Even cats and children know that," said Douglas.

"Thank you," said Julie.

I was sitting in the middle. I turned mostly towards Julie as I talked.

"He said they liked to have some friends who weren't rich people or government people, people they could think of as eccentric or independent or artistic, sometimes a starveling artist

Caroline could get her hooks into, to torment and show off and be bountiful with."

"Sounds as if he didn't like his friends much," Julie said.

"I don't know if he'd think of it that way. Liking or disliking. I expected them to be physically intimidating, at least I expected her to be, but they were little people. Keith was very fussy and hospitable. He had little freckled hands. I think of his hands because he was always handing you a drink or something to eat or a cushion for your back. Caroline was a wisp. She had long limp hair and a high white forehead and she wore a gray cotton dress with a hood. No makeup. I felt big and gaudy. She stood with her head bent and her hands up the sleeves of the dress while the men talked about the house. It was new. Then she said in her wispy voice how much she loved the way it was in the winter with the snow deep outside and the white rugs and the white furniture. Keith seemed rather embarrassed by her and said it was like a squash court, no depth perception. I felt sympathetic because she seemed just on the verge of making some sort of fool of herself. She seemed to be pleading with you to reassure her, and yet reassuring her seemed to involve you in a kind of fakery. She was like that. There was such a strain around her. Every subject seemed to get caught up in such emotional extravagance and fakery. The man I was with got very brusque with her, and I thought that was mean. I thought, even if she's faking, it shows she wants to feel something, doesn't it, oughtn't decent people to help her? She just didn't seem to know how.

"We sat out on a deck having drinks. Their house guest appeared. His name was Martin and he was in his early twenties. Maybe a bit older. He had a pretty superior style. Caroline asked him in a very submissive way if he would get some blankets—it was chilly on the deck—and when he went off she said he was a playwright. She said he was just a marvelous, marvelous playwright but his plays were too European to be successful here, they were too spare and rigorous. Too spare and rigorous. Then she said, oh, the state of the theater, the state of literature in this country, it is an embarrassment, isn't it? It is the triumph of the second-rate. I thought, she mustn't know that I am a contributor to this sorry situation. Because at that time I was the assistant editor of a little magazine, you know, it was *Thousand Islands*, and I had published a poem or two. But right then she asked if I could put Martin in touch with some of the people I knew through the magazine. Straight from insult to asking favors, in that suffering sensitive little voice. I began to think she was a bitch, all right. When Martin came back with the blankets she went into a fit of shivering that was practically a ballet act and thanked him as if she was going to weep. He just dumped a blanket on her, and that way I knew they were lovers. The man I was with had told me she had lovers. What he said was, Caroline's a sexual monster. I asked if he had ever slept with her, and he said oh, yes, long ago. I wanted to ask something about his not liking her, hadn't that been any sort, of impediment, but I knew that would be a very stupid question.

"Martin asked me to go for a walk. We walked down a great flight of steps and sat on a bench by the water, and he turned out to be sinister. He was vicious about some people he said he knew, in the theater in Montreal. He said that Caroline used to be fat and after she lost weight she had to have tucks taken in her belly, because the skin was so loose. He had a stuffy smell. He smoked those little cigars. I began to feel sorry for Caroline all over again. This is what you have to put up with, for the sake of your fantasies. If you have to have a literary-genius lover, this is what you're liable to end up with. If you're a fake, worse fakes will get you. That was what I was thinking.

"Well. Dinner. There was lots of wine, and brandy afterwards, and Keith kept fussing, but nobody was easy. Martin was poisonous in an obvious sneering way, trying to get one up on everybody, but Caroline was poisonous in an exquisitely moral way, she'd take every topic and twist it, so that somebody seemed crass. Martin and the man I was with finally got into a filthy argument, it was filthy mean, and Caroline cooed and whimpered. The man I was with got up and said he was going to bed, and Martin wrapped himself up in a big sulk and Caroline all of a sudden started being sweet to Keith, drinking brandy with him, ignoring Martin.

"I went to my room and the man I was with was there, in bed, though we'd been given separate rooms. Caroline was very decorous in spite of all. He stayed the night. He was furious. Before, during, and after making love, he kept on the subject of Martin, what a slimy fraud he was, and I agreed. But he's their problem, I said. So he said, they're welcome to him, the posturing shit, and at last he went to sleep and I did too, but in the middle of the night I woke up. I wakened with a revelation. Occasionally you do. I rearranged myself and listened to his breathing, and I thought—he's in love with Caroline. I knew it. I knew it. I was trying not to know it, not just because it wasn't encouraging but also because it didn't seem decent, for me to know it. But once you know something like that you never can really stop. Everything seemed clear to me. For instance Martin. That was an arrangement. She'd arranged to have the old lover and the new lover there together, just to stir things up. There was something so crude about it, but that didn't mean it wouldn't work. There was something crude about *her*. All that poetic stuff, the sensibility stuff, it was crudely done; she wasn't a talented fake, but that didn't matter. What matters is to want to do it enough. To have the will to disturb. To be a femme fatale you don't have to be slinky and sensuous and disastrously beautiful, you just have to have the will to disturb.

"And I thought, why should I be surprised? Isn't this just what you always hear? How love isn't rational, or in one's best interests, it doesn't have anything to do with normal preferences?"

"Where do you always hear that?" Douglas said.

"It's standard. There's the intelligent sort of love that makes an intelligent choice. That's the kind you're supposed to get married on. Then there's the kind that's anything but intelligent, that's like a possession. And that's the one, that's the one, everybody really values. That's the one nobody wants to have missed out on.

Standard," said Douglas.

"You know what I mean. You know it's true. All sorts of hackneyed notions are true."

"Hackneyed," he said. "That's a word you don't often hear."

"That's a sad story," Julie said.

"Yours were sad too," I said.

"Mine were really sort of ridiculous. Did you ask him if he was in love with her?"

"Asking wouldn't have got me anywhere," I said. "He'd brought me there to counter her with. I was his sensible choice. I was the woman he liked. I couldn't stand that. I couldn't stand it. It was so humiliating. I got very touchy and depressed. I told him he didn't really love me. That was enough. He wouldn't stand for anybody telling him things about himself."

We stopped at a country church within sight of the highway.

"Something to soothe the spirit, after all these hard-luck stories, and before the Sunday traffic," Douglas said.

We walked around the graveyard first, looking at the oldest tomb-
stones, reading names and dates aloud.

I read out a verse I found.

> *"Afflictions sore long time she bore,*
> *Physicians were in vain,*
> *Till God did please to give her ease,*
> *And waft her from her Pain."*

"Waft," I said. "That sounds nice."

Then I felt something go over me—a shadow, a chastening. I
heard the silly sound of my own voice against the truth of the lives laid
down here. Lives pressed down, like layers of rotting fabric, disintegrating dark leaves. The old pain and privation. How strange, indulged,
and culpable they would find us—three middle-aged people still
stirred up about love, or sex.

The church was unlocked. Julie said that was very trusting of
them, even Anglican churches which were supposed to be open all the
time were usually locked up nowadays, because of vandals. She said
she was surprised the diocese let them keep it open.

"How do you know about dioceses?" said Douglas.

"My father was a parson. Couldn't you guess?"

It was colder inside the church than outside. Julie went ahead,
looking at the Roll of Honour, and memorial plaques on the walls. I
looked over the back of the last pew at a row of footstools, where people could kneel to pray. Each stool was covered with needlework, in a
different design.

Douglas put his hand on my shoulder blade, not around my
shoulders. If Julie turned she wouldn't notice. He brushed his hand
down my back and settled at my waist, applying a slight pressure to the
ribs before he passed behind me and walked up the outer aisle, ready
to explain something to Julie. She was trying to read the Latin on a
stained-glass window.

On one footstool was the Cross of St. George, on another the
Cross of St. Andrew.

I hadn't expected there would be any announcement from him,
either while I was telling the story, or after it was over. I did not think
that he would tell me that I was right, or that I was wrong. I heard him

translating, Julie laughing, but I couldn't attend. I felt that I had been overtaken—stumped by a truth about myself, or at least a fact, that I couldn't do anything about. A pressure of the hand, with no promise about it, could admonish and comfort me. Something unresolved could become permanent. I could be always bent on knowing, and always in the dark, about what was important to him, and what was not.

On another footstool there was a dove on a blue ground, with the olive branch in its mouth; on another a lamp, with lines of straight golden stitching to show its munificent rays; on another a white lily. No—it was a trillium. When I made this discovery, I called out for Douglas and Julie to come, and see it. I was pleased with this homely emblem, among the more ancient and exotic. I think I became rather boisterous, from then on. In fact all three of us did, as if we had each one, secretly, come upon an unacknowledged spring of hopefulness. When we stopped for gas, Julie and I exclaimed at the sight of Douglas's credit cards, and declared that we didn't want to go back to Toronto. We talked of how we would all run away to Nova Scotia, and live off the credit cards. Then when the crackdown came we would go into hiding, change our names, take up humble occupations. Julie and I would work as barmaids. Douglas could set traps for lobsters. Then we could all be happy.

EXCHANGE

Ray Bradbury

THERE WERE TOO MANY CARDS IN THE FILE, TOO MANY BOOKS ON THE shelves, too many children laughing in the children's room, too many newspapers to fold and stash on the racks . . .

All in all, too much. Miss Adams pushed her gray hair back over her lined brow, adjusted her gold-rimmed pince-nez, and rang the small silver bell on the library desk, at the same time switching off and on all the lights. The exodus of adults and children was exhausting. Miss Ingraham, the assistant librarian, had gone home early because her father was sick, so it left the burden of stamping, filing, and checking books squarely on Miss Adams' shoulders.

Finally the last book was stamped, the last child fed through the great brass doors, the doors locked, and with immense weariness, Miss Adams moved back up through a silence of forty years of books and being keeper of the books, stood for a long moment by the main desk.

She laid her glasses down on the green blotter, and pressed the bridge of her small-boned nose between thumb and forefinger and held it, eyes shut. What a racket! Children who fingerpainted or cartooned frontispieces or rattled their roller skates. High school students arriving with laughters, departing with mindless songs!

Taking up her rubber stamp, she probed the files, weeding out errors, her fingers whispering between Dante and Darwin.

A moment later she heard the rapping on the front-door glass and saw a man's shadow outside, wanting in. She shook her head. The figure pleaded silently, making gestures.

Sighing, Miss Adams opened the door, saw a young man in uniform, and said, "It's late. We're closed." She glanced at his insignia and added, "Captain."

"Hold on!" said the captain. "Remember me?" And repeated it, as she hesitated.

"Remember?"

She studied his face, trying to bring light out of shadow. "Yes, I think I do," she said at last. "You once borrowed books here."

"Right."

"Many years ago," she added. "Now I almost have you placed."

As he stood waiting she tried to see him in those other years, but his younger face did not come clear, or a name with it, and his hand reached out now to take hers.

"May I come in?"

"Well." She hesitated. "Yes."

She led the way up the steps into the immense twilight of books. The young officer looked around and let his breath out slowly, then reached to take a book and hold it to his nose, inhaling, then almost laughing.

"Don't mind me, Miss Adams. You ever smell new books? Binding, pages, print. Like fresh bread when you're hungry." He glanced around. "I'm hungry now, but don't even know what for."

There was a moment of silence, so she asked him how long he might stay.

"Just a few hours. I'm on the train from New York to L.A., so I came up from Chicago to see old places, old friends." His eyes were troubled and he fretted his cap, turning it in his long, slender fingers.

She said gently, "Is anything wrong? Anything I can help you with?"

He glanced out the window at the dark town, with just a few lights in the windows of the small houses across the way.

"I was surprised," he said.

"By what?"

"I don't know what I expected. Pretty damn dumb," he said, looking from her to the windows, "to expect that when I went away, everyone froze in place waiting for me to come home. That when I stepped off the train, all my old pals would unfreeze, run down, meet me at the station. Silly."

"No," she said, more easily now. "I think we all imagine that. I visited Paris as a young girl, went back to France when I was forty, and was outraged that no one had waited, buildings had vanished, and all the hotel staff where I had once lived had died, retired, or traveled."

He nodded at this, but could not seem to go on.

"Did anyone know you were coming?" she asked.

"I wrote a few, but no answers. I figured, hell, they're busy, but they'll be *there*. They weren't."

She felt the next words come off her lips and was faintly surprised. "I'm still here," she said.

"You *are*," he said with a quick smile. "And I can't tell you how glad I am."

He was gazing at her now with such intensity that she had to look away. "You know," she said, "I must confess you look familiar, but I don't quite fit your face with the boy who came here—"

"Twenty years ago! And as for what *he* looked like, that other one, me, well—"

He brought out a smallish wallet which held a dozen pictures and handed over a photograph of a boy perhaps twelve years old, with an impish smile and wild blond hair, looking as if he might catapult out of the frame.

"Ah, yes." Miss Adams adjusted her pince-nez and closed her eyes to remember. "That one. Spaulding. William Henry Spaulding?"

He nodded and peered at the picture in her hands anxiously.

"Was I a lot of trouble?"

"Yes." She nodded and held the picture closer and glanced up at him. "A fiend." She handed the picture back, "But I loved you."

"Did you?" he said and smiled more broadly.

"In spite of you, yes."

He waited a moment and then said, "Do you *still* love me?"

She looked to left and right as if the dark stacks held the answer. "It's a little early to know, isn't it?"

"Forgive."

"No, no, a good question. Time will tell. Let's not stand like your frozen friends who didn't move. Come along. I've just had some late-night coffee. There may be some left. Give me your cap. Take off that coat. The file index is there. Go look up your old library cards for the hell—heck—of it."

"Are they still *there?*" In amaze.

"Librarians save everything. You never know who's coming in on the next train. Go."

When she came back with the coffee, he stood staring down into the index file like a bird fixing its gaze on a half-empty nest. He handed her one of the old purple-stamped cards.

"Migawd," he said, "I took out a lot of books."

"Ten at a time. I said no, but you took them. And," she added, "*read* them! Here." She put his cup on top of the file and waited while he drew out canceled card after card and laughed quietly.

"I can't believe. I must not have lived anywhere else but here. May I take this with me, to sit?"

He showed the cards. She nodded. "Can you show me around? I mean, maybe I've forgotten something."

She shook her head and took his elbow. "I doubt that. Come on. Over here, of course, is the adult section."

"I begged you to let me cross over when I was thirteen. 'You're not ready,' you said. But—"

"I let you cross over anyway?"

"You did. And much thanks."

Another thought came to him as he looked down at her.

"You used to be taller than me," he said.

She looked up at him, amused.

"I've noticed that happens quite often in my life, but I can still do *this.*"

Before he could move, she grabbed his chin in her thumb and forefinger and held tight. His eyes rolled.

He said:

"I remember. When I was really bad you'd hold on and put your face down close and scowl. The scowl did it. After ten seconds of your holding my chin very tight, I behaved for days."

She nodded, released his chin. He rubbed it and as they moved on he ducked his head, not looking at her.

"Forgive, I hope you won't be upset, but when I was a boy I used to look up and see you behind your desk, so near but far away, and, how can I say this, I used to think that you were Mrs. God, and that the library was a whole world, and that no matter what part of the world or what people or thing I wanted to see and read, you'd find and give it to me." He stopped, his face coloring. "You *did,* too. You had the world ready for me every time I asked. There was always a place I hadn't seen, a country I hadn't visited where you took me. I've never forgotten."

She looked around, slowly, at the thousands of books. She felt her heart move quietly. "Did you really call me what you just said?"

"Mrs. God? Oh, yes. Often. Always."

"Come along," she said at last.

They walked around the rooms together and then downstairs to the newspaper files, and coming back up, he suddenly leaned against the banister, holding tight.

"Miss Adams," he said.

"What is it, Captain?"

He exhaled. "I'm scared. I don't want to leave. I'm afraid."

Her hand, all by itself, took his arm and she finally said, there in the shadows, 'Sometimes—I'm afraid, too. What frightens *you?*"

"I don't want to go away without saying goodbye. If I never return, I want to see all my friends, shake hands, slap them on the back, I don't know, make jokes." He stopped and waited, then went on. "But I walk around town and nobody knows me. Everyone's gone."

The pendulum on the wall clock slid back and forth, shining, with the merest of sounds.

Hardly knowing where she was going, Miss Adams took his arm and guided him up the last steps, away from the marble vaults below, to a final, brightly decorated room, where he glanced around and shook his head.

"There's no one here, either."

"Do you believe that?"

"Well, where are they? Do any of my old pals ever come visit, borrow books, bring them back late?"

"Not often," she said. "But listen. Do you realize Thomas Wolfe was wrong?"

"Wolfe? The great literary beast? Wrong?"

"The *title* of one of his books."

"You Can't Go Home Again?" he guessed.

"That's it. He was wrong. *This* is home. Your friends are still here. This was your summer place."

"Yes. Myths. Legends. Mummies. Aztec kings. Wicked sisters

who spat toads. Where I really lived. But I don't see my people."

"Well."

And before he could speak, she switched on a green-shaded lamp that shed a private light on a small table.

"Isn't this nice?" she said. "Most libraries today, too much light. There should be shadows, don't you think? Some mystery, yes? So that late nights the beasts can prowl out of the stacks and crouch by this jungle light to turn the pages with their breath. Am I crazy?"

"Not that I noticed."

"Good. Sit. Now that I know who you are, it all comes back."

"It couldn't possibly."

"No? You'll see."

She vanished into the stacks and came out with ten books that she placed upright, their pages a trifle spread so they could stand and he could read the titles.

"The summer of 1930, when you were, what? ten, you read all of these in one week."

"Oz? Dorothy? The Wizard? Oh, *yes.*"

She placed still others nearby. *"Alice in Wonderland. Through the Looking-Glass.* A month later you reborrowed both. 'But,' I said, 'you've already *read* them!' 'But,' you said, 'not enough so I can speak. I want to be able to *tell* them out *loud.*'

"My God," he said quietly, "did I say that?"

"You did. Here's more you read a dozen times. Greek myths, Roman, Egyptian. Norse myths, Chinese. You were *ravenous.*

"King Tut arrived from the tomb when I was three. His picture in the Rotogravure started me. What else have you there?"

"Tarzan of the Apes. You borrowed it . . .'"

"Three dozen times! *John Carter, Warlord of Mars,* four dozen. My God, dear lady, how come you remember all this?"

"You never left. Summertimes you were here when I unlocked the doors. You went home for lunch but sometimes brought sandwiches and sat out by the stone lion at noon. Your father pulled you home by your ear some nights when you stayed late. How could I forget a boy like that?"

"But still—"

"You never played, never ran out in baseball weather, or football, I imagine. Why?"

He glanced toward the front door. *"They* were waiting for me."

"They?"

"You know. The ones who never borrowed books, never read. They. Them. *Those."*

She looked and remembered. "Ah, yes. The bullies. Why did they chase you?"

"Because they knew I loved books and didn't much care for them."

"It's a wonder you survived. I used to watch you getting, reading hunchbacked, late afternoons. You looked so lonely."

"No. I had *these.* Company."

"Here's more."

She put down *Ivanhoe, Robin Hood,* and *Treasure Island.*

"Oh," he said, "and dear and strange Mr. Poe. How I loved his Red Death."

"You took it so often I told you to keep it on permanent loan unless someone else asked. Someone did, six months later, and when you brought it in I could see it was a terrible blow. A few days later I let you have Poe for another year. I don't recall, did you ever—?"

"It's out in California. Shall I—"

"No, no. Please. Well, here are *your* books. Let me bring others."

She came out not carrying many books but one at a time, as if each one were, indeed, special.

She began to make a circle inside the other Stonehenge circle and as she placed the books, in lonely splendor, he said their names and then the names of the authors who had written them and then the names of those who had sat across from him so many years ago and read the books quietly or sometimes whispered the finest parts aloud, so beautifully that no one said Quiet or Silence or even *Shh!*

She placed the first book and there was a wild field of broom and a wind blowing a young woman across that field as it began to snow and someone, far away, called "Kathy" and as the snows fell he saw a girl he had walked to school in the sixth grade seated across the table, her eyes fixed to the windblown field and the snow and the lost woman in another time of winter.

A second book was set in place and a black and beauteous horse raced across a summer field of green and on that horse was another girl, who hid behind the book and dared to pass him notes when he was twelve.

And then there was the far ghost with a snowmaiden face whose hair was a long golden harp played by the summer airs; she who was always sailing to Byzantium where Emperors were drowsed by golden birds that sang in clockwork cages at sunset and dawn. She who always skirted the outer rim of school and went to swim in the deep lake ten thousand afternoons ago and never came out, so was never found, but suddenly now she made landfall here in the green-shaded light and opened Yeats to at last sail home from Byzantium.

And on her right: John Huff, whose name came clearer than the rest, who claimed to have climbed every tree in town and fallen from none, who had raced through watermelon patches treading melons, never touching earth, to knock down rainfalls of chestnuts with one blow, who yodeled at your sun-up window and wrote the same Mark Twain book report in four different grades before the teachers caught on, at which he said, vanishing, "Just call me Huck."

And to *his* right, the pale son of the town hotel owner who looked as if he had gone sleepless forever, who swore every empty house was haunted and took you there to prove it, with a juicy tongue, compressed nose, and throat garglings that sounded the long October demise, the terrible and unutterable fall of the House of Usher.

And next to him was yet another girl.

And next to her . . .

And just beyond . .

Miss Adams placed a final book and he recalled the fair creature, long ago, when such things were left unsaid, glancing up at him one day when he was an unknowing twelve and she was a wise thirteen to quietly say: "I am Beauty. And you, are *you* the Beast?"

Now, late in time, he wanted to answer that small and wondrous ghost: "No. He hides in the stacks and when the clock strikes three, will prowl forth to drink."

And it was finished, all the books were placed, the outer ring of his selves and the inner ring of remembered faces, deathless, with summer and autumn names.

He sat for a long moment and then another long moment and then, one by one, reached for and took all of the books that had been his, and still were, and opened them and read and shut them and took

another until he reached the end of the outer circle and then went to
touch and turn and find the raft on the river, the field of broom where
the storms lived, and the pasture with the black and beauteous horse
and its lovely rider. Behind him, he heard the lady librarian quietly
back away to leave him with words . . .

A long while later he sat back, rubbed his eyes, and looked
around at the fortress, the encirclement, the Roman encampment of
books, and nodded, his eyes wet.

"Yes."

He heard her move behind him.

"Yes, *what?*"

"What you said, Thomas Wolfe, the title of that book of his.
Wrong. Everything's *here*. Nothing's changed."

"Nothing will as long as I can help it," she said.

"Don't ever go away."

"I won't if you'll come back more often."

Just then, from below the town, not so very far off, a train whistle blew. She said:

"Is that *yours?*"

"No, but the one soon after," he said and got up and moved
around the small monuments that stood very tall and, one by one, shut
the covers, his lips moving to sound the old titles and the old, dear
names.

"Do we *have* to put them back on the shelves?" he said.

She looked at him and at the double circle and after a long
moment said, "Tomorrow will do. Why?"

"Maybe," he said, "during the night, because of the color of those
lamps, green, the jungle, maybe those creatures you mentioned will
come out and turn the pages with their breath. And maybe—"

"What else?"

"Maybe my friends, who've hid in the stacks all these years, will
come out, too."

"They're already here," she said quietly.

"Yes." He nodded. "They are."

And still he could not move.

She backed off across the room without making any sound, and
when she reached her desk she called back, the last call of the night.

.   "Closing time. Closing time, children."

And turned the lights quickly off and then on and then halfway between; a library twilight.

He moved from the table with the double circle of books and came to her and said, "I can go now."

"Yes," she said. "William Henry Spaulding. You *can.*"

They walked together as she turned out the lights, turned out the lights, one by one. She helped him into his coat and then, hardly thinking to do so, he took her hand and kissed her fingers.

It was so abrupt, she almost laughed, but then she said, "Remember what Edith Wharton said when Henry James did what you just did?"

"What?"

""The flavor starts at the *elbow.*""

They broke into laughter together and he turned and went down the marble steps toward the stained-glass entry. At the bottom of the stairs he looked up at her and said:

"Tonight, when you're going to sleep, remember what I called you when I was twelve, and say it out loud."

"I don't remember," she said.

"Yes, you do."

Below the town, a train whistle blew again. He opened the front door, stepped out, and he was gone.

Her hand on the last light switch, looking in at the double circle of books on the far table, she thought: What *was* it he called me?

"Oh, *yes,*" she said a moment later.

And switched off the light.

THE LIBRARY OF BABEL

Jorge Luis Borges

> By this art you may contemplate the
> variation of the 23 letters . . .
> —*The Anatomy of Melancholy,*
> Part 2, Sect. II, Mem. IV.

THE UNIVERSE (WHICH OTHERS CALL THE LIBRARY) IS COMPOSED OF AN indefinite, perhaps an infinite, number of hexagonal galleries, with enormous ventilation shafts in the middle, encircled by very low railings. From any hexagon the upper or lower stories are visible, interminably. The distribution of the galleries is invariable. Twenty shelves— five long shelves per side—cover all sides except two; their height, which is that of each floor, scarcely exceeds that of an average librarian. One of the free sides gives upon a narrow entrance way, which leads to another gallery, identical to the first and to all the others. To the left and to the right of the entrance way are two miniature rooms. One allows standing room for sleeping, the other, the satisfaction of fecal necessities. Through this section passes the spiral staircase, which plunges down into the abyss and rises up to the heights. In the entrance way hangs a mirror, which faithfully duplicates appearances. People are in the habit of inferring from this mirror that the Library is not infinite (if it really were, why this illusory duplication?); I prefer to dream that the polished surfaces feign and promise infinity. . . .

Light comes from some spherical fruits called by the name of lamps. There are two, running transversally, in each hexagon. The light they emit is insufficient, incessant.

Like all men of the Library, I have traveled in my youth. I have journeyed in search of a book, perhaps of the catalogue of catalogues;

now that my eyes can scarcely decipher what I write, I am preparing
to die a few leagues from the hexagon in which I was born. Once dead,
there will not lack pious hands to hurl me over the banister; my sepul-
chre shall be the unfathomable air: my body will sink lengthily and will
corrupt and dissolve in the wind engendered by the fall, which is infinite. I affirm that the Library is interminable. The idealists argue that
the hexagonal halls are a necessary form of absolute space or, at least,
of our intuition of space. They contend that a triangular or pentagonal
hall is inconceivable. (The mystics claim that to them ecstasy reveals
a round chamber containing a great book with a continuous back cir-
cling the walls of the room; but their testimony is suspect; their words,
obscure. That cyclical book is God.) Let it suffice me, for the time
being, to repeat the classic dictum: *The Library is a sphere whose con-
summate center is any hexagon, and whose circumference is inaccessible.*

Five shelves correspond to each one of the walls of each hexagon;
each shelf contains thirty-two books of a uniform format; each book is
made up of four hundred and ten pages; each page, of forty lines; each line,
of some eighty black letters. There are also letters on the spine of each
book; these letters do not indicate or prefigure what the pages will say. I
know that such a lack of relevance, at one time, seemed mysterious. Before
summarizing the solution (whose disclosure, despite its tragic implications,
is perhaps the capital fact of this history), I want to recall certain axioms.

The first: The Library exists *ab aeterno*. No reasonable mind can
doubt this truth, whose immediate corollary is the future eternity of
the world. Man, the imperfect librarian, may be the work of chance or
of malevolent demiurges; the universe, with its elegant endowment of
shelves, of enigmatic volumes, of indefatigable ladders for the voyager,
and of privies for the seated librarian, can only be the work of a god.
In order to perceive the distance which exists between the divine and
the human, it is enough to compare the rude tremulous symbols which
my fallible hand scribbles on the end pages of a book with the organic letters inside: exact, delicate, intensely black, inimitably symmetric.

The second: *The number of orthographic symbols is twenty-five.**
This bit of evidence permitted the formulation, three hundred years

---

*The original manuscript of the present note does not contain digits or capital letters.
The punctuation is limited to the comma and the period. These two signs, plus the
space sign and the twenty-two letters of the alphabet, make up the twenty-five sufficient symbols enumerated by the unknown author.

ago, of a general theory of the Library and the satisfactory resolution of the problem which no conjecture had yet made clear: the formless and chaotic nature of almost all books. One of these books, which my father saw in a hexagon of the circuit number fifteen ninety-four, was composed of the letters MCV perversely repeated from the first line to the last. Another, very much consulted in this zone, is a mere labyrinth of letters, but on the next-to-the-last page, one may read *O Time your pyramids*. As is well known: for one reasonable line or one straightforward note there are leagues of insensate cacaphony, of verbal farragoes and incoherencies. (I know of a wild region whose librarians repudiate the vain superstitious custom of seeking any sense in books and compare it to looking for meaning in dreams or in the chaotic lines of one's hands. . . . They admit that the inventors of writing imitated the twenty-five natural symbols, but they maintain that this application is accidental and that books in themselves mean nothing. This opinion— we shall see—is not altogether false.)

For a long time it was believed that these impenetrable books belonged to past or remote languages. It is true that the most ancient men, the first librarians, made use of a language quite different from the one we speak today; it is true that some miles to the right the language is dialectical and that ninety stories up it is incomprehensible. All this, I repeat, is true; but four hundred and ten pages of unvarying MCVs do not correspond to any language, however dialectical or rudimentary it might be. Some librarians insinuated that each letter could influence the next, and that the value of MCV on the third line of page 71 was not the same as that of the same series in another position on another page; but this vague thesis did not prosper. Still other men thought in terms of cryptographs; this conjecture has come to be universally accepted, though not in the sense in which it was formulated by its inventors.

Five hundred years ago, the chief of an upper hexagon* came upon a book as confusing as all the rest but which contained nearly two pages of homogenous lines. He showed his find to an ambulant decipherer, who told him the lines were written in Portuguese. Others

---

*Formerly, for each three hexagons there was one man. Suicide and pulmonary diseases have destroyed this proportion. My memory recalls scenes of unspeakable melancholy: there have been many nights when I have ventured down corridors and polished staircases without encountering a single librarian.

told him they were in Yiddish. In less than a century the nature of the language was finally established: it was a Samoyed-Lithuanian dialect of Guarani, with classical Arabic inflections. The contents were also deciphered: notions of combinational analysis, illustrated by examples of variations with unlimited repetition. These examples made it possible for a librarian of genius to discover the fundamental law of the Library. This thinker observed that all the books, however diverse, are made up of uniform elements: the period, the comma, the space, the twenty-two letters of the alphabet. He also adduced a circumstance confirmed by all travelers: *There are not, in the whole vast Library, two identical books.* From all these incontrovertible premises he deduced that the Library is total and that its shelves contain all the possible combinations of the twenty-odd orthographic symbols (whose number, though vast, is not infinite); that is, everything which can be expressed, in all languages. Everything is there: the minute history of the future, the autobiographies of the archangels, the faithful catalogue of the Library, thousands and thousands of false catalogues, a demonstration of the fallacy of these catalogues, a demonstration of the fallacy of the true catalogue, the Gnostic gospel of Basilides, the commentary on this gospel, the commentary on the commentary of this gospel, the veridical account of your death, a version of each book in all languages, the interpolations of every book in all books.

When it was proclaimed that the Library comprised all books, the first impression was one of extravagant joy. All men felt themselves lords of a secret, intact treasure. There was no personal or universal problem whose eloquent solution did not exist—in some hexagon. The universe was justified, the universe suddenly expanded to the limitless dimensions of hope. At that time there was much talk of the Vindications: books of apology and prophecy, which vindicated for all time the actions of every man in the world and established a store of prodigious arcana for the future. Thousands of covetous persons abandoned their dear natal hexagons and crowded up the stairs, urged on by the vain aim of finding their Vindication. These pilgrims disputed in the narrow corridors, hurled dark maledictions, strangled each other on the divine stairways, flung the deceitful books to the bottom of the tunnels, and died as they were thrown into space by men from remote regions. Some went mad. . . .

The Vindications do exist. I have myself seen two of these books, which were concerned with future people, people who were perhaps not imaginary. But the searchers did not remember that the calculable possibility of a man's finding his own book, or some perfidious variation of his own book, is close to zero.

The clarification of the basic mysteries of humanity—the origin of the Library and of time—was also expected. It is credible that those grave mysteries can be explained in words: if the language of the philosophers does not suffice, the multiform Library will have produced the unexpected language required and the necessary vocabularies and grammars for this language.

It is now four centuries since men have been wearying the hexagons. . . .

There are official searchers, *inquisitors*. I have observed them carrying out their functions: they are always exhausted. They speak of a staircase without steps where they were almost killed. They speak of galleries and stairs with the local librarian. From time to time they will pick up the nearest book and leaf through its pages, in search of infamous words. Obviously, no one expects to discover anything.

The uncommon hope was followed, naturally enough, by deep depression. The certainty that some shelf in some hexagon contained precious books and that these books were inaccessible seemed almost intolerable. A blasphemous sect suggested that all searches be given up and that men everywhere shuffle letters and symbols until they succeeded in composing, by means of an improbable stroke of luck, the canonical books. The authorities found themselves obliged to issue severe orders. The sect disappeared, but in my childhood I still saw old men who would hide out in the privies for long periods of time, and, with metal disks in a forbidden dicebox, feebly mimic the divine disorder.

Other men, inversely, thought that the primary task was to eliminate useless works. They would invade the hexagons, exhibiting credentials which were not always false, skim through a volume with annoyance, and then condemn entire bookshelves to destruction: their ascetic, hygenic fury is responsible for the senseless loss of millions of books. Their name is execrated; but those who mourn the "treasures" destroyed by this frenzy, overlook two notorious facts. One: the Library is so enormous that any reduction undertaken by humans is infinitesimal. Two: each book is unique, irreplaceable, but (inasmuch as the

Library is total) there are always several hundreds of thousands of imperfect facsimiles—of works which differ only by one letter or one comma. Contrary to public opinion, I dare suppose that the consequences of the depredations committed by the Purifiers have been exaggerated by the horror which these fanatics provoked. They were spurred by the delirium of storming the books in the Crimson Hexagon: books of a smaller than ordinary format, omnipotent, illustrated, magical.

We know, too, of another superstition of that time: the Man of the Book. In some shelf of some hexagon, men reasoned, there must exist a book which is the cipher and perfect compendium of *all the rest*: some librarian has perused it, and it is analogous to a god. Vestiges of the worship of that remote functionary still persist in the language of this zone. Many pilgrimages have sought Him out. For a century they trod the most diverse routes in vain. How to locate the secret hexagon which harbored it? Someone proposed a regressive approach: in order to locate book A, first consult book B which will indicate the location of A; in order to locate book B, first consult book C, and so on ad infinitum. . .

I have squandered and consumed my years in adventures of this type. To me, it does not seem unlikely that on some shelf of the universe there lies a total book.* I pray the unknown gods that some man—even if only one man, and though it have been thousands of years ago!—may have examined and read it. If honor and wisdom and happiness are not for me, let them be for others. May heaven exist, though my place be in hell. Let me be outraged and annihilated, but may Thy enormous Library be justified, for one instant, in one being.

The impious assert that absurdities are the norm in the Library and that anything reasonable (even humble and pure coherence) is an almost miraculous exception. They speak (I know) of "the febrile Library, whose hazardous volumes run the constant risk of being changed into others and in which everything is affirmed, denied, and confused as by a divinity in delirium." These words, which not only denounce disorder but exemplify it as well, manifestly demonstrate the

*I repeat: it is enough that a book be possible for it to exist. Only the impossible is excluded. For example: no book is also a stairway, though doubtless there are books that discuss and deny and demonstrate this possibility and others whose structure corresponds to that of a stairway.

bad taste of the speakers and their desperate ignorance. Actually, the Library includes all verbal structures, all the variations allowed by the twenty-five orthographic symbols, but it does not permit of one absolute absurdity. It is pointless to observe that the best book in the numerous hexagons under my administration is entitled *Combed Clap of Thunder;* or that another is called *The Plaster Cramp;* and still another *Axaxaxas Mlö.* Such propositions as are contained in these titles, at first sight incoherent, doubtless yield a cryptographic or allegorical justification. Since they are verbal, these justifications already figure, *ex hypothesi,* in the Library. I can not combine certain letters, as *dhcmrlchtdj,* which the divine Library has not already foreseen in combination, and which in one of its secret languages does not encompass some terrible meaning. No one can articulate a syllable which is not full of tenderness and fear, and which is not, in one of those languages, the powerful name of some god. To speak is to fall into tautologies. This useless and wordy epistle itself already exists in one of the thirty volumes of the five shelves in one of the uncountable hexagons-and so does its refutation. (An *n* number of possible languages makes use of the same vocabulary; in some of them, the symbol *library* admits of the correct definition *ubiquitous and everlasting system of hexagonal galleries,* but *library* is *bread* or *pyramid* or anything else, and the seven words which define it possess another value. You who read me, are you sure you understand my language?)

Methodical writing distracts me from the present condition of men. But the certainty that everything has been already written nullifies or makes phantoms of us all. I know of districts where the youth prostrate themselves before books and barbarously kiss the pages, though they do not know how to make out a single letter. Epidemics, heretical disagreements, the pilgrimages which inevitably degenerate into banditry, have decimated the population. I believe I have mentioned the suicides, more frequent each year. Perhaps I am deceived by old age and fear, but I suspect that the human species—the unique human species—is on the road to extinction, while the Library will last on forever: illuminated, solitary, infinite, perfectly immovable, filled with precious volumes, useless, incorruptible, secret.

Infinite I have just written. I have not interpolated this adjective merely from rhetorical habit. It is not illogical, I say, to think that the world is infinite. Those who judge it to be limited, postulate that in remote places the corridors and stairs and hexagons could inconceivably cease—a manifest absurdity. Those who imagined it to be limitless forget that the possible number of books is limited. I dare insinuate the following solution to this ancient problem: *The Library is limitless and periodic*. If an eternal voyager were to traverse it in any direction, he would find, after many centuries, that the same volumes are repeated in the same disorder (which, repeated, would constitute an order: Order itself). My solitude rejoices in this elegant hope.*

Mar del Plata
1941

—Translated by ANTHONY KERRIGAN

*Letizia Alvarez de Toledo has observed that the vast Library is useless. Strictly speaking, *one single volume* should suffice: a single volume of ordinary format, printed in nine or ten type body, and consisting of an infinite number of infinitely thin pages. (At the beginning of the seventeenth century, Cavalieri said that any solid body is the superposition of an infinite number of planes.) This silky vade mecum would scarcely be handy: each apparent leaf of the book would divide into other analogous leaves. The inconceivable central leaf would have no reverse.

ABOUT THE AUTHORS

ISAAC BABEL (1894-1941) Short story writer, novelist, and playwright, Babel was born in the Jewish ghetto of Odessa and became the first major Russian Jewish author to write in Russian. Among his best-known works are *Odessa Tales* and *Red Cavalry*. Charged with espionage and arrested in 1939, Babel died in a Siberian labor camp in 1941.

GINA BERRIAULT (1926-1999). Winner of the National Book Critics Circle Award and the PEN/Faulkner Book Award for her short story collection *Women In Their Beds*, Berriault was also the author of two earlier short story collections and four novels. She lived in Northern California.

JORGE LUIS BORGES (1899-1986). Born in Buenos Aires in 1899 and educated in Europe, Borges is considered one of the greatest writers in the Spanish language, a master of brilliantly imaginative short fiction, poetry, and literary and philosophical essays. He worked as Director of the National Library of Argentina and was a professor of English at the University of Buenos Aires.

ANTHONY BOUCHER (1911-1968). One of the most important figures in 20th century mystery and detective fiction, Boucher was a novelist, editor, and—perhaps most importantly—a critic who wrote the "Criminals at Large" column for the *New York Times* from 1951 until his death in 1968. He was a founder of the Mystery Writers of

America and for nine years was the editor of the *Magazine of Fantasy and Science Fiction*. The "Bouchercon," the oldest and largest annual convention of mystery fans, is named in his honor.

RAY BRADBURY (1920-). Bradbury was born in Waukegan, Illinois but grew up in Southern California and credits reading at the Los Angeles Public Library for much of his early education. The author of *The Martian Chronicles, The Illustrated Man, Fahrenheit 451* and countless other modern classics, Bradbury is a master of speculative and imaginative fiction. The National Book Foundation recently honored him with its Medal for Distinguished Contribution to American Letters. He lives in Los Angeles.

WALTER R. BROOKS (1886-1958). Born in Rome, New York, Brooks was a novelist, editor, reviewer and author of the classic Freddy the Pig books for children. He was also a prolific author of more than two hundred short stories for adults, twenty-six of which featured a talking horse named "Ed," who became the inspiration for the celebrated 1960's TV series "Mr. Ed."

 ITALO CALVINO (1923-1985). Born in Cuba, Calvino grew up in San Remo, Italy and was a member of the partisan movement during the German occupation of northern Italy during World War II. This experience was the catalyst for his first novel *The Path to the Nest of Spiders*. Among his other acclaimed works of fiction—many of them dreamlike and fantastic—are *The Baron in the Trees, Cosmicomics,* and *If on a Winter's Night a Traveler*.

JOHN CHEEVER (1922-1982). One of the greatest American writers of the 20th century John Cheever was a winner of the National Book Award, the National Medal for Literature and the Pulitzer Prize. Though he remains indelibly linked with the *New Yorker*, which published 121 of his short stories, he was also the author of five acclaimed novels, including *The Wapshot Chronicle* and *The Wapshot Scandal*.

MARIA DABROWSKA (1889-1965). The celebrated Polish author was born in Russow to a family of cultured but impoverished landowners. Privately educated, she began writing in 1914 and established her reputation with her 1926 cycle of stories *People from Over Yonder.* Her tetralogy *Nights and Days* has been compared with Tolstoy.

ZONA GALE (1874-1938). Born in Portage, Wisconsin, Gale graduated from the University of Wisconsin in 1895 and later earned a master's degree in 1899. Becoming a journalist for the New York *Evening World,* she began publishing short stories in 1903 and subsequently wrote novels, poetry, biography and plays. She won the Pulitzer Prize for drama in 1921 for *Miss Lulu Bett.* She served as chairman of the Wisconsin Free Library Commission.

JOANNE GREENBERG (1932-). Greenberg is the author of sixteen novels, including such acclaimed titles as *I Never Promised You a Rose Garden, In This Sign,* and *Of Such Small Differences.* An adjunct professor at the Colorado School of Mines, she is an expert in working with the deaf. She has received honorary doctorates from Gallaudet University and Western Maryland College. She lives in Colorado.

M. R. JAMES (1862-1936). Noted scholar and antiquary Montague Rhodes James was Provost of King's College Cambridge. As an author he was a master of the supernatural and is widely regarded as the father of the modern ghost story. *The Collected Ghost Stories of M. R. James* was published in 1931.

SUE KAUFMAN (1926-1977). Born on Long Island, New York, Sue Kaufman graduated from Vassar College and worked for a time as assistant fiction editor of *Mademoiselle* magazine. From 1949 until her death in 1977 she was a free-lance writer of fiction, including short stories and novels like *Dairy of a Mad Housewife* and *Falling Bodies.*

LISA KOGER (1953-). Raised in West Virginia, Koger received her M.F.A. from the Iowa Writer's Workshop and earned other degrees from West Virginia University and the University of Tennessee. Her stories, many of which focus on the lives of the Appalachian middle class, have appeared in *Seventeen, Ploughshares,* and *Kennesaw Review.* She lives in Kentucky.

URSULA K. LeGUIN (1929-). Born into a scholarly family in Berkeley, California, LeGuin is herself a scholar. Educated at Radcliffe and Columbia University, she is a profoundly original writer and one of the foremost contemporary authors of fantasy and science fiction. She is the winner of a National Book Award, a Pushcart Prize and a remarkable total of ten Hugo and Nebula Awards. She lives in Oregon.

LORRIE MOORE (1957-). A professor of English at the University of Wisconsin in Madison, Moore is author of the novels *Who Will Run the Frog Hospital?* and *Anagrams.* Her short story collections include *Like Life, Self-Help* and *Birds of America,* which was a finalist for the National book Critics Circle Award. Her work has been published in *The New Yorker, The Best American Short Stories,* and *Prize Stories: The O. Henry Awards.*

ALICE MUNRO (1931-). Widely regarded as one of the greatest contemporary short story writers, Canadian author Alice Munro is the author of ten books, including *The Moons of Jupiter, The Love of a Good Woman,* winner of the National Book Critics' Circle Award, and *Who Do You Think You Are?* which was shortlisted for the Booker Prize. A three-time winner of the prestigious Governor General's Award, she lives in Ontario, Canada.

FRANCINE PROSE (1947-). The author of ten acclaimed works of fiction including *Hunters and Gatherers* and *Guided Tours of Hell,* Prose is a contributing editor to *Harper's* magazine and has taught at the Iowa Writer's Workshop and Johns Hopkins University. Her latest novel is *Blue Angel.* She lives in New York.

SAKI (H. H. MUNRO) (1870-1916). Born in Burma, Munro was raised by his aunts in England. He began a career as a journalist in 1896. As a writer of short stories under the pen name "Saki" (borrowed from "The Rubaiyat of Omar Khayyam"), he was a master of the macabre and the savagely satirical. Though officially overage, he volunteered for military service in World War I and was killed by a sniper's bullet in France.